One man wants to be King. The lives of millions are in his hands. Can SAS: Vigilant stop him?

SIMON DALEY

HACKED

ULTIMATE WARRIORS - ULTIMATE PUNISHERS

SAS: VIGILANT SERIES BOOK TWO

Copyright © 2023 by Simon Daley

The right of Simon Daley to be identified as the Author of the Work has been asserted by him in accordance with the Copyright, Designs and Patents Act 1988.

All rights reserved.

No part of this publication may be reproduced, distributed, or transmitted in any form or by any means, including photocopying, recording, or other electronic or mechanical methods, without the prior written permission of the publisher, except as permitted by U.S. copyright law. For permission requests, contact simondaleybooks.co.uk.

The story, all names, characters, and incidents portrayed in this production are fictitious. No identification with actual persons (living or deceased), places, buildings, and products is intended or should be inferred.

Book Cover by Caroline

1st edition 2024

This book is dedicated to the men and women of our armed forces and emergency services. Without them the world would be a much darker place.

So many acts of heroism and selflessness go unrecognised. They don't seek our thanks, and we don't thank them often enough.

The SAS are not superheroes. They are at times superhuman, but they are also very human. I hope I have captured some of that humanity in the characters of this book.

WE ARE THE PILGRIMS MASTER: WE SHALL GO
ALWAYS A LITTLE FURTHER: IT MAY BE
BEYOND THAT LITTLE BLUE MOUNTAIN BARRED WITH
SNOW.
ACROSS THAT ANGRY OR THAT GLIMMERING SEA
by James Elroy Flecker

Contents

1. Chapter 1   1
2. Chapter 2   5
3. Chapter 3   10
4. Chapter 4   14
5. Chapter 5   18
6. Chapter 6   20
7. Chapter 7   22
8. Chapter 8   29
9. Chapter 9   33
10. Chapter 10   36
11. Chapter 11   42
12. Chapter 12   47
13. Chapter 13   53
14. Chapter 14   57
15. Chapter 15   63
16. Chapter 16   71
17. Chapter 17   78

18.	Chapter 18	87
19.	Chapter 19	92
20.	Chapter 20	96
21.	Chapter 21	99
22.	Chapter 22	101
23.	Chapter 23	110
24.	Chapter 24	116
25.	Chapter 25	118
26.	Chapter 26	128
27.	Chapter 27	130
28.	Chapter 28	136
29.	Chapter 29	140
30.	Chapter 30	146
31.	Chapter 31	149
32.	Chapter 32	157
33.	Chapter 33	160
34.	Chapter 34	164
35.	Chapter 35	166
36.	Chapter 36	171
37.	Chapter 37	174
38.	Chapter 38	182
39.	Chapter 39	191
40.	Chapter 40	197
41.	Chapter 41	202

42.	Chapter 42	205
43.	Chapter 43	210
44.	Chapter 44	216
45.	Chapter 45	229
46.	Chapter 46	234
47.	Chapter 47	236
48.	Chapter 48	238
49.	Chapter 49	240
50.	Chapter 50	241
51.	Chapter 51	243
52.	Chapter 52	246
53.	Chapter 53	248
54.	Chapter 54	252
55.	Chapter 55	254
56.	Chapter 56	258
57.	Chapter 57	260
58.	Chapter 58	264
59.	Chapter 59	267
60.	Chapter 60	269
61.	Chapter 61	274
62.	Chapter 62	278
63.	Chapter 63	282
64.	Chapter 64	287
65.	Chapter 65	289

66.	Chapter 66	292
67.	Chapter 67	296
68.	Chapter 68	299
69.	Chapter 69	301
70.	Chapter 70	304
71.	Chapter 71	306
72.	Chapter 72	309
73.	Chapter 73	317
74.	Chapter 74	322
75.	Chapter 75	324
76.	Chapter 76	326
77.	Chapter 77	336
78.	Chapter 78	346
	Also By	348
	Acknowledgements	349
	About the Author	350

Chapter One

Her eyes bore into him, they screamed at him. At once pleading, warning, beseeching him. He was transfixed, the noise, the shouts and screams around him were a distant murmur. The world shrunk into a tiny slot of light and those dark, dark eyes. Red rimmed from crying, wide with fear, they were still beautiful as he saw them now. Too far away to make out the amber and gold flecks in the chestnut brown, but he knew they were there.

The image softened, it took all of his effort and strength to refocus. The edges became watery but he knew how the metamorphosis worked, it would slowly merge two faces until the woman was lost, the face became that of the woman he loved; Esmé - his ex-wife.

Fighting the change, through force of will, he kept the image of the woman. He felt his finger twitch, the memory of the trigger pull, the slow motion reaction as the rounds struck the woman in the face, ripping through her skull. The crimson exit, followed by the flash as her hand spasmed releasing the detonator switch.

He didn't feel the pain of the shrapnel hitting him or the blast throwing him through the air, all he could feel was the pressure he had exerted on the trigger.

Waking with a start, it took a moment to work out where he was. Sweat coated his body, it felt cool as the ceiling fan turned silently above him. He hadn't planned the nap and regretted giving the dreams an opportunity to spoil a beautiful day.

The medals in his hand threw beams of reflected light over the ceiling. Caribbean sunshine was bright but that wasn't the cause of the moisture in his eyes.

He had been SAS, the best Special Forces unit in the world. These medals, the memories, a few scars and a skill set even hardened professional soldiers could only dream about, were all he had to show for his service he thought to himself. Actually, he realised, that wasn't true, he still had his team. They had been SAS; now they were something else. Not mercenaries; the £12 million they'd taken from an IRA bomb maker meant they never need work for money again. No longer part of the British Army; that career was over thanks to the snakes in Whitehall. They were free to help those who had no-one else to turn to. Vigilantes was a term that had led to them becoming known as Vigilant. It was certainly vigilante behaviour in London that saw them take down the Kosanians, along with some of their feral foot soldiers. The thought of the trafficked women and children they'd saved gave him clarity about their purpose. They were the wrong side of the law for sure, but he knew they were still the good guys.

Wiping his eyes with the back of his free hand, he picked up the box laying the medals into the velvet lining. They'd be kept secure here in his safe deposit box at RBC Royal Bank Cayman Islands. He'd opened the account on his 21st birthday, with his father. This was still where he kept his family valuables. It was a long way from home but for Capt *JT* St John-Templeman home had for a long time been a barracks in Hereford.

Now, three months after leaving the British Army, JT and his team had become Vigilant. He still found himself trying to make sense of all that had happened.

The media and legal furore over the killing of an Afghan woman had disappeared when he and the team had been given medical discharges from the Regiment. None of that sat comfortably with him. The mercurial Hamilton had come in to save them, but how far can you trust a spy from MI6, or whoever it is he worked for. Hamilton seemed to be answerable to no-one and he thought of Vigilant as his private army.

The music starting up on the terrace brought JT back to the present. Brothers in Arms by Dire Straits played for the umpteenth time in the last couple of days. Rambahadur *Rambo* Gurung, Vigilant's ex Gurkha, expert climber and world-class sniper, was a terrible singer. His guitar playing not much better. Still, it made JT happy to see Rambo doing his thing. They no longer had a rank structure but he was still in charge, the team were his to look after.

Pretty soon they'd all have completed their current missions around the world and the team would be together for some R&R on the Cayman beach.

Ezekiel, or Easy as he was known, was due in tomorrow too. The kid, whose cry for help had started them on this journey, was a financial and cyber whizz. In the last three months, Hamilton had arranged for him to be trained by GCHQ's finest minds to hone his skills. The kid was going to be a valuable part of Vigilant. His job this coming week was to sort out numbered bank accounts for each of the team. They were making sure that whatever happened, they would be financially secure. It had been Easy who booked the villa JT was standing in. The kid had undeniably great taste; it was spacious and well-appointed without being ostentatious.

He looked down at the private jetty which held their dive boat that they'd use this week. Sun, sea and scuba - the perfect recipe for a relaxing break.

Rambo started on a new Dire Straits song, Romeo and Juliet weren't to be allowed to commit suicide, it was their turn to be murdered.

JT knew he couldn't complain, after London, they'd all become murderers.

Chapter Two

The door of the first class lounge was a step too far. Looking down at his clothes he remembered what his Aunty had told him; "Ezekiel, *good* people don't have to dress to impress."

His shoes shone as he'd polished them every day for a week. They were new and he'd worn them in the house to break them in. They'd cost him a lot of money, but they were an investment.

'Are you going in?'

The voice made him jump, he spun around to find himself face to face with a woman. Her lips were vibrant red. She gently bit her lower lip with perfect white teeth as she tried to hide the amusement that lit up her eyes.

'Errm...' was all he could manage.

'I'm so sorry, I did not mean to startle you,' she said, gently touching her fingertips to his arm.

He looked down at his feet as he couldn't meet her gaze. She was the most beautiful woman he had ever seen.

'This is the first class lounge, is this where you are looking for?'

Her voice had such warmth that he had to concentrate to separate the feeling of the words from their meaning.

'I have a ticket,' he blurted out in a voice at least an octave higher than his own. He could feel her watching him but still couldn't look into her face.

'You know, these places can be very intimidating when you are travelling alone. Perhaps if you were to come into the lounge as my guest?'

'No, no thank you very much but I couldn't ask you to do that.' At last, he met her eyes finding only warmth emanating from the sort of blue reserved for the sky in dreams.

'You would be doing me a real favour. If I go in there alone, it will be a matter of time before some boring man tries to hit on me. I'd have to listen to him brag about his sports cars or some other inane nonsense. Please, escort me in and we can pass the time in pleasant company? Unless of course you are meeting someone else?'

'No, I am on my own.'

'A gentleman would normally introduce himself to a lady,' she said, with a playful smile.

'I'm sorry. My name is Ezekiel but everyone calls me Easy.'

'Well then Easy, I am very pleased to meet you. My name is Rosamunde but my friends, of which you are the newest, call me Rosa.'

'Pleased to meet you Rosa,' he said, feeling suddenly more at ease.

'Then it's settled,' she said, taking his arm and walking him through the automatic doors.

All eyes in the lounge were on them as they were shown to some comfortable leather chairs. She undid her coat, dropping it onto an adjacent chair. Her black dress had white detailing around the neckline and cuffs. Easy felt sure he'd seen it before somewhere, maybe in a movie. He fought the urge to stare.

'Easy, do you mind if I ask how old you are?' Rosa asked as she sat down with a well-practiced but seemingly effortless elegance.

'I'm 18, why?'

'Ah, wonderful, I was about to order Champagne but not if I'd be drinking alone.' She lifted a manicured hand and instantly the steward appeared.

***

Outside the first class lounge, two men stood up and walked to where they could talk without being overheard. One man positioned himself so he could see the lounge doors.

'Who the hell is the kid?'

'No idea, there was nothing in the brief about a kid.'

'Maybe she knows him from the island?'

'Don't think so, did you see the shock in his face when she spoke to him?'

'Yeah, he looked petrified. Mind you so would I be. Three weeks we've been following her and I still can't get over how hot she is!'

'That she is, that she is.'

'Do we tell the boss?'

'I'll message him when she boards the plane as arranged.'

'What if they're travelling together?'

'Then they'll both get picked up in Grand Cayman. Our job was to make sure she gets on the plane. The rest is their problem.'

***

'How wonderful, we'll be on the same aeroplane!' said Rosa. 'What takes you to the Caymans?'

'Business, well, sort of business. I'm meeting my friends and they're taking me scuba diving, fishing too.'

'What sort of business are you in Easy?' she asked him with a quizzical look.

'Crypto investing mostly, but also some property.'

'At 18? That is amazing! I've heard about crypto obviously but don't know much about it really.'

'I could teach you if you like?' Easy offered, then instantly regretted sounding too keen.

'I fear I am too old to learn new tricks Easy. I have difficulty enough keeping on top of things,' she said then sipped her Champagne.

Easy watched her rub her thumb against her empty ring finger. The faintest white line suggested it had recently held a wedding ring. 'Are you meeting your husband in the Caymans?' he asked her.

A sadness came over her face. He watched her shoulders droop just a little before she gathered herself. 'My husband and I, are no longer together, Easy. I am on my way to sort out some paperwork at the bank, then I will be returning home to England.'

'I'm sorry, I didn't mean to be so personal,' said Easy.

'Not at all, not at all. It's all quite recent, but I'm ready for a new life.' She smiled at him and not for the first time, Easy felt his heart skip a beat.

'Can I ask you something?'

'Ask away, but remember there are some things a gentleman would never ask a lady.' She winked at him and he felt the colour rise in his cheeks.

'It's a little embarrassing, for me.'

'Go on,' she said, intrigued.

'I've never flown first class before. Can you tell me what I'm supposed to do, when we board the aeroplane?' He tried but failed to maintain eye contact with her, but he knew instinctively, she wouldn't judge him.

Chapter Three

'All go to plan?' asked JT.

'Yep, two vehicles in place, with keys in the magnetic boxes. They're parked where we discussed, GPS trackers are tested and working. Joe's solar gizmo will keep them charged up ready to deploy, whenever we need them,' said Taff.

Thomas *Taff* Michaels had been the Sergeant of JT's SAS team and very much his right hand man. The big Welshman was rarely without a smile, no matter what was thrown at him. In the SAS he'd faced the worst the enemy could muster with skill and a cunning to match his exceptional calm.

Joe Paterson was the team's comms and electronics expert. A rough Glaswegian accent belied an intelligence and technical ability second, he conceded, only to his sister Sandra. Sandra was a rising star in the Special Reconnaissance Regiment, for some the Army really was a family affair.

'Excellent work Taff. How soon can you get over here to the Caymans?'

'As soon as humanly possible. Manilla is a bit humid at this time of year for my liking,' Taff chuckled into the phone. 'How's the weather been?'

'A lot better than Porto Novo, it rained for pretty much the whole 5 days we were there.'

'All sorted in Benin?'

'Yeah, Africa is Africa but, as usual, Hamilton's contacts came up trumps. We purchased a compound for the price of a London garage. Kit and vehicles are all set up.'

'You think we're doing the right thing, preparing all these sites I mean, we might never use them?'

'Well, as Hamilton said, we don't have the back up or resources of the Regiment or Her Majesty's Government any more so we're preparing and planning, just in case.'

'Talking of Mr Hamilton, is he joining us on the beach?'

'No, he's in London with his MI6 or whoever pals. So far it's just me and Rambo. Easy arrives tomorrow, Cooky and Posty are finishing up in El Salvador, so should be here the day after.'

Josiah Cook and Patrick *Posty* Harrower, were the other members of the six-man team. Cooky, the quiet but huge man of Jamaican descent was a cook in name only. His bravery and fighting ability, especially at close quarters was well known not just in the team but throughout the Regiment.

Posty often referred to himself as the token Northern Irishman, often joking he was in the team just so they would always have someone in the home nations to support at football. The real reason being that he was the Method of Entry and Demolition expert. If you wanted something blown up or blown in, he was your man.

'What about Rory?' asked Taff.

Detective Inspector Rory Maxwell, a Counter Terrorism officer was an old friend of JT. He had become caught up in the mission to take down the Kosanians. Forced to kill a bent officer in self-defence, it had sealed his fate to become the 8th member of Vigilant.

'He's stuck at New Scotland Yard, some case he wants to see through before he turns in his warrant card.'

'He's a good lad. The Met's loss will be our gain.'

'Very true, we'll see what the future holds but his contacts will come in handy.'

'Ok Boss, I'll update you with an ETA.'

'Cold beer waiting.'

'Good man, speak soon.'

JT hung up the phone thinking about Taff's insistence on still calling him Boss. They'd been discharged from the SAS six months ago, but old habits die hard. The truth was he liked looking after his men, his team, and they liked him being their boss.

Checking the remote cameras at the new compound in Porto Novo, JT saw Paulo the caretaker working away, hoeing the flower beds outside the long low built house. Hamilton had put him in touch with Paulo de Souza, an older man originally from Mozambique, who had fought with the Rhodesian forces in the late 1970s. It was difficult to tell exactly how old he was, his skin was wrinkled but the muscles underneath were wiry and strong.

Importantly, he knew his way around weapons, how to maintain them and, if necessary, how to use them.

Paulo's wife Claudine came into view, leaving one of the service quarters carrying a pile of washing to hang in the late afternoon sun. It made JT happy to think that this couple might live happily in the compound, without it ever having to be used by his team. He had questioned Hamilton's choice of location at the planning meeting, but knew there would be something in the pipeline that would reveal itself in good time.

Once the bank accounts set up here in Grand Cayman, they had a week of team rest and recuperation planned. Afterward he'd be heading back to Bordeaux, where he had the beginnings of a relationship to nurture, with his ex-wife.

Chapter Four

Easy stood up from his comfortable 1st class pod, stretching as he looked out onto the greenery beyond the runway of Nassau airport. The Bahamas were as he'd expected, sunny with blue skies. He was excited to spend 24 hours here for his layover.

He turned looking across the cabin to where his new friend Rosa was being handed her carry-on, by the ever attentive stewardess.

The same stewardess had offered him several drinks throughout the flight as he'd been unable to sleep. He'd read his book and watched a movie but mostly he'd listened to some music and spent the time thinking. He'd tried to think about the bank accounts he was going to set up for the Vigilant team, but his mind just kept wandering back to Rosa.

He wasn't stupid, she was way out of his league and old enough to be his mother, but nonetheless he was absolutely captivated by her.

She looked back in his direction, giving him a smile. Her smile made him blush and did something funny to his tummy. He smiled back, feeling himself standing taller, puffing out his chest a little more.

They were meeting for dinner later, at her favourite restaurant in Bahamas called *Sapodilla*. She'd told him the dress code was smart casual, then on seeing his confusion, added that they would share a taxi on the way from the airport. She was taking him shopping.

Such was his excitement he started to head for the exit, when the stewardess caught him by the elbow. She smiled then said, in a low voice, 'Your shoes, sir?' nodding in the direction back to his seat.

An hour later, he found himself trying on a floral shirt and Bermuda shorts in *Bonneville Bones*, an uncomfortably fashionable boutique in Harbour Bay.

'Ooh, now, give me a twirl!' said Rosa, from her chair as she sipped Champagne.

'I'm not sure it's really me,' said Easy, catching sight of himself in the mirror.

'Nonsense, the green of the shirt sits perfectly with your skin tone,' mused Rosa, 'I think you look rather dashing.'

Her smile was so disarming he'd have worn anything she selected, but as he looked at himself again in the mirror, he thought he could just about pull it off.

***

Outside the shop a man leaned against the bonnet of his car. His dark sunglasses shaded his eyes and the wide brim of his hat cast a shadow that obscured his face. He held his phone to his ear, nodding as he listened to the voice on the other end.

'Carlo, find out who this kid is and what the hell he is doing with my wife.' Carlo's boss sounded irritable.

Carlo knew that this woman no longer considered herself his boss's wife, but he knew better than to correct him. 'Yes, boss, I got the passenger manifest, I think his name is Ezekiel Olu-'

'Think?' his boss interrupted, 'I don't pay you to think!' The growl down the phone made no less menacing by the distance.

'Yes of course Boss,' said Carlo, 'I meant that I know that is the name on his ticket, but I will confirm that's his real identity.'

'Make sure you do; she will be in Grand Cayman in around 24 hours. I want to know everything before she lands, understood?'

'Yes Boss,' replied Carlo. His boss had already hung up.

He waited another 5 minutes until he saw the woman and the kid leave the shop, before they climbed into the waiting taxi. He had already paid the driver to call him with the details of where he dropped them off. He knew the woman was booked into a suite at The Four Seasons Ocean Club, but wanted to know if the kid went with her.

Carlo approached the assistant in the shop, asking to speak to the manager. A moment later, a tall skinny man emerged from an office behind the cash desk.

'How may I help you today, sir?' he asked Carlo.

'Might we speak in private?' asked Carlo, taking off his sunglasses, he walked toward the open office door.

'Of course, this way sir,' said the manager, gesturing toward the door, Carlo was already half way through.

Carlo stood in the office, taking in the neat desk with an Apple Mac and an open magazine catalogue with pictures of men's clothes.

The manager saw Carlo looking at the catalogue. 'We like to stay up to date with fashion, whilst also catering for those with a taste for the classics.' he said, taking in Carlo's attire.

'I'm sure you do. I'm looking for some assistance.'

'How may I assist, Mister...?' the manager prompted Carlo.

'I am Detective Superintendent Laurent of the Caribbean Financial Action Task Force,' said Carlo, flashing a card in his wallet. 'I need the details used by the woman and young man who have just left.'

'You think they are fraudsters?' asked the worried looking manager.

'They are persons of interest. I don't yet know if they are legitimate. How did they pay?'

'Let me check,' said the manager, sitting down, pulling the computer keyboard forward.

A few key strokes later he turned the screen toward Carlo and pointed. 'The Gentleman used a credit card in the name of E Olufemi.'

'Did your staff check his ID?'

'Yes, it says here he showed a UK passport.'

'Ok, thank you. If I require a formal statement I will be back in touch,' said Carlo making his way out of the office.

Carlo walked to a nearby cafe to order himself a coffee. After 10 minutes he received a call from the taxi driver. He now knew exactly where to find Ezekiel Olufemi. The only question was, what should he do with him?

Chapter Five

Easy showered before changing into his new clothes. Taking a coke from the mini bar he stood on the balcony, looking over the hotel gardens to the sea. It was breathtaking and the warm evening air felt good on his skin. It was a long way from his home in London.

Picking up his mobile phone, he was about to dial his Aunty when the phone rang in his hand. 'Hello JT, switching to video,' he said, placing his drink down.

'Hey Easy, just checking to see-, wow, that's some view kid!' exclaimed JT, as Easy panned the camera around.

'Yes, it is rather special,' replied a grinning Easy.

'How's the journey been so far?'

'Amazing! Truly wonderful...beautiful!' gushed Easy.

'Jings, British Airways must have upped their game!'

'Oh, not the flight, although that too was amazing.'

'So, what's got you so excited?'

'I met a lady at the airport. We're having dinner together tonight, here in Nassau.'

'A lady? What kind of lady Easy?' the amused questioning tone suggested JT was ready to make fun of him.

'Her name is Rosa, she's the most beautiful woman I've ever seen. She looks like a model, from a magazine or something. She took me shopping for clothes for tonight.'

'Oh, Easy, you need to be careful kid. These women hang around airports, looking for wealthy tourists they can sponge off for a couple of weeks.'

'No, you don't understand, we met at the first class lounge at Heathrow. She is obviously quite rich, and very classy. She is also going to Grand Cayman to her bank. I think she has recently divorced.'

'Divorced huh, and she's picked up a young buck to ease her pain?'

'No, she is way older than I am, I think she just wanted to look after me, maybe have some company.'

'Do we need to have a chat about the birds and bees kid?' JT asked, with what Easy knew was good-humoured mockery.

'I'm going to call Aunty now so goodbye, I'll see you tomorrow,' said Easy.

'Sure thing Easy, I'll pick you up at the airport tomorrow. Have a nice time tonight with Mrs Robinson.'

Easy hung up the phone thinking that he hadn't even asked Rosa her surname.

Chapter Six

'It's Carlo, boss, I've confirmed who the kid is.'

'And?'

'He's an 18 year old kid from London. He was a passenger on the same flight as Mrs Bergstrom. The boys at Heathrow saw them talking outside the 1st class lounge.'

'Name?'

'Ezekiel Olufemi.'

'And who is Ezekiel Olufemi?'

'That's the thing boss, he's nobody. He's a Nigerian kid living in London and just left school. A shitty high school at that. He's flown first class, so he must have money from somewhere.'

'What are you thinking Carlo, drugs?'

'He's booked on the same flight to Grand Cayman as your wife tomorrow. It may just be coincidence, but it doesn't feel right, we can't risk him getting in the way tomorrow.'

'Agreed, what do you suggest we do about it?'

'I will have him detained at Cayman Immigration, then we continue as planned.'

'Yes, do that. Rosa must not get to the bank under any circumstances.'

'Boss, just how far do you want us to go?'

'I love my wife very much Carlo, but if needs must, then do whatever is required.'

Carlo had killed, or arranged for others to kill, people on behalf of his boss. All of them had been men, all were necessary. He'd felt nothing for any of them but the prospect of killing Rosa Bergstrom made him feel queasy in his stomach. He hoped there would be an alternative ending that meant he didn't have to hurt the woman who had been nothing but kind to him and his family.

Later that evening he watched Easy leave his hotel before following the taxi to the Sapodilla restaurant. The kid looked nervous, fidgeting with his clothes before he entered the restaurant.

Carlo walked out of the car park, into the shadowy gardens. He found a position with a clear view of the restaurants terrace. He'd been here before on a security detail for the Bergstroms, so had scoped out the gardens. The Bougainvillea that grew up as a tall shrub with its beautiful delicate purple flowers was dense enough to give him cover in the low light. He ensured he could still see the terrace clearly. Realising he was leaning against the same Palm tree as the first time he'd been here, he felt the rough ridges in the bark. The slightly angled trunk made for a great leaning spot, he settled himself into position.

Back then Mr and Mrs Bergstrom had seemed so happy. He was always mindful that Mrs Bergstrom didn't know the details of her husband's business. That was a good thing. Some things a wife, especially Carlo's own, just should not know.

Six months ago, Carlo would never have guessed how things would play out. Things were different now, they would never be the same again.

Chapter Seven

Easy stood at the desk while the maître d' finished a phone call. The man smiled, holding up a hand by way of apology. Easy willed himself not to sound nervous but he felt a lump growing in his throat.

'Good evening Sir, welcome to Sapodilla. Do you have a reservation with us this evening?'

'Ye, ye, yes,' stammered Easy.

'Wonderful, under what name Sir?'

Easy felt panicked, Rosa had booked the table and he didn't know her surname. 'I'm not sure which name she has booked under.'

'Ah, perhaps I can assist. At what time is your table booked and for how many guests?'

'It's a table for two at 7:30.'

'Then we have two possible tables,' said the maître d'.

'The lady I am meeting, her name is Rosa, but I don't know her surname. I think she must come here quite often.'

'Can you describe the lady in question Sir?'

'Yes, she has blonde hair and she, she is the most beautiful woman in the world,' said Easy, earnestly.

'In that case sir, if you would like to follow me, your table is this way,' the maître d' replied, as he smiled giving a nod.

Easy sat awkwardly as the maître d' slid in his chair. He looked around at the terrace and realised the table was set farther apart from the others. There was no privacy but at least their conversation wouldn't be so easily overheard.

'Would you like to see a drinks menu while you wait sir? Or perhaps I can tempt you with our special cocktail? Tonight, we are serving the Sapodilla Americano. I can highly recommend it, we import the finest French, not Italian, Vermouth mixed it with our own blended botanical bitters, finished with a squeeze of bitter orange grown here in our gardens. We serve with a splash of soda and lots of ice.'

'Does it come with an olive?' Easy's look betrayed him as a cocktail novice.

'Well sir, it can, but allow me to suggest a slice of our namesake, the Sapodilla fruit.'

'Sounds perfect then,' said Easy.

'Right away, Sir.'

Easy forced himself not to watch the door, instead turning to look over the dark gardens where occasional lights illuminated flowering shrubs and trees. He heard someone whistling a tune from somewhere in the darkness. It was a haunting tune that he recognised but couldn't think of the song. The whistling continued as he tried to identify where in the gardens it was coming from. Eventually he located the position as a dark area under a big tree but as he stared to try to see who was whistling it stopped.

'Your drink sir,' announced a waiter, who stood with a tray perfectly balanced on his upturned hand.

Easy turned to thank him, the waiter stood by the table waiting, making Easy wonder if he was supposed to tip him.

Seeing the confusion in Easy's face, the waiter said, 'If you would like to try your drink sir, then I can bring you something else if you'd prefer?'

Easy took a sip of the drink, the flavour explosion made his eyes pop, bitter yet sweet with aromas of something new. It was wonderful in his mouth, he took another sip before thanking the waiter again. He saw the maître d' looking over at his table and Easy gave him an enthusiastic smile, receiving a small bow in return.

Ten minutes later, right on time, Rosa breezed through the door where she was met by the effusive maître d'. Easy watched as he bowed to kiss her hand, like something from a movie.

She was radiant and Easy sprang to his feet to welcome her. Her dress was a plain off-white linen, that looked as though it had been made for her. Her jewellery matched the flower she wore in her hair. There was something ethereal yet effortless about the woman and every eye in the restaurant followed her across the terrace.

'Good evening Rosa,' said Easy, using her name to let everyone know she had already shared that treasure with him.

'Good evening Easy,' she smiled at him with an admiring appraisal of his new outfit. 'Please, sit,' she said, as the maître d' helped her take her seat. 'I trust Jean Paul here, has been looking after you?' she asked gesturing to the maître d'.

'Yes, he has made me very welcome,' replied Easy.

'Excellent.'

'Might I offer you an aperitif Mrs Bergstrom,' asked Jean Paul.

'Yes please, but no more Mrs Bergstrom, you must call me Rosa.'

'As you wish, what may I bring you?'

Rosa looked at Easy's glass, 'I'll have whatever my handsome companion is having.'

'It's very good,' said Easy, keenly.

'Shall I bring you a fresh glass, sir?'

'Yes please, I'd like that.'

'Right away,' said Jean Paul, then set off leaving them alone.

'Rosa Bergstrom,' said Easy.

'Yes, my married name.'

'I didn't know what name the table would be booked under. I told Jean Paul I was meeting the most beautiful woman in the world, he knew it must be you,' he said, with sincerity.

'Oh Easy, such flattery is lovely, but the exaggeration quite unnecessary!' She smiled at him, touching her cheek coyly.

After dinner was finished Easy excused himself to use the bathroom. Washing his hands, he thought about their conversation realising Rosa had skilfully avoided telling him very much about herself. She showed lots of interest in him, his story and his future aspirations. He couldn't tell her about Vigilant, but neither could he bring himself to lie to her. In the end he'd told her that he was involved in security, that his specialism involved cyber security. At this she'd become very interested saying her ex-husband was in the same field.

Easy had explained he was in training but he hadn't heard of *Strom-Sec* her husband's company. He'd known he'd have to explain how a trainee could afford a first class ticket so told her a little of his trading in Bitcoin, how he used the arbitrage between prices in the UK and Nigeria.

Rosa had raised an eyebrow at the mention of Nigeria but said no more other than to ask if he still had family there.

Easy returned to the table, absentmindedly whistling the tune he'd heard from the garden earlier.

Rosa spun in her seat to face him, 'That tune, why are you whistling that tune?'

Her concerned look took Easy aback. 'I don't know, I'm not even sure what the tune is. I heard someone whistle it earlier.'

'Where Easy, where did you hear it? Think!' The tremor in her voice was easily discernible. 'When?' her eyes darting around the restaurant.

'I'm not sure, why what's the matter?' He stood beside her but when she leaned away from him he instinctively stepped back. 'Please Rosa, I don't understand, it's just a tune I heard someone whistle. It must be one of those ear-worm thingies.'

'Easy, sit down please,' said Rosa still looking around the restaurant. 'Think, when did you hear that tune being whistled?'

Easy thought for a moment, 'Someone was whistling out in the gardens, before you arrived. I recognise the tune bit don't know what it's called.'

Rosa visibly paled as he spoke. Looking quickly out into the darkness of the gardens she picked up her bag and stood. 'We should go now Easy,' she said quickly, 'I'll drop you back at your hotel.'

Before he could respond, she walked off to speak to Jean Paul, the maître d'. Easy followed, stopping to offer Jean Paul his credit card.

'The Bergstroms have an account with us Sir, the bill is settled. Your taxi awaits,' said Jean Paul ushering Easy to the door.

Outside, the taxi driver was closing the door of the taxi before he opened the opposite side for Easy. He climbed in and sat staring forward, unsure what he'd done wrong or what he should say.

After a few minutes Rosa broke the silence, 'Concierto de Aranjuez.'

'I'm sorry, I don't know what that means,' said Easy not sure where to look.

'The music. You were whistling a tune by Joachim Rodrigo.'

'Ok, I didn't know the name but I recognised the tune. I'm very sorry that I upset you.'

'Oh Easy, I'm the one who is sorry. That music just took me back, to another time and place.'

Easy turned to her leaving a silence for her to fill.

'One of Knut's men used to whistle that tune all the time.'

'Knut?'

'My ex-husband. Knut Bergstrom. His security man is called Carlo. He accompanied us when we travelled, I would always hear him whistling that tune. He told me once it was because my maiden name is Hawthorne. Apparently the Basque word for Hawthorn is Arantza, the piece of music by Joaquin Rodrigo is called Concierto de Aranjuez. The Aranjuez is the Royal Palace near Madrid.'

'Do you think this Carlo is here? Is he following you?' asked Easy, looking back to see if their taxi was being followed.

'It wouldn't surprise me. Knut isn't taking my leaving him very well.' Rosa looked at Easy her face and tone now very serious, 'Easy, it may be dangerous for you to be seen with me. I will drop you at your hotel tonight but tomorrow we should behave like strangers at the airport and on the flight to Grand Cayman.'

'But why, who are you afraid of Rosa?' with more emotion in his voice than he meant to show.

'My husband is not the man I thought he was Easy. I was blinded by his charm and the public act he put on. He is not the man of his public persona.' She stopped to take a steadying breath, 'I control the Cayman bank accounts. He has been trying to prevent me from accessing the money. That's why I am here in person.'

'Do you think he would try to hurt you?'

'Three months ago, I'd have thought you mad to suggest it, but now, now I am not so sure.' She turned away, but not before Easy saw the tears come. He offered her his handkerchief, internally thanking

Hamilton for teaching him that a gentleman always carried one, for just such an occasion.

'Rosa, my friends that I am meeting with in Grand Cayman, I can't tell you too much about them, but they can protect you.'

'Protect me how?'

'They are soldiers, or were soldiers. Now they help people.'

'Do you mean they are mercenaries?'

'No, they don't need to be paid, they just help people who need help. They helped me, now I am working with them.'

The taxi stopped outside Easy's hotel and the driver opened the rear door for him.

'Once I have completed the business at Butterfield's, then I will be free of Knut. Free to begin a new life.'

'I will see you tomorrow, please don't worry, my friends and I will make sure no-one gets in the way of your new life.'

'Good night, sweet boy.'

'Good night Rosa.'

Easy stood watching the taxi drive away into the night. His mind was racing, he needed to speak with JT and Hamilton, but first he had to do some research. Who was Knut Bergstrom and who was Carlo?

Chapter Eight

JT parked the car in the short stay car park before wandering into the arrivals hall at Owen Roberts International Airport. The airport was pretty small but it had decent air conditioning and a place called *The Brew Hut* selling iced coffee.

With his drink in hand, he checked the arrivals board confirming Easy's plane had landed five minutes ago. He'd be through baggage reclaim and customs in another 10 minutes or so.

Thinking back to meeting Easy for the first time, when he had audaciously sought their help, JT marvelled at the maturity of the kid and his skill set. If they were going to take Vigilant forward, then Easy would be a valuable part of the team.

Their future as some sort of vigilante force still felt a bit ridiculous to him. When the team had discussed it, the movies *Seven Samurai* and *Magnificent Seven* had been mentioned, alongside *Robin Hood* and *Equalizer*. But those were all make believe, this was very, very real. They had killed the Kosanian gangsters and the Sheik's network of sexual predators, because it was necessary; the right thing to do. The IRA guys were terrorists, he felt good about taking them down; removing their weaponry from the streets. They had put the weapons to good use, if necessary they would do so again.

He clearly remembered the faces of the IRA bomb-maker and the American they'd dealt with, but the Sheik and his men were a bit of a blur.

The one face he could always see clearly, that still haunted him, though thankfully it was less often as time went on, was the Afghan woman. He would always see her eyes as she opened her coat to show him the bomb vest. She had saved his life knowing that she was going to die and begging him to be the one to kill her. Instinctively his hand went to the scar in his abdomen where the bomb fragment had hit him.

Shaking himself out of that memory, he took a sip of his drink, the slurping noise from the straw made him look around to see who had heard it. No-one paid him any attention. In his shorts and linen shirt, he looked like 50% of the relaxed people waiting to greet someone at the arrivals gate. The other 50% wore business attire of varying degrees. From suits with shirt a tie, to a uniform or two among the chauffeurs and hotel pick up service guys.

Through the huge, partially tinted windows, JT could see a line of executive cars parked up behind the row of shuttle minibuses.

A uniformed police officer, wearing an immaculately pressed white shirt and red stripe on the leg of his black trousers, was faux marching along the row of parked vehicles.

JT watched as a big man climbed out of a black SUV with tinted windows to speak with the police officer. The big man gestured dismissively for the officer to go away, with a shooing motion. JT expected to watch a confrontation take place, automatically starting to move in the direction of the exit. The cop was armed, but the big guy looked pretty menacing, something about him made JT's sixth sense tingle. Before he could get to the automatic doors, and much to his surprise, the officer spun on his heels, marching off away from the guy. JT watched the big guy smirk leaning in to talk to someone else in the darkened vehicle.

Just then, a murmur came from the waiting greeters as the arrivals gate opened and the first of the passengers emerged. First came a young couple, with a baby each in their arms, who were instantly surrounded by a joyous family.

The next person to walk through the sliding door made women stare, men stood a little straighter. She was tall and very elegant, with blonde hair tied back in a bow. When she took off her sunglasses, there was a split second of silence as everyone gawped at her beauty.

A man stepped forward holding a name board, JT moved to see the name. *BERGSTROM.*

The man waiting to greet her wore a grey suit with matching hat, but to JT's eye he was definitely more security than driver.

The arrivals door whooshed back open, JT turned to look for Easy but instead an older man, in a gaudy shirt and panama hat, strutted out with an unlit cigar in his mouth. A driver rushed over to take the man's briefcase before they wandered over to the exit.

JT caught sight of the beautiful woman outside, surprised to see her being shown to the black SUV. She stopped abruptly at the open rear door, then was pushed unceremoniously in by the driver who had met her at the gate. He jumped into the rear beside her, before the vehicle sped off. Grabbing his phone from his pocket, JT tried but failed to get a photo of the vehicle's number plate.

The crowd moved as more people came through the arrivals gate. JT turned but couldn't see any sign of Easy. He checked his phone, the last message from Easy was from 15 minutes ago saying, **Just landed,** accompanied by a smiling emoji with sunglasses.

After a few more minutes the crowd of greeters had dispersed, only one other person stood waiting against the rope barrier. She was a driver, holding a name board, but JT couldn't see the name.

He tried calling Easy's phone but it rang out, so he sent a message, **OK?**. No reply came.

Ten minutes later, a disgruntled Easy came through the automatic doors. He looked around at the almost empty terminal building, then his face dropped when he saw the name on the last remaining driver's board, *HAWTHORNE*.

Chapter Nine

'She's in trouble! We have to find her!' Easy said, urgently.

'Find who?' asked JT, though he had a feeling he already knew.

'Rosa!' said Easy.

'Bergstrom?' asked JT, to Easy's back as he was walking over to talk to the driver.

'Are you waiting for Rosa?' Easy asked the woman.

'*No sah*, I is waiting for *Awtorn, she soon come me tinks.*' she replied, in a thick Caymanian accent as she looked past him to the arrivals door.

'You didn't see her come through already?' asked Easy.

'Nevah met the lady, I stannin' here, wid me board, whole time though.'

JT approached asking, 'who arranged your pick up?'

'I works for Ritz-Carlton. You know dis lady I meant collect?'

'I do,' said Easy.

'You not together though?'

'No, I got held up at Customs.'

'Thanks for your help Miss,' said JT, taking Easy by the elbow, walking him toward the exit.

Easy looked left and right scanning the terminal as they walked.

'She's gone Easy,' said JT. 'I saw who took her.'

'You saw her?'

'Everyone saw her Easy, she's as beautiful as you said.'

'How did you know it was her?'

'She was met by a guy with a board that said, *BERGSTROM*. He looked legit, but then he walked her to a black SUV that I saw a goon at earlier.'

'A goon?'

'Yeah, a big guy, there was someone else in the car too. The driver shoved her in the back, then they sped off.'

'Aren't there usually Police outside at an Airport? I haven't seen one yet.'

'I think the big guy scared him off, or told him to make himself scarce. I couldn't get the number plate of the SUV but this isn't a big island, there can't be too many around.'

'It might have been Carlo.'

'Who is Carlo?'

'He is security for her husband, or rather her ex-husband. She told me about him last night when she got spooked.'

'Okay, listen, let's get back to the villa, it's only 15 minutes away, we'll pick up Rambo. On the way, you can tell me everything you know.'

'How is the phone signal?'

'There's 4G available, the Wi-Fi seems good at the villa, why?'

Easy pulled his laptop out of his bag, opening it. 'Airport CCTV.'

'Good idea kid, how long will that take?'

'Depends on their security, but I'll have it before we get to the villa. I told her we'd help her.'

JT drove the hired Jeep Wrangler out of the car park, heading up Dorcy Drive, passing the 19-81 Brewing Company, then the Esso filling station. 'Listen Easy, what exactly have you told this woman about us?'

'Nothing really, just that we help people.'

'Help people?'

'That's we do isn't it? Vigilant help people, Rosa needs our help.'

'Yes, I suppose it is, but we can't go around advertising or offering out our services. We're supposed to be a secret.'

'Don't you want to help Rosa?'

'Of course I want to help her, the guys will all be up for helping, but in future-'

'Slow down, in fact go back into the filling station.' Easy told JT not letting him finish his sentence.

JT indicated before pulling into a lay-by to do a U turn. 'What did you see?'

'I just want to check the CCTV cameras, if they're facing the right way they'd have caught all of the vehicles heading West and North. If the SUV didn't come this way then they've gone South to the quieter end of the island.'

'Smart thinking. You understand what I'm saying about us being secret though, right kid?'

Easy opened the maps app on his phone, 'There's another filling station just the other side of the airport,' he zoomed in on the name. 'It's called *Jose's Rubis*, we should head there to check their cameras too. We might get lucky. And yes, I do understand, we're a secret.'

Chapter Ten

Rosa blinked as the hood was removed, instantly hit by the musty smell from the warehouse.

She had been dragged from the car and placed on a hard wooden chair in the middle of the dirty concrete floor. Looking around she saw the only windows were high up next to the roof. The walls appeared to be made of old wooden planks. There were piles of sacks full of something bulky, apparently left to decay, much like the building.

A man she didn't recognise stood before her, but she had decided not to let him look her in the eye.

He crouched before her, placing his hand on her knee to steady himself as he bent forward to pull the tape from her mouth. 'Mrs Bergstrom, please do not scream or shout out. It would be a waste of time, as there is no one to hear you. Secondly, it is surely a sin to cover any part of such a beautiful face.'

She nodded, then forced herself not to recoil as he touched her face. The pain made her wince as he ripped the tape from her mouth.

'My apologies Mrs Bergstrom, I know from experience, it is better to rip the band aid off.' He smiled at her, but made no attempt to get back up from where he crouched.

Rosa felt her skin crawl, the beginnings of nausea churning in her stomach. She looked around taking in as many details of the building as she could. She looked at the windows, which were old and filthy. The roof was supported by metal beams that looked held together by rust and cobwebs. There was no obvious door that she could see, the entrance must be behind her, beyond the SUV she'd been brought here in. If there was a rear door, she guessed it would be behind the stack of sacks and boxes to the left. The light and shadows from the window told her roughly where the sun was, she had been driven around hooded, for somewhere between 40 minutes and an hour. She knew Grand Cayman wasn't a big place, with the airport pretty central so thought they had driven her about to disorientate her. It had worked, she had no concept of where she was on the island.

'Thirsty?' the man asked her.

She nodded, then thought about the movies she'd seen when someone had been kidnapped. Make yourself human, try to strike up a relationship with your captors; make it harder for them to kill you.

'Please may I have some water? In my bag I have some pills, they're for my migraines.'

'You do not look to have a migraine.' Another man's voice stated, from behind her. The man's accent had a hint of soft German.

'They're preventative, please they are very important.'

'What happens if you don't take them?' asked the big man still crouched in front of her.

'Stress makes a migraine more likely and then I'm a mess. It can last days.'

'Give her the medicine,' said the German, 'tomorrow she must to go to the bank.'

'The bank?' she asked, but was already aware of what they had planned for her.

'Tomorrow you will attend the bank, to transfer the money that belongs to your husband into another account.'

'And then?' she asked trying to turn herself far enough to see who had spoken.

'Once the transfer is complete, you will be free to go, when the boss gives his permission.'

'And if I don't transfer the money?'

'Mrs Bergstrom, I have no wish to cause you any harm or alarm. Believe me when I say that my colleague, there in front of you, will take great pleasure in persuading you. Gary can be, *very* persuasive.'

Rosa looked at the man crouching in front of her, he grinned at her, licking his lips.

'I'd have to take my time, make sure I enjoy every inch of you, Mrs Bergstrom. The boss says that if you don't play along, then I can have you to do what I want with.' He stood in front of her, pushing his crotch toward her face making her twist away in the chair as he roared with laughter.

Rosa stayed silent, trying to gather her thoughts. Her mind raced, she knew that as she'd seen Gary's face he was going to kill her. The thought of what else he was going to do to her, made the thought of being dead more appealing.

The German guy handed her a bottle of water from over her shoulder. 'What is the name of your pills?'

'Migraleve, they're in the white box.'

'How many?'

'I take one a day, usually before a meal.'

'I can offer you only a biscuit.'

They are not here for the long haul then thought Rosa. Probably thinking they can frighten me into doing the transfer at the bank tomorrow. They'll pretend they're going to release me, kill me as soon as possible, then be on the next flight out of here.

'You do know that I arranged to collect bearer bonds when I close the accounts?'

'What does that mean?' asked the German.

'It means, tomorrow at 10:30 I am supposed to meet the manager at Butterfield's, a Mr Jeffries, to sign the closure paperwork. As tomorrow is Friday, the bonds will be ready for collection on Monday.'

'Monday? That is impossible. Tomorrow you will tell them you changed your mind, make the transfer instead.'

'I can't, it's too late now. The transaction has already started, all $50,000,000 is in bonds awaiting my signature. As Knut will no doubt have worked out, I changed the account so I must attend in person. The bank has a statutory three day compliance or whatever check, which means I, and I alone, must pick them up on Monday.'

'Very clever Mrs Bergstrom, very clever indeed,' the German said, his tone showed no concern.

'So, you can see that it is futile to hold me here. Knut cannot have the money, he'll just have to live with it.'

'An apt phrase you used, very apt,' said the German.

'What do you mean?' asked Rosa, although the dread in her stomach told her she already knew the answer.

'Your husband is insistent that the money belongs to him. My instructions are that I should persuade you, through whatever means necessary, to hand over the money. If you do so, then I am to let you live and walk away.'

'And if I don't?'

'Then Mrs Bergstrom, I will have to unleash Gary, for him to take his pleasure with you. Fifty million dollars' worth of pleasure could last weeks, though I doubt very much you will find the experience pleasurable. If you die in the process then Mr Bergstrom will inherit the money, as you are still officially married, no? It makes sense to walk away Mrs Bergstrom. You are a very beautiful woman, you will have your pick of rich suitors in no time.'

'I don't need a rich man; I can take care of myself thank-you very much!' Rosa hissed.

'As you wish Mrs Bergstrom, as you wish. We will escort you to the bank tomorrow, you will sign the papers. On Monday we will return you to the bank to retrieve the bonds. After which, you will stay here with Gary, until I am safely off the island. Then you will be free to do as you please.'

'Whatever you say,' said Rosa, as she made a plan to call the police from the bank, and wait for the cavalry. How could these guys be so stupid to think she would just roll over for them, for Knut. The thought of him made the bile rise in her stomach. His lies, his criminality and how he took her for a complete fool, made the anger in her boil.

She was dragged back to the present, as an object was fastened around her neck. It was covered in cloth that felt like silk, like a heavy necklace.

'What is this?' she asked, as she squirmed in the chair.

'A little persuader that I prepared for you,' said the German.

'What do you mean, persuader?'

'I am going to untie your hands now Mrs Bergstrom, but before I do so, I must warn you that your new neck attire is very dangerous. You should not attempt to remove it. In a moment, you will see that I have used your favourite Hermes scarf to wrap it. Inside the scarf is a coil of detonating cord, the clasp is a remote trigger. The device also has a proximity switch, which means that if you and I are too far apart while it is armed, then it will activate.'

'Activate?' Rosa felt herself shrink in the chair. She barely noticed the knife slice through the tape that had held her hands to the chair.

'Detonation cord is an explosive Mrs Bergstrom. Should this particular charge detonate, then it will part your head from your shoulders. You won't feel a thing I assure you, so please do not fret.'

Gary grinned at her as he sliced the tape at her ankles.

'Now, we will sort out some food Mrs Bergstrom. I am thinking of sending Gary for pizza and beer. What do you think?'

Chapter Eleven

Detective Inspector Rory Maxwell sat at his desk at New Scotland Yard, when a mobile phone in his desk drawer vibrated. Opening the drawer, he saw the message on the screen was just two letters; **JT**.

Switching off his computer he picked up the file on his desk. The file was the last case he was working on, before he quit the force and the Counter Terrorist Unit for good.

He was to be a fully-fledged member of Vigilant, the thought of which excited and scared him in equal measure. The last three months had been a whirlwind. From helping out his friend, to being abducted, to killing a corrupt colleague in self-defence, it beggared belief how much his life had changed. Superintendent Steve Harper and Chief Inspector Ella Misu were dead, their criminal gang along with them. They continued to cast a shadow over him, he knew that would always be the case.

The Counter Terrorism Unit was the most secure part of the building at New Scotland Yard, but after what had happened with Harper and Misu, he no longer trusted anyone.

Misu was a plant who was part of, perhaps even heir to, the Kosanian crime gang. She had embedded herself into the Metropolitan Police Service. Her intelligence paired with her good looks, meant no-one was suspicious of her accelerated rise through the ranks. It became apparent later that Superintendent Steve Harper was also corrupt and working for the Kosanians. He and his wife had grown very wealthy, as they facilitated some of the Kosanians activities, arranging for a blind eye to be turned to others.

Vigilant raided the country house the Kosanians had filled with trafficked or kidnapped women and children. They were destined to be sexual playthings for a depraved Sheik and his friends. Maxwell had tried to confront Harper, but ended up being ambushed and taken prisoner. He'd had a narrow escape, with Easy to thank for taking out the Kosanian hitman who was about to kill him.

Then Misu had tried to mow him down with a car, he'd been forced to shoot her through the windscreen. It was self-defence, but there was no way he could report it. Hamilton had made sure there was no trace of him ever having been at the scene.

Hamilton had become a regular part of his life, both in and out of work, as he fed Maxwell information that had been obtained unofficially. They had talked about it at length over Hamilton's favourite 21 year old Macallan whisky. They were both married to their jobs, with Maxwell now divorced. Hamilton had been widowed after the IRA murdered his wife.

They had formed a friendship of sorts, a good working relationship, but Maxwell knew he could never fully trust Hamilton. He was a spy after all, and everyone knows you can never trust a spy! The man seemed to play 3D chess in his mind appearing to be always a step, or three, ahead of everyone else. Some of that was down to his access to intelligence, the incredibly illegal network of systems and operators he seemed to have at his disposal. But then, if you have no-one to answer to, you can do as you please, thought Maxwell.

He locked away the file he'd been working on. It was a bizarre fact that he already knew who the culprit was. Hamilton had passed information to him, that identified a man called Zane Elm as the eco-terrorist who had sent explosive packages to several MPs, the CEOs of every oil company and bank based in the UK. None of the principals had been hurt, but a mail room lady had lost a hand, while another had suffered burns across his chest and face. Now it was Rory's job to work back from knowing the who, to build a case against Elm as if routine, and legal, police work had discovered the who, the how and the why.

Zane Elm had been arrested three times; once for gluing himself to the road outside the Scottish Parliament in Edinburgh, once for throwing soup over a Rembrandt painting in the National Gallery. The last occasion was eight months ago, when Elm had breached the perimeter fence at RAF Lossiemouth air base, almost making it to one of the Typhoon fighters based there, before an RAF Police dog dragged him screaming to the ground.

The first two episodes had seen him almost applauded from the bench in the Magistrates Courts, the judge seemed to think it was all a jolly jape. The incident at RAF Lossiemouth however, saw him sentenced to a year in prison. He'd been released under the early release system after six months. Within a week of his release, the campaign of letter bombs had begun.

Elm was the poster boy of so many middle class eco warrior wannabes. They had no idea of the lengths the guy would go, to push his agenda. He obviously wasn't working alone either. Packages had been sent simultaneously, from across the country, which was a message in itself; *we're everywhere!*

It was late, but still warm in London, so Maxwell left his jacket, making his way out through the security exits.

'Goodnight Guv,' said DC Maria Charalambous, the duty night-shift desk officer.

'I'll be back Maria, just going to clear my head,' replied Maxwell, as he walked past her desk. He turned, mock tip toeing back, to help himself to a piece of the baklava Maria's father made.

Maria looked up, pushing some of the mass of black curly hair from her face, 'Help yourself Guv, you'll be doing me a favour.'

'You're not a fan of your Dad's cooking?' Maxwell replied, as he pushed the moist square of honey soaked pastry into his mouth.

'Problem is, I'm too big a fan. If I eat much more, I'll have to be surgically removed from this seat!'

Maxwell sniggered as he walked away chewing, waving back over his shoulder.

Out on the street, he walked along the Victoria Embankment into Whitehall Gardens before taking a seat on a bench by the Korean War Memorial. The Ministry of Defence building was behind him, as he looked out towards the Thames.

Taking the phone from his pocket, he considered for a second how Hamilton had given the Vigilant Team these phones. He'd explained they ran through a black hole at GCHQ, so they were completely secure and untraceable.

He didn't yet know Hamilton that well, but well enough to know, there was no way the man wasn't party to every message or call made on one of the phones.

Pushing that thought aside, he called JT's number.

'Rory, we need your help,' said JT.

'No social chit chat or preamble then? What's up, the Pina Coladas gone off?'

'Sorry, but it's serious Rory, we have a situation.'

Maxwell sat upright, all business despite the fact he'd been at work for the last 14 hours, 'I'm listening.'

'Do you know the names Rosamunde and Knut Bergstrom?'

'I've heard of Knut Bergstrom, he's the corporate cyber security guy. His company *StromSec* are who you call when hackers have got into your system. Or, if you've any sense, you get him in before they hack you. The Met use his company, as do most Government departments, why?'

'Shit, I think this could be even more of a problem than we realised.'

'Hang on, I think I read his name a couple of weeks ago in a bulletin. StromSec won a contract from the Government, to protect the Air Traffic Control service in the UK and Ireland.'

'Rory, I think Bergstrom may not be legit, and his wife Rosamunde has been taken.'

'Taken?'

'Yes, I saw her bundled into a car at the airport. It's a long story, but she befriended Easy, they were on the same flight.'

'Is Easy ok?'

'He's fine, upset, but fine. Can you find out what you can about Bergstrom and get back to me, asap?'

'Of course, have you spoken to Hamilton yet?'

'No, he's my next call.'

'Okay, I'm heading back to the office. I'll liaise with Hamilton and get back to you.'

'Thanks Rory.'

'No worries.'

'Oh, and Rory, hurry up and finish that case, Vigilant needs you!'

Chapter Twelve

Hamilton sat in the corner of the dining-room at his club. The East India Club, in London's St James's Square, was old fashioned enough to preserve traditions, such as no phones in the dining-room. However, as he was the only gentleman left so late in the evening, no-one was going to complain.

He pulled the phone from his jacket pocket, the screen read **JT**. He smiled at the use of the most succinct of messages, an unnecessary but pleasant attempt at a code.

Pressing the pre-set for JT's number, he folded his newspaper, adjusting it to fill in 19 across on the cryptic crossword; the clue had read, *The river of literal Yoruba head, named my Hebrew light, going solo. 7 letters.* '*ORINOCO,*' he muttered, as he wrote with his ancient fountain pen.

'Ori what?' asked JT as he answered the phone.

'19 across - *Orinoco*'

'Sorry, I don't follow, Orinoco, as in the river?'

'The clue read, *The river of literal Yoruba head, named my Hebrew light, going solo.* There is a Yoruba religious tradition of sorts, called ORI, which also happens to be Hebrew for; *my light.* Then *going solo* leads us to *NO COmpany*. Quite clever I thought, although I did have the first letter from 8 down; *POLYAMOROUS.*'

'Hamilton, sorry to interrupt your crossword, but we have a situation.'

'I gathered this wasn't a social call.'

'Do you know of a Knut Bergstrom and his cyber security company, *StromSec*?'

'I've certainly heard of them, but not had the pleasure of meeting Bergstrom himself. They run cyber security for quite a few Government departments as I understand it.'

'And soon to run the Air Traffic Control security too.'

'Ah yes, I recall someone mentioning something about that. It's a big contract.'

'Do you know anything about Knut himself and his wife Rosamunde, she's better known as Rosa?'

'Not much at all, as I recall he is based between the UK and Switzerland, he runs *StromSec* across the world. He famously prevented or repaired a hack on a hospital server in Zurich, that's how he made his name. Then there was a big data breach at the German Ministry of Justice; he managed to sort that one too. After that there was a clamour for his company's protection.'

'Nothing about the wife?'

'No, but I've just googled her as we speak, she's a very attractive lady. Something of a trophy wife perhaps? Knut looks rather small and geekish stood next to her on red carpets.'

'She was taken, at the airport here in Grand Cayman, an hour or so ago.'

'Taken? As in against her will?'

'Certainly looked that way. They switched the pick-up driver. I saw them bundle her into a SUV outside the terminal.'

'How does this involve you and/or Vigilant? There's a reasonable Police Service in the Caymans.'

'She befriended Easy on the way here; they ended up travelling together. Easy was stopped at Customs for no apparent reason, conveniently meaning she was on her own when she exited arrivals.'

'Is Easy ok?' asked Hamilton with genuine concern.

'He's fine, he's accessing CCTV as we speak. There's a gap in the airport CCTV that just happens to be when the incident took place. Easy thinks it's been wiped.'

'I'll have some enquiries made, see what we know about the Bergstroms. I'll get straight back to you.'

'Do you think this might be something to do with Government contracts?'

'I don't know, but everything is possible, until it's not. Perhaps there is a more obvious motive?'

'Such as?'

'Like you, everyone is in Grand Cayman for one reason only, that reason is the motive behind the majority of crimes; money. My advice is to follow the money. It is always enlightening.'

'Follow the money, got it.'

'Found it!' came Easy's voice in the background, as he spun his laptop to show an image of a black SUV.

'We've got a lead at this end. I'll await your call.'

'Indeed, when are you expecting the rest of the team?'

'They should all be here by Sunday morning.'

'Excellent, this could be a nice little job for Vigilant.'

'Let's see,' said JT, but realised Hamilton had already hung up.

'I've got the registration number, it's registered to a company called Exec Fleet based in Georgetown.'

'Can you get into their system?'

'Give me a minute, their firewall is pretty decent.'

'Which way was it headed?'

'North, they came this way,' said Easy, without looking up from his lap top.

'Rambo, go head into town, find us the biggest most detailed map of the island you can.'

'Will do. Anything else?'

JT thought for a moment, 'Yeah, go see about the possibility of hiring a helicopter.'

'Seriously?' asked Rambo, with a grin.

'Why not, we've all spent the last couple of months getting our licence, might as well put it to good use?'

'How long for?'

'I don't know. Easy, did Rosa tell you when she was due to fly back?'

'Tuesday, she said, she was booked on the early flight.'

'Then whatever is going on is likely to be over by Tuesday. If they'll let you book it for the next week then go for it. See if we can use the helipad over by the tennis club too.'

'I'm on it. Do I have a budget?'

'No, doesn't matter what it costs!' chirped Easy.

'Roger that!' said Rambo, heading for the door.

'Why can't this island have ANPR cameras like the UK? That would make finding the car a lot easier?' asked Easy.

'It's a little island and not the sort of place cars get stolen, or there be much crime at all, I wouldn't think.' replied JT.

'No, I know, it's just frustrating. I wish they had more criminals here!'

'There's plenty of them using the banks here to hide their ill-gotten gains, some might say we're doing the same thing.'

'When Rambo is back, can we drive around a bit, you never know we might see the SUV?'

'Sure thing, when we have the map we can cross off streets as we check them.'

'It's probably a waste of time I know, but at least we'll be doing something.'

'It's reconnaisance kid, that's never a waste of time. Always good to know the lay of the land.'

'I wish the rest of the team could be here, we could split up and search faster.'

'Cooky and Posty will be here Saturday lunchtime, they're arriving in Miami tomorrow. Taff and Joe are due first thing Sunday morning.'

'Can't they come quicker?'

'They're on the first available flight.'

JT's phone rang, he answered switching on speaker phone. 'Sorry boss, no dice with the helicopter people. They're booked solid for the weekend with folk from a cruise ship,' said Rambo.

'Did you offer them more money?' asked Easy.

'Yep, they said the cruise ships are their main income, so they can't let them down.'

'Wait there, give me a couple of minutes,' said Easy.

'What's your plan?' asked JT.

'They're about to get a whole lot of cancellations,' said Easy, typing away furiously.

'Ok!' said JT, once again impressed by Easy's skills and lateral thinking.

'Tell them you're scouting for a Russian billionaire who wants to buy property here.'

'Good idea. I got a couple of maps boss, there are thousands of villas and hotels north of the airport. Most of the industrial infrastructure too. It'll be a needle in a haystack trying to find a black SUV.'

'We've got to try!' Easy replied, a little louder than necessary.

'Don't worry, we'll find her,' JT tried to reassure him.

'I'm in. I'm cancelling the bookings from tomorrow morning until next Thursday morning. Rambo go ask them to check their bookings.'

'Won't that look a bit suspicious?'

'Yeah, but enough money will make them forget about that.'

'I'll go try again,' said Rambo.

'Good lad, tell them we'll take good care of their chopper. What is they have?'

'It's a Eurocopter AS350 B2, its liveried to look like an aquarium.'

'Seriously?'

'Yeah it's a tour guide set up, 10 minute buzz round the island sort of thing.'

'Capacity?'

'1+6 without much kit.'

'The decal might help, it'll look like just another tour. Go offer them $100k for five days, they can't refuse that kind of money, especially after their bookings *cancelled* on them last minute.'

'I'm on it, call you back when the deal is done.'

Chapter Thirteen

Rambo drove at a sedate pace through Georgetown with JT and Easy each holding street maps. JT marked off the streets they'd checked looking for a black SUV and any buildings with garages or places to store a vehicle. There were lots of car-ports attached to houses, but not too many garages which made their job slightly easier, but still pretty close to impossible.

Easy was marking off CCTV cameras, but they were few and far between. Those that he found he photographed on his phone, to show the direction they were pointed.

Georgetown formed the fulcrum between the two halves of the island on the map. To the north ran the vertical section all the way up to West Bay. It held most of the tourist resorts, including the famous seven mile beach, which in reality was just over five miles long.

Running horizontally on the map, an urban area stretch from Georgetown to Bodden Town. Beyond that was mostly green space as far as Sparrowhawk Bay, with small settlements around the coastline, all connected by the A3 road.

'Boss, we haven't eaten since breakfast, it's nearly closing time for most places. Should we stop and pick something up?' asked Rambo.

'Yes, good idea, according to this map there's a couple of places round the corner. Looks like a fried chicken place and a crab shack.'

'Crab sounds good to me,' said Rambo, licking his lips.

'I'm not hungry,' Easy declared from the back seat.

'Need to eat kid, we'll be half an hour tops, then we can hit the road again.'

'Yeah ok, but I vote chicken, crabs are just big sea spiders. I'm not eating spiders!'

'Ok kid, you have chicken, Rambo can have the sea spider.'

Rambo pulled into a carpark shared by six small retail units. He parked next to an old pick up truck that looked as if it came straight off a farm and hadn't been washed in a while. In the rear window of the cab was a sticker, with the regimental badge of the Cayman Islands Regiment.

Sitting in the passenger seat was a young man who looked like a local and wearing a British Army green t-shirt. He nodded at JT as he got out of the passenger seat.

'Good evening,' said JT.

'Evenin' Sah,' replied the soldier, with a relaxed toothy grin.

'Food good here?' asked JT.

'I like the crab 'ere, Mama Pat is a great cook, best in town.'

'Better than MRE packs I'll bet?' asked JT referring to the British Army ration pack.

'Yes Sah, much better. You military yourself?'

'Retired, I served 12 years.'

'You see much action?'

'A bit, Afghanistan and a couple of other places. How about you? I didn't know The Caymans had a regiment.'

'Yes Sah, we been running just a couple of years. We always recruiting but there's not so many volunteers. We got a few officers come from England, proper Sandhurst officers too.'

'I see, where are you based, I might know some of them?'

'Our barracks are at Combermere, Sah. You'd be made most welcome I'm sure.'

'Thanks, what sort of strength do you have?'

'We is around 98, as I says we struggle to recruit.'

'Is your kit all the same as the regular army?'

'We mostly train for emergency disaster type o' ting, but we got some kit. I tink it must be same.'

'What sort of weapons do you use? Can't be much use for say an L129A1 out here?'

'Ah now, we do have one long range sharpshooter rifle Sah, but not too many of us is trained with it. No, we use the SA80, but we also get Glock 17 sidearms to train with.'

'Decent kit!'

'Not bad Sah. Must admit, I like the Heckler n Koch them Naval Reserve guys have.'

'Naval Reserve?'

'Yes Sah, they have their little base over at the harbour. They share their little interceptor boat with the Police. They call themselves the Pirate chasers!' said the young soldier laughing.

'Boss, I'm going to get some cash from the ATM.' said a hungry Rambo in an apparent attempt to hurry JT along.

'Ok, be right with you.' said JT. He turned to the young soldier and offered his hand. 'Nice meeting you soldier, and thank you for your service.'

'Nice to meet you too Sah, enjoy your crab!'

Easy had been listening to the conversation from the back of the car while reviewing the photographs he'd taken of CCTV cameras. He got out of the vehicle as Rambo returned handing Easy some cash.

'That should buy you some chicken Easy, though you really are missing out with the err, sea spider!' He smiled at Easy hoping to cheer him up a little.

Easy took the cash with a nod and a muttered, 'Thank you.'

'Funny thing, the ATM was from a bank called *Butterfields*, now that is the weirdest bank name I've ever heard.'

Easy stopped in his tracks, 'That's it, that's what she said.'

'What who said?' asked JT.

'Rosa, she said she was going to *Butterfields* but I didn't know what it meant and was too embarrassed to ask. It's her bank, *Butterfields Bank*.'

'Okay...' said a confused Rambo.

'She was going to her bank tomorrow; we can wait for her to show up at the bank.'

'Won't there be more than one branch?' asked Rambo.

'It'll be the HQ, that's where they handle the bigger transactions. If this is all about money, I doubt the amounts will be small,' said JT.

'Okay,' said Easy, 'let's get to the bank.'

'It's 9pm kid, the bank is closed. Meantime, let's eat,' JT told him.

Easy looked a little crestfallen but nodded and trudged toward the restaurant.

'What was the squaddie saying to it?' asked Rambo.

'He's Cayman Islands Regiment. They're more emergency relief than soldiers. They respond to hurricanes, earthquakes and the like. Importantly though, they have an armoury as do the Naval Reserve. If we should end up having to negotiate with brass and lead; we might just have to borrow some kit.'

Chapter Fourteen

Rosa was allowed to use the bathroom alone. *Bathroom* was an exaggeration, it consisted of a disgusting stained toilet bowl, without a seat, and a cracked grimy sink. There was no running water, so a bucket of water that smelled of the sea, sat beside the toilet for flushing. A separate 5-gallon tub of fresh water sat beside the sink for washing.

Only one shard of the broken mirror was left in the frame. Rosa used it to try to get a look at the device around her neck. It was wrapped in her Hermes scarf and felt like a coil of rope was inside. She had no idea what detonator cord felt like, or how reactive it was, so didn't dare touch it too much. At the back of the loop behind her neck, she gently touched a small box about the size and shape of a matchbox. She felt the cool, smooth surface through the silk scarf and thought it must be metal, though it didn't feel particularly heavy. She knew it wouldn't take much electronic hardware to be a trigger of some kind, she'd seen such things in movies.

'Hurry up in there!' came the shout from Gary.

The salivating attack dog just stared at her incessantly. He gave her the creeps. She knew exactly what he wanted to do to her. The thought made her sick to her stomach. She also knew she had to survive this somehow. Knut may have won this battle but she would make sure he lost the war.

It was seven weeks since she'd found out the truth. Her husband, the celebrated cyber security expert, was a con man, a thief, willing for people to die just so that he could make more money. He was already rich beyond any one person's needs. He had the houses, his collection of cars, use of the company jet whenever he wished. They had mixed in the best circles, were patrons of the arts; everyone said how fabulous their life was. He had financed her hobbies and her charitable works. He even came with her to open the orphanages in Bangladesh and Nigeria.

How could she have missed it? How did he hide it from her, this whole other side of his personality.

If she hadn't made him a drink, and taken it into his study while he was on the phone, then she might never have known. He'd been a bit drunk, so didn't hear her come in as he was speaking on the conference call.

She'd stood listening, not to snoop, not at first, but waiting for a gap in the conversation so as not to disturb him.

Instead, she had listened as Knut instructed one of his staff to target a Hospital in the Czech Republic, with a DDoS attack. He said this would make them more amenable to a contract with *StromSec*. They would appear as a white knight, to restore the Hospital servers.

Worse than that, he spoke about the million euros his guys had extorted from a factory in Denmark, after using a Ransomware attack to close down their system. He laughed when he explained how inflated the price was that he would offer them, to *protect* their system from future attacks. Knut was not only offering to protect the hen house; he was also the fox.

'Mrs Bergstrom, you must come soon, the pizza will be all gone,' said the German, from outside the bathroom door.

'I'm not hungry,' she replied.

'As you wish Mrs Bergstrom, but I cannot promise you in the morning a decent breakfast.'

She listened to his footsteps as he walked away, then splashed some more water on her face. She used a paper towel to pat her face and hands dry, then looked for a bin. When it was obvious there was no bin she crumpled it into a ball throwing it beside the other dozen or so on the floor.

Opening the door, she instinctively knew Gary would be waiting for her. He forced her to squeeze by him, trying to induce some bodily contact. It was like an electric shock when his hand stroked her back, guiding her past.

'There's a good girl. Come get some grub now, we wouldn't want you getting all skinny now would we. Much better to have something to hold on to!' His snigger was part grunt.

Rosa walked into the warehouse, over to where the German sat at a rickety table with two pizza boxes in front of him. She really didn't want to eat, but somehow felt safer with the German than with Gary.

On the table were half a dozen bottles of White Tip beer. The condensation on them told her they were cold.

'I'll take a beer,' she told the German.

He lifted a beer and took a knife from his belt which he used to prize off the lid.

'Aren't you joining me?' she asked him glancing at the remaining beers.

'Why not?' said the German, with the faintest of smiles. For the first time she saw that he had braces on his lower teeth.

'I had braces too,' she told him. He looked a little confused until she pointed at her own teeth.

'Ah, mein brackets,' he said, nodding as he opened his bottle of beer.

'I had them as a teenager, I hated them.'

'Yes, they are not popular with young people. My brackets are more practical than cosmetic Mrs Bergstrom.'

'Please, call me Rosa,' she told him taking a sip from her bottle.

'As you wish, Rosa,' he replied, after a long slug of his beer.

'What is your name?'

'Jurgen.'

'I've never heard Knut mention a Jurgen before. How long have you worked for *StromSec*.'

'Ah, I have worked for Mr Bergstrom for 5 years, but the work I carry out on his behalf is not something he would likely discuss.' He looked at her without emotion or any hostility.

'What is it you do for him, exactly?' she asked, unsure if she really wanted to know.

'My role is most often to deliver messages, to ensure the good conduct of other employees.' He had a slightly self-satisfied look, as if happy with his word play.

'And kidnapping?' she asked, with an intensity that took Jurgen by surprise.

'Mr Bergstrom pays me well. For that reason I am asked to carry out tasks that are somewhat distasteful, but necessary.'

'Kidnapping a woman and threatening to kill her, upsets your *sensibilities*?'

'Mrs Bergstrom, I assure you I take no pleasure in this business, unlike my colleague Gary who relishes such tasks. Tomorrow you will complete your paperwork at the bank. On Monday you will collect the bonds. As I have stated my mission is to take possession of the money. To return it to Mr Bergstrom. Then, when he is satisfied, you will be free to resume.'

Rosa looked him in the eye then lifted a slice of pizza and started eating. She stopped, mid bite, when Gary appeared beside her. He moved quietly, for such a big man, she thought.

Gary reached for a slice of pizza with one hand and a beer with the other. He used his teeth to open the bottle spitting the lid onto the floor. He slurped the pizza noisily into his mouth, pulling a chair closer to Rosa with his foot, before sitting unnecessarily close to her.

'Good pizza, huh?' he said to Rosa.

When Rosa ignored him he kicked the leg of her chair making her spill some beer.

'I said, it's good pizza.'

'I've had better,' she replied.

'Well, you'll be having the best before too long Mrs Bergstrom, the best you've ever had!' He moved toward her, so that his mouth was close to her ear, 'you're going to love it,' he whispered.

'Eat your pizza, then go relieve Peter,' Jurgen told Gary. 'Keep an eye on the road, there shouldn't be anyone coming this way until first thing tomorrow.'

'I'm not sitting out there all night,' said Gary, as he chewed on his pizza.

'You'll sit there as long as you're told,' said Jurgen. 'You can take four hour shifts with Peter.'

'You aren't my boss!' said Gary.

'Right now, I am, but the boss will be here tomorrow morning. You can tell him how you're too important to keep watch.'

'Yeah right, I like my internal organs on the inside, thanks very much.'

'Knut is coming here?' asked Rosa.

'No, your *husband* is the big boss, but our immediate boss is coming tomorrow.' Gary replied, with emphasis on the word *husband*.

'Who is your immediate boss?'

'You'll know soon enough Mrs Bergstrom,' said Gary, as he got up from the table, brushing his hand against her hip with a juvenile giggle. He reached for another slice of pizza, pushing it all into his mouth as he walked away.

When he had left, disappearing behind the tarpaulin wall, Rosa turned to Jurgen, who sat with his usual impassive face, 'I'd rather die than let that animal touch me.'

Jurgen nodded, looking her in the eye as if measuring her, 'Good choice, Rosa, a very good choice.'

Chapter Fifteen

After midnight Cayman time, JT, Easy and Rambo sat around the lap top, on an encrypted video call with Hamilton and Maxwell.

'We've driven every street north of the airport. No sign of the SUV but there were over a hundred buildings big enough the conceal it,' said JT.

'127,' chirped in Easy.

'What did you guys find out? Anything useful?'

'I'll go first if I may?' said Maxwell, 'I need to be at a briefing in 40 minutes.'

'Of course dear boy,' replied Hamilton.

'Thanks, here's what I could find; the Bergstroms have a flat in Kensington, but their main abode in the UK appears to be in the Cotswolds. They own an estate near Charlbury, pretty close to Blenheim Palace. I spoke to a contact over in Oxfordshire who says it's a grand old pile, with its own solar panel farm. That caused a bit of resentment with the locals, who don't like new money. Apparently Mrs Bergstrom is a sweetheart and won the planning committee over by paying for upgrades at the local primary school. She's really in to kids charities, but oddly they don't have any kids of their own. Mr Bergstrom is described as a bit socially awkward. Bit of a geek by all accounts. He belts around the country roads in his collection of sports cars, but always has a Range Rover following him, which appears to be his personal security. Not sure who he needs protecting from out there, mind.'

'Anything about their divorcing?' asked JT.

'No, but there was a report of an argument of sorts at the train station. It was a couple of months ago. Taxi driver reported picking her up and dropping her at the train station. He was sitting admiring her when she got out of the taxi. A Range Rover screeches up and Mr Bergstrom runs up to the platform. Driver couldn't hear what was being said, he got told to clear off by the security guy who'd been driving the Range Rover. Apparently the driver stopped along the road and watched until Mrs Bergstrom safely boarded the train on her own. The driver plays darts with a local cop so told him about it. The cop put something on the database but it wasn't followed up.'

'Do we know any more about the security?'

'No, they keep themselves to themselves, they're only seen when Mr Bergstrom is on the move. He does seem to travel a lot, but then he's running a worldwide cyber security firm. There's staff at the house but they are all, even the gardeners are from outside the area. They all live in the old farm workers lodges in the grounds.'

'You mentioned *StromSec* have the contract for the Met systems. Any more on that?'

'Yeah, I asked the guys responsible, they said the vetting was top tier; had to be sanctioned at the highest levels in the Home Office. *StromSec* and Bergstrom are squeaky clean. The guy who heads up the Cybercrime Division reckons Bergstrom is a genius. He says the speed at which he can identify and nullify threats or breaches is incredible. He's never seen anything like it. As of next month, *StromSec* will be protecting the Home Office, most of the UK Police Forces, Air Traffic

Control, I reckon it's only a matter of time before they get a contract for the MoD.'

'That is a perfect example of when groupthink is a portal to disaster,' interjected Hamilton.

'How do you mean?' asked Maxwell.

'If *StromSec* are the single point of failure, if they themselves are compromised, then the whole pack of cards comes tumbling down.'

'Did you know about all this?' asked JT.

'Not before you flagged the name to me and I actioned some digging. Suffice to say the Home Secretary and I have had stern words. She is an obstinate woman, like most of her Political class, she has neither the intellect nor ability to see beyond her budget or reputation.'

'Gents, I need to run, but I'll check back in later,' said Maxwell, with a wave, cutting his connection.

'I have some more intelligence for you,' continued Hamilton, 'but, as yet, I don't have the full picture. I had someone look into Mrs Bergstrom; how she spends her time when she's not jetting around with Mr Bergstrom. She is heavily involved in charitable work, quite the patron of the arts. As Rory attested, she is mostly concerned with the welfare of children. She has built and funded two orphanages. One in Bangladesh, the other in Nigeria. Bangladesh is an affiliation with the Order of the Little Sisters of the Poor. It all seems legitimate, I'm told she met Mother Teresa herself, when a child, travelling with her parents. She has a 1st class Honours Degree from St Andrews in International Development, so not just a pretty face.

I checked further into the Nigerian connection, this is where things became a little murky. Ezekiel, please forgive my pronunciation, feel free to correct me with any local knowledge. It seems the Nigerian orphanage is in the town of Birnin Kebbi in the Kebbi region. The area is some 500 miles North of Lagos and notable for very little.

Birnin Kebbi is a sizeable town, perhaps even a small city, situated in the hinterland of the fertile coastal areas, on the edge of the semi-arid north. The GDP of the area is above average for rural Nigeria, but it has very little by way of natural resources, unless you count farm land and sunshine.

All of which begs the question of the attraction for the Bergstroms. Mrs Bergstrom's orphanage could have been built and been welcomed anywhere in Nigeria. There are countless areas that would be considered more needy and deserving.

This made me consider what else the Bergstroms were involved in around that area. I have discovered that Mr Bergstrom has financed the building of a satellite hub, at the Federal University of Birnin Kebbi. This hub is based in Arungu a very small town north of Sir Ahmadu Bello International Airport. My staff sent me a link to the satellite imagery of Arungu. Bizarrely the town, and the University buildings look more like a military base than a rural backwater with a school. It has its own solar power farm, satellite dishes that would put the Pentagon to shame, and what appears to be a formidable security fence, with guard towers no less.'

'What do they teach there?' asked JT.

'According to the University it is a research centre for Computer Science and Artificial Intelligence. It is worth noting that the University is by and large, a pedagogical establishment, by which I mean they churn out 100 or so teachers a year. The curriculum seems to focus on humanities, so no obvious link to IT or AI.'

'So, it's a cover for something,' said JT.

'It appears that way, certainly.'

'Well, maybe Mrs Bergstrom can shed some light on it all, when we find her.'

'You're confident you can do so?'

'She told Easy that she was coming to do business at Butterfields Bank tomorrow. We're going to recce the place, we'll see if she keeps her appointment.'

'If she does?'

'Then we'll make sure she is safe and there of her own free will.'

'And if she's not?'

'Then we'll have to change that.'

'Are you in a position to take on such a mission?'

'We'll play it by ear but it's a public place, the bank will have security so I don't anticipate it getting ugly.'

'Butterfields have offices here in London and Jersey, I'm sure I can find someone to get access to a contact in the Cayman staff.'

'That would be great, maybe see if you can get one of us inside the bank, for when she's in there. Easy knows her, so best if it's him.'

'Agreed, leave it with me.'

'We're going to try to get some kip. We'll look to be plotted up by 8. The bank is open from 9:30 according to the website. Be good if the rest of the team were here, but we'll just have to manage with the three of us on the ground.'

'I can try to arrange some kit delivered from Belize, but I fear it wouldn't arrive before later tomorrow,' said Hamilton.

'We'll see the lay of the land, then work out what we need. At the moment we're hoping this is an ex-marital tiff, so we can help Rosa on her way.'

'I'll also be looking further into this Nigeria business; this chap Bergstrom has some questions to answer.'

'Agreed.'

After closing down the video call JT and the others headed to bed. While the two experienced soldiers got to sleep pretty quickly, Easy lay awake, going over the conversations he'd had with Rosa.

Picking up his lap top he tried to put himself in the shoes of those who had taken Rosa. It was obviously a well-planned operation, so he thought about where it started. Rory said the argument at the train station had been a couple of months ago. He wished that intel had been more precise, but thought back to Rosa touching her ring finger. The tan line on her finger had suggested it was recently that she stopped wearing a wedding ring. Three months, he decided, was a reasonable timescale.

Her husband knew she was coming to Grand Cayman, but it seemed unlikely he'd have a permanent crew here on the island. That meant logistics had to be organised and timed.

They had both flown first class with BA, he'd booked his flights online three weeks before, as an upgrade to his original premium economy tickets. If he could get into the BA booking system, then he'd have an idea of when Rosa made firm plans to come to the island.

He set to work on the programme that Hamilton's tech guy had given him. He'd called it *Safe Cracker*, as it was designed to get into a system, and get back out without leaving a trace. A minute later, he was into the BA system, via what must have been a well-worn route, used by the Secret Service.

Searching under the route along with the name Rosamunde, Easy was a little disappointed to see the surname used was Bergstrom. He surmised that she wouldn't have had time to change her passport, so it made sense.

The ticket was booked three weeks ago and the return flight was for scheduled for Tuesday morning. He hoped more than anything she would be on that flight.

On a whim, he searched for flights booked in the name Knut Bergstrom. There were none listed. He puzzled over this for a while, then checked the *StromSec* website; there it was, the photo of the company jet. Zooming in, he could make out the aircraft identifier *G-STRM*. From there he accessed the Civil Aviation Authority site to search flight-plans registered for the Bombardier Challenger 300 aircraft.

Easy sat bolt upright when he saw the next flight plan, it had been registered only yesterday; Oxford Airport, UK to Santiago de Cuba International airport, Monday morning. A quick search showed Santiago de Cuba airport was only 400 miles or so from where he sat.

He typed a message to Hamilton, updating him on what he'd found. He would tell JT in the morning, it was best to let him sleep.

Next Easy went back to thinking about logistics. The men who took Rosa needed somewhere to keep her and somewhere to keep their SUV off the road. They had to hire somewhere private, they wouldn't risk being seen, so definitely weren't using a hotel. Most of the villas were on the beach, with neighbours pretty close by. If he were to do it, thought Easy, then he would rent a warehouse or a lock up of some description. They might have a contact who could lend them somewhere, but more likely they'd have had to rent somewhere.

Where would you go to rent somewhere like that in Grand Cayman. A quick search showed there were only three estate agents offering non domestic properties. There was a dearth of options according to their websites.

It didn't take long for *safe cracker* to open up the websites, but there were no obvious rental properties removed in the last month. Could they have bought somewhere, he asked himself. Back in the websites for properties being sold there were three industrial units sold in the last three months.

He marked each of them on the map. Two of the three appeared from the map to be remote enough to fit the bill.

Checking his watch, Easy yawned realising he could manage an hour or two of sleep before morning. He brushed his teeth and lay on top of the bed in the cool breeze coming through the patio door. With thoughts of Rosa swirling in his mind he dropped off into a fitful sleep.

Chapter Sixteen

Knut Bergstrom sat at his desk looking at the bank of six screens. The screen holding his attention was a video feed showing his wife sleeping on a blow up bed. He watched as her chest gently moved as she breathed. She looked at peace. She looked as beautiful as the first time he saw her. She looked far too far away. He wanted her home. He wanted to sit her down, to let him explain to her the reality of the situation. He wanted her to see the beauty of what he was doing.

A message appeared on another screen. Bergstrom saw it was from Lev Andreyev, or as he preferred to be called, Major Andreyev. **I AM WAITING**.

Another message followed, **YOU KNOW WHAT TO DO.**

Bergstrom sighed; the man irritated him no end, but his 30 strong detachment of Wagner Group troops were an essential, if very expensive, part of his operation in Nigeria.

The system he'd developed should have been self-sustaining but the interruption to power supply in Abuja had caused a temporary blip. The *call centre* as he liked to think of it, had been offline for almost a month, and had so far cost him $500,000. The call centre was based in the business district in Abuja. Under normal circumstances it would have been a safe and reliable set up.

The office manager had paid the necessary bribes to push along the electricity company to carry out the necessary repairs. Still nothing had happened. It became quickly apparent that the issue concerned a building housing a dozen squatters under which the damaged cables ran. The court process to remove the squatters was taking far too long. It was time to take matters in hand.

Bergstrom pressed the send button pushing 300,000 Swiss Francs into the account, through which he paid the Wagner mercenaries. He'd never liked the Russians, but had to admit they were as effective as they were ruthless. The fact that their price had been raised twice in the last 12 months was a minor annoyance, but if they understood how much money he would be making, then they'd be charging so much more.

Since he set up the call centre, with its 120 staff all calling unsuspecting victims in English speaking countries, it had quickly paid for itself. It had also paid for the University buildings as well as the millions of dollars of equipment and staff - including the Wagners. A tiny percentage also paid for Rosa's stupid orphanage, to keep the brats clothed and fed. If she had known the money came from scamming old people out of their life savings or from fools falling for investment scams, he wondered how she'd have balanced the needs of the kids against the victims.

Rosa's fascination with children had caused them to attend fertility clinics, even attempting IVF. He had spent a lot of time and money making sure the Doctors played along with his ruse of wanting kids. The small operation he'd endured while Rosa was visiting her parents in New Zealand had been well worth the post procedural discomfort.

He had never wanted kids. He didn't like the noisy little brats. It was a real test of his love for his wife, that he accompanied her to visit those bloody orphanages. The memory of the smell in Bangladesh, having photographs taken with a snotty nosed kid sat on his knee, made him squirm.

Rosa had shone in amongst all the dirt and squalor. Somehow, she had remained pristine while he sweated and creased with a reddened face and thin hair slick to his head. She was simply the most beautiful woman he had ever met and he loved her dearly. The fact that she had betrayed him by leaving, caused his skin to itch. The psoriasis ointments did very little to help. He had been advised to get some sun light on his skin instead of hiding away in front of his screens.

He would be in Cuba by Monday. If Rosa could be persuaded to come to her senses, then she could help him buy what would be their forever home. The 50 million dollars she was trying to steal from him, was going to pay for a huge estate in the Cuban highlands with their land running down from the mountains all the way to their private beach. The money had no links to him should the authorities ever think to start digging. It was the perfect route to anonymity. The transaction was supposed to happen two months ago, but he was paying such a premium he knew they'd wait until he was ready.

He'd already purchased a sea plane, just so they could travel throughout the Caribbean and Central America at their leisure. They could have lunch in Jamaica, or date night in Cancun. He smiled at the thought of whisking her away, her falling back in love with him again.

He was so close to bringing his whole plan together. It would earn him riches beyond even his own comprehension. They would make him a trillionaire and all he had to do was press a button. Soon he could walk away from the University project, close it down when, at last, it carried out the job he'd built it for. No more would he have to deal with those disgustingly arrogant Russians. His life of crime would be behind him. *StromSec* would be the saviour of the Western World.

The ping of a message arriving made him start and he knocked the glass of his favourite Black Tot Rum over. He tutted at the waste of the Master Blenders Reserve, then used the sleeve of his cardigan to wipe away the spilled liquid, before taking it off, and throwing it into the corner.

The message read, **IS IT DONE?**

He typed a reply, **The money is in the account Major.**

NOT WHAT I MEANT, came the terse response, followed by, **MAKE SURE NO-ONE RETURNS TO THAT BUILDING. SEND THEM A MESSAGE.**

Bergstrom rubbed his fists into his eyes, he hadn't slept. He had been at his desk for nearly 24 hours. Eventually he forced himself to send a message which appeared on a different screen; **Do it now, please.**

OK came the reply.

Simultaneously a live feed from a body cam replaced the image of the sleeping Rosa.

The image showed a corrugated metal sheet being pulled aside, revealing the dark interior of a building that had suffered fire damage. The fire damage was from the last failed attempt to resolve the problem.

Another man, this one wearing a military style uniform, entered the periphery of the body-cam feed, there were two of them. They climbed a bare concrete staircase, where despite some more natural light, it was still quite dark.

Suddenly, a bright muzzle flash illuminated the scene, then the other man's weapon also fired. The men moved forward, as five bodies came into view. They lay on the floor, collapsed on top of each other.

The camera showed mattresses and tarpaulins being dragged aside and more muzzle flashes.

Bergstrom got up from his seat. He stood, fascinated, watching the images as first a woman, then a child's dead body were revealed behind a makeshift cardboard shelter. The images continued, Bergstrom found himself a little frustrated that there was no sound to accompany them.

A message appeared, **ONE LEFT. INSTRUCTIONS?**

As discussed, do the cross. Hang it somewhere visible. typed Bergstrom.

STAND BY.

The body cam images showed a skinny African man, who looked to be in his late teens, being dragged across the floor by a rope secured around his neck. Knut could see the pock marks of acne scarring on the man's face as the camera pushed up close to him. A scaffold plank came into view propped up against a concrete pillar next to where a tarpaulin masked the large void left by a missing window. The man was dragged to his feet, stood with his back against the plank. The rope forming the noose around his neck was used to attach him to scaffold plank, another binding used to secure his feet.

Bergstrom fought the urge to tell them to step back so he could take in the whole scene, but satisfied himself with the messy footage along with his knowledge of what would come next.

As if reading his mind, the operative stepped away from the trussed up squatter. The camera caught a second, shorter scaffold plank being inserted behind the man's back horizontally. His arms were tied to the plank, into a cruciform shape. The young man was wide eyed with fear. The same fear appeared to paralyse him, he wasn't struggling as the wooden cross was pushed to the edge of the window void. The end of the rope securing his neck to the scaffold board was tied around the concrete support pillar. With a grunt of exertion, the two operatives lifted the cross to balance on the window ledge.

From where he lay tied to the planks, the young African man, stared up at the charred concrete ceiling. He found himself thinking of his grandmother's hut, with the blackened roof caused by the cooking fire. He knew he was going to die. Tears formed in the corners of his eyes that he blinked past his long dark lashes. He had been struggling to survive on the streets, and squatting for so long he knew life was cheap. He had nothing, death had been a close companion for as long as he could remember.

SAY WHEN, appeared on the screen.

Bergstrom thought for a moment then replied, **Go outside to let me see it happen.**

STAND BY. Came the the response before the body cam images showed the operative making his way down and out of the building. The body cam image changed as it was unhooked to became hand held.

A blade cut deep across the squatter's stomach, his screams lost in the gag stuffed in his mouth. For a fraction of a second, the wooden cross teetered on the edge, a metaphor for the fragile balance of life, before gravity won. It slid out, down the side of the building.

Bergstrom was mesmerised, watching the man on the cross swing like a pendulum back and forth on the rope. It took a few seconds to register that blood was pouring from the man, painting an arc, like a gruesome smile, across the concrete facade.

Only when the cross finally came to rest, did Bergstrom realise that the bare chested man had been cut across his abdomen. His intestines were hanging from the wound. He hadn't ordered that to happen, but decided he was impressed by the thoughtful touch.

Bergstrom debated whether to let Andreyev stew for a while about the end of the squatter problem. He walked toward the door before turning back. *Manners maketh the man*, he thought to himself, as he typed a one word message.

Done.

Chapter Seventeen

JT was showered and shaved by 0545. He felt well rested, despite just five hours of sleep. For the first time in a while, he couldn't remember his dream. His mind seemed to know it needed the space to prepare for whatever today threw up at them.

He heard Rambo moving out on the terrace. He knew he'd be completing his Qi Gong, a type of Tai Chi based yoga. JT had considered joining him, but instead stood in front of the stove frying bacon.

The patio doors slid open revealing a naked Rambo. He stood wiping the sheen of sweat from his face with a towel. 'Namaste Boss! Smell's good, I'm mighty hungry!' he said, with his usual happy smile.

'Namaste Rambo, go wake Easy please. Haven't heard him yet.'

'Sure boss,' said Rambo, as he padded towards the bedroom door.

'Maybe put something on first, don't want you scaring the kid into being a vegetarian!' said JT, with a wink.

'Ah, good point!' said Rambo, wrapping his towel around himself as a sarong. Rambo opened the bedroom door, gently wafting it back and forth to let the smell of cooking bacon make its way in. When that didn't have the desired effect he walked in, touching Easy on the shoulder.

Easy woke with a start, blinking several times as he took in his surroundings.

'Good morning, sleep well?' asked a cheery Rambo.

'Umm, yes, I mean no, I mean...I don't know really,' replied Easy rubbing his face with his hands.

'Boss has breakfast ready, I suggest a cold shower to wake up. See you at the table in three minutes.'

'Three minutes? Not four or two and a half then?' said Easy, sitting up, swinging his legs off the bed.

Rambo laughed, 'Any more than three minutes is a waste of water, any less, then you missed a bit!' He offered Easy a hand pulling him to his feet.

'Three minutes it is then,' replied Easy, shuffling toward the ensuite.

Five minutes later they were sat at the table with plates of bacon and eggs served with orange juice. A pot of strong coffee steamed its nutty aroma competing with the bacon.

JT watched the difference between Rambo and Easy eating. One, a Special Forces soldier well used to eating fast, taking on enough fuel to last a long time, without over filling in a way that would impact performance. SAS training had often seen them run five or six miles straight after a meal, just to reinforce that very point. Easy, on the other hand, used his cutlery, cutting his food into bitesize pieces, keeping his plate neat and tidy. His Aunty had brought the kid up well.

He was quite something this kid, he'd made more than enough money to keep himself, and his Aunty, in the lap of luxury with his Bitcoin stuff. He even owned an upmarket property in London, but instead chose to live with his Aunty on a housing estate. JT knew what it meant to have somewhere less comfortable, but that felt more like home. He had felt the same way about the barracks at Hereford, or *Home* as he and the rest of the Regiment referred to it.

The three men ate on in silence, other than the quiet humming of a Dire Straits song from Rambo, as he worked his way through another mouthful. There was time enough to discuss their plans when they did their briefing, for now, each of them was welcome to his own thoughts.

JT scrunched up his face and shook his head when something occurred to him. He was supposed to call Esmé last night. He had completely forgotten. He looked at his watch, working out what the time in Bordeaux would be. France was seven hours ahead so 13:00hrs. She would be out to lunch somewhere, probably with clients. Undoubtedly some rich people looking to buy property in the beautiful old city, or perhaps a place at the beach in Arcachon. Esmé had built quite a reputation as an interior designer in Bordeaux since their divorce. The toll of his being in the Regiment had been too much for her. The fact they'd met again in Bordeaux still amazed him. After his discharge from the Regiment, the whole team had been discharged en masse, they had gone on holiday to Bordeaux. It was a favourite city to visit, but it had been Hamilton who had suggested it. Hamilton had also suggested breakfast at the Orangerie in Parc Public. Esmé had been there, the coincidence still niggled at him and -

'Want me to piece that, boss?'

Rambo's voice shook JT from his thoughts. 'Eh, yeah thanks Rambo.' JT replied looking at his half-finished breakfast.

'Piece?' asked Easy.

'Yeah make a left over sandwich to take with us for later,' Rambo explained, as he spread butter on slices of bread.

'Why *piece*?'

'I don't really know, it's a word the boys use for a sandwich. Don't know why,' said Rambo, dumping the bacon from JT's plate onto the bread in front of him. 'I'm doing cheese and ham for mine, what do you want?'

'I'm pretty stuffed thanks, I don't think I need one,' replied Easy, patting his stomach.

'You've a lot to learn kid,' said Rambo, 'never know where your next meal is coming from when you're working. You've got to prepare when you can. I'll do you one of those peanut butter and banana numbers you like.'

'Okay, thanks Rambo.'

'No worries, you're team *Vigilant*,' he said, in a deep theatrical voice and a grin, while making a V sign on his chest. He often did the voice in jest, as if they were comic book superheroes. 'Vigilant takes care of their own!' He finished with a wink, before wandering off to the fridge, juggling some bananas as he went.

Easy cleared the dishes away, as JT spread out the street map on the table.

JT's phone rang, it was Hamilton.

'Good morning, Gentlemen.'

'Good morning, Hamilton.'

'I have some good news. I spoke with the someone at Butterfields HQ this morning. He called the client manager in Grand Cayman - apparently he wasn't too impressed at being woken at 4am, but needs must. His name is Jeffries, he's an ex-pat. As luck would have it, he is the person meeting with your Mrs Bergstrom at 10:30. I've asked him to meet with you prior to opening time this morning. He says he'll be playing at the South Sound Squash Club from seven until eight. He'll meet you in the car park at 8. He drives a racing green vintage Jaguar.'

'That's great news thanks. What did you tell him about us?'

'Simply that I was calling on behalf of Her Majesty's Government, and that he should not mention anything about it to anyone else.'

'Did he say why she's meeting him today?'

'He was hesitant, but it seems that Mrs Bergstrom has arranged to withdraw $50million from her account.'

'Sorry, did you say withdraw $50m?' asked JT incredulously.

'Yes, three weeks ago she began the process of converting the cash into bearer bonds.'

'I didn't know they were still a thing?'

'Yes, they are no longer permitted in the US, but the rest of the world is still happy to accept them.'

'Why bearer bonds I wonder, there are far easier ways to move money?'

'They have no digital trail,' said Easy, over JT's shoulder as he moved to take a seat next to JT.

'Her husband is an IT genius, perhaps she doesn't want him to know where she keeps her money,' offered Hamilton.

'He's her ex-husband,' answered Easy. 'I think maybe she wants to disappear.'

'$50million would certainly allow her to start afresh, assume a new identity. The question then, would be why? Why does she feel the need to disappear?' said Hamilton.

'Did you find anything else on him?' asked JT.

'Very little actually, surprisingly so. Born in Zurich, the illegitimate son of the Norwegian Ambassador and one of his staff. It seems he was packed off to boarding schools in Switzerland then Norway while his father divorced. The family moved around the world in diplomatic circles. Nothing of note until he appeared as the youngest ever graduate of University of Science and Technology in Trondheim. He graduated with a 1st class distinction at the age of 15. Then he moved to the US, graduating from MIT with a Masters in System Design. He came to the UK, did his PhD at Oxford, reading Artificial Intelligence Design. He wrote a thesis on *Cyber Wars*.

His parents died two days before his graduation from MIT. Some sort of car accident, on the way to the airport to fly to Boston. As the only child, he inherited a decent sized estate. Set himself up in business as a Cyber Security expert. Hacking on an industrial scale was only just beginning; he offered a solution at just the right time. Hence *StromSec* became a leader in the field.

Since then, he lived quietly. He appears your archetypal computer nerd, until he met Mrs Bergstrom at a charity event. They are by any standards an odd couple, but from what I can gather, she was on the rebound from an abusive relationship with some flash football player. Knut Bergstrom was as far to the opposite end of the spectrum as you could find.

Mrs Bergstrom set about refashioning, in a literal sense, her new beau, he was given a new wardrobe, a new house and access to a completely different social circle. It's very obviously not his thing, as he's socially awkward, being dragged around parties and events.

They set up a foundation, building orphanages in Bangladesh and Nigeria, as we've discussed previously. It appears they are Mrs Bergstrom's pet projects, while he provides the money. He seems to have set up some sort of business in Abuja which funds the Nigerian orphanage. He owns a building in the financial district, the rental profits go direct to the orphanage.

Bangladesh works differently; there's a monthly stipend sent to them for their running costs.'

'He sounds like your regular philanthropic rich dude, with a trophy wife,' said JT.

'Ex-wife,' said Easy.

'Yes, ex-wife. Are they divorced yet?'

'No, they are still married, although they have been separated for a couple of months. She moved into a flat in Brighton with one of her friends, and it seems, took a few weeks to lick her wounds, but is now ready to move on.'

'What caused the split?'

'I don't know. It's usually infidelity, but that seems unlikely considering Knut had landed the woman of his dreams.'

'And lots of other men's,' said JT, nudging an unimpressed Easy.

'They had been trying for a baby. I'm told they had been attending the very best IVF specialists but to no avail. That sort of thing can put a huge strain on a relationship.'

'I don't think that's it,' said Easy. 'She was scared, I mean proper scared when she thought that Marco character was around. You don't snatch your wife at the airport if it's just about having a baby.'

'No, I agree,' said JT, 'there's something bigger going on for sure.'

'I have a meeting with one of the boffins at GCHQ shortly, I want to discuss the awarding of contracts to *StromSec,* and Bergstrom's vetting. If there's the risk of something malevolent going on, I want to know we are prepared, and that any failure can be mitigated.'

'Okay, we'll do our briefing, then get on the road to meet this Jeffries guy.'

'Best of luck Gentlemen,' said Hamilton.

'You too,' said JT, ending the call.

'I found something out last night, when I couldn't sleep,' said Easy.

'Go on,' said JT.

'Bergstrom has a private jet, there's a flight-plan filed, from Oxford to Cuba.'

'Ok...?' said JT.

'It's arriving on Monday.'

'Cuba is pretty close-'

'400 miles,' interrupted Easy, 'give or take.'

'You think he's heading here? Why not just fly straight to Grand Cayman?'

'I don't know, but I do know that Cuba wouldn't share any info, with say the UK Government, unlike the Caymans.'

'Yeah, good point. Ok, anything else, or shall we get back to the briefing?'

'I hacked into the BA website, Rosa only booked her ticket three weeks ago. I used that date to check listings with letting agents, for lockups and things. I think I've narrowed it down to two places in the North that fit the bill. I made a few guesses, but they're here,' he said, pointing to the map, 'and here, this one. Both are near the airport, neither have immediate neighbours. There's no google maps street view or anything, but the satellite images makes them both big enough to keep an SUV, they'd make a decent hideout.'

'Ok, good work kid. Let's hope we can get this all sorted out at the bank, then we don't need to go searching for hideouts.'

'What's the plan boss?' asked Rambo.

'I want you to find an OP somewhere around this corner,' said JT, pointing out an intersection on the map. 'It should give clear sight of this road coming past the bank, this road that goes north, the opposite road heading south, then east. We know they've used the SUV and after the way they behaved at the airport, I don't think they're overly worried about surveillance, or that anyone is looking for them.'

'Easy and I will get into the bank at opening time with this Jeffries guy, we'll try to make sure he speaks to Rosa in private. She knows him, so she should feel safer. If the goons try to prevent that from happening, I'm thinking we get Jeffries to hand her a note or something. Between me and the bank security guy, we should manage to subdue anyone else there. We know there's be metal detectors at the door so they won't be armed. Then, we either call the cops, or we get Rosa out of there and make a plan to get her off the island.'

'Sounds straight forward enough,' said Rambo.

'That's what worries me,' said JT, 'they must know Rosa could just scream, the bank would get locked down until the cavalry arrive. No, there's something else going on here, so we'll just have to be on our toes. As you know, I don't like a lack of planning, but it is what it is.'

'I have the schematics from the planning department for the inside of the bank,' said Easy, bringing them up on his lap top. 'There are offices behind the teller counter and a row of consulting rooms down the right. There's a lift and stairs to the basement, which must be the vault where the safe deposit boxes are kept. Maybe we could get Rosa down there, away from whoever brings her in?'

'Good idea, we'll speak to this Jeffries guy to see what usually happens in the bank,' said JT, folding the map. 'Rambo we'll drop you off on the way to the squash club, any issues with getting an OP you can let us know, and we'll have a rethink. Right, grab anything you need, we hit the road in five.'

Chapter Eighteen

Rosa woke up a little stiff, exhausted after an uncomfortable night on a folding camp bed. Her mouth felt dry and furry after not being able to brush her teeth. She dreaded to think how she must look in yesterday's make up and having slept in yesterday's clothes.

As if to answer her question, she found that Gary was sitting at the table watching her, the look on his face suggested she must still be desirable. Ignoring him, she sat up to slip on her shoes. As she moved, the weight of the explosive necklace around her neck shifted, reminding her of its presence. It wasn't something she would easily forget.

Jurgen had told her it would detonate if he was too far away, so he must be here somewhere, wherever this place was. The only thing she knew for sure was that she was in Grand Cayman, not too far from the airport as she'd heard the sound of aeroplanes. Apart from the occasional sea bird and a scurrying lizard she hadn't heard any other noise from outside. This place must be pretty remote, she thought.

'I need to use the bathroom,' she said, loudly enough to address anyone in the building other than Gary.

Jurgen appeared, he was bare chested, half of his face covered in shaving foam. 'Good morning, Mrs Bergstrom. Of course, be my guest,' he said, gesturing to the toilet.

'Is there a possibility of my being allowed to clean up and change my clothes? I can't exactly walk into the bank looking like this, can I?'

'Look good enough to me!' said Gary, with his trademark lecherous smirk.

'The facilities here are not ideal, I apologise for that,' said Jurgen, 'however, I will see what can be done.'

'Thank you. My toothbrush and things are in my bag, can I have it please?'

'Of course.' replied Jurgen, giving a nod to Gary, who picked it up and walked over to where Rosa stood.

Gary stopped a step short, holding out the bag, forcing Rosa to come to him in some sort of pathetic power play. Rosa stepped forward, reaching for her bag without looking at him. She wasn't surprised when he moved the bag closer to himself, to try to draw her in.

Grabbing the bag from him, she shook her head at his childish giggle. She saw that Jurgen stood impassively like an uninterested observer.

Rosa went to the bathroom, trying to ignore the grime and unpleasant smells. She used paper towels to create a makeshift toilet seat, using a fresh one to pick up the others in a bundle when she'd finished. There was still no bin, so she reluctantly threw them on the floor beside the growing pile.

Brushing her teeth made her feel slightly more human. Her compact mirror was much better than the dirty shard above the sink. The phone was missing from her bag, as she knew it would be. She tried to position her compact, hoping to get a look at the clasp on the scarf bound necklace around her neck. The clasp was enclosed in a little metal box with a tiny screw to keep the lid in place. The temptation to try to force open the box was almost too much for her, but she knew nothing about explosives, and the risk of triggering it was not worth thinking about.

She packed up her bag after trying in vain to brush her hair, giving up she tied it back instead.

'I have a solution for your bathing needs, Mrs Bergstrom,' announced Jurgen, when Rosa appeared from the bathroom. 'Please, follow me.' He pulled back a huge tarpaulin hung from the ceiling, that made an effective curtain wall.

Rosa was surprised to see that behind the tarpaulin was a boat shed. But rather than a boat, the shed contained a sea plane. The plane had been winched partially out of the water on a slip way and took up most of the space.

On the floor was a large bucket into which Jurgen poured fresh water from a 5 gallon drum. He threw in a sponge which looked like it had been used for cleaning the aeroplane and stood back admiring his handiwork.

'Am I supposed to take a bath in that?' Rosa chided him.

Jurgen looked, by his granite featured standards, a little crestfallen, 'It is not ideal, but the best I can provide in the circumstances, Mrs Bergstrom.'

Rosa realised that she was alienating the one person who seemed to have Gary under control, so tried a conciliatory tone, 'Yes, I'm sorry Jurgen, thank you for trying.' She smiled at him giving a little puppy dog eyes look, but he didn't seem to register it.

'I have found you some soap,' he said, pointing to a bottle of Lynx body wash.

Rosa read the label, she knew instantly it would be Gary's.

'Also, you may borrow my towel. It is a little damp I am afraid,' he told her, removing the towel from his shoulder to drape over the rear fuselage of the aeroplane.

'What about this?' asked Rosa, pointing to the scarf around her neck.

'A yes, it might not be wise to get it wet. I will remove it for you presently,' said Jurgen, as he went back through the tarpaulin wall.

Rosa looked urgently around the shed, searching for a means of escape. The doors were closed but light permeated through the water beneath them. There must be a gap, she was a strong swimmer so as soon as the necklace was off she would dive into the water.

Jurgen returned carrying a small screwdriver, but to Rosa's anguish, he also brought Gary. Gary wore an even more lecherous look than before, grinning like the cat who got the cream.

Jurgen stepped behind Rosa, after a few seconds he had opened the box to unhook the necklace. 'Now you will be able to bathe Mrs Bergstrom. Without this little device, I must however leave Gary here, to watch over you, in case you were thinking of attempting escape.'

Rosa stood with her shoulders slumped, contemplating going without washing. She needed this to be over, to make that happen she would have to go through with the appointment at the bank. The bank would definitely think there was something amiss if she turned up looking like a rough sleeper. She would just have to get on with it.

When Jurgen left, Gary took up a position sat on an oil drum in the corner watching her every move. Turning away from him she slipped out of her dress, hanging it over the wing support where it met the fuselage by the door. She looked into the aeroplane, noting it had three seats. One for the pilot, with a small two seat bench in the rear.

'Come on, I haven't got all day,' said Gary, obviously enjoying himself.

Rosa contemplated washing in her underwear but as she had nothing to change into she stripped naked keeping her back to Gary. She picked up the sponge, but on seeing it was covered in windscreen bugs, threw it aside. She quickly splashed water over herself, deciding against using the highly perfumed Lynx body wash.

She stood up after splashing water on her face, feeling, as much as hearing, Gary approach her. She froze momentarily, waiting to feel his hand touch her skin. When it didn't come, she looked around to see him walking around her, with his phone in his hand. He was videoing her, nodding his pleasure as he went.

With the anger growing again in her stomach, she knew what she would do if it came down to it. That animal Gary would not have his fun with her, she would rather die.

Chapter Nineteen

'I'm on the roof of the library,' said Rambo. 'Good line of sight. Light traffic. I can't find anyone plotted up.'

'Good work Rambo, we're just arriving at the squash club. We'll check in after we've finished here.' said JT, slipping the phone back in his pocket.

'That's him over there,' said Easy, 'I saw his photo on the bank website.'

They pulled in next to Jeffries who was leaning on his Jaguar. He was wearing sportswear, looking lean and fit, like a regular squash player. His bald head was well tanned, and his face a little wrinkled, despite being in his late 30s.

'Mr Jeffries, thank you for meeting with us.'

'Not a problem, it's not every day the CEO calls to tell me I have to meet with the Secret Service.'

He looked at Easy, a question appearing on his face, 'You *are* the Secret Service?'

'Not a question we're at liberty to answer, Mr Jeffries,' replied JT.

'Ah of course, you could tell me but you'd have to kill me!' He laughed at his own joke, but his smile soon faded when he was met with straight faces.

'Mr Jeffries what have you been told?'

'Only that you are interested in my client Mrs Bergstrom, or Hawthorne, as she told me she now prefers to be known. I have been told to give you any assistance I can. That gentlemen, is all I know.'

'Your appointment is at 10:30 correct?'

'Yes, I have some paperwork to prepare first, so we arranged 10:30.'

'Have you met Mrs Berg..., sorry Ms Hawthorne before?' asked JT.

'Yes, a couple of times. I opened the account for her.'

'So, you will recognise her?'

'Yes of course, she is, not to put too fine a point on it, a very memorable lady.'

'How do you mean?'

'She is very beautiful, not someone you're likely to forget!' Jeffries was smiling at a memory, then forced himself to be more professional.

'Mr Jeffries, please explain to us the security arrangements at the bank. I assume you have armed security?'

'Yes, we have Evan, he's our security guard, he is armed.'

'Metal detectors at the entrance?'

'Yes, it's a standard set up, much like an airport. We have an x-ray scanner, all brief cases etc go through there.'

'If something happens within the bank, what is the protocol?'

'The doors have an automatic shutter system. The vault locks itself down, so it can't be opened. Do you think someone will try to rob the bank? They'd be fools to try!'

'No, we have no information to suggest that. Tell me about how you conduct meetings.'

'In what way?' asked Jeffries.

'Where do you meet clients; do you take them to a private room, or use an open plan desk?'

'Our clients come to us, in part, for our discretion, all meetings are held in my office.'

'Can people in the rest of the bank see into your office?'

'Yes, the wall is glass, but I can switch them to privacy mode, if a client requests. It's a flick of a switch and the window becomes opaque.'

'Does Ms Hawthorne usually request that to happen?'

Jeffries thought for a moment, 'No, she doesn't.'

'You're sure?'

'Yes, definitely. I've had some of my colleagues trying to ogle her, when passing by the window.'

'Is there somewhere in your office one of us could wait, out of sight?'

'No, I'm sorry, my office is minimalist.'

'Is there an office nearby where we could wait without being seen?'

'Yes, my colleague Gilfudsdottir is on leave, you can use her office next door, it has the same privacy glass.'

'Excellent, we'd be much obliged.'

'Of course.'

'What is the meeting for today?'

'Ms Hawthorne asked me to arrange the exchange of money from her account, into Bearer Bonds.'

'$50 million?'

'Yes, you are well informed,' said Jeffries, with an appreciative nod.

'Did she say why?'

'No, she asked my advice on legal ways to make money untraceable. She wanted something without a digital footprint, for such a large amount, Bearer Bonds seemed appropriate.'

'So, she can just walk out this morning with $50 million in certificates in her handbag.'

'Not this morning, no. The bank has a cooling off period, when we are supposed to do security checks. To be honest, it's an excuse for us to try to persuade them to keep their money with us.'

'How long is this cooling off period?'

'Three days, we have an appointment set up for Monday afternoon.'

'Interesting, what time?'

'4:30, she asked for the very end of the day.'

'Her flight out is booked for early Tuesday morning. She's leaving it as late as possible,' said Easy.

'What does $50million in bearer bonds look like?' asked JT.

'There are 100 x $500,000 certificates.'

'Bits of paper? I've only seen them in movies.'

'There's more to them than that but essentially yes, bits of paper. They are seen very rarely nowadays, especially as they are now illegal in the US.'

'In that case,' said JT, 'I have another favour to ask.'

Chapter Twenty

Inside the bank it was refreshingly cool, with the sort of air conditioning you would expect in an establishment set up for wealthy clients.

JT thought about Rambo on the roof, grateful that the temperature at this time of the morning was still pleasant, compared to the hot humid conditions forecast for the afternoon.

JT was sitting at the beautiful antique desk of Sally Gilfudsdottir, while she was back home in Iceland on holiday. 'Sit Rep please, Rambo,' he said, into his phone.

'All quiet so far Boss, traffic has quietened down a little again post rush hour.'

JT looked up as Jeffries walked in carrying a tray with tea and biscuits.

'Lapsang Souchong?' asked Jeffries, as he placed the tray down on the desk.

JT looked at Easy who smiled and said, 'Thought it couldn't hurt to ask, as it's your favourite.'

Not for the first time, JT found himself impressed by the kid's thoughtfulness. 'You're a star, thank you both,' he said, covering the phone with his hand. Then he set the phone down, switching it to speaker phone mode. 'Rambo, these guys are spoiling me, my favourite tea, for the first time since we arrived on the island!'

'Very nice!' said Rambo, with a chuckle.

'Let's keep this line open, she's due in 25 minutes.'

'Roger that...wait one boss.' said Rambo.

'What's up?' said JT, putting down his cup.

'There's a red soft top just done its second drive past of the bank. I noticed it had the roof up first time round. Seemed strange having a soft top but keeping it up on a day like this.'

'Is it parking?'

'No, it's taken a right. I've lost eyes on. Probably nothing.'

'Good spot Rambo, let us know if it reappears.'

'Will do boss.'

'Let me log on to that terminal,' said Jeffries, 'and I can bring up the CCTV for outside the building if that would help?'

JT nodded toward Easy who turned around his laptop to show he had already accessed the feed.

'How did you...?' blustered Jeffries, then nodded, composing himself. 'I'll leave you Gents to it, must get back to the exciting world of banking. You know where I am if you need anything.'

'Thanks, you've been a great help,' said JT.

Jeffries closed the door behind him, walking next door into his own office. He was feeling more than a little nervous so decided he should get back to work to take his mind off things.

He tapped the space bar to reawaken his computer, finding a message from Easy. He was in the bank's internal messaging system. The message read, **Thanks again for all your help Mr Jeffries. We can use this messaging system to communicate while Rosa is in your office. Please put your desk phone in conference call mode.**

Jeffries looked at his phone which immediately rang. He pressed the conference call button as instructed.

JT's voice came across the speaker. 'Testing.'

'I can hear you,' said Jeffries.

'Likewise, good strength, clear and readable, Mr Jeffries. We'll leave this line open.'

'Yes, yes of course.'

'Mr Jeffries, just a reminder that you cannot discuss any of this, *any of this*, with anyone else. You do understand?' asked JT.

'Yes, I understand perfectly. Just my luck, the most exciting thing to happen to me since I came to Cayman, or indeed ever, but I can't tell anyone about it. James Bond is next door, but I can't even tell my fiancé!'

'I promise you; James Bond is not real Mr Jeffries.'

'Okay, but he's the only spy I know the name of.'

'That's kind of the point, Mr Jeffries.'

Jeffries gave a gentle resigned laugh.

'Oh, Mr Jeffries, one more thing,' said JT.

'Yes?'

'Excellent tea, thanks again.'

Chapter Twenty-One

Rosa applied make up as best she could, but still thought she looked a mess.

'Time to go Mrs Bergstrom,' announced Jurgen, who had changed into a lightweight suit. He was wearing mirrored aviator sunglasses and carried a small holdall with him.

'I'm ready as I'll ever be,' said Rosa, lifting up her handbag.

'Then let's get this done, we can pick up lunch on the way back.'

Rosa followed him to the car, and he opened the rear door for her to climb in. After closing the door, he walked around the vehicle, then climbed into the rear seat beside her.

A man she hadn't seen before, opened one half of the big garage doors, before Gary got into the driver's seat and started up the engine. He fiddled with the radio, selecting some awful Euro pop, then with his right hand tapping merrily on the wheel, drove out into the sunshine.

The darkened windows in the rear gave a real contrast with the bright light through the windscreen, Rosa reached into her bag to get her Chanel sunglasses.

A thought occurred to her as her fingers touched her steel nail file, she looked at Jurgen, as he sat impassively next to her. Could she stab him with the nail file? Could she get hold of the little trigger device he kept on his person, and run off from the car?

She looked at Gary in the front seat, and knew she wouldn't be able to outrun him, so it would have to be somewhere in town. Somewhere with people around, who could help her, could protect her. She wondered if she might see a Police car or maybe one of the guards at a jewellery store, or at the bank.

She looked back to Jurgen and realised that no matter what he had done to her, she wouldn't be able to kill him. She couldn't see herself stabbing another person. Gary was another matter, he was more animal than human.

With a sigh, she turned to look out of the window at the industrial units edging a body of water. Her mind wandered as he considered her options. If she gave them the money and they took it to Knut, they were surely going to kill her. This money was important Knut, it was probably the only reason she was still alive now. She knew about his plans, her threat to tell the authorities if he followed through with them, was she now realised futile. He would either have her killed or he was confident he could get away with it, maybe both. She also knew he would hate the fact that she'd left him. He wouldn't be able to cope with the fact that she'd seen him for what he was. He would want her back if at all possible, he'd try to pretend none of it had ever happened. That's what was keeping her alive, his desperation. She wondered if she could agree to go to Cuba, to wait for a time to escape. The thought of even seeing Knut made her nauseous.

'Would you like some water?' asked Jurgen, taking a bottle from his rucksack.

'No, thank you,' was all she could say, despite the screaming that was going on in her head.

Chapter Twenty-Two

'Black SUV approaching from the North.'

'Occupants?' asked JT.

'Can't tell from the privacy glass, white male driver,' said Rambo, peering through the tourist grade binoculars, 'he's a big lad, about 30 I'd say.'

JT looked at his watch it was 10:28. 'Show time,' he said, more for Jeffries' benefit than anything else. 'Mr Jeffries, just act as if it's a normal day at the office.'

'Yes, I'll try.'

'Vehicle coming to stop outside the bank,' said Rambo.

'Got it,' said Easy, as he typed on his laptop.

The SUV stopped right outside the door of the bank, Jurgen stepped out of the rear door on the road side of the vehicle. Easy moved the camera to get a close up taking a screenshot. The man's sunglasses glinted in the sun and covered some of his face.

The driver opened his door to get out, Easy got a close up of his face. He had a sneering smile in the screenshot. He opened the rear door, giving a little mock bow as Rosa stepped out of the vehicle.

Easy could see she wasn't her usual pristine self, her face looked drawn beneath her sunglasses.

Jurgen walked round to join Rosa while sweeping his gaze up and down the street. Then he walked forward opening the door of the bank ushering Rosa inside.

Easy fired off the images of the two men to Hamilton asking him to run them through facial recognition.

Rosa and Jurgen made their way through the security checks before Jeffries walked forward to meet them. He offered his hand to Rosa, 'Good morning Ms Hawthorne, how lovely to see you again.'

'Good morning, likewise Mr Jeffries,' replied Rosa, without a smile.

'And you are Mr...?' said Jeffries, turning to Jurgen who kept on his sunglasses but made no attempt to reply.

'This is Jurgen, he is...my minder,' interjected Rosa.

'Ah, then please follow me to my office,' Jeffries turned, hoping they didn't spot the slight tremor in his voice.

Jurgen made to walk with them but Rosa turned to him, 'You can wait over there, Jurgen,' she said, pointing to some leather chairs.

'I should stay with you Mrs Bergstrom,' replied Jurgen, stepping closer to her.

'I'll be perfectly, *safe*,' said Rosa, pointing to her scarf.

Jurgen hesitated, then showed her the trigger mechanism in his hand, before he skulked off to the chairs.

Rosa followed Jeffries into his office taking a seat in front of his desk as he closed the door.

Jeffries slid a piece of paper in front of her for her to read. It said, *You are about to hear a voice you will recognise, please do not react, keep looking at Mr Jeffries.*

'Ready,' said Jeffries, when she had read it.

'Rosa, it's me, it's Easy,' came a voice from the speaker phone.

'Easy? How? Where are you? What's happening?'

'Do you remember, I said my friends I was meeting could help? Well I'm in the office next door with one of them now.'

'But how did you know?'

'JT saw them take you at the airport. Have they hurt you?'

'No, I'm not injured. Not yet anyway. Who is JT?'

'Good morning Rosa. I am JT, as Easy says we are going to help you. We won't have long. I'm assuming you are here under duress?'

'That's a bit of an understatement!' said Rosa touching her scarf.

'Is there any reason why we can't call in the Police?'

'Yes, that man outside, his name is Jurgen. He works for my ex-husband.'

'What kind of hold does he have over you?'

'My scarf contains an explosive, he has a trigger mechanism in his hand.'

'What?' exclaimed Easy.

JT held up a hand to quieten him, 'What kind of explosive Rosa?' he asked.

'He said it's made of something called detonating cord. The trigger will go off if I get too far away from him.'

'Shit!' said Jeffries, pushing his chair back from his desk.

'Jeffries, calm down. They won't risk harming Rosa until they get what they want. Rosa, how is the explosive fastened, can it be removed?'

'Jurgen used a little screwdriver this morning to let me wash. There's a little metal box at the back. It looked like one end had a hook when he took it off.'

'Okay that's good to know.'

'Is detonation cord dangerous?'

'Yes, it's essentially a plastic tube filled with a high explosive called PETN. It's used to initiate a bigger explosive material.'

'Shit, can it go off by itself?' she asked, trying to keep the panic at bay.

'Unlikely, it's pretty stable, but best not to fiddle about with it.' JT tried to sound relaxed for Rosa's benefit. 'Rosa, we're going to get you out of this, try to stay calm, just do what they want.'

'They want the $50 million, I told them it's not available until Monday. Gary on the other hand...'

'Who is Gary?'

'He drove the car to bring us here, he's outside.'

'Ok, what does Gary want?'

'He wants...me,' she sniffed and gathered herself before continuing. 'He's a pervert. He watched me having a wash this morning. The dirty bastard was filming me, on his phone. He's an animal.'

'Where are they keeping you Rosa?'

'I'm not sure. It's a big shed by the water, there's a sea plane in the back, like a boat-shed sort of place with a slip way.'

'Jeffries, does that sound familiar?'

'No, not really, sea planes are quite common here. They tend to be around the Grand Sound, as it's fairly sheltered.'

Easy chipped in, 'Rosa, is it a modern building? What's it made of?'

'It's old, made of wooden planks. The roof is corrugated metal and the windows are really high up so I can't see out.'

'Did you see any other buildings nearby?'

'No, after we drove for a little bit, just maybe 40 seconds or something, there were industrial buildings.'

'Anything that would stand out like a landmark or anything?'

'No, I don't think so, it was very scruffy. |There were lots of rusty old cars stacked up.'

'Do you mean like a scrap yard?' asked Jeffries.

'Yes, like a scrap yard.'

'There's a scrap yard on Sparky's Drive, near the quarry.'

'Yes, I saw a big dusty lorry with sand or something heaped up in the back.'

'I think, I know where it is,' said Easy showing JT his laptop screen. 'This is one of the properties that was for rent. It still shows as for rent but if they've only taken it recently, maybe the website hasn't been updated.'

'He's coming!' said Jeffries, as he spotted Jurgen stand up and walk toward his office.

'Shit, stall him, we need more time,' said JT.

Jeffries made a show of standing up to point to something in the document in front of Rosa and deliberately knocked over his coffee cup.

'Oh, I'm so terribly sorry!' he was saying, as Jurgen opened the door to the office.

'What is taking so long Mrs Bergstrom?' asked Jurgen to Rosa's back.

'Entirely my fault,' said Jeffries, using tissues to mop up the spillage. 'I'll have to reprint these documents. Again, I'm so terribly sorry Ms Hawthorne, I will have you on your way, momentarily.'

'Oh, don't worry Mr Jeffries, Jurgen and I are just going to grab some lunch later, so we have some time...' she turned in her seat to face Jurgen, 'to kill.'

Jurgen stood staring at her from the doorway, until Jeffries ushered him back out, saying he should take a seat outside and that he'd have the documents reprinted right away.

Jurgen skulked back to the seat, taking a phone from his pocket to start typing a message.

With the door closed again, Jeffries went back to his desk. 'Ok we're alone again,' he said for the benefit of JT and Easy.

'Good work Jeffries,' said JT.

'Thank you,' said Jeffries sounding drained.

'You'd best print something,' JT reminded him.

'Yes, of course,' said Jeffries, as he started bashing away at the keyboard.

'Rosa, how many of them are there?'

'Three men, I think, Jurgen told Gary to do four hour stints with someone called Peter.'

'Have you actually seen three men or just heard their names?'

'I saw the Peter guy for the first time this morning, he opened up the shed door for Gary to drive out.'

'Did you see any weapons?'

'Gary has one of those holster things that wraps over your shoulder, I saw him fiddling with a gun at one point.'

'Was it a hand gun?'

'Yes, like a pistol.'

'Anything else?'

'Not that I saw, but something about Jurgen makes me think he's ex-military.'

'Is he the one in charge?'

'Yes, but he said their Boss was arriving today.'

'Mr Bergstrom is arriving?'

'No, he called Knut the *big Boss*, this is someone else, I think it may be Carlo. He is Security for my ex-husband.'

'Mr Bergstrom's jet is flying to Cuba on Monday,' said Easy.

'Ah yes, he's been going on about Cuba for a while. He said we'd retire there, to live like King and Queen.'

'Why Cuba, that seems an unusual choice?' asked JT.

'I know, I said I didn't want to go, but he kept going on about being untouchable there.'

'Is that why you left him?' asked Easy.

'No, I left him because he's a criminal. He's dangerous and he could get lots of people killed.'

'How so?' asked JT.

'Everyone thinks he's the good guy battling against hackers, but it's him.'

'Sorry, I don't follow,' said JT.

'Knut *is* the hacker. He gets in to people's servers or whatever, then extorts money out of them. Then he rides in like the white knight to save the day, makes the systems secure. He charges the same people he's extorted a lot of money from, to keep their system *safe*. He's got them all fooled.'

'How do you know all this Rosa; do you have any proof?'

'Why, don't you believe me?'

'Yes we believe you, but with proof we can go the authorities, have him arrested.'

'I heard him on the phone. I had gone into his office, he didn't know I was there. I heard everything.'

'Is he working alone?'

'He has a whole team working on it. He's created a base at the University in Nigeria. He told me has protection from Russians. Even the call centre in Abuja is full of scammers. The bastard's been using that to finance the orphanage.'

'Okay Rosa. I think we're pushing it keeping Jurgen waiting, we don't want him getting suspicious.'

'Do I have to go back with him now?'

'Yes, we'll need time to assess what they're up to. We know they'll have to bring you back here on Monday.'

'If Gary comes near me…I would sooner die,' said Rosa with conviction.

'They're counting on you coming back here to collect the money, I don't think they'll hurt you before then.'

'And after?'

'We'll make sure they don't get a chance to hurt you Rosa, I promise,' said Easy.

'Thank you Easy, I'm sorry you've been dragged into this.'

'It's what we do Rosa, we help people.'

JT looked at Easy, he was right, this is what Vigilant were created for. 'Rambo, get back to the car, head for the scrap yard on Sparky's Drive. See if you can find an OP with a view of buildings on the waters edge. Somewhere big enough to house a sea plane.'

'Will do boss. What about transport for you guys?'

'We'll sort ourselves out, get going before they leave here, I think we've pushed it far enough for today.'

'Jurgen is moving again,' said Jeffries.

'Okay, time to go. Stay strong Rosa.'

'I'll try. Just promise something.'

'Go on.'

'Whatever happens to me, you'll stop Knut. Stop him and make him pay.'

'Yes, we will. That's a promise.'

Rosa left with Jurgen, and the black SUV drove off as they watched on the CCTV feed.

JT sat for a moment thinking, cultivating an embryonic plan, until Jeffries walked into the office.

'What happens now?' asked Jeffries.

'We're going to work out a plan to protect Rosa,' said JT.

'And make Knut Bergstrom pay,' added Easy.

'I've made the arrangements for Monday as you requested,' said Jeffries. 'Is there anything else I can do for you Gentlemen?'

'You were great today, thanks for all your help.'

Pride covered Jeffries face, 'My pleasure, anything to help!' he said grinning.

'That Jaguar of yours,' said JT.

'Ah yes, she's my pride and joy. 1961 E-type drop hood. Naturally aspirated 3.8-litre straight six. One of only 5 or so remaining, she's my...' Jeffries noted JT's slightly disinterested look, it caused his heart to sink. 'What about her?' he asked nervously.

JT flashed him a friendly smile, 'We're going to need the keys.'

Chapter Twenty-Three

Rambo lay prone, keeping himself out of sight, as he watched for the black SUV. Adjusting his position he reached for his phone as it buzzed in his pocket.

'Sit Rep please Rambo,' said JT, as he adjusted the seat of the Jaguar.

'No sign of them yet boss. They should be here about now, if they came straight from the bank.'

'You had a couple minutes start on them.'

'Yeah, I put the foot down a bit too.'

'Where are you plotted up?'

'I'm three cars up, in a really old American number, sort of thing you'd see in Havana.'

'Can you see any potential buildings for their hideout?'

'Sure can, there's a big old boat builders shed about 600 metres away. Fits the bill perfectly.'

'Any movement?'

'Nothing so far. I've eyes on the closed front doors, and one side wall. Might be someone inside, or on the shady side of the building.'

'Anything else?'

'I'm sending you a photo now Boss. You'll see it's sitting on a little inlet, some kind of natural harbour maybe. Must be pretty sheltered in there; good for a sea plane.'

'Big enough to take off and land?'

'No idea, I don't know much about them, but it looks like it's about 500 metres long. My guess is that it would depend on the wind.'

'There's always a sea breeze here, so it's feasible I guess.'

'Do we have a plan?'

'Not yet Rambo, it seems we have until Monday. Until then we can recce the place, and hopefully Rory or Hamilton can find us some more info on them.'

'Roger that, I'm good up here for a few hours at least but I'm going to need some water and if you could drum up a Schmidt and Bender 50mm scope, preferably with my L118A1 attached, I'd be very comfy up here.'

'Not sure we can find you a sniper rifle Rambo, but we'll sort out water and provisions.'

'Spoilsports!'

'Keep us updated, I think we're going to go visit some sailors.'

'Some what?'

'Sailors. We'll fill you in later.'

JT drove the Jaguar across Georgetown until he reached the dock where the Royal Naval Reserve station was located. Parking up behind a truck, he donned his sunglasses and a baseball cap before taking a walk along the quayside.

As he approached the Reserve station, two men left the building, locking up on their way out. They exited the razor-wired compound, securing the heavily padlocked gate as JT approached them.

'Good morning,' he greeted them with a broad smile.

'Good morning,' they replied, eyeing him suspiciously.

JT let his arms hang loosely by his sides, slightly turning his empty hands toward them, hoping they would pick up on the subliminal *no threat* message. 'Are you guys the Navy?'

'Naval Reservists,' answered the closest man.

'Cool, that must be pretty exciting!' JT flashed them his friendliest smile, taking off his sunglasses allowing them to look him in the eye.

'What can we do for you Sah?' asked the younger man, who appeared keen to get on with his day.

'I'm Nick Donald, I work for Paramount Cinematic Location Services. We're planning to do some filming around here, for the next Mission Impossible movie. Maybe you know the franchise?' said JT, keeping his smile in place.

'You mean Tom Cruise an' all dem, want come film, here?'

'Yeah Tom loves the Caymans, and he's a big fan of the Navy, thinks you guys are the unsung heroes. I probably shouldn't tell you this, but the film is going to include Navy patrol boats taking on pirates and drug smugglers. Is that what you guys do?'

'Yeah, that's our jobs right enough.'

'They'll be looking for extras, and technical advisors, maybe you guys could earn some cash, it sure does pay well.'

The younger man turned to his friend, 'Hear dat Dom, we gonna be famous, gonna be movie stars man!'

The older man laughed, shaking his head, 'You too ugly, Pickleboy. They just want good lookin' fellas, like me!'

JT laughed along. 'There'll be plenty of work for everyone, assuming of course they choose this location. I have to fly to Puerto Rico tomorrow, the American base there have invited us to have a look-see.'

'You don't want go der, you need dis place,' said the one called Pickleboy.

'Is there someone on site can show me around, maybe the Commander?'

'No, we closed for de weekend now, nobody back here until Wednesday. Commander be back on deck Wednesday morning, 0700 sharp.'

'Ah ok, that's a pity. In that case I'll get going, thanks for your help chaps,' said JT, turning to leave.

'Hold up there, Sah,' said Dom. 'We can give you a quick look now, if you like?'

'Really? That would be amazing, if it's not too much trouble. Mind if I bring my assistant?'

'No, go for it, we'll get opening up.'

JT jogged over to the Jaguar, quickly explaining the ruse to Easy. 'Try to get some photos, and ideas of how we might overcome the security.'

They trotted over to join the two waiting sailors. 'Dom, Pickleboy, this is my assistant Zeke, do you mind if he takes some pictures?'

'Not suppose take no photos inside, Sah.'

'Ah ok, no problem, just thought we could get some action shots with you guys, show them to Tom and the Director, but not to worry.'

The two sailors looked at each other and grinned, 'You take many photos as you like Sah, just be makin' sure you get my good side!'

Dom used a swipe card to open the main door of the building, then punched a four digit code into the antiquated alarm system. Easy held his phone discreetly filming the keypad. After a cursory tour of the building, they had a peep inside the control room with the radar station, and a host of ageing computer equipment, the sailors started warming to their task.

JT saw an opportunity. 'You guys must use real guns and things? The ones we use filming are imitations. What kind of guns do you use?'

'We use Heckler and Koch, MP5 and MP7 mostly,' said Dom.

'Right, Heppler and Gough. Which ones are those again?' asked JT.

'Heckler and Koch, you heard of H n K surely?'

'Well yes, I think so, I don't know much about guns to be honest.'

'You wanna see them?' asked Pickleboy.

'That would be great, maybe we can get some photos of you guys holding them?'

'Not sure about dis now, Pickleboy,' said Dom.

'Don't worry if it's not possible,' said JT.

'Come on Dom man, 5 minutes not doin' no harm. I wanna be in a movie!' said Pickleboy, almost pleading with his friend.

'Shit, come on den, armoury dis way.'

Easy saw the electronic keypad wondering how he might overcome the security, then to his surprise, Joe typed in an eight digit code without any effort to cover it up. 19591959, the date of Cayman independence repeated. Easy couldn't quite believe how lax the security was. Then he realised no-one was ever likely to try to rob the Royal Navy.

When the heavy metal door was pulled open, it revealed what was essentially a large cupboard with 30 carbines in racks down one wall. Shelves full of magazines and ammunition boxes were on the opposite wall.

JT pointed to the top row of carbines and to two longer weapons. 'What are the big ones?'

'They be sniper rifles, they called L96. Bit stupid us having them, we got no-one trained yet. I been waiting 18 months for my sniper course, last one cancelled 'cause of 'urricane Nicole.'

'That does seem a waste, such things belong in the hands of people who can use them though. What does the bit on top do, is that a silencer?'

'Jeez no man, that be the scope. It's 50mm, L96 can take out something at about a mile away, in the right hands.'

'Will you be able to do that?'

'Sure,' said Pickleboy, 'Probly could now, but I need a certificate first.'

'Ah yes, well I hope you get to do the course soon. What does a silencer look like then?'

'We *professionals* call dem *suppressors*, we only got these four, here,' said Joe, pulling open a drawer.

'Wow, you guys are ready for war!' said JT.

'Yeah, we ready alright!' said Pickleboy.

'Can we get some photos of you guys holding the guns?' asked JT.

'Sure ting,' said Pickleboy, grabbing an MP7 from the rack. 'Fire away!'

Chapter Twenty-Four

Gary returned to the SUV carrying a shopping bag with an array of sandwiches and a salad bowl.

'I have some goodies here folks,' he said, as he started bringing items out of the shopping bag. 'Let me see, there's a Pastrami on Rye, Honey Roast ham with pickle, plain old cheese for Peter, but for the adventurous among us, duck in hoisin sauce with lettuce in a wrap. To wash it down, we have a chilled little Argentinian Torrontes number from,' he paused as he read the label, 'from the Rio Negro region. It came highly recommended!' He grinned in the rear view mirror.

'What's with the wine?' asked Jurgen.

'Thought me and Mrs B here could have a nice little romantic lunch, you know get her in the mood like,' he licked his lips at her.

'You make me sick,' said Rosa.

'Well Mrs B, you and me are going to be spending some quality time together. It's up to you how much you want to enjoy it, I know I will!' His immature giggle was cut short when Jurgen placed a hand on his shoulder.

'Which part of the boss is coming didn't you understand? You touch her without his say so, you will not see out the day.'

'Yeah okay, okay, I'm just having a little fun,' said Gary, starting the car engine.

'Well, do not.' Jurgen turned to Rosa, 'Mrs Bergstrom, please just continue to do as you are asked, by Monday afternoon this will all be over.'

'You mean I'll be dead,' replied Rosa, without emotion.

'I sincerely hope that will be avoided. My understanding is that we are to take you, and the money, to Cuba where you will be reunited with your husband.'

'He is my ex-husband. I have no intention of being reunited with him in Cuba, or anywhere else for that matter.'

'I hope you will reconsider, as the alternative is somewhat less pleasant. You have the weekend to think it over.'

Chapter Twenty-Five

The SUV made its way out of Georgetown through the outlying industrial area on Sparky's Drive. They passed the scrap yard at the same time as Rambo was calling JT.

'Boss the SUV is on its way past me now. They're heading for the boat-shed.'

'Roger that, see if you can get a head count.'

'One half of the door opening now, just one operative but shit -'

'What's up?'

'There's another car in there, it's a red convertible with a tan roof. Got to be the same one I saw cruising the bank earlier.'

'That's probably Carlo,' said Easy.

'Ok,' said JT, 'now we have to assume there are at least four of them.'

'Do we go in and get her?' asked Easy.

'Too risky kid, we don't know what kind of firepower they have in there. There's always a risk to the principal. Especially if the principal is wearing a detonator around her neck.'

'Isn't that what you guys trained in the Killer House for?'

'It's the Killing House, and yes we trained all the time for hostage rescue situations, but there are just too many unknowns at the moment. We have until Monday to figure this all out. By then we'll have the full team back together.'

'Looks like they're having to reposition the cars, the other door is being opening. Confirming there are two males inside the building. Neither of them were in the black SUV at the bank earlier.'

'Can you get a photo?' asked Easy.

'Too far away for my phone camera I'm afraid.'

'We badly need some kit,' said JT.

'Then let's go shopping. What we can't buy in Georgetown, maybe the other guys can bring with them?'

'Good idea kid. Rambo can you survive another couple of hours up there?'

'Sure thing Boss, I've got a sea bird of some description to keep me company, but if it shits on me, I'll have to wring its neck.'

'It's meant to be good luck remember! Ok, you look after the wildlife. We'll get back asap.'

'Rambo, can you see any security cameras in the scrap yard, or any of the places nearby?'

'There's a camera on the front of the office opposite here, it's an engineering firm, what are you thinking?'

'Could it be repositioned, to have a line of sight of the boat-shed?'

'Looks like it might be rotatable to that position, yeah.'

'What's the name of the company?'

'Cay, that's Charlie Alpha Yankee, Fabrications.'

Easy brought up the website, 'Okay thanks, I'll see if I can get into their security system remotely, we might be able to keep an electronic eye on the place. Free you up from the birds nest.'

'Sounds good to me, my feathered friend here looks like he's had a big lunch!'

***

Pulling up outside an electronics shop, JT dropped Easy off as he went in search of a drone and a few other gizmos.

JT went to find a decent digital camera, and a load of provisions consisting mostly of biscuits, protein bars and lots of bottles of water. Unfortunately, Georgetown didn't have an Army Navy store. The gents outfitters were geared toward Caribbean Gentleman's Sports club attire; good old shorts and loud, patterned shirts.

The only place he knew, that might hold some tactical clothing, was the same place they would be borrowing some weapons from.

Easy appeared with armfuls of boxes, having to make two trips back and forward, to get it all into the car.

'Did you buy enough kit?'

'It's all packaging really, drones are pretty fragile.'

'Get everything you wanted?'

'I think we'll manage with what I've got. It's at times like this we could do with Hamilton, with his Aladdin's cave of kit.'

'Yeah, he's got all the Gucci stuff has our Mr Hamilton. Anywhere else you want to go?'

'I could do with going back to the villa to prepare all this stuff. I can also be getting access to the camera at Cay Fabrication.'

'I took a call from Taff, all four of the guys won't be getting in until Monday morning now, storm over Florida. It would be better if they were here already, but we'll keep a lid on things until then.'

'Unless there's a chance to rescue Rosa.'

'Yeah kid, if the right opportunity presents itself, we'll get her out.'

'When do we go get the guns from the Navy place?'

'I think we try tonight. Those guys said they were closed for the weekend, so nobody should be any the wiser. Can you override the security system?'

'It's simple enough, the card reader at the front is ancient, from about the year 2000 or something.'

'Oi, cheeky bugger, less of the ancient!' said JT, chuckling.

'Oh yeah, sorry I forgot, Grandpa! Seriously though, the security in there was shocking. The alarm code is 1959 the year Cayman became an Independent Territory, and wait for it - the armoury was 19591959! They're not big on imagination here huh?'

'Bloody hell, pity help them if they ever get invaded.'

'They have been, by bankers with great taste in classic sports cars!'

As the sun started to sink beneath the horizon, they parked outside Cay Fabrications. Easy typed on his lap top until the CCTV camera began to rotate slowly, to face the direction of the boat-shed.

'Damn,' said Easy, 'it's about 5 degrees short of optimal, if I try to zoom in we'll miss most of the boat-shed.'

'Can it be moved manually?' asked Rambo.

'Probably,' said Easy

45 seconds later, Rambo was on the roof, leaning over the edge, gripping the camera. 'Tell me when.'

'Up a bit, bit more, bit more, stop! That's about perfect, now we'll have 24 hour coverage. The camera has infra-red too, so we can pretty much see in the dark.'

'The lights are on in the boat-shed. The windows are either covered up or filthy, but now it's dark you can see bits of light,' said Rambo, as he got back into the Jeep.

'Ready when you are,' JT told Easy.

Easy reached his hand out of the car window, placing his new drone on the roof. He lifted the radio control handset up, pulling the lever to make the drone take off vertically. He left it hovering about 30m high, as he pressed a button on his laptop to split the screen between CCTV coverage with the feed from the tiny high res camera on the drone.

A touch of the joystick made the drone tilt forward, it took off in the direction of the boat-shed. Before it got there, Easy sent it higher, then flew in a wide slow circle while the camera was fixed on the target.

'That's quite some flying kid,' said JT, appreciatively.

'The drone is doing most of the work. $800 dollars gets you self-stabilising, perfect for the 4K camera. The eight blades give excellent manoeuvrability.'

'If you say so Inspector Gadget.' said Rambo, staring at the screen.

'It's not a whisper quiet model, so I don't want to get too close in. Anything you want to see closer up?'

'Get a video with as much detail of the building structure as you can, particularly entry points. Get the windows, doors, any roof lights etc. Then get as much of the immediate terrain as you can. Look for cover points, somewhere we can get close without being seen. Heaven forbid we need them but let's find some defensive positions in case they have a shed full of serious fire power. Too many unknowns for my liking.'

After 10 minutes of flying while recording video footage, Easy pressed a button on the remote control handset before setting set it down.

'Are you just dumping it?' asked Rambo.

'No, it's on its way back, on auto pilot. It uses GPS, along with the camera, to return to its exact take off location.'

'Bloody hell, what will they think of next?' said Rambo.

'Well, they're working on an...wait, that was rhetorical wasn't it?' asked Easy.

'Yeah kid, you just keep all that stuff up in your super brain, to deploy when necessary! Me, I'll stick to climbing and shooting.'

'Talking of which,' said JT, looking out at the dark sky, 'it's time to go borrow some kit.'

'Borrow?'

'It's Her Majesty's Navy's kit ,so if we can get it back to them in one piece, then we probably should.'

'Maybe we could keep it as a stash here on the island?'

'Next time we come back it'll be to use the banking facilities, no guns required.'

'Fingers crossed!' said Rambo, with a snort.

They drove both vehicles down to the quayside, parking well away from the Naval Reserve's yard. Using the shadows created by a jetty linked to the cruise ship terminal, they made their way forward. They located a point where the razor wire fence stopped, perpendicular to a tall sturdy wooden pole, which was a legacy of the old port infrastructure.

To prevent anyone climbing, more razor wire had been coiled around the pole around eight feet above ground level.

JT stood with his back to the pole and with Easy's help, Rambo climbed up to stand on top of JT's shoulders. From here he could safely reach above the razor wire, allowing him to wrap a length of rope around its trunk. Holding the rope diagonally across his shoulders he leaned back until he was almost horizontal with his feet against the trunk pushing against the rope.

Then, much to Easy's amazement, Rambo walked slowly up the trunk of the pole, shuffling the rope up as he went. Near the top of the pole, he changed position to wrap his legs around the trunk as he tied off a longer length of rope.

He gave a thumbs up to JT who gathered the length of rope, took a couple of steps back then ran forward swinging out over the edge of the jetty and around the fence, landing quietly in a crouch.

He gave Easy a nod, throwing the rope back in an arc for him to catch. The rope hit Easy in the face, causing him to let out an involuntary yelp, when it smacked his nose.

JT came up to the fence, 'Got to move, we're a bit exposed here. Strong grip, take three or four steps back then run. Let yourself swing, like you did over the river as a kid.'

'I was brought up in Central London remember, we didn't play near rivers as they're full of shopping trolleys, and dead gangsters,' replied Easy.

'Yeah ok. Just grip tight and swing like I did.'

Easy took a step back, holding on for dear life, he threw himself out into the darkness over the 30 foot drop to the water. His inertia took him wide, his legs kicking out at the apex of the swing until he was heading round the fence back to dry land. He swung his feet forward getting ready to land as he'd watched JT do moments before, but as his feet made contact with the concrete edge his grip failed and he fell backwards toward the water.

A strong hand grabbed Easy's flailing arm as JT reached out for him, but his momentum was such that he pulled JT forward and over the edge. At the last second, JT grabbed the rope with his free hand, a searing pain shot through his shoulder as he took the weight of Easy with his free arm. From the top of the pole Rambo adjusted the ropes trying to winch his companions back to safety. JT pushed his feet back over the edge, gripping with his heels as it took all his might to keep his grip on Easy's arm.

'You need to climb up me,' JT growled through gritted teeth.

Easy lifted his arm, grabbing for JT's trouser belt. JT felt his hand start to slip on the rope as Easy pulled himself up, finally supporting his own weight. With two hands now free, JT worked hand over hand to pull himself up. After what felt like an eternity Easy managed to grab the quayside, pulling himself up over the edge. Too tired to do much else, he threw his weight onto JT's legs to anchor him to the quayside. He lay panting for a few seconds, before he helped pull JT to safety.

They lay in a heap until eventually JT rolled over pulling himself onto his knees. He knelt, holding his arm, which was on fire and seemed virtually immobile.

'I'm sorry,' panted Easy.

'No time for apologies, we need to move and I only have one good arm.'

'Do you need a doctor?'

'No, I need you to help me get some heavy weapons out of that building, then get us out of here.'

Easy ran to the door, producing a small electronic gadget which flashed twice. The door lock mechanism clicked and swung open. He typed in the four digit code to disable the alarm, then switched on the torch of his phone.

JT followed him to the armoury, again Easy punched in the eight digit number then pulled open the armoury door. The internal light came on automatically as JT stepped into the room grabbing a kit bag as he did so, laying it open on the floor.

'Grab four of those MP5s with the folding stocks and get the suppressors out of that drawer,' he told Easy.

JT put two MP5s and 12 full Magazines in his bag. He picked it up with his good hand, slinging it over his shoulder. 'Let's get out of here,' he said, 'make sure we wipe down anything we touched on the way out.'

Back out at the exit point they found Rambo waiting for them. 'Figured you guys might need a hand with the kit,' he told them taking the bags from each of them, slinging them across his chest.

He effortlessly, almost gracefully stepped off the quayside, swinging around the fence without a sound. He swung the rope back to where Easy caught it. Rambo had fashioned a loop in the rope, Easy slipped his hand through feeling the reassuring grip around his wrist. This time he stepped off in a more controlled fashion landing perfectly.

JT followed suit but let out the faintest grunt when he landed.

Back in the vehicles they drove off until JT pulled over at a 24 hour pharmacy to pick up some pain killers and kinesiology physio's tape. He also bought a bag of ice and some vodka from an off licence.

Back at the villa, Easy started cooking a dinner of linguini with lemon and garlic. He separately cooked up some shelled prawns with a mountain of grated Grana Padano cheese.

JT walked in bare chested but with several lengths of blue tape up his arm and over his shoulder. He also had the bag of ice strapped to his shoulder.

'How is it?' asked Easy.

'Dr Rambo here tells me I've torn my deltoid and tricep muscles, I may never use my arm again.'

Easy looked shocked and dismayed, he turned to Rambo for confirmation.

'I told him it was a sprain and not to be such a drama queen,' said Rambo, heading for a shower.

'Thankfully, it's my left arm.'

'Because you shoot right handed?'

'No, because I use my right hand to wipe my arse!' He winked and gave Easy a nudge, 'Don't worry kid, it'll heal soon enough.'

'Do you want me to pour you a drink?' asked Easy picking up the bottle of vodka.

'Christ no, that stuffs for taking off the tape, the glue is a bugger to get off! You can open me a beer though and pass me four of those Ibuprofen.'

Chapter Twenty-Six

Knut Bergstrom drove out of his gates, turning left, heading toward Burhampton. The unmistakable throaty engine roar of his Porsche 911, was a delight to his ears. The long road that ran along the south wall of his estate was poker straight for almost a mile. It had been resurfaced, thanks to a decent donation he'd made to a local council official.

Flooring the accelerator, the rear end fish tailed before he gleefully pulled her back, slipping up through the gears, with the rev counter red lining each time.

112 mph was his record on this straight, although that had been in the Veyron. The Porsche hit 80 mph before he eased up, fighting the urge to touch the brake, he pushed the tyres to hold the line of the long curve ahead.

He was panting slightly when his watch beeped to say his heart rate had reached 120. The slightly damp patch in his armpits, and wide grin, were all the evidence left when he took the car, at a slightly more sedate pace, on the three mile circuit around the estate boundary to the east gate.

This was the last chance he'd have to drive her. He'd disposed of all the other cars over the last few weeks, as he prepared for Cuba. He'd driven hard bargains for all of them, even though he wouldn't need the money, and all of the cars had made him a handsome profit. There was a principal involved, it was a game, he simply had to win.

The Porsche, he had sold to some *city wanker*, who thought he was someone in London. Knut had played him for a fool, by hacking into his emails and reading how much, he'd told his friends, he was willing to pay. The guy was willing to pay above the market rate, and was offering an excellent price. Knut wasn't satisfied with that, so set up a phoney bidding war by getting the guys business nemesis involved. He wasn't really involved, but Knut cloned his social media to create fake bragging posts, about how he was going to *pay whatever it took* to get the 911.

In the end, Knut squeezed an extra £30k out of the guy. He had already decided he would buy Rosa a gift with it for when she came back, *if* she came back. He desperately wanted her in his life, but if he couldn't have her, he would make sure no-one else did.

The sadness he felt at the thought of losing his wife briefly threatened to overwhelm him. To cheer himself up, he took his shotgun from the gun cabinet and stomped down to the ornamental fish pond. He stood on the little faux Japanese bridge throwing a handful of fish food pellets. A maelstrom of gold, orange and white Koi, that Rosa had loved so much, erupted at the surface as they competed for the food.

Knut fired both barrels into the water, turning it red instantly. It churned, as a couple of injured fish tried to make their way out of the soup of their companions remains.

It's survival of the fittest Knut told himself, and he was born to survive.

Chapter Twenty-Seven

Saturday morning was market day in Georgetown, so the streets were busy as Marco walked around. He was killing time before his meeting at the *Bread n Cocoa* Vegan Bistro. It wasn't his sort of place, neither was it the sort of place you would expect to find a contract killer. Then again, Gabriela Carmenez was not your run of the mill killer.

Carmenez, or Gabbi as she preferred to be called, was a diminutive 5'2" tall and so skinny she could wear kids clothes; in fact, she often did. Her superpower was that everyone who met her underestimated her, by the time they'd realised their mistake, they were already dead or dying.

Gabbi had a reputation among those knew her identity, those people were few and far between. She was expensive, but if you wanted someone taken out, and for everyone to assume it was an accident or even natural causes, then she was your woman.

Carlo walked in, looking around in what, compared to the sunshine outside, was the cool, dimly lit interior of the cafe. A woman behind the counter waved him toward an empty table. The table was in the middle of the room, but those that he would have preferred, allowing him to have his back against the wall, all had reserved signs on them.

As he sat down, the woman came from behind the counter to take his order. She recommended the fresh mango-lime juice, with a piece of pie made of honey and coconut milk with fresh Goji berries.

'Sounds good to me, can I also have some coffee, black, with a glass of water please?'

'Come right up sah.' said the woman, as she bustled off back behind the counter.

As he waited, Marco looked around at the few customers. A girl pushed past him to reach the table behind him. He had left his Beretta back at the boat-shed as it was too hot for a jacket and difficult to conceal. Instead, he wore his trusty knife in its sheath on his belt. Instinctively he reached down to touch the hilt as he had 1000 times before and his father had before him. This time, however, all he found was the leather stud fastening lying impotently over his belt.

Marco turned to the table behind him, two girls were playing chess at the table. The girl who had pushed past him was sitting facing him. She had masses of brown curly hair, neat red framed glasses, and looked to be about 12. The girl with her back to him however, had black hair wearing an oversized denim jacket that disguised her shape. He knew this must be Gabbi, so placed his hand on her shoulder to turn her round.

As his fingertips touched the denim he felt a different sensation; cold steel against his neck. His twisted position had left him vulnerable, exposing his carotid artery perfectly for his attacker.

'Do not ever touch a girl, unless she explicitly gives you her consent. In the case of a child, you better have the consent of her Papa too,' came a soft voice, with a South American accent.

Marco started to turn back around, slowly, but as he did the pressure from the knife on his neck increased. 'Please may I turn around?' he asked.

'There now, you are already learning, Señor,' she said, the knife was removed from his neck.

Marco turned very slowly, by the time he was back fully around, Gabbi Carmenez was sitting opposite him, eating a piece of his pie. She wrinkled her nose, pushing the plate toward him.

'A little too sweet for me,' she said, then used the straw to take a sip of his mango-lime juice. 'Much better.'

'Gabbi, I have some business to discuss with you, in private.'

'Naturally. We shall visit the roof terrace, when you are finished.'

'I'm fine, I didn't really want this anyway.'

'You must eat some and drink the coffee. Otherwise, you will insult the lady who owns this place, she is very proud.'

'But you didn't like her cake,' said Carlo.

'Yes, but you are the one who ordered it!' With that, she stood, walking away to climb the stairs to the roof, without looking back to see if he was following.

Carlo spooned a couple of mouthfuls of the cake which was, as expected, very sweet. The bitter black coffee burned his tongue, but the flavour juxtaposition was a pleasant surprise. He left a big tip on the table, then made his way upstairs.

On the roof, he found Gabbi, sat on the parapet wall waiting for him. She looked very relaxed and impossible to age. She could be anywhere from 15 to 25, her clothes were fashionable without being flashy. Marco knew she must be a wealthy woman by now. Her services were much sought after throughout Central America, and he knew of at least one job she'd carried out in the United States. He knew about that job because he had ordered it, on Mr Bergstrom's behalf. Marco was here looking to procure her services, once again on behalf of his boss. This time was different, there was something personal involved too. He would be hiring her to do a job, a job he didn't want to do himself.

'How big a tip did you leave?' she asked him as he approached her.

'Big enough, I didn't see a bill but I left $100, so more than enough.'

'Good, I like to know that people can expect to be well rewarded for their work.' The look she gave him told him everything he needed to know about the negotiation he was about to enter.

'I always pay well; you should know that by now, Gabbi.'

'You pay what I ask you to pay, because you know I have skills that you do not have, that no-one else has.'

'You are very good at what you do Gabbi, but let's not pretend you are the only killer for hire out there. I have five or six on speed dial, who will all kill for a fraction of what you charge.'

'And yet, here you are Marco.' There was no malice in her voice, no triumphalism, though she knew she had the upper hand; instead, she sounded almost bored.

'Yes, here I am,' said Marco, 'and here you are too. Let's not pretend that you are not looking for work. We both know careers in your line of work are short, you need to make money, while you can. This job also has the benefit of being right here, on the island.'

'You misunderstand if you think I am in need of money, Marco. Tell me what you need, I will tell you if it is interesting enough for me to want to do it.'

'My employer is looking to undertake some housecleaning.'

'I'm listening.'

'On Monday evening I will be leaving the Island. I hope to have one passenger with me, but if they choose not to travel then they will be part of the required clean up.'

'Monday doesn't give me much time to prepare. How many?'

'Three or possibly four.'

'Details...?'

'There are three men, they are armed, and currently guarding the fourth person. She will hopefully be leaving with me, but if not they will all be in one location.'

'Where exactly?'

'Here in Georgetown, they will be in a boat-shed across town when I leave.'

'Special requests?'

'I want them clean and preferably not easily identifiable. They came in by sea plane, so there is no record of them arriving on the island. I will be leaving on the sea plane.'

'Fire?'

'Yes, a fire would work, with your usual *accident* set up, that will work very well.'

'As I don't have much time to plan, can you get me too close to them?'

'Yes, I'll introduce you as an associate on Monday. I can tell them that my boss has sent you to look after the woman.'

'I rarely get the opportunity to work on women. Who is she?'

'She is my bosses wife, but if she refuses to come with me and return to him, then he is willing to become a widower.'

'Hmm, such work at very short notice is risky, my price may be too expensive for your liking.'

'I will be taking possession of $500,000 bearer bonds on Monday afternoon. One of them will be yours when the task is completed.'

'How will the handover take place if you have already left with, or without, the woman?'

'I have a man here on the island, his name is Kirkland, he will pay you.'

'Hmm, you would not try to cheat me of payment, now would you Marco?'

'It would be more than my life is worth Gabbi, more than my life is worth.' Marco took a piece of paper from his pocket, handing it to her, 'this is the address of the boat-shed. I will pick you up from here at midday on Monday.'

'Very well, I will be ready.'

Marco turned, walking away, but as he reached the doorway to the stairs he froze as Gabbi called his name. As he turned, his knife slammed point first into the doorframe a few inches from his head.

'Don't forget your knife!'

Marco left the cafe, after remembering to thank the lady behind the counter, and passing the two girls, still playing chess. He noticed that the girl he had mistaken for Gabbi was winning, very close to check mate.

Back in his car he made a call as the electronic soft top motor purred, opening the car to the sky.

'This is Kirkland,' came a man's gravelly voice.

'It's all set for Monday. She will contact you to arrange a meet. Do not make the mistake of underestimating her.'

'Understood.'

Chapter Twenty-Eight

JT watched, as Rambo taught Easy how to strip down a Heckler and Koch carbine. First the MP5 and then the MP7. Easy was proficient; from the moving parts he could rebuild the weapon, checking its firing mechanism. He was, by Regiment standards, ludicrously slow. JT thought back to the hundreds of drills he had carried out in the dark, or blindfolded, until he could strip and rebuild a weapon in 20 seconds.

Heckler and Koch were incredibly reliable, but any weapon can jam, especially if not maintained properly. It was why soldiers, or at least professional soldiers, spent so much time cleaning and looking after their weapons. They cleaned as if their lives depended on it; because they did.

JT picked up an MP7 feeling the heft in one hand. His shoulder injury still caused him pain, but worse than that was the loss of dexterity. He had visited a physiotherapist yesterday, after finding one on the island who worked Sundays who had a free appointment. In the end he had gone to the Squash and Tennis Club, where they met Jeffries, to see their club physio. The Swedish man had manipulated and massaged JT's shoulder, all the while scolding him for not using a harness while kite surfing. It had been the best excuse JT could think of to explain the wrenching injury; it seemed to satisfy the big Swede.

The prognosis for the shoulder was that it should heal in time, but that he would likely need treatment on scar tissue, with months of rehab exercises.

The physio had taped up his shoulder but also given him a sling. He suggested the healing time would be much improved, if it was kept immobile for the next two weeks.

JT had left promising to limit its use as much as possible. He doubted it was a promise he'd be keeping. He looked at his watch, wincing at the pain as he rotated his wrist. While popping Ibuprofen tablets, coupled with Advil, he opened the freezer, pulling out a bag of frozen peas.

'Still hurting boss?' asked Rambo, looking up from the magazine he was reloading.

'Yeah, it's pretty effing sore!' replied JT, looking disgruntled.

'Maybe you should have let me fall?' asked Easy, who had apologised a thousand times already.

'Don't be daft kid. We're a team, we look after each other, it's why we usually work in pairs.'

JT noted Easy hadn't made eye contact with him, but then realised he was watching something on his laptop.

'Movement?' asked JT.

'The red soft top just arrived back,' said Easy, 'still no sign of Rosa.'

'Well, she'll have to come out of there tomorrow, her appointment at the bank is at 4:30, if she's not come out by four then we'll start to worry, but not before then. These guys have a lot of money riding on this, 50 million reasons to keep her safe and well.'

'What about afterwards?' asked Easy.

'Afterwards they'll have us to deal with, we'll have four more of us tomorrow too.'

'What time do the guys arrive,' asked Rambo.

'Their flight is due in at 10:40, we can pick up the hire car while we wait for them, so back here by 11:30 if all goes to time.'

'What time do you want us plotted up at the bank?'

'If we can be in position by 15:00 that would be ideal. We have Easy's video of the boat-shed and terrain to brief the guys. They can get set up while we're at the bank.'

'What do we do if they don't take her back to boat-shed?' asked Easy.

'We will be following them so we can react to whatever happens, but I can't see them going anywhere else. They'll feel safe there, most likely get ready to exfil.'

'What if they kill her, or leave her with the explosive scarf as they drive off?'

'We're not going to let them do either of those things. We need to be in position to take out Jurgen, he's the trigger man. Once we neutralise the threat, we'll get that scarf off of Rosa. They won't be expecting us, so we can hit them all simultaneously.'

'You make it sound simple,' said Easy, unconvinced.

'I'm not suggesting it's simple, or even straightforward. Remember, we were trained for this, hostage rescue was a big part of our training schedule. We have the team; we have the kit, most importantly we have the element of surprise. We hit them hard and fast.'

'What about our ex-fil boss?' asked Rambo.

'I had a look at the road around the quarry. There's a back way in that looks as if it's an old access road. Both of the hire cars we're using are 4x4, so we'll get through there okay. From there, it's through a couple of bushes onto Dyke Road, that takes us to Minerva Road and the bridge to the little islet where the heliport is. Tomorrow morning, we park up the Heli, if we need to beat a retreat, then we fly out of here. If, however, it looks like we're clear, then we'll wash down the cars by the heliport, head back to the villa and assume our role as tourists.'

'Are you going to manage with your arm in a sling?' asked Easy.

'The rest of the guys can do the heavy lifting, but if push comes to shove, I've still got one good arm.'

Chapter Twenty-Nine

'Today is the day, Mrs Bergstrom,' said Marco. 'We can be in Cuba, in time for you to enjoy a drink with Mr Bergstrom, tonight.'

'Knut is my *ex*-husband Marco. You can't honestly think I even want to speak to Knut after this?' asked Rosa, gesturing at the men sat at the table.

'Please consider what you are saying Mrs Bergstrom. Your husband has made it very clear, he wishes you to be on the flight with me, to Cuba. My instructions are very clear if you should refuse.'

'Your man Gary over there, has made it quite clear what he intends doing with me, if I don't leave with you...' Rosa stopped as she fought back tears.

Carlo handed her a handkerchief, 'I am truly very sorry it has come to this Mrs Bergstrom. I pray you will change your mind.'

'If I don't, will you leave me, to that animal?' she sobbed.

'He will not be permitted to hurt you Mrs Bergstrom, you have my word.'

'That's good to know, thank you Carlo,' said Rosa. After a moment a thought occurred to her, 'What is it you do for Knut, Marco?'

'I am security.'

'What does that entail exactly?'

'Mr Bergstrom has me do what is necessary to protect him, his business interests and yourself, obviously.'

'Do you know what he plans to do? Do you know what *StromSec* really does, how he makes his money?'

'I know only what he thinks necessary to tell me.'

'People will die Carlo, when he takes down a system, or shuts down a hospital, people die.' She looked Carlo in the eye, realising that he was showing little to no emotion despite what she had said. Even if he already knew of Knut's plans, he must still feel pity for those who would die. She had seen him with his family, he was a loving husband and father. Then it hit her. She knew then that Knut would have Carlo kill her, if she didn't go back to him. She knew too much to live. 'You're going to kill me, aren't you Carlo? That's your instructions isn't it?'

'I promise you, I could never hurt you, Mrs Bergstrom.'

'Then you'll get one of this lot to do it.'

'These men will not hurt you Mrs Bergstrom, you have my word.'

'Then what will happen?'

'I have arranged for a young woman to come here, to look after you when I am not around. Then when you return from the bank, we will leave together for Cuba, and you can live. Your life will be different, but you will live Mrs Bergstrom, you will live.'

Rosa lay down on her camp bed, curled into the foetal position, screaming silently inside her head.

When Carlo left, she heard him start the car engine as the door was opened to let him out.

Gary appeared back from re-securing the door to crouch down beside her. 'Don't you worry about what Carlo says, when he leaves later with the money, you and me have a date remember. I've been sorely looking forward to it, nothing is going to get in our way of having some fun!'

***

Easy watched the CCTV feed of the boat-shed, relaying to JT that the red car was on the move, with only the driver in the vehicle.

'Ok, let's get this other hire car sorted for the guys arriving, we can get things moving,' said JT.

A few minutes later Rambo emerged from the car hire office with a set of keys for a Jeep Wrangler. This one had a canvas roof on the rear section and Rambo rolled it away before taking up the driver's seat.

Easy was already working out how he would be able to launch his drone from the rear of the vehicle, when it was parked somewhere near the boat-shed. He knew this was what he brought to the team. They worked hard at cross-skilling but wherever possible they let the experts do their thing.

They chose a petrol station outside the airport where they knew there was no CCTV. Completely filling the tanks on the vehicles, not because they thought they were going to drive far, Grand Cayman is a small island after all, but this was part of the ritual before a mission. They were crossing the things off that they could in preparedness, but deep down they knew there were too many unknowns. They were stepping into the danger zone.

Rambo bought a petrol can, which he filled from the pump marked Gasoline. He also bought a 5 litre bottle of oil and a pack of hand towels, this would create a makeshift smoke screen, should they need it.

Setting off in good time, they drove to the terminal building to see Taff, Joe, Cooky and Posty emerge separately onto the street before heading for the car park. Without fanfare, they were picked up, away from the terminal CCTV cameras. Each vehicle headed for the villa using different routes.

Once at the villa, the new arrivals dumped their bags and immediately inspected the weapons laid out for them, as Easy made pots of tea and coffee.

JT stood over the map of Georgetown, arranging markers highlighting the routes and positions of buildings. Easy had his laptop ready to show the video footage from his drone, along with the cameras he had commandeered.

When everyone was ready, the briefing began. Before JT was able to speak, his phone rang. He quickly switched the call from Rory Maxwell to speaker phone, 'Rory we're on the clock here, about to start a briefing. What have you got for us?'

'You're going to want to hear this, Hamilton just sent it over.'

'Of course, we're listening.'

'Between us, we've got a definitive ID on one of the men. The driver is Gary Simpson, he's 31, he was an army brat born in Gibraltar. He was kicked out of the British Army for psychological reasons, then joined the Foreign Legion. After three years, they didn't want him either. He was alleged to have raped and tortured several women, in a village in Gabon. After they kicked him out, he found work in security and seems he now works for *StromSec*. We found photos of him in Knut Bergstrom's security detail, when he was in Belarus last year.'

'He sounds a charmer,' said JT, 'thanks Rory, anything on the others?'

'Hamilton found a passenger manifest, from the *StromSec* private jet landing in Hong Kong a couple of months ago. There were four men listed, other than Bergstrom himself. From that list, we've ID'd the guy who went into the bank with Mrs Bergstrom as Jurgen Spitz. He's German/Italian, from one of those Alpine border villages. He is ex Bundesnachrichtendienst or BND. From what Hamilton could find out, the guy was a foot soldier working in Rome, but suddenly handed in his notice and went to work for *StromSec*. Told his bosses the pay available in the private sector was too good to turn down.

There was also a Peter Müller, he's 38, Swiss born and wait for it, an ex Papal Security guard. He had the full jester/clown outfit at the Vatican, as you know they're a well-trained bunch.'

'Yes they are, we've done some training with them, and the Italian SF guys. I seem to remember they were proud of the term 'mercenaries', but fiercely loyal to the Church. It sounds like he may have been more loyal to C for cash, rather than the Holy See,' said JT, causing a few smiles and rolled eyes among his team.

'Last, but by no means least, is Marco Angelucci, he is Bergstrom's head of security. The only one officially on the books of *StromSec*. He seems to be Bergstrom's Mr Fixit, and is most often found by his side. His name is a complete misnomer too, the guy is no Angel. Brought up in Rome, he was an enforcer for the Mafia Capitale. They were decimated in 2014 by a huge, very public, crackdown. Marco was sentenced to 12 years in prison, alongside Massimo Tollonati aka *The last King of Rome.* But, in the usual Italian style, some corrupt Judge in their Supreme Court set them all free, after six months. Marco had his hands full while in prison protecting Tollonati. He was suspected of killing five inmates in his six months inside but nothing was ever proven.

After he was released from prison, Tollonati allegedly retired from one life of crime and joined another, by going into Far Right Italian politics. Marco was cut loose, but how he ended up working for Bergstrom, we don't know. He's been on the payroll for the last four years.'

'This all great intel, thanks Rory.'

'What's the plan?'

'We're working it out right now, but the mission is to get Rosa Bergstrom to safety. The rest of it is up to them, if they want to go toe to toe; we put them down.'

'What about the local Police?'

'We can't trust them, after what I saw at the Airport, they were either scared or being paid to walk away. We will try to avoid them, if we can.'

'I'd suggest a couple of hoax calls, as far away from your position as possible. A good old fashioned bomb hoax, or jewellery store robbery, will keep their limited resources tied up.'

'Good idea, that's what we'll do. We'll be operating in Georgetown, in the mid-point, so we'll send them to either end of the island.'

'Did you get any more on Bergstrom's plane going to Cuba?'

'Yes, we confirmed he is on board, and on his way. Even Hamilton can find very little out about our Mr Bergstrom. He appears to be clean, but we know there's something going on, Hamilton thinks it's linked to Nigeria. We'll keep searching.'

'Excellent, thanks again Rory.'

'No problem, and best of luck, look after yourselves.'

'We'll do our best,' said JT, rubbing his hand over his damaged shoulder.

Chapter Thirty

Marco parked the car inside the boat-shed, then opened the door to let Gabbi out of the passenger side. Gabbi was wearing denim shorts and a hello kitty t-shirt which made her look like a teenager. Marco knew it was part of her methodology; making people discount her as a threat; giving herself the ultimate advantage of surprise.

As they walked in, Gary let out a wolf whistle that was immediately silenced by a look from Marco. Gabbi looked around wide eyed, playing the part of teenage girl perfectly.

'Everyone, this is Gabbi, she will be looking after Mrs Bergstrom; helping her to make herself presentable for going to the bank. She will also be doing some housekeeping after we leave, to make sure we leave no trace of being here.'

Gabbi walked over to Rosa and stood staring at her for a few seconds. She could see how beautiful Rosa was even with her creased clothes and dishevelled hair. Gabbi handed her a plastic bag and said, 'It's for you Ma'am. The man says you were size 10 so I picked this one. You are very beautiful Ma'am.'

Rosa looked at the sweet smile from this young girl, but found she could say nothing, instead she nodded her thanks.

Gabbi stepped forward, lifting the dress out of the bag. It was a floaty beach dress in golden yellow. Gabbi had to lift her hands above her head to stop it trailing on the floor.

Marco placed a small holdall, that could have been a school bag, on the floor beside Gabbi. 'There's shampoo and things in there, Gabbi here will help you.'

'I won't be letting that animal film me bathing again, I'd rather stay dirty,' said Rosa, finding her voice.

Marco spun and marched up to Gary with his hand out, 'Give me your phone.'

'Woah, it's just a bit-'

Marco pulled the knife from his belt, pressing the tip into the soft skin under Gary's chin 'Phone,' he repeated quietly.

Gary took his phone from his pocket, placing it into Marco's hand.

'Did you send it to anyone?'

'No, it's for my personal use only, you can't blame a man for-' Gary stopped mid-sentence when Marco dropped the phone onto the concrete floor, stamping on it angrily until it was smashed into pieces.

'If you really want to have fun with a female, then I suggest you try your charms on Gabbi here, once I have left. I'm sure she will surprise you for one so young.'

Rosa took Gabbi's hand, 'Come on Gabbi, come help me get ready.' Rosa picked up the holdall, walking with Gabbi to stand in front of Jurgen. 'Take it off,' she told him.

Jurgen undid the screw then unclipped the det cord necklace.

Rosa led Gabbi beyond the tarpaulin to where the bucket and fresh water lay. 'Don't worry, Gabbi, I won't let them hurt you.'

'I'm not worried Ma'am,' said Gabbi, in a sweet, innocent voice, 'I've met men like them before. I know how to deal with them.'

Rosa grabbed her in a hug, holding her close. 'Someone will rescue us Gabbi, I just know it,' she whispered to her.

Gabbi stepped back and looked at Rosa as if appraising her. 'Let me wash your beautiful hair Ma'am, I always wanted blonde hair.'

Chapter Thirty-One

'That's us in position,' reported Taff.

'How's the OPs?" asked JT.

'Not perfect but adequate. We've no cover from the air, but clear eyes on the target.'

'Any difficulty getting in?'

'No, we waited as discussed, until after the SUV left the boathouse. The soft top left too, definitely that Marco guy driving. He had the roof up still, which is a bit weird if you ask me, but maybe he's a fan of air conditioning.'

'So just one guy left behind minding the fort?'

'Yeah, saw him close up the doors. He's not overtly armed, they all look fairly relaxed.'

'Did you get eyes on Rosa?'

'Negative, the SUV has privacy glass, so can't confirm who's in the vehicle.'

'Roger that, we're in position at the bank. Rambo has the high ground. We're in the adjacent office.'

'They should be with you imminently.' Taff said.

'Yes, Jeffries is primed. If an opportunity arises we'll intervene here. If the scarf is still in play then we'll hold off; revert to the contain and negotiate plan. We'll keep this line open, updates as and when Taff.'

'Will do boss.'

A moment later Rambo gave an update. 'The red soft top is back, he's having a slow drive past the bank. I can see the SUV on its way, 30 seconds out.'

'Marco is taking the scout role,' said JT.

'I'll keep an eye on him, but for now he's parking up, 50 metres West of you.'

'Roger that.'

'Here's the SUV now, parking up right outside.'

'We've got them on the bank CCTV,' said Easy.

As they had on the previous visit to the bank, Gary stayed with the vehicle while Jurgen walked in with Rosa. She turned heads in her golden yellow dress. Her hair had a natural beach tousled look, that models and photographers spent hours trying to create. Again, she wore the Hermes scarf around her neck with the navy, white and gold colours giving a contrast to the bright but plain dress.

'She's wearing the scarf. Repeat she's wearing the scarf.' JT told the team.

'Shit,' said Easy, zooming in on Rosa as she walked through the security scanner. 'Why doesn't it set off the security alarm?'

'It's mostly high explosives in a plastic tubing. Judging by the bulk of it, there's a few strands braided together or wrapped around something. Probably an actual necklace, or maybe a length of para-cord or something.'

'We've got to get it off her.'

'I know kid, I know. But until we can secure the trigger device from our friend Jurgen, then it's too risky. He can set that thing off before we get to him.'

Jeffries left his office after setting up the conference call with the room next door. He greeted Rosa and referred to Jurgen by name. This surprised Jurgen, but he knew this was how these people ingratiated themselves.

Without being told, Jurgen handed the briefcase he was carrying to Rosa, then made his way to the waiting area. He took a long look around the bank before sitting down. Noting that the office next to Jeffries' had the privacy glass activated again, he tried to see inside, but there were only the faintest shadows visible. Some rich schmuck moving their money around to avoid paying taxes, he thought to himself. On a whim, he said, 'Wait!' He said it loud enough that everyone in the public area of the bank stopped to look at him. He approached Rosa and Jeffries at the door to his office. 'You can do this out here,' he told them. 'Sign the papers, and put the bonds in the briefcase. Then we go.'

Jeffries looked shocked and Rosa said nothing.

'That would be most unusual,' said Jeffries. 'This is a very large transaction. I think it would be better if Ms Hawthorne completed it in private.'

'Her name is Mrs Bergstrom, and you will do this out here.' said Jurgen, taking a step closer to Rosa, showing her something in his hand.

'It's ok Jeffries, let's just get this over with,' said a resigned Rosa.

'Very well, as you wish. I will bring the papers to you directly. Perhaps Ms Hawthorne, you would like to take a seat in the waiting area. I will ensure no-one overhears us.' He winked at Rosa before retreating into his office.

'Did you hear all that?' Jeffries said aloud, gathering papers up on his desk.

'Yes we did.'

'Do you have your mobile phone with you?' asked Easy.

'Yes, it's here on my desk, why?'

'Dial your office number, connect your mobile in to the conference call.'

'Ah yes, give me a second.' Jeffries connected his mobile phone, placing it inside a document folder.

'Try to leave it beside them, when you go to the vault,' said JT.

'Yes, I'll do that,' said Jeffries. He took a deep steadying breath before heading out of his office.

When he reached the waiting area, Jeffries pulled the heavy coffee table closer to Rosa. He placed the document folder containing his phone on the shelf beneath, beside the untouched glossy magazines about private jets and super yachts.

'I will just need two signatures from you, here and then here, Ms Hawthorne,' said Jeffries, pointing to two documents and handing her his pen.

'This is a nice pen,' she said, admiring the sleek black writing instrument.

'It's by Conway Stewart, they are an old client of the bank in London. I rather think we are their biggest customer. We gift these pens to clients, when they open accounts with us. You should have received one, when you opened your account, Ms Hawthorne?'

'Enough about the pen, complete our business here Jeffries, and as I have told you, her name is Mrs Bergstrom,' said Jurgen.

Rosa ignored him and carried on speaking to Jeffries. 'The setting up of the account was handled by my *ex-husband,* but I doubt he'd have been interested in a pen. He's more of a digital person.'

'Then you must have mine,' said Jeffries.

'Unless she has changed her mind, then she won't be needing any pen,' said Jurgen, sounding uncharacteristically stressed, 'and for the last time, get on with it.'

'Very well. I will need a few moments to collect the bonds from the vault. Perhaps Jurgen, you would care to accompany me to count them, save some time?'

Jurgen considered this as he looked around the bank. 'No, just bring them here. You will make sure they are all present and correct, or I must return to seek compensation, from *you personally*.' He spoke with a level voice, but the look he gave Jeffries carried all of the required threat.

'The man is just doing his job Jurgen, there's no need for unpleasantries.'

'I wish to have this matter concluded. One way or another, I intend being on a flight out of here later this evening.'

'And me?' asked Rosa.

'I sincerely hope you will be on a different flight, Mrs Bergstrom, but your future is in your own hands.'

Rosa touched the scarf at her neck. 'Yes I think you are correct.'

***

Ten minutes later they were leaving the bank, with Jurgen carrying the briefcase and a dejected looking Rosa walking in front of him.

'They're coming out,' said JT, as he and Easy made their way out of the office. JT stopped to shake Jeffries' hand. 'Thanks for all your help, Jeffries.'

'Any time, any time. Do you need to borrow the Jaguar again?'

'No, thank you. We're all set this time.'

'Ok, can you let me know how it all works out?'

'We'll try,' lied JT, making his way through security to the door of the bank.

'Good to go,' said Rambo, 'the soft top is following them, they're headed back the way they came.'

'Get to the Jeep Rambo, I want to get there right behind them.'

'On my way down.'

With Rambo driving and JT in the passenger seat, Easy set up his lap top in the rear seat. As he brought up the commandeered CCTV from Cay Fabrication, he was met by the perturbed face of an engineer, who was using a cherry picker to reach and reposition the camera. 'We're losing the CCTV,' he told JT.

'Okay, it's served its' purpose anyway,' said JT, over his shoulder. Pulling his phone from his shirt pocket, he pressed speaker phone function, 'Sit rep please Taff.'

'We're in position boss, the guy opened up both doors about a minute ago. He was standing waiting for them to come back, but he took a phone call and he's gone back inside.'

'They're about four minutes out, we're not too far behind them.'

'Standby, there's movement on the water side. Looks like they're winching open the doors to the slip way.'

'They must be getting the sea plane ready. Shit!' said JT, spinning scenarios around in his head. 'We can't move until we get that scarf away from Rosa.'

'I'll get the drone up,' said Easy, from the back seat.

'Boss, we can probably get inside the shed, while the guy's busy at the other side? We'll see if there's somewhere we can lay up.'

'Go for it Taff, but be careful, you've got three minutes to get back out if there's nowhere suitable.'

'Roger, moving now.'

Taff and Joe sprinted from cover, up to the boat-shed. Easy's drone camera gave the others a live feed to their phones, as Taff and Joe readied their MP5s. They took a quick look inside, then disappeared into the shadowy darkness.

Inside the boat-shed, the two men moved silently forward, finding a gap behind a stack of bulging sacks, next to the external wall. They heard the winch stop, followed by the sounds of a man walking back into the shed.

The man appeared to be talking to himself, 'Not long now, soon this will all be over. We can all get out of this shit-hole.' The sound of approaching vehicles prompted the man to make his way back to the front of the shed.

Rambo parked up beside the scrap yard, before leaning over to watch the screen of Easy's laptop. Easy kept the drone in position until the cars were parked in the shed and the doors were closed. Flying the drone closer, they could see Cooky and Posty in position, crouched between an overturned oil drum and some scrubby bushes. Easy took the drone high and wide to get a view from the seaward side. The doors were fully open, the seaplane bobbing in the little internal dock.

Inside the boat-shed, Marco shouted instructions to the other men, 'Get this place cleaned up. One of you wipe down the cars. No fingerprints, no trace please gentlemen.'

The sounds of people scurrying around reached JT through the open line on Taff's phone. Then he heard Marco deliver an ultimatum to Rosa, 'Mrs Bergstrom, this is it, decision time. Please just come with me. I will be leaving in one minute. You must be on that plane with me.'

'Or?'

'Stop with the silly games Mrs Bergstrom,' Marco's voice held mix of anger and exasperation, 'get on the plane now, or you die here. I cannot be responsible for how you die, but our friend Gary over there has requested the task.'

Rosa looked at Gary, then at Gabbi, who was standing beside her.

'You should go Rosa,' said Gabbi. 'Someone so beautiful, does not deserve to die in this place.'

'Thank you Gabbi,' said Rosa taking Gabbi's hand, 'but I won't leave you here.'

'I am at home here. I have work to do. Do not worry for me, I will be fine.'

'There now, do the sensible thing Mrs Bergstrom, I am leaving now. It is decision time; do you want to live?'

Gabbi pushed her forward with a strength that surprised Rosa.

'It seems I have no choice.'

'Excellent, now let's get out of here.'

Rosa followed Carlo out to the seaplane. He helped her up and into the rear seat, before passing her the briefcase containing the bearer bonds.

'Can't forget the all-important money!' said Rosa, sarcastically.

'$50 million dollars will buy you the most beautiful house in all of Cuba.' Carlo told her.

He climbed into the pilot's seat, fastening his safety harness, before flicking some switches to start the engine. The backdraft from the propeller shifted the tarpaulin curtain, ruffling Gabbi's hair, as she stood waving farewell to Rosa.

Rosa pressed a hand to the window as the seaplane inched out of the dock, easing through the doors into the lagoon beyond. 'Be safe little one,' she mouthed.

Chapter Thirty-Two

Rosa looked back from the rear seat of the sea plane. 'We can't just leave her here with that monster!' she pleaded. 'We can take her with us, there's room in here.'

'Don't worry, Gabbi can take care of herself.'

'She's a child Marco!'

'She is much older, and a whole lot tougher, than she looks. I wouldn't like to be in Gary's shoes if he tries to lay a finger on her.' Marco turned the sea plane left out of the boat-shed. The engine noise changing pitch as he accelerated toward the end of the lagoon.

Rosa looked back again and thought she saw two figures running toward the boat-shed. She was sure it must be Easy's friends. Vigilant were too late to save her, but maybe they could save Gabbi.

With the windows open, the breeze meant that even over the noise of the aircraft engine, they could hear the sound of suppressed gunfire. Three distinct but almost simultaneous double pops.

'Double taps, excellent work Gabbi,' muttered Marco, as he checked some dials getting the seaplane into position facing up the lagoon, into the breeze.

'The necklace!' exclaimed Rosa, suddenly remembering the explosive charge around her neck.

'Don't worry Mrs Bergstrom, I took this from Jurgen.' Marco fished the trigger device from his shirt pocket, showing it to her over his shoulder. 'It's safe, we'll be in Cuba before you know it,' he told her as he placed the trigger device in a little compartment on the dashboard.

'Can I take it off, please?' asked Rosa.

Marco slipped the knife from his belt and passed it back to her. 'Be careful, it is very sharp, but you can use it on the screw. I'd suggest waiting until we are in the air, this may be a little bumpy,' he said, pushing forward the throttle, as the seaplane started to gather speed. He began to whistle Rodrigo as the floats cut across the water, until the sea plane slowly began to gain altitude.

Rosa wasted no time, using the point of the knife on the little screw. After a few seconds she was holding the necklace in her hand despite being pushed back into her seat by the speed of the aircraft. She looked at the briefcase that contained the $50 million in bearer bonds. She made her decision.

Tucking the necklace under the pilot seat, she wrapped it around one of the metal supports. Undoing her seatbelt she forced herself forward. She looked at the knife held tightly in her hand. She paused for a moment, and screwed her eyes shut then drove the knife into Marco's side. She felt the knife scrape bone as it found a way through his ribs and into his lung. He screamed, the aircraft lurched throwing Rosa back into her seat. Gathering herself, she reached for the door handle, pushing it open. The door crashed back as the wind force worked against her. As Marco groaned and fought the controls of the seaplane, it rolled slightly, causing the weight of the door to make it swing open. Rosa pushed herself forward, then in a moment of clarity, grabbed the trigger device from the cubby hole, before throwing herself out of the door.

Falling backwards, Rosa looked back up at the sea plane. The impact of hitting the water knocked the air from her lungs. She choked on the salt water as she fought to reach the surface. Coughing out the water she had swallowed, she looked up in time to see the cockpit of the seaplane explode. The aircraft spun steadily downward, crashing into the sea. As it fell, she saw paper certificates floating down through the air, burning as they went.

Chapter Thirty-Three

'Three down,' reported Taff, 'but there's a kid in here,' he said, as Gabbi appeared from behind the tarpaulin.

'Who is it?' asked JT.

'No idea, standby.' Taff lowered his weapon, watching Gabbi take in the scene in an almost bemused way. She didn't look frightened, which he put down to shock. 'It's ok, sweetheart, we're no going to hurt you.'

Gabbi stood looking at him, as she tried to work out what was going on. These men were very professional, it was good shooting to put down all three of Carlo's men so quickly. The man speaking to her spoke in English, but his accent was strange to her. He had a kindly face, and had obviously assumed she was a child, so she decided to go along with it. Her job had been to kill the three men and these guys, whoever they were, had done the job for her. Now, all she had to do was collect her payment as arranged; this would turn out to be a very good day. Unless of course these guys turned her over to the cops, but she doubted that. They hadn't identified themselves, just told Carlo's men to put their hands up. That idiot Gary had reached for a gun, paying the price for having the brain of a *burro*. Gabbi knew that no-one, not even she, could draw and fire a weapon quicker than these guys could pull a trigger. The double tap shooting told her that these guys were probably military, most likely Special Forces.

'What's your name sweetheart?' asked Taff

'Gabriella,' she replied, applying her best puppy dog eyes.

'What are you doing here, Gabriella?' asked Taff.

'The man made me come, to look after the lady, to wash her hair.'

'I see. Where do you live?'

'Here in town,' she pointed, 'just five minutes to walk. I don't have my bike.'

'Is there someone at home, to look after you?'

'Yes, my mama. She is at home, with my little brother.'

'Ok, then I think you should run along home. Probably best that you don't tell anyone what happened here,' said Taff.

'They were bad men. They would have hurt me, if you hadn't come. Thank you.'

'Hang on a second, Gabriella.' Taff had a quick chat with JT on his phone, they agreed to let Gabbi get on her way. 'Ok Gabriella, you can head home, to your mama.'

Gabbi reached for her hold all looking at Taff, 'May I take my schoolbag, it has shampoo and things that are barely used.'

'Of course, help yourself,' said Taff, with a smile.

Gabbi reached into the bag, her fingers touching her SIG Sauer P365. She hesitated for a moment, then decided that these men didn't deserve to die, especially as they were not part of her contract. Zipping up her bag, she slipped it over her shoulder before walking out into the sunshine, then jogging happily across the waste-ground.

'Bye!' she called as she ran past Cooky and Posty, who were still in position covering the front of the building.

The explosion in the aircraft made everyone look up, they all feared the worst. Panicked, Easy flew the drone in that direction. In the water he saw something that made his heart jump. It was Rosa, somehow she was alive. Rambo gunned the Jeep engine, driving as close to the shore as he could, before he and Easy leaped from the vehicle diving into the sea.

Rosa spun around in the water to see two men dive in and start swimming out toward her. She'd never seen one of them before, but the other she knew, even from this distance, was a young man called Easy.

***

'Let's get the hell out of here,' said JT, driving with one arm as Rambo and Easy climbed in, after helping Rosa into the car.

The other members of the team followed in the second Jeep, as they made their way into the quarry site. The quarry had closed as usual at 4pm, but they were able to lift the gate from its hinges, then put it back again once they'd driven through, leaving the padlock and chain intact.

A quick circuit round the quarry, after finding a parked lorry barring their original way, led them to the service road. Once through the road to the line of bushes, they found a bare patch, just big enough to drive through. Out onto the road they stopped while Cooky ran back. Using a large palm frond, he brushed away their tyre tracks.

A minute later, they were at the Helipad, both vehicles were parked with two wheels in the water. They got to work washing down the now dusty vehicles, and put all of the weapons in kit bags, that they hid in bushes along the water's edge.

Posty, had started up the Eurocopters engine, letting it idle while they waited to see if they were being followed.

After 10 minutes, when no-one came, Posty picked up a message from Air Traffic Control that there had been an accident involving a light aircraft. Aircraft were advised to avoid the area, as the Coastguard made their way to investigate.

Easy had been monitoring the Police radio frequency, there was no talk about gun shots. All available officers were dealing with the hoax bomb call Maxwell had suggested.

They waited another 10 minutes, then decided they would split up. With Posty and Cooky taking Rosa and Easy in the helicopter, the others took long, circuitous routes back to the villa. They left the weapons hidden, making plans to come back for them later.

As Posty piloted the helicopter out to sea, he told Air Traffic Control that he had some tourists aboard heading for Little Cayman, on a sightseeing trip. He acknowledged the message re the downed sea plane, offering his assistance, but was told the Coastguard were on scene and had the matter in hand. The ATC operator confirmed that the seaplane had exploded, they did not anticipate survivors.

Chapter Thirty-Four

From her vantage point, Gabbi had watched Rosa fall from the aircraft and hit the water, as the explosion erupted in the cockpit.

Very good, thought Gabbi, as she watched the two men help Rosa from the water, *beautiful people should not die in such ugly ways*.

Waiting until the cars had driven off, she returned to the boat-shed. The bodies of the three men lay where they had fallen. She examined their faces before going through their pockets. None of them carried ID, which told her they were at least semi professional, or were controlled by someone who was. Marco had always struck her as if he knew how to play the game, but he had also contracted out work to her.

Pushing over a half empty drum of aircraft fuel, she rolled it over to the dead men. Looking at Gary with his face contorted, either in shock or pain, she felt a little cheated that she hadn't had the pleasure of killing him. She looked at him again, then spat in his face after offering a little prayer. She prayed that the hell he was going to, was of the very worst kind. She pumped fuel over the bodies, and over the piles of sacks against the wall. As she stepped backward she created a wide puddle of gasoline. She locked open the fuel pump lever allowing it to continue pouring fuel over the floor.

On the way out of the door, she took a lighter from her holdall, lit some paper and threw it into the pooling fuel. The whoosh caught her by surprise, as the room behind her ignited, and she giggled as she started running across the waste ground, back to her parked car.

From her car, she watched the boat-shed burn, throwing a column of black smoke into the air. The dancing, swirling plume looked delicate and almost graceful against the topaz blue sky. Orange and gold flames licked out of the windows beneath the metal roof which sang out it's distress, as it began to warp. The two cars hissed and popped as tyres exploded before their fuel tanks erupted with a throaty roar. At this distance Gabbi was spared the nauseating smell of burning human flesh. It always reminded her of barbecued pork; whenever possible she tried to be well away from the fires she set, or at the very least least upwind.

The goosebumps on her skin, and the tiny beads of sweat in the small of her back, were something she always got after a job. This was slightly different, as she hadn't actually killed anyone. The feeling took her back to a job a few years back in Argentina. That job had come from Marco too, and she took a second to recall the young girls's face. Her name had been Catalina and Gabbi had killed her father. That night in Buenos Aires, she had merely encouraged the man to take his own life, rather than pull the trigger herself. It always amazed her, the sheer spectrum of men that existed in the world. Some men, like Catalina's father, would die protecting their children, others were happy to destroy their own children. Gabbi had no intention of having kids of her own, but if she knew that if she did, she would happily kill all the men in the world, to protect them.

Chapter Thirty-Five

Later that evening, in the hours of darkness, Posty landed the helicopter back at the helipad. He was met by Rambo in the Jeep. They loaded the weapons into the vehicle before driving back to the villa, where the rest of the team were waiting.

Rosa looked around the team, at the men who Easy had explained, were known as Vigilant. She stood in her damp clothes, finding she was suddenly very tired and cold. 'Do you think I might have a bath?' she asked the room.

'Of course. You can use the bath in my ensuite,' said Easy, showing her into his room.

Rosa borrowed a guest robe as she ran hot water into the bath. She found some luxury complimentary toiletries by the bath, noticing they were unused. She uncapped the bath soak, smelling the heady, musky scent before pouring it under the hot running water.

Half an hour later, she walked out into the living area, wearing her bathrobe and hair wrapped in a towel.

The men all stopped what they were doing, a sudden hush fell over them.

Rosa looked at them all, then took a deep breath, 'Who does a girl have to kill to get a drink around here?'

Her joke fell a little flat, but the men gave her a smile and Easy jumped up to give her a seat.

Rambo made his way to the fridge and opened it, 'We can offer you some beer, or some industrial cleaner masquerading as vodka?'

'There's some rum in the cupboard,' said JT, 'it was in the welcome pack.'

'I have some Cognac in my bag?' offered Joe. 'Picked it up in Duty Free on the way here.'

'I'd love a Cognac, if that's not too much trouble?'

'Of course,' said Joe, before he trotted upstairs to fetch the bottle from his bag. He came back holding a bottle in his hand, 'I'm not sure if it's any good, I bought it because I liked the name, *Bisquit and Dubouché*. I just thought it sounded funny!' he grinned, handing the bottle to Rosa.

'It's a new one on me, but had I seen it, I'd have chosen this one too.' She smiled at Joe who felt himself blush a little as he dropped into his seat. 'Might I have a glass, or should I sip from the bottle?'

'Oops, sorry!' said Joe, laughing at himself.

'I have a glass here for you,' said Rambo.

'Oh thank you. Anyone going to join me?'

'We have some work to do I'm afraid,' said JT.

'Work?'

'We borrowed the weapons you saw today. It would make life easier for all concerned, if we can return them tonight.'

'You can borrow guns? I had no idea.'

'Neither do the people we borrowed them from,' said JT. 'Thankfully, Taff lifted a 9mm Beretta from one of the men who held you captive, so we can even replace the six rounds that were fired today. The Naval Reserve need never be any the wiser.'

'Which one of you is Taff?' said Rosa, looking around the men.

'My apologies, please allow me to introduce everyone. Easy, you already know, obviously. I am JT, we spoke on the telephone on Friday in the bank.'

'Yes, I recognised your voice.'

'This is Rambo, who was with us at the bank. Then we have Taff, Joe, Posty was your pilot today and Cooky was flying shotgun.' said JT, pointing out the members of the team who nodded or held their hands up when their names were mentioned.

'Very pleased to meet you all. I am Rosa Hawthorne, previously I was Bergstrom, but I think you know that already. I have to thank you for rescuing me today. I firmly believed I was going to die. I am now $50million poorer, but I'm alive, so a fair exchange I would say.'

'Actually, you may not be as poor as you think.' JT told her.

'How so?' asked Rosa, taking a sip of her Cognac.

'I had Jeffries swap out the bearer bonds with photocopies. The real bonds are safely tucked up in a safe deposit box at the bank. Jeffries was great incidentally, I hope you'll keep your account with him.'

'I can't believe it!' said Rosa, shocked. 'I'd already written the money off. I owe you all so much. Mr Jeffries too.'

'It's what we do,' said Easy.

'Just who are you guys? I heard the name Vigilant, but don't quite understand. Are you part of the Military, or Secret Service or something?'

'Something like that, Rosa.' JT gave her a look that made it obvious it was all they would say on the matter.

'It's need to know, and I don't need to know.' She smiled, saluting each of them with her glass. 'Whoever you are, I owe you my life. I will forever be in your debt.'

'There are another two members of the team, who are currently back in the UK. They are both very interested in your husband, sorry *ex-husband,* and his business affairs. When we have sorted out the weapons, perhaps you would be so kind as to fill them in on what you know?'

'It would be my pleasure.'

'Excellent. Rambo, same system as before re the fence swing?' said JT, rubbing his shoulder.

'Maybe Easy can lend us his gadget, to get past the door security?' said Rambo.

'I can do it this time, no problem,' said Easy.

'No offence mate, but it's probably safer if we let the guys with more training handle this stuff.' Rambo said, gently.

Easy turned to Rosa to explain. 'I slipped and fell, but JT caught me. That's how he hurt his shoulder,' he told her.

'Ah, I did wonder about the sling,' said Rosa.

'It's nothing, but Rambo is right Easy, your skills are better utilised here with your computer. Our youngest team mate is a bit of a genius, Rosa.'

'Wonderful, I could tell he is very smart.'

'That's settled then, Rambo take Cooky and Posty with you. Taff and Joe can provide backup from the second Jeep. There's obvious racking for the weapons, the suppressors were in a drawer under the magazines.'

'I'll replace the six rounds before we put them back obviously, but what about the Beretta?'

'Let's keep it somewhere handy, but if we don't need it, we can dump it some place safe before we leave.'

'Will do boss. We'll get going now. See you in a couple of hours.'

'Good stuff, keep us updated.'

'Will do.'

JT switched on the TV to check the local news on CIGTV. The lead story concerned the plane crash and a fire at a sea plane shed where three people had died. The news reader announced the body of the pilot had been recovered, and that the Police were considering the two incidents linked. They were considering the possibility of it being a fight between rival drug dealers.

The news reader also said the efforts of the Police had been hampered, by officers having to attend a hoax bomb call, just before the plane crash incident. They were appealing for any witnesses, but said that they did not suspect any danger to islanders.

'What's with the fire?' asked Easy.

'I don't know, but we didn't do it, so either it was the mother of all coincidences, or someone else did it when we left.'

'Who would do that though?'

'I don't know, but whether they meant to or not, they've done us a favour. It'll take weeks if not months, before they identify the bodies. Marco has previous, and Mafia connections, so that'll take them down a path well away from us.'

'Is my ex-husband involved with the Mafia?' asked Rosa.

'He could be,' said JT, 'but when the others are back we'll have that call with the guys in the UK, we'll try to work it all out. Meantime, there's a washer dryer in the utility room. I'm sure if you ask Easy nicely, he'll wash your dress for you until you can get something else to wear tomorrow.'

'I had a suitcase with me, but I don't know if it ever left the airport.'

'Your flight home is tomorrow, so you can just pick it back up on the way through?'

'Yes, I suppose I can.'

Chapter Thirty-Six

Gabbi sat in her parked car playing chess with her cousin Francesca. She was the girl who had been in the cafe playing chess, when Marco had come to meet her.

It seemed a pity he was dead, as it was an end to a potential income stream. Having said that, the $500,000 she was about to receive would go a long way to securing her retirement, she thought.

She had arrived 30 minutes early, to meet the man Marco had called Kirkland. She didn't know if that was his real name, and didn't care. As long as she was paid, that was all that mattered.

Marco was gone, but whoever he worked for had hired her to kill the three men, and if necessary the beautiful woman, Rosa. The fact that someone else had pulled the trigger was inconsequential, as far as she was concerned. The men were dead and she had returned to set fire to the building as part of the plan. She had earned the money, and was about to collect her reward. Francesca had asked to come along for the ride, this was a good day.

Gabbi moved her knight, in what she knew was called the *Queen's Knight Defence*. Francesca had called it the *Nimzowitsch Queen Pawn Defence* when Gabbi moved, giving her a knowing smile.

They were both aware of a car driving past them, which turned in the road up ahead, then returned, stopping 50 metres ahead of them. The driver flashed his headlights twice before Gabbi returned the gesture.

A man got out of the drivers' seat with some difficulty. He produced a walking cane from the vehicle, leaning on it as he took a few steps forward, then stopped, lifting his free hand to show he held an envelope.

Gabbi patted Francesca on the knee, then climbed out of the car. She looked around her, then walked toward the man.

'Gabbi?' he asked, in an American accent.

She nodded, 'Kirkland?'

'Yes, I am to give you this, from Marco.' He gave the envelope a little wave.

Gabbi stepped forward, and as she got closer realised the man was not as old as she had first thought. He looked physically strong for someone with a walking stick.

'Here you are,' he said, holding out his hand, forcing her to step closer.

As she reached out her hand to grasp the envelope, the man flicked up the walking stick, the end of which revealed a blade which he thrust deep into her abdomen.

Gabbi stayed bent forward with one hand touching the envelope, until she felt her legs buckle, falling to her knees. She looked up at the man wide-eyed and saw he was shaking his head.

He pulled the blade from her belly with a twist, causing a rush of blood from the wound. 'It's nothing personal kid, you know how it is.'

Clutching at her wound, Gabbi tried to resist as Kirkland lifted her head.

'Quicker this way kid,' he said, as he slit her throat, then pushed her into the gutter.

Suddenly cured of his limp, he walked toward the car, where Francesca sat in the passenger seat staring at him. When he reached the car, he opened the door ready to stab the young girl, but as the door opened he froze, visibly shocked, at the sight of the SIG Sauer in her hand.

Francesca shot him with two quick shots to his centre mass. The upward trajectory of the rounds, at such close range, meant they ripped their way through vital organs, smashing bone as they went. Kirkland fell back into the road, dead before he hit the ground. From where she sat, Francesca emptied the rest of the magazine into him, before wiping down the gun as Gabbi had taught her, throwing it at the spreadeagled Kirkland.'

With a last look at Gabbi's lifeless body, she gathered up her chess set, placing the board and box of pieces in her bag. She wiped down the surfaces she'd touched in the car, then started the long walk home.

Chapter Thirty-Seven

Following JT's instructions, it took Rambo and the guys less than four minutes to break in, and get back out of the Naval Reserve building. The weapons they returned were even cleaner than when they'd borrowed them. Taff joked that it was possibly the only time they'd be fired in anger.

On the way back to the villa they picked up some groceries and a long woman's t-shirt with a picture of a dolphin on the front.

Back at the villa, they put all of their clothes they'd worn that day in the washer dryer, then showered before sitting down at the long dinner table.

JT told them they would forego the usual debrief until they were safely off the island.

Easy set up his laptop, dialling up Maxwell in London and Hamilton, who was currently being driven back from an emergency meeting, with the head of National Air Traffic Service and her erstwhile security chief.

'Hi Rory,' said JT, 'we're just getting Hamilton on line.'

'I'm here Gentlemen.' Hamilton announced.

'Thanks both, realise it's very early for you both.'

'Rather than early, it's very late. I've just come from a lengthy meeting with Julia Walsh at NATS.'

'You both got the message that Rosa Hawthorne, formerly Mrs Bergstrom, is here with us?' asked JT, making sure everyone knew who was listening.

'Yes,' confirmed Maxwell.

'Good evening Ms Hawthorne, so glad you're able to join us,' said Hamilton.

'Thank you Mr?'

'My apologies, hopefully we will have the opportunity to meet in person in the future. Please, call me Hamilton.'

'That would be lovely Mr Hamilton. May I ask, are you the boss of Team Vigilant?'

'Not in any literal sense, no. I am something of an administrator you might say. Why, do you feel they need a *boss*?' he asked playfully. 'JT does an excellent job leading the team, wouldn't you say?'

'I only asked as I wanted to say thank you, these men rescued me. Oh, and I believe they deserve a pay rise!' Rosa smiled at the men around the table, which was met by a mixture of blank and amused looks.

'I don't believe remuneration is the driver for Vigilant, Ms Hawthorne, besides, they set their own rate of pay.'

Rosa thought for a moment, 'Do you mean they are mercenaries?'

This caused some incredulous looks from the Team, and a short laugh from Hamilton.

'We're not mercenaries Rosa, what we are is complicated, but we are not guns for hire.'

'Then what-'

JT raised a hand, 'We'll explain some more in good time, but right now we should be finding out who, and what, we are dealing with. I get the feeling this isn't over yet.' He turned back to face the laptop. 'Hamilton, what do we know?'

'I have been digging in to *StromSec* and our Mr Bergstrom. He is a tricky customer to pin down. He has been very careful to cover his tracks, so not a lot of information is readily available. Perhaps Ms Hawthorne could tell us what she knows, that may help fill in the blanks?'

'Rosa?' prompted JT.

'Knut is planning something. I'm not sure what exactly, but he said people would have to die for him to get full value out of his project. He is not the man I married. The Knut I married, was a shy, quite introverted man. He was very gentle, and kind - quite the opposite of my previous partner.' She felt the need to explain herself further. 'I came from an abusive relationship, with a complete narcissist, Knut was nothing like that. He cared about people, poor people, especially children. We built two orphanages, he made sure the kids had a future. In Abuja, there's a call centre that Knut owns, all of the children are guaranteed a job there when they leave the orphanage. He cares about education, he always said that it would be Africans, or people from the Indian subcontinent, that would change the world in the future. He even built a whole new college at a University in Nigeria, to teach local young people about Cyber skills and programming.'

'Yes, we know about the University link,' said Hamilton, 'have you ever visited the University, Ms Hawthorne?'

'Only once, I went to the Grand Opening.'

'Did it seem strange to you, that the buildings were so far away from the rest of the campus?'

'No, Knut explained it to me. He said it would give more job opportunities in the smaller towns. He created a power supply for the people in the area who didn't have one. It was nearer the airport too, so that they could have guest lecturers and techy people visit more regularly.'

'Were there armed guards there when you visited?'

'There were security men there, Knut told me they'd been hired in conjunction with the Nigerian Government, as there had been trouble with terrorists. It was those Boko Haram guys, the ones who kidnapped all those girls.'

'Boko Haram usually operate in the North East of the country. There is a mostly Muslim community in the Birnin Kebbi region, there are certainly militant factions in the area, but no recorded attacks around the University. The security men, Europeans or Africans?' asked Hamilton.

'They were Russian. I remember Knut talking to one of them, he looked very scary. Knut called him Major something. It was a Russian sounding name. Knut told me they were Government sanctioned, they were all ex Russian soldiers.'

'Wagner?' asked JT.

'I don't think that was the name,' said Rosa, 'it sounded more Russian.'

'Andreyev?' asked Hamilton.

'Yes, that sounds about right. Who is Wagner?'

'JT is correct, they are indeed Wagner. The Wagner Group are a Russian PMC; Private Military Company. PMC's *are* mercenaries and increasingly used throughout the world. They have infiltrated much of Africa, usually operating at the behest of local Governments, shoring up dictators or fighting insurgencies. They operate as a proxy for the Russian state, but also undertake private security work if the price is right. They won't come cheap, but are a private army for hire.'

'Why would Knut's University need an army?' asked Rosa.

'That is a very good question, and one we are trying to answer. Did Knut mention what his project was, or how it would work?'

'He never spoke to me about work, he always said it was boring cyber security programming, and best left to the geeks. The only reason I know about the project at all is that I walked into his office, he was so busy on a call he didn't notice me come in. I don't know who he was speaking to, but they had a Russian accent, or I assumed they were Russian. I didn't want to disturb him mid flow, so stood there like a fool, holding the drink I'd made him in my hand.'

'What was he saying?' asked Hamilton.

'They were discussing when to activate something he called, *Trojansk Hest?* The Russian man said they were estimating over 250,000 people would die. That aeroplanes would fall from the sky, all over Europe.' Rosa paused, her face paled as she replayed the scene in her head.

'Anything else?'

'I dropped the glass I was holding and ran out of the room. When Knut found me, he tried to tell me that it was all about a computer game, or simulation or something. But I *knew*, I knew it was real. His voice, when he didn't know I was listening, was different. He sounded excited at the prospect of people dying.'

'What did you do next?'

'I left, went to stay with my friend in Cornwall. Of course, he found me and tried to woo me back. I told him that if I was to even consider going back to him, he would have to tell me everything.' Rosa stopped, turning to Joe, 'Do you think I might have another brandy?'

'Coming right up,' said Joe, leaving the table.

'Knut told me that he had found a group of hackers in Nigeria, that they were hitting bigger and bigger companies with Ransomware. Apparently they were some of the best hackers he'd come across. He'd been battling with them to create a code to stop them. Then he had a light bulb moment as he described it, he realised they could form a partnership. He said they were attacking companies and holding the servers to ransom. Knut would then get the business to protect them from future attacks. Knut advertised heavily, after they arranged a hack where he was able to defeat it and save the day. Companies were falling over themselves to hire *StromSec*.'

'Governments too,' said Hamilton.

'Yes, he said he was able to procure the biggest contracts. That was when he came up with his master plan. Rather than holding companies to ransom he could hold entire countries, even continents to ransom.'

'Continents?' asked JT.

Rosa shrugged, 'That's what he said.'

'It begins to make sense now,' said Hamilton.

'What does?' asked JT.

'Air Traffic Control. *StromSec* have been given access to both the UK and French Air Traffic Control Systems, while they work on a security tender. They offered to do the preliminary work for free, as a gesture of good will, to show what they are offering. *StromSec* could easily have uploaded their *Trojansk Hest* - that's Norwegian for Trojan Horse - they would effectively have control of the skies over Western Europe, and the Western Mediterranean.'

'Surely the NATS boffins would be able to spot it?' asked Maxwell.

'Only if they know to be looking, and what they're looking for,' said Hamilton.

'It could be as simple as a kill switch,' said Easy.

'What do you mean?' asked JT.

'They could just turn the system off, prevent it from being switched back on.'

'How would that make planes fall from the sky?' asked Maxwell.

'They would simply run out of fuel,' said Hamilton. 'Without Air Traffic Control the aeroplanes can't land. They would be routed to circle near airports until they literally ran out of fuel. It's genius.'

'Genius? It's bloody madness!' said JT.

'Yes of course, but consider this; how much would a Government, or indeed several Governments, be willing to pay to prevent such a thing occurring. It would be a simple choice, pay however many millions are demanded, or watch people die and your economy be buried with them.'

'Billions,' said Rosa.

'Billions?' asked JT.

'He said he would be a Trillionaire when they all paid up.'

'If he's going to be a Trillionaire why go to all the trouble for your $50million?'

'It's not just the money, it's me he wants back. Or at least he did. I believe I was going to be murdered if I didn't get on that plane to Cuba with Marco. The money was to pay for an estate in Cuba where we were meant to live after…he said there was no extradition treaties, should anyone ever work it out and come looking for him.'

'How did you get the $50million in the first place?' asked JT.

'He transferred it into my bank account, in an attempt to woo me back. I had the bank account after I split from my footballer ex. Terry paid me £500,000 when I signed an NDA not to go public about his abuse. So, the account was in my name only and required me to sign in person to access funds.'

'Terry Waltham was your ex?' asked Posty.

'Sadly yes, he's a horrible man, despite what his adoring fans think.'

'Well, that's my Chelsea season ticket plans going in the bin then,' said Posty, with a wink.

'Ok, so you know his plan now Hamilton, the techy guys at your end can close him down I'm guessing?' said JT.

'I don't believe it's that simple. If he gets a whiff of our techs snooping around, then he may just activate the Trojan Horse programme.'

'So, have him arrested. I'm sure the Americans will have plenty of people in Cuba that can rendition him for you.'

'Again, not so simple sadly. We have our own man - or rather woman - in Havana still. I am reliably informed that Mr Bergstrom's jet took off over an hour ago.'

'Ok, so where's he heading?'

'Morocco, but that's a refuelling stop before his final destination - Nigeria.'

'So, you'll have the Nigerians arrest him?'

'No, I don't believe that is how this will have to play out.'

'Why not, you have enough evidence surely?'

'Any arrest will bring this whole matter into the public domain. Just imagine the furore and economic impact if the public lost faith in the air traffic control system. The world would grind to a halt. That may have some of the eco cultists cheering in the short term, but economies, especially the UK, would be decimated. Someone has to pay for the hospitals and welfare state. The country would collapse,' said Hamilton, gravely.

JT shook his head, then sighed, 'Why do I get the feeling Vigilant are going to Nigeria?'

Chapter Thirty-Eight

JT had managed almost four hours of sleep on the flight. The stresses of the last couple of days had left him exhausted, which when combined with the pain meds he'd taken, meant he'd slept soundly.

There was no time for separate and dispersed entry routes into Benin for the Vigilant team so they were all on board the same Air France flight from Charles De Gaulle to Cotonou.

'Welcome to Benin Sir!' the smiling Air Steward stood to attention, looking remarkably crisp after a long flight.

'Thank you,' said JT, as he adjusted the shoulder strap on his back pack.

'Are you here on Business or is this a social visit?' asked the Steward, as they waited for the disembarkation steps to arrive at the aircraft door.

'Bit of both really, we're headed up into the W National Park for a bit a recce.'

'A recce?' asked the Steward.

'We're filmmakers, we're doing some location scoping for a documentary series on the African Bush Elephants up there.'

'That sounds amazing, I've never been on safari. In fact, I'd never heard of W National Park.'

'It's called W because of the shape of the Niger river; it looks like a W carved out of the land. The park is shared between three countries, it's here in Benin but it crosses the borders with Niger and Burkina Faso. The elephants don't care about the borders someone drew on a map; they just roam wherever they please.'

'Wow, I'm so jealous, it sounds like you're going on quite an adventure.'

'More than you know,' said JT, stepping off the aeroplane into the hot and humid African morning.

As JT and the team headed for the terminal, he checked his phone, reading a message from Hamilton saying the other's had arrived safely in the UK.

Easy had travelled with Rosa Hawthorne to London, where they were met by Rory Maxwell to be driven to Hamilton's place in the country.

Easy had immediately gone to work in Hamilton's secret underground bunker. The bunker was a top secret survivor of the Cold War, Hamilton had requisitioned it, modernising it to be a Command and Control centre for Vigilant. Kitted out with access to all UK intelligence databases, and through them, several of the major players across the globe, the bunker was state of the art, despite being built more than half a century ago.

JT and Hamilton had debated the best course of action to keep Rosa safe, until they had dealt with her ex-husband. Rory had to return to work at New Scotland Yard, so Hamilton wanted to ship Rosa up to the teams' castle in the Highlands of Scotland. Rosa had steadfastly refused to go, saying she wanted to stay so she could know what was going on.

In his typically cryptic fashion, Hamilton had responded with a crossword clue when JT asked what he thought of Rosa, now that he'd met her in person. Most men, in fact most people, would have commented first on how beautiful the woman was, but not Hamilton, though he could patently see it for himself.

Instead, his message read; **1 Across - 12 letters, Shrewdness. Start sweating before reaching California enroute to LA or San Diego for example**.

JT had no idea what he meant, so quickly messaged Rory for an explanation.

It's the start of PERSPIration for the sweating. Then CA for California. Then LA and San Diego are each a CITY. PERSPICACITY = Shrewdness, came Rory's reply.

How do you know this stuff?, texted JT.

We needed something to do on the nightshift, crosswords are good for the mind, you should try it sometime! LOL

I'll wait until you're retired and can teach me!

PERSPICACITY - you think she's sharp. JT replied to Hamilton.

She is very sharp and situationally aware, which begs the question; why did it take her so long to see through Knut Bergstrom?

He's obviously very careful and smart too.

Indeed, which makes him very dangerous.

Agreed, we'll let you know when we reach the compound.

Excellent, I have already put Easy to work, he'll be sending you over some files for your planning and briefing.

Great thanks. typed JT.

And very well deduced on the crossword clue.

You mean you're impressed that I know what PERSPICACITY means? typed a grinning JT.

Not at all, I was impressed that you thought to ask Rory so quickly!

The team got through border control quickly, using their documentary makers cover story. They were met outside the terminal by Paulo and Claudine de Souza, in two fairly battered but serviceable, Toyota Landcruisers.

It was an hour's drive, from Cotonou airport to the compound, with a stop to pick up supplies enroute.

When they reached the compound, they offloaded the baskets of live chickens, bags of yams and peanuts into the main house, then their own kit into the bunkhouses.

Parked next to the bunkhouses were three ATV quad-bikes, each equipped with seats for a pillion passenger in front of black steel luggage racks. On either side of the racks, were fitted jerry can style petrol cans.

The de Souzas had been busy, preparing everything they could from the list they'd been sent, just 24 hours before. The one obviously missing item, made itself known as it approached. The thrum of the blades and pitchy whine of the Soloviev D-25 engines, gave no clue to the size of the beast as it lumbered towards them. It flew less than 100 feet above ground level, and as it came closer, the pilot tilted the nose toward them in a nod of acknowledgement. The Mil Mi-10K, which NATO designated *Harke-B,* was a relic, but it's very presence was a reminder that the Russians built some solid helicopters. Unlike its predecessor, the Mi-10 *Harke,* this aircraft had shorter legs but was still a flying crane. It had been designed and used to transport equipment including vehicles into drop zones, using an underslung winch or cargo net.

The team stood in wonder as the pilot expertly set the huge machine down onto a flat area at the far end of the compound. None of them had noted the circle of small rocks designating the landing area.

The pilot quickly geared down the engines, killing the power to stop the storm of sand and grit it was creating. A few seconds after the rotors came to a halt the side door slid back and a set of steps were fixed for the 2.5 metre drop to the ground. Down the ladder came the pilot who seemed to be taking his time. When he reached the ground, he ignored the assembled team, instead walking around his aircraft, carefully inspecting it.

'Everything okay Bob?' called Paulo.

The reply was a wave and a grin, as the pilot took off his hat, revealing a shock of dazzlingly white hair.

Bob approached the team, limping as he came, and looking like he should be in a care home rather than out here in the African sunshine.

'Excuse me a second Paulo,' said Bob, with a wink, as he walked past him to where Claudine stood with her arms extended.

The pair embraced, with a warmth that suggested they were the oldest of friends, and ended with a noisy kiss on the cheek from Claudine.

'Now, it's your turn!' said Bob, turning to Paulo. The men hugged each other like brothers.

'She's a beaut,' said Paulo, gesturing to the helicopter.

'She's an antique, but like us, she's still functioning,' said Bob, with a grin and a slap on Paulo's shoulder.

'She's ok to fly without a co-pilot?' asked Paulo.

'I did have a co-pilot,' said Bob, then put his fingers in his mouth to let out a loud whistle.

The team turned to look at the helicopter, as a huge Rhodesian Ridgeback dog climbed gingerly down the first few steps, then jumped the last six feet to the ground. The beast bounded happily up to Bob, before taking up a position by his side, staring watchfully at the team.

'This is Erasmus, he's my co-pilot, and brother in arms,' said Bob, scratching behind the dog's ears.

'Is he friendly?' asked JT, who was stood closest to the dog and receiving the brunt of his stare.

'Free!' said Bob.

Erasmus sprung up wagging his tail, having a good sniff at each of the team in turn.

'What happened to Mabel?' asked Claudine.

'Bastard poachers got her about two months ago. The dirty animals set a trap, when they knew we'd be trailing them. They took the tusks off Betsy, one of the old girls in the Pendjari. We tracked them for four days, they knew they couldn't escape the dog. They rigged a sprung spear and it caught Mabel in the flank, punctured her lung. I couldn't do anything for her, had to put her out of her misery.' Bob explained, then shook his head at the memory.

'Did you get them?' asked Paulo.

'I got one, they'd left him trailing behind as a look out. The silly bugger shot me in the leg, then thought he could beg for his life when I got to him. I told him, I didn't mind him shooting me, but that he'd have to pay for Mabel.'

'You killed him, I hope,' said Claudine.

'I staked him to the ground, tied a sack around his foot.'

'What was in the sack?' asked Paulo.

'I found him a Puffy to keep him company,' said Bob, matter of factly.

'What's a Puffy?' asked JT.

'It's a Puff Adder,' explained Bob, 'pretty venomous, their bites are excruciatingly painful. Untreated their bites kill an adult in 24 hours or so, but they're the worst 24 hours imaginable.'

'That'll teach him.'

'I'd have thought up something better for the little shit, but I was bleeding pretty heavily,' said Bob. 'I had 20 miles or so to get back to my truck.'

'You walked 20 miles after getting shot in the leg?'

'There aren't too many buses out in the bush mister. You walk or you die.'

'I hear you,' said JT, with genuine admiration.

'Allow me to introduce you properly Bob,' said Paolo, 'this is JT, he leads this team. This is Rambo, Taff, Cooky, Joe and Posty.'

Bob shook hands with each of them in turn. 'Should I ask what you gents are doing here in Benin, or is it better I don't know?'

JT looked at Paulo who nodded then said, 'Perhaps I should explain who Bob is. He is too shy to tell you exactly himself, so I will try to sum up something of his history. Bob was with the Rhodesian Selous Scouts, a bit of a legend in his day. He was considered one of the best white trackers in the Rhodesian Forces. He was tasked with hunting down the Zanla and Zipra hunting parties that terrorised Rhodesian farmers, near the border with Mozambique. So successful was he, that the Zanla, who were the Zimbabwe African National Liberation Army and then the Zipra or Zimbabwe People's Revolutionary Army put a bounty on his head. At one point his head was worth, what was it Bob, 10,000 US dollars?'

'It topped out at 15,000 in 1980,' said Bob, with a shrug.

'After the war, Bob and I went to South Africa. We did some work there before it became increasingly difficult to be a white man in Africa. Thankfully there were plenty of miners and oil companies looking for trustworthy security, so we found work. But there was always the threat of repercussions, so we couldn't return to Rhodesia or to Mozambique. Which took us first to Rwanda and DRC, then we found our way here to Benin. We helped set up the National Parks Anti-Poaching Division.'

'That's what the chopper is for?' asked JT.

'No, she's for transporting elephants,' said Bob. 'Elephants and humans don't mix too well. We have an agreement with the farmers around the edges of the W. If the elephants get onto their land, start eating crops or whatever, we dart them, and lift them back into the bush.'

'How old is that thing?' asked JT.

'Older than you are, but she's been well looked after. The Russian's supplied lots of these birds to their African allies, but never really taught them how to look after them. There's a few in Congo and Angola that barely flew after they were delivered. They're great for spare parts, the dry conditions they were kept in mean they've not just rusted away.'

'Bob knows Hamilton well JT, you're safe to discuss your mission with him.'

'Ah, you're Hamilton's lads are you? That makes some sense now.'

'In what way?' asked JT.

'Paulo here just told me he needed the chopper, that I should make up some story of a request from the Nigerians, to move a rogue bull elephant.'

'Who does the chopper belong to?' asked JT.

'It officially belongs to the Bush Elephant Trust, but seeing as I'm the only one that flies, and maintains the old girl, she's pretty much mine.'

'How do you know Hamilton?' asked JT.

Bob looked at Paulo, receiving a nod of permission. 'We did some work together over the years, when Brits got kidnapped, or when friends of his, or of Her Majesty, needed some assistance. He's a good man is Hamilton, doesn't get caught up in the niceties when the chips are down.'

'Sounds like the Hamilton we know'

'How about you lads then? You Special Forces, MI6 or what?'

'We're ex SAS.'

'And now?'

'Now, we're helping people, in a less official way,' said JT, unsatisfied with his own answer.

'They're called Vigilant,' said Claudine. 'You men need to stop with the poker faces and get on with it, we're on the clock. Besides, dinner needs prepared and I'm not doing it on my own.'

Bob laughed with a deep rumble which turned into a hacking cough. 'Need to get back on the fags,' he spluttered.

'How long have you been stopped this time?' asked Paulo, putting his arm around Bob's shoulders and leading him toward the house.

Bob looked at his watch, '3 days, 14 hours and 37 minutes!'

Chapter Thirty-Nine

Twelve hours earlier, Knut Bergstrom sat in the General Aviation Terminal of the El Massira Airport in Agadir, Morocco. The delay, caused in his opinion by the typically inept North African laissez faire attitude, had added to his already foul mood.

He hadn't slept for 36 hours, as he had waited for Marco to bring Rosa to him in Cuba. Then when he failed to arrive he had received news of the explosion aboard the sea plane. The Cayman authorities had found the remains of a man but there was no trace of Rosa. It made no sense, as the last message he'd had from Carlo was that he had Rosa, and the Bearer Bonds, aboard the aircraft. Now Rosa and the $50million were missing.

The Cuban's had accepted his explanation that he had an emergency to take care of, rather than complete as planned on the deal for the estate. He was probably paying five times what the place was worth, but that was the price for the complete anonymity he sought. The villagers being cleared from their homes would be well compensated, and rehoused outside the 25 square miles of the estate.

The money would be replaced soon enough, but to him, Rosa was irreplaceable.

He had fluctuated, between a grief that came close to consuming him, and a belief that somehow she was still alive.

The team that had intercepted Rosa at the airport were all dead, as part of the clean-up plan, now there was no-one left to tell him exactly what had happened.

'Mr Bergstrom, I am Hassan Mansouri, the manager here. The aircraft is now refuelled and ready when you are Sir,' said the obsequious representative of MA Aviation Services.

Knut shutdown his laptop before slipping it into his backpack.

'Once again, my sincerest apologies for the delay, the defective equipment has been replaced. I guarantee we will meet your every satisfaction, the next time you transit with us.'

Knut walked out of the terminal building without responding or looking in the man's direction.

Mansouri lifted his mobile phone to his ear as he watched Knut walk across the tarmac. 'Mr Hamilton, I have kept him as long as possible, as you requested, but he is boarding now.'

'Thank you Hassan, you've been a great help,' said Hamilton.

'It is nothing. My family and I owe you our lives Mr Hamilton, I wish I could do more.'

'Not at all Hassan, the delay you have caused, will be of great benefit to my people.'

'Mr Hamilton, if you had not rescued us from Tripoli-'

'Let's not talk anymore about that now Hassan. How are Asmaa and the children?'

'They are all doing splendidly, praise be to Allah, and yourself of course.'

'Glad to hear it Hassan. I must dash now; I have a call I must make. Goodbye for now.'

'Goodbye Mr Hamilton.'

Hamilton dialled the number for JT.

'Hamilton, we were just talking about you,' answered JT.

'Really, in what context?' asked Hamilton, as he typed something on his keyboard.

'We've just met a friend of yours.'

'Ah, Bob! He's a good man, and don't be fooled by his age, he's tough as old boots. There are very few people in the world that can do what he does.'

'Which is what exactly?'

'He has a skillset that in many facets would match your own, but when it comes to bush craft, you would need a lifetime to learn half of what he knows.'

'I can believe that. He's quite the pilot too, he flies antiques.'

'Ah he brought the Mil Mi-10K then.'

'How did you know that?'

'I supplied the aircraft back in 2018, gave it to the Elephant charity on proviso they employed Bob. Used the donation of a benefactor, to allow him to maintain the aircraft. She's quite the workhorse. Easier to operate than the Mi-10s with those huge long legs.'

'You're definitely the most resourceful person I've ever met, but couldn't you have drummed up a Chinook?'

'A charity with access to a Chinook? I don't think that would have washed - even in the continent where anything goes. It pays to be prepared, and to have people in place we can trust.'

'Did you know in advance we'd be going to Nigeria?'

'Not at all. Paulo and Claudine are in Benin simply due to its proximity to several countries where we maintain an interest.'

'So, the places you've had us set up safe-houses and depots across the world are random?'

'Not random, no not random at all. All of the locations provide regional cover. It is always possible that they may never be used, but sadly the world doesn't like to be at peace for long.'

'You can say that again,' said JT, as he watched Claudine lift a live chicken from a basket, wringing its neck as if it was second nature.

'Bergstrom is about to take off from Agadir, he'll land in Nigeria in around six hours. I have a man on the ground in Birnin Kebbi. He is based in Lagos, so won't be able to operate easily without attracting attention. It seems the Gwandu Emirate is happy to receive handsome homage from Bergstrom's University annexe. They are consequently very protective of their cash cow. Easy has access to CCTV at Sir Ahmadu Bello Airport. We'll know when Bergstrom arrives, but we will have too many blind-spots for my liking once he heads for the University, assuming of course that is where he heads.'

'We're going to stick out like sore thumbs in Nigeria, so we need to get in and out sharpish.'

'The University annexe is rural, and the security guards make sure the locals are disincentivised to get too close. The satellite imagery Easy is procuring, should hopefully provide you with sufficient detail to select OPs, entry and egress points etc.'

'The plan is still to take Bergstrom alive and destroy his facility?'

'That would be the ideal, however, if Bergstrom decides to go down with his ship, then that cannot be helped. Easy will talk you through the satellite link to download the software, that part of the plan is essential. If Bergstrom has planted his code into everywhere that he has a cyber security contract, then we cannot risk the possibility of his triggering it. The future of the world as we know it depends on this JT.'

'Oh, no pressure then!' said JT.

'It's why I've sent my best people to sort it out,' said Hamilton.

'We are a team of six, we have an old couple and a limping old man for a pilot. Wouldn't it be easier to order a missile strike?'

'Firstly, do not underestimate your three new friends, they are hand selected, and have been operating longer than you have been alive. I'd trust any of them with my life. I suggest you learn to do the same. As for missile strikes that is out of the question. Just think of the international treaties and laws that would be broken.'

'The Americans never seem to worry about international law. Can't you ask them to help?' JT asked.

'Our America cousins are very often a law unto themselves, but no, the less they know of this matter the better. We are cousins, but we don't always take the same view on who should make decisions. Besides, we still need to get our hands on the code.'

JT watched as Claudine threw three freshly killed chickens to Posty, Joe and Taff, sending them off to pluck the dead birds, followed closely by Erasmus the dog.

'Looks like we're all getting roped into making dinner here,' said JT, into the phone as Paulo appeared carrying a bag on yams with a big bucket of water.

'Claudine makes an amazing dish of chicken and yams in a peanut sauce, I can highly recommend it.'

'I think that's what's on tonight's menu,' said JT, walking toward where Cooky had joined Paulo to start peeling yams.

'Excellent, you chaps might be in the bush for a while, so eat while you can. Call me back when you've sorted out your logistics.'

'Will do,' said JT, ending the call.

'What can I do to help?' JT asked Claudine.

'You're coming with me and Bob, bring your best sniper, Rambo I believe, with you.'

'Yes Ma'am, where are we going?'

'Call me Claudine. We are going to prep some rifles for hunting.'

'What are we hunting?'

'Some of Africas most dangerous animals. I believe they're called Wagner Russians.'

Chapter Forty

Easy sat facing the bank of monitors in the underground bunker, sipping from a can of Coke. He watched the images change, from pixelated mosaics to clear images, as the military grade software decoded the satellite imagery.

He could clearly see the four watch towers that formed the corners of the compound, and the 200 metres long stretches of fences topped with razor wire. What had really grabbed his attention was the area of ground around the outside of the perimeter fence. A strip, of approximately five metres deep, had been cleared of plant life and raked smooth. It must be so the security guys can see if anyone has been near the fence, he thought to himself. It seemed a practical, but slightly old fashioned, security measure considering the state of the art computing equipment it was protecting. Something about it bothered him, so he made a note to speak to JT about it.

The next image was of the big satellite dishes situated 50 metres from the buildings. They sat upon concrete plinths with industrial cabling running from them. The cables sat in a metal conduit, built on top of concrete pillars, that led to a metal box the size of a garden hut. Another set of cables came out of the rear of the metal box and into the main building.

The satellite dishes faced slightly different azimuth's, which told Easy they were utilising different satellites. One of them was undoubtedly using NigComSat-1R. Easy's research had told him it was a Chinese built DFH-4 satellite, it had replaced its predecessor NatComSat-1 that had deorbited in 2009. It was the imaging from this very satellite that Easy was using.

The second dish seemed to be tracking NigeriaSat-2. This intrigued Easy as he'd found out the satellite, which had been built in the UK by Surrey Satellite Technology Ltd, had reached its End of Life date on 31st December 2021. The ground link for the satellite had been based in Abuja, but should have been switched off. The fact that the dish was still tracking that satellite suggested it was somehow still operational, and it may no longer be controlled by NASRDA the National Space Research and Development Agency of Nigeria. So, if it was no longer the Government Agency who controlled it, then maybe Bergstrom had somehow commandeered it thought Easy. It might explain how he planned to control whatever it was he had planned, without it being traced back to him.

Working his way sequentially through the images of the compound, and its surrounds, he took still images of the adjacent savannah. Studying shadows and vegetation clusters, he was able to pick out a dozen possible OPs within 400m of the fence line. There were no living trees within 50 metres, that suggested the land had been cleared, but mother nature had fought back with thickets of bushes springing up randomly.

Easy stood to stretch his legs, then decided to head upstairs and out through the cabin, to get some fresh air. It was the first time he'd been in the bunker for any length of time on his own. He found himself wondering where Rosa was, and what she was doing. He knew she was staying at Hamilton's house in the old church, but he wondered how she was filling her time.

Outside the cabin he took long slow breaths of the clean woodland air and decided to call Rosa. On the third ring she answered.

'Hello Easy,' she said.

'How did you know it was me?' he asked.

'Hamilton is downstairs cooking and no-one else is likely to call me on this number.'

'Ah of course, how are you?'

'I'm fine, this old place is lovely, but I have a feeling I might go a little stir crazy if I can't go out at some point.'

'Hopefully this will be over soon, and you can be free to go wherever you want to.'

'I've been thinking about that. I've realised I have nowhere to go, or at least nowhere I *have* to go.'

'What has Mr Hamilton said about you staying there? I know he suggested the Castle in Scotland.'

'He showed me some photos, it looks stunning. For sure I'd love to visit, but it's a bit remote, there'd be no-one else there, but a caretaker.'

'Yes, it is probably not an ideal place to be on your own, but it's also a very safe place for you until this is over.'

'For now, Hamilton says I can stay here with him. Where are you?'

'I'm at the command and control room, working. I've just come up for some air.'

'Come up? Is it in a basement someplace.'

'Something like that, yes.' Easy replied, remembering he was sworn to secrecy.

'I see, another secret. I'll stop asking questions!' sighed Rosa.

'I'm sorry, it's just something I'm not allowed to discuss,' said Easy.

'Don't worry, I understand. I just don't like being kept in the dark.'

'Mr Hamilton is the one to tell you things, maybe he can share more, after this is all over.'

'He's already told me about a hotel spa place, Palmerston House I think he called it, that's being done up after an explosion. He asked if I'd ever thought of running such a place.'

'Ah that's a fantastic idea, you would be brilliant at that. Did he tell you much about the place?'

'Only that it's quite near London, and that you guys use it for training, but that the plan is to reopen it as a hotel to make it pay for itself.'

'You should definitely consider it. I've only had what you might call a birds eye view of the place, but I've seen the renovation plans and it'll be amazing.'

'Well, let's see how everything works out, you never know.'

'Rosa, don't forget you have $50 million dollars still, you can do whatever you want.'

'That's not my money Easy, it's dirty and I don't want it. I'm thinking of giving it all to charity, maybe open some more orphanages.'

'Great idea, you should definitely do that.'

'I'd love to give it back to whoever Knut took it from, but I wouldn't know where to start.'

'I doubt we could locate the victims very easily, but once this is over, I can try to help you look for them.'

'You keep saying, *once this is over*, Easy, what does that actually mean?'

'Once we have stopped your ex-husband.'

'What happens to him then, will he go to prison...or is the plan to kill him?'

'I know they'll try not to kill him; they'll want to interrogate him.'

'I wouldn't mind.'

'You mean interrogating him?'
'No, I mean him being killed.'

Chapter Forty-One

Knut Bergstroms' Bombardier Challenger 300 touched down at Sir Amadullah Bello International Airport, just after noon. The heat that greeted him was a shock after the air-conditioned 17 degrees, he insisted upon, in the aircraft. It was the exact same temperature that awaited him in the Cadillac Escalade, parked 30 feet from the aircraft steps.

He contemplated telling them to bring the car closer, but he was already late. Fighting an impending headache from lack of sleep, and an over indulgence of coffee, his mood was foul.

As he stepped down the stairs, an umbrella opened from behind and above him, as his new personal security woman, Laila, took her close protection duties seriously.

At the bottom of the stairs, Knut took the umbrella from her, after all he didn't require that level of cosseting, especially in front of the Russians, besides, Laila's hands should be free to do what he was really paying her for.

Major Lev Andreyev waited beside the Escalade, looking bronzed from the African sun which had turned his well-muscled arms a dark brown. He was wearing a camouflage peaked cap with the red stripes and gold star insignia, befitting a Major of the Russian Armed Forces. The line, between official Russian Forces and Wagner Forces ,was blurred at the best of times, but here in Africa, especially so. Wagner were sanctioned by Moscow, they did virtually nothing without the tacit approval of the Kremlin. Russia was fighting many proxy wars as she tried to turn a foot hold in Africa into a controlling interest.

Knut knew of the Russian desire to lay claim to the mineral riches of African countries along with their Chinese allies. Their intention to control the rare earth minerals and other African bounties, as well as the Continent itself, was not his problem.

He was creating a personal *Shangri-La* in Cuba that would be sheltered from whatever battles the rest of the world engaged in. He thought of his plan as a smash and grab, that was the absolute beauty of it. Sure, he could terrorise the world; keep using their fear of cyber-attacks to milk more money from them, but there was always the risk of it unravelling and his being identified. No, the best plan was to hit them with, what the Jihadist terrorists like to call, a *spectacular*. Hit them where it really hurt, forcing them to pay big, so that he and Rosa-

'You are late Mr Bergstrom,' interrupted Andreyev, in a way that made Knut stand a little straighter.

'Yes, I am well aware of that thank you Andreyev,' replied Knut deliberately using just the man's surname as he knew it would annoy him.

'You should address me at all times as Major Andreyev,' snarled Andreyev.

Laila stepped between the men and faced up to Andreyev which made him sneer at her.

'Tell your little girlfriend to get the fuck out of my face Mr Bergstrom, before I have to slap some sense into her.'

Laila looked to Bergstrom for permission to escalate but Bergstrom shook his head as he climbed into the rear of the vehicle.

'He should not speak to you that way Mr Bergstrom,' said Laila, when she joined him in the vehicle. 'It is most disrespectful, he needs reminded that you are his employer.'

Bergstrom looked at his security woman and wondered how good it would be to watch her use all of her Mossad training to beat Andreyev to a pulp. He had seen her in action at the *interview* and the demonstration her broker had set up. He was quite confident that the muscle bound Russian mercenary would be no match for her in hand to hand combat.

'He is a beast of burden Laila, an animal I employ to keep other animals at bay, he is best tolerated or ignored. His men are useful in that I don't have to deal with the locals. The Emir is paid his levy and stays out of my business. Meanwhile the local Hausa or Fulani can kidnap each other and fight to their hearts content. They know, however, to stay well clear of our operations.'

'He thinks he is in charge, that is a dangerous arrangement.'

'That's exactly what I want him to think. He knows nothing of my plans. When I am finished here, he and his ilk will be the perfect patsies to take the blame.'

'You said they were all to die?'

'Dead men are easier to pin the blame on Laila. For now we let him think what he wants to think, within reason of course. When the time comes you can kill him, if you want to teach him some manners while doing so, you have my blessing.'

Chapter Forty-Two

'These were the best images I could get from the CCTV. Bergstrom arrives with a woman, they're met by the big Russian dude, Andreyev,' said Easy.

'Do we know who the woman is?' asked JT.

'Her name is Laila Acker,' said Hamilton.

'You know her?' asked JT.

'I know of her. She was with Mossad until fairly recently. Suspected of infiltrating, then executing a Pro Palestinian terrorist group based in Dusseldorf. That group had links to London, they had support as high as the Mayor of our once great city. Hence my interest, and how I know of Ms Acker.'

'What is she doing with Bergstrom?'

'It's a good question, but I would think she will be working in a personal security or bodyguard function. I know she was very highly regarded in Mossad circles, but Political interference has seen quite a few of their operatives move on, often into the private sector.'

'Okay, that's good to know, we can add her to the list with the Wagner guys.'

'What has your guy on the ground come up with?'

'He is in situ, he's only been able to confirm what we've seen from the satellite images. The security makes it look more like a prisoner of war camp than a University facility. The locals are all well aware not to go near the place, even the food is dropped off at a storage facility half a mile from the entrance.'

'What about staff, there must be folk going in and out, to work?'

'It seems entirely self-contained. There are accommodation blocks, a laundry, even sports facilities within the fences. My man says none of the locals are employed there. A small number of Pilipino women are bused back and forward to the airport, every two months. They live in a small house outside the complex.'

'What about students, it's meant to be a university?' asked JT.

'There are no matriculation records with the University proper, it seems to operate independently.'

'How does that work; it doesn't make sense?'

'In Nigeria, just as in most, if not all of Africa, money can make anything make sense, JT. Corruption is endemic, a way of life.'

'Okay, so it sounds as if there's no way to gain access, other than through the fence and past the Wagner guards,' said JT.

'There's something else. Let me show you the images,' said Easy, from his desk in the bunker 3,000 miles away. He brought up images of the ground immediately outside the fence.

'Mines?' asked Taff, when he saw the prepared ground.

'Maybe, maybe pressure sensors?' said JT.

'Doubt that,' chipped in Bob, 'too many animals moving around out there, they'd be setting off them constantly. Same with mines, bigger animals would be blowing up regularly.'

'I think I may have something else related to that,' said Easy. 'When I was looking for potential OPs I noticed these, they're all around the camp.' Easy shared images of animal carcasses in various states of decay but mostly their stripped and bleached bones.

'Target practice,' said Bob, 'the guards in the towers will be picking off anything that wanders in. Bastards aren't even eating them, just leaving them to rot and be scavenged. Look at that one,' he said, pointing at an image, 'that's an antelope and next to it is a jackal. They've shot the jackal while it was feeding on the antelope corpse.'

'Sport or security?' asked JT.

'I'd say sport, if they were worried about animals triggering mines, they could put up another fence to create a no-man's land. No, I think they're having fun or using the animals for target practice. That jackal would have been smaller than Erasmus here,' he ran his hand along the ridge of hair along the dog's spine. 'It's also 5-600 yards out from the fence line, that's pretty decent shooting, it wasn't using an Assault Rifle neither.'

'Agreed, they have at least one sniper rifle in there, we'd best assume there's one based in each tower.'

'Are all Wagner troops that well trained?' asked Paulo, 'I thought they were mostly rent a grunts?'

'No, they have drawn from some of the Russian Special Forces, several Spetsnaz officers hold higher ranks in the Wagner organisation,' said Hamilton, 'I believe the troops stationed here are drawn from Units based in Angola and Central African Republic. The right money buys you the right skill set, so it's possible Bergstrom has chosen from the elite.'

'Ok,' began JT, 'I've had a look at the images Easy sent, I have the bones of a plan about how we get in. If we can do so quietly, then so much the better, but if not, we'll just have to force our way in. Bob, Paulo and Claudine are going to help. Bob can get us reasonably close with his Heli-monster, so if all goes according to plan, we can ex-fil the way we came in. Hamilton I'll need your guy to source us a vehicle and some fuel, I'll send you co-ordinates of where he can leave them. Can we utilise him on the incursion?'

'He is more of an observer than combatant, but he'll make himself available.'

'Ok, that's sorted then. We have our cache of weapons here, but ideally I'd have liked some heavier fire power in case they spot us on the way in.'

'I can operate the drones from here,' said Easy, 'and if you rig them as we discussed, they can deliver a bang. I'd just need the satellite phone transmitter set up, within two kilometres.'

'Can't we just fly in some high explosives and wreck the place?' asked Posty.

'We need to try to get the code, that means accessing one of the computers inside. If, however we can't do that, then yes we'll be wrecking the place.'

'Do we have anything that goes bang big enough for that?' asked Taff.

'Paulo here tells me there's two mines out west in Zamfara, where we should hopefully be able to pick up some ordinance. It's a trek, but it might be worth it from another point of view. There's a fair bit of terrorist activity over in Zamfara. The miners get *taxed*, by the guys with guns. They've been raiding further and further east, as the miners have been refusing to work, and that's cut the money supply. We might just make the authorities think it was the terrorists who attacked the University. We'll leave some clues from the mine, for the cops or whoever to find. I'd rather the Wagner guys look elsewhere too, if they should want to avenge their fallen comrades.'

'Sounds like a plan,' said Taff.

'Our only issue is fuel. We can get from a fuel stop off up North in Benin, over to the mines then down to the University, but we wouldn't make it all the way back here. We'd have to try to land somewhere, then make our way back here at ground level.'

'We can stash the ATVs on the way out, you guys can use them to get back here,' suggested Paulo.

'There's only three of them, there'll be nine or maybe ten of us,' said JT.

'Don't worry about us,' said Paulo, 'we'll make our own way back.'

'I wouldn't be comfortable with that, what if we are pursued?'

'Then I'd rather be in the bush than back here. The bush is a great place to disappear, if you know how,' said Paulo.

'Ok, this is your theatre of operations, you'll know better than I will.'

'That's settled then.' said Paulo. 'Bob and I will work out where we can drop supplies, for the trip back.'

Chapter Forty-Three

The diesel generators kicked in as the sun dropped close to the horizon, and the air conditioning didn't miss a beat. A constant 17 degrees, not only suited Knut, but kept his beloved computers purring away happily.

The system he had created was completely isolated, the servers churned through the data harvested from the foolish Government Departments who had given *StromSec* access to their systems.

The beauty of his scheme was that the genuine technical teams at *StromSec,* worked very hard to protect the very same systems he was taking control of. These powerful machines, hidden away in the fake Nigerian University Annexe, were playing war games with the systems his company was hired to protect.

Sometimes the war games were like 3D chess, while others were blunt force attacks that were more brutal in nature but, with the right defences, easier to rebuff. When a suitably complex or cunning attack plan was formulated, Knut could unleash it with the press of a button. The *StromSec* teams would lay battle with the attacking virus, with Knut ensuring they were victorious, but only after an arduous, hard fought battle. The customers would be falling over themselves to thank *StromSec*. They'd happily keep paying the ever rising fees, for the type of protection only *StromSec* could provide.

To keep the customers attention, Knut would occasionally bolster the attack with something new and unexpected. Something that even his own staff didn't recognise, so that the system was infected, requiring a ransom to be paid to call off the dogs. An occasional leak to the media, made sure everyone was aware of the very real dangers hackers posed.

It was a good business plan that Knut's endeavours could easily have brought in 10s of millions each year from. However, it was not without risk, there was always someone smarter, or luckier, out there who could ruin his scheme by identifying his methods or coding. All coders have a signature, Knut was no different. It was a personal language, or accent, that pervaded code. Once you knew how to listen out for that accent, it was a matter of time before you found the person or group it belonged to.

His *spectacular,* would ensure that he was never found. He would disappear, with wealth to rival Elon Musk, and 90% of the countries of the world. He had no intention of travelling to sample what the world had to offer, no, he would pay the world to come to him, in his own little kingdom, in Cuba.

The only thing missing was Rosa. He was convinced that she was alive, and turned his attention to finding her. He would give himself another 48 hours, then he would unleash the code. It would take 24 hours for the code to completely disable the UK, Irish and French air traffic control systems. By which time he would be back in Cuba, letting the terror of planes falling from the sky shock the world, before he sent his demands. The ransom payments, in multiple crypto currencies, would be diverted between 15,000 accounts and wallets before being siphoned through banks in Argentina, Belarus, Lichtenstein and Switzerland. The authorities would be confident of tracking the payments, until that is Knut's code made their systems crash, leaving them completely blind. The Home Office network in London had given him access to Interpol. Once over the shock of how antiquated their systems were, Knut had installed a sleeper code; one that would be activated the same day as the Governments transferred their payments. Western Europe would become virtually lawless, allowing Knut to create time for his agents to work at laundering the money. By the time it reached him, it would be completely untraceable.

Knut enjoyed the knowledge that Andreyev, and his knucklehead soldiers outside, knew nothing of what was going on. They were convinced they were protecting a huge, but low level, scamming network that facilitated old ladies handing over their pensions. The call centre in Abuja was just such a network, but its job had been to provide the millions in funds to build this place, and to pay for its up keep. It was a neat solution, keeping a firewall between Knut and the financing of the operation. His name was on the lease for the call centre, but it was one of 30 or so similar enterprises in the Abuja business district, as *Nigerian Princes* plied their trade on a global stage. The orphanage was the perfect cover, with all of the rental profit from the building going straight to the kids upkeep; placing Knut as a very arms-length benefactor.

Knut rubbed his eyes; he was still fighting back the migraine that was threatening in the background, but he didn't want to take any of his medication. The tablets made him drowsy, and more often than not, he would be forced to sleep them off, but thankfully they would take the migraine with them.

Right now, he had to focus, he had to confirm Rosa was still alive. He had to find her. She would be coming with him to Cuba, whether she wanted to or not. Once they were together again, once she could see for herself the paradise that would become their home, then she would want to stay, he knew it.

A knock at the door gave Knut a start, no-one was allowed in here, in his sanctum, so he was unused to being disturbed. He could see from the CCTV camera buried in the door frame that it was Laila. She had been in his employ for just three weeks, and although she was growing on him, he did not yet know her as well as he had Carlo. Carlo had been easy to manipulate, he would do whatever he was ordered to do. Laila had yet to be tested, but the way she stood up to Andreyev, who anyone could see was a formidable man, had made Knut happy with his choice.

Knut unlocked and opened the door. He saw Laila try to look beyond him into the room, so pulled the door closed as he stepped into the corridor.

'What can I do for you Laila?' he asked her.

'I am ascertaining the layout of the complex.'

'This area is private, only I am allowed access.'

'I understand, but if I am to do my job Mr Bergstrom, I require to know where you are, and the obstacles to overcome or utilise.'

Laila's eyes were so dark they gave nothing away. She seemed devoid of emotion, and not for the first time Knut thought he would love to know what she was thinking.

'We are in a secure compound, with 20 heavily armed men protecting the perimeter, I think you can rest easy in here Laila.'

'They are what causes me concern Mr Bergstrom. I have no experience of working with Wagner, but their reputation is far from satisfactory. They are only interested in money, for the right price would sell their babushkas.'

'What they do with their Grandmothers is not our concern Laila,' said Knut. 'Aren't you also being paid to be here?'.

Laila looked almost offended, perhaps she was human after all thought Knut. 'I am paid to do my job, but with my services also come my loyalty, the same cannot be said for Andreyev or his men.'

'Then it's a good thing I am paying them very well.' Knut checked no-one else was within earshot before continuing, 'Besides, very soon we won't be needing their services any longer.'

'You said there was to be a delay in our leaving this place, how long do you anticipate our being here Mr Bergstrom.'

'I plan to be out of here within the next 24-36 hours at the latest Laila, and please, call me Knut.'

'I would rather call you Mr Bergstrom, if you don't mind, sir.'

'Ok, have it your way,' said Knut, with an amused shake of his head. 'If it makes you feel better, you can have a quick look in here, it's just me, my desk and a wall full of servers.'

He opened the door and stood back to allow her in. 'The door is steel plated; the air system is independent; capable of recycling air for up to a month. There is only one way in or out. There's a camera in the corridor outside, to show anyone at the door.'

Laila took in the room, turning to look at everything from floor to ceiling. 'No windows, no fire escape. You have provisions, should they be required, Mr Bergstrom?'

'Yes, there's a fully stocked kitchen, a private bathroom and a bed, should I decide to stay over in here. It's essentially a hotel room with a server suite.'

'But no room service?'

'No, no room service. Apart from myself, you are the only one to have set foot in here, since I powered it up.'

'And the Russians?'

'They leave me alone to work. They have plenty to keep themselves amused, outside.'

'Then I too shall leave you alone to work Mr Bergstrom, my apologies for disturbing you,' said Laila, heading for the door.

Knut watched her check the locks and feel the heft of the door itself, she gave a little nod of apparent approval as she left. Once again, he was sure he'd made the right choice in Laila.

Knut returned to his desk and started typing, he accessed the Grand Cayman airport records, quickly finding what he was looking for. The passenger manifest, for the British Airways flight to Jamaica, had a list of 159 passengers, but the security list showed there had been a full complement of 160. Someone had removed a passengers' details, Knut didn't have time to work out how that had been done, but he felt sure it must be Rosa. Now he just had to follow the trail.

Chapter Forty-Four

The first drop was some rations and water canisters. Hung from a rope, while Paulo guided Bob to hover the Mi-10K over a huge isolated Acacia tree, the sack was nestled into the canopy, from where it would be retrievable, but safe from scavengers.

Noting the geo location of the tree electronically, the Vigilant team hoped they wouldn't need to find it again, as that would mean their exfil plans had fallen apart. Paulo and Bob were satisfied they could identify the location by eye, after noting some other distinguishing markers in the landscape.

Beneath the helicopter hung the cargo net, containing the three ATV quad-bikes. Any locals seeing the helicopter would assume it was delivering the vehicles up country, possibly for use by the Government sponsored game wardens.

At a designated spot, the ATVs were placed gently on the hard savannah grassland, before the chopper continued to Malanville, a decent sized northern town, near the border with Niger. Malanville held the fuelling depot for aircraft working in the W National Park, so no questions would be asked when Bob filled up the MK-10K to the brim, as well as two back up reserve fuel drums.

The next part of the journey took them across the border into Niger, then south west into Nigerian airspace. North West Nigeria was mostly savannah and desert, so the team were able to fly low to the ground, avoiding the Nigerian Air Force radar. Bob had already switched off his transponder, flying a path avoiding townships and settlements.

After a nervous two hours of flying, Bob set down in an area between the two mines. The team split in two, taking off in a jog to cover the remaining three miles.

When JT's trio reached the first mine, they located the explosives store easily. It was the only building with a well maintained roof and positioned well away from the other buildings.

The steel door was padlocked, covered in signs and stickers, all denoting it as dangerous.

Posty jemmied the door then went inside, letting out a whistle at what he saw. Inside were several sealed drums of Ammonium Nitrate powder. Ammonium Nitrate, when mixed with fuel oil, made ANFO, the most commonly used blasting agent in mines. It was not as accurate, or as easy to use, as C4 or other plastic explosives, but Posty knew it could make quite a bang.

There was a small, but robust looking, lockable metal cabinet, that bizarrely had the key left in the lock. Inside the cabinet were boxes of blasting caps and a roll of detonation cord. Posty gathered up all of the supplies he could fit in his back pack, before selecting two extra containers of Ammonium Nitrate, which he handed to JT and Posty.

The jog back to the chopper took a little longer with their extra baggage, but they got back within 45 minutes.

Five minutes later the 2nd team got back. They had found just three rolls of detonating cord, several emulsion explosive fuses and a manual firing device. Happy with the haul, Posty declared he had everything he'd need to do the job.

Bob lifted the chopper back into the air, heading to the landing zone, two miles north of the target.

As the wheels touched the ground, the Vigilant team jumped clear of the aircraft, spreading themselves out in firing positions.

Bob powered down the rotors, after a few moments the only sound was the ticking of the cooling engines. As the team sorted their gear, Bob pumped fuel from the reserve drums into the main tank, but kept a little back to fill two plastic bottles.

'Ready to move out in two minutes,' said JT, 'where are you hiding the keys for the chopper?'

Bob laughed, 'They're staying right in the ignition. Don't want to be pissing about locating keys if we're being chased!'

'What if someone finds the chopper?'

'Erasmus here, will be looking after things while we're gone, no-one will be getting inside!' he said, scratching the dog's ear.

JT was sceptical, but then looked up to the loading bay door to see the huge Erasmus, looking even more menacing from above. 'Let's go.'

The team set off, covering the first mile at a brisk walking pace, but then waited up until the sun disappeared and instant equatorial darkness fell. They had brought night vision goggles for everyone, though Bob brought his own, that he used for night-time flying in the bush.

From the wait point they split up, with teams of two heading out around the perimeter, to take up position from where they could engage the towers. Bob stayed with JT and Rambo as they were headed to the closest OP, due to his injured leg that made him limp.

JT noticed Bob never complained, despite what was obviously still a painful injury. He was impressed that the older man kept up with them, and seemed to move silently through the long grass. At one point, Bob held up his hand to halt their progress, the team watched in awe as a leopard appeared from the grass 20 feet in front of them. The leopard stopped, sniffing the air, her eyes glowing green in their night vision view. The long, streamlined cat ambled on, disappearing back into the grass with a flick of its tail.

'Glad you're with us Bob,' whispered JT.

'Just be glad she wasn't a Lion; Leopards are solitary, but if we come across a pride, then we're in trouble.'

'Would they attack us?' asked JT.

'Depends on when they last ate, or if they feel threatened by us,' said Bob.

'Can we out run them?' asked Rambo.

'I can, but you can't,' said Bob.

'You've got an injured leg and I'm half your age, there's no way you can outrun them if I can't,' said Rambo, indignantly.

'Forgot to mention, the first thing I'm going to do, is shoot you in the foot!'

Bob laughed at his own joke until he was shushed by a grinning JT. 'Heads in the game guys, not heads in the big game!'

Bob offered to site the satellite phone control box in the bushes closest to the fence. He made his way, in his usual silent fashion, through the grass until he reached a suitable bush, thick enough to make sure the kit couldn't be seen, but only 300 metres from the fence line. He returned a few moments later, with a small python wrapped around his wrist.

'This little guy was living in the bush, wouldn't want him getting hurt when that thing goes pop later. There's very little grass around the bush I chose, so less chance of a fire taking hold. There's a time and a place for bush fires, this ain't one of them.'

'Ok, let's move forward into position. Rambo, you get a sight on the guard in the tower.'

With the satellite phone in place and acting as a receiver/transmitter, the team were able to send each other text messages, rather than risk being overheard in the near silent night. Even the insects seemed to be in whisper mode. Their NVGs meant the team could have their phones in dark mode too, preventing screen light giving away their positions.

When the third message arrived, to tell JT that the teams were all in place, it was time to send up the drone. The Martlet MI-3 drone had an impressive 20km datalink range, but for tonight that was overkill. The MI-3 had a 90 minute fly time and more importantly a 3kg payload limit. 3kg of ANFO - Ammonium Nitrate Fuel Oil - explosive was enough to destroy a bus, but to be really effective it had to be in an enclosed space. The miners that typically used ANFO, drilled holes into rock, then packed ANFO inside before setting a detonator cap to initiate it.

The MI-3 took off into the air from the halt point, a mile behind them, flying silently over their heads. The only way they knew of its presence, was the live video feed it was providing.

Easy was guiding the drone from the UK, thanks to the satellite link. He used a map overlay on his screen, from previous satellite images, to guide the drone around the facility, in a pre-agreed pattern.

JT and the team watched the images, building a mental image of their respective targets; deciding how they would move, once inside the complex.

Paulo and Claudine were farthest from the complex, they had to make their way through the solar panel farm to reach the satellite dishes. First though, they had to get through the fence and past the guard in the tower. The guard was the easy part though once Claudine had him in the crosshairs of the Leupold Mark IV night vision scope of her M2010 sniper rifle. The suppressor would lower the sound to roughly 130 decibels, but, in the quiet of the African night, it would not make much difference. When she fired, everyone awake within a mile radius would know about it.

JT sent a text message, confirming there were four guards in the towers, as expected, with two more on a foot patrol around the complex. The fact that they were smoking and chatting as they ambled around, told JT they weren't expecting visitors. Three of the tower guards were sitting down, with one illuminated by the light of a screen where he appeared to be watching a football match, the others appeared to be reading.

Something bothered JT. These guys were all Wagner, they wouldn't come cheap, and they were here to do a job. So why were they so relaxed? He typed a message to Easy; **They're too relaxed. They must have some kind of early warning system, see if you can find it.**

JT watched the images from the drone camera, as Easy swept it around the perimeter of the fence line. There was nothing obvious. **Go further out. 50m increments.** typed JT. **There's something out there, there has to be.**

Easy flew the drone slowly in another circuit, still nothing. On the third circuit the drone was flying 150 metres out from the fence line, it was Bob who spotted it. He tapped JT on the shoulder, motioning for JT to follow him, while Rambo stayed in place with his rifle trained on the watch tower.

Back at the wait point, Bob pointed at the screen, explaining what he'd seen, or rather what he'd not seen. 'There's a straight line in the vegetation.'

'Meaning?'

'There are no straight lines in nature, if it exists, it's because humans created it.'

'You think there's a camera?'

'Or a movement sensor or whatever. The bush where I put the satellite kit must have been this side of it.'

'We need to disable it, or we'll wake the whole place up before we can reach the fence.'

'Maybe that's not a bad thing.'

'What do you mean?'

'Give me ten minutes, I'll show you.' said Bob, as he moved off into the darkness.

There's a straight line where the vegetation has been cut back Easy, see if you can find whatever is at the ends of it. JT typed after watching Bob merge with the African fauna, then disappear.

Easy flew the drone, following the straight line to where it ended at a mound, from the air it looked like a termite mound. Following the line, he found a tree stump, that had apparently been cut down with a chainsaw, and the fallen tree dragged further out from the fence line.

Continuing the circuit, he found a series of 12 straight lines cut out of the vegetation each with a notable structure at the end. Not wanting to fly too close, he zoomed in at each one and found a lens pointing along the line. Either cameras or PIR sensors he guessed.

Bob appeared back, and to JT's surprise, he found him holding Pangolin. The big, scaly, lizard like creature twisted and writhed as Bob held it carefully at arm's length.

'This guy will show us what those sneaky Russian bastards have up their sleeves. Get your eye in the sky to follow me, he can let me know when I'm approaching the line.'

Bob headed off into the grass, quickly becoming invisible, again JT had to marvel at the stealth of the man.

When Bob was six feet from the line where the vegetation abruptly ended, he slowed down to get a good look at the edge of the grass.

From his pocket he produced three juicy grubs, letting the Pangolin sniff them before he threw them out onto the bare ground. He put the Pangolin down gently. As he knew it would, it curled into a ball using its thick keratin scales as a protective shield. Bob retreated, heading back to where JT and Rambo were waiting.

'What now?' asked JT.

'Now we let the little guy have a snack.'

A few moments later, they watched the images from the drone camera as the Pangolin appeared from the edge of the grass, apparently no worse off from being handled by Bob. It's long thin tongue tasting the air as it scented the grubs. After a second or two of hesitation, it lumbered out of the grass to munch on the closest grub. Before it had finished chewing it was on the move to the second grub, another foot or so into the open.

The shrill alarm sounded at the same time as floodlights, on top of the two closest watchtowers, illuminated the savannah with dazzling light. Rambo let out a grunt as his eye was blasted with the intense light from his night vision scope.

Easy took the drone higher into the air, and it was his images that alerted the team to how quick the Wagner force were at deploying. Despite their sleepy and relaxed demeanour, as soon as the alarm sounded they all jumped into professional mode. The guards in the towers took up firing positions with their assault rifles, the two guards on foot patrol raced to the sector that was now illuminated, throwing themselves into a prone position, pointing their weapons out into the savannah night. Shouting could be heard from the compound as a booming voice shouted in Russian, 'Report!'

The two guards facing out to the now illuminated side were scanning the ground looking for movement. Eventually one of them spotted the Pangolin and shouted, 'False alarm. It's an Armadillo!'

'Then shoot the fucking thing!'

'Yes Major!'

The guard raised his rifle and fired a three round burst at the Pangolin all falling 2 ft short. The Pangolin scarpered off into the long savannah grass.

'You got it?' asked the Major.

'Yes sir, I believe so,' said the guard.

'You believe so? You either hit it or you didn't man!' The Major sounded furious.

'Yes sir, I hit it, I'm sure.'

'Then go out there and get it, I don't want the fucking thing waking everyone up again!'

'Yes Major, right away.'

'You go with him Dmitri. Sukov you man the tower,' he told the two foot patrol guards.

JT watched carefully, as the two men left the facility via a pedestrian gate under the tower, and how they walked across the ploughed area immediately outside the fence. At least it's not mined, he thought to himself.

Leaving Rambo in situ with his rifle trained on the tower, JT drew his combat knife, motioning for Bob to do the same. Bob led the way in a circuitous route around to where the Pangolin had made it's escape. The long grass gave some cover, but they took up position where an animal track led between two thickets of bushes.

The two Russian soldiers approached slowly, their eyes peeled to the ground, hoping for a blood trail or some animal tracks to follow.

'I thought you said you hit it, Ilya?' said Dmitri.

'I don't know, but I wasn't going to tell the Major that, was I?'

'Was it definitely an Armadillo?'

'Fucked if I know, it was something like that, big fat armoured lizard thing.'

'Maybe they're bulletproof?' Dmitri said, laughing at his friend.

'Let's just find the thing so we can get back inside, there's lions and stuff out here.'

Dmitri stepped between the bushes, turning his head to reply to Ilya when Bob clamped his hand over his mouth stabbing him three times in rapid succession to the kidneys.

Ilya looked up, shocked, not quite able to compute what had happened, but before he could raise his weapon JT jumped up from his crouched position in the bush driving his combat knife through the Russians' throat. The blade sliced through his windpipe and up at an angle severing his spinal cord. Ilyas' eyes went wide and he managed the slightest gurgle before he collapsed forward. JT grabbed him, dragging his limp body into the bush.

Easy captured the action from above so everyone knew what had happened.

When they send out the guys to find these two, we'll take them out, then we hit the towers. Easy, get another drone up for camera duties. You can fly this loaded one into the accommodation block when they open the door. JT typed.

Ok, came the response.

Another drone, a smaller Mi-1 took off from the wait point, and the images switched from the Mi-3. After five minutes, they could see Sukov, the guard in the tower, becoming anxious. He was scanning the ground with his binoculars until the timed lights switched themselves off. The savannah once again plunged into inky darkness.

Apparently not daring to disturb the Major, or the guards who had gone back to bed, he climbed down from the tower, pacing back and forward at the fence, staring out into the night.

Come on, come find your buddies, thought JT, as he watched the man consider his next move.

Eventually, Sukov couldn't help himself, leaving via the pedestrian gate before switching on his torch and following the clear footprints left by his friends. He moved slowly, scanning his torch left and right before returning it to the ground, to follow the footsteps. 'Dmitri, Ilya,' he hissed, 'for fuck sake, find the Armadillo and get back in.'

There was no reply. He kept inching forward until he accidentally tripped the motion sensor. As he did so, the lights illuminated everything around him and set off the alarm. His shock at tripping the alarm, was nothing compared to the shock of finding himself face to face with Bob, who sliced his machete into the man's neck, felling him instantly, causing a spray of blood, as the man fell bucking to the ground.

This time, the alarm didn't get quite the same response, as the men in the accommodation block assumed it to be a false alarm. The door was thrown open as the Major, followed by his three closest lieutenants, made his way out.

Rambo shot out the flood lights, and as he did, Claudine, Taff and Cooky all fired their rifles, taking out the three guards at the other towers.

Easy flew the Mi-3 drone into the open door of the accommodation block, knocking a half asleep Russian off his feet as he did and crashing the drone inside the building. The explosion blasted a hole in the wall, ripping through the sheet metal roof, quickly turning the block into an inferno. Agonised screams could be heard, as those not killed instantly were burned, or blasted by the building fabric being turned into shrapnel.

Now the team could turn to vocal comms and JT said, 'We're going in, we have access through a gate.' He took off from cover, followed by

Rambo and Bob. They reached the gate and ran inside, immediately coming under fire from Major Andreyev and his three surviving men. JT and the others took cover behind the low concrete platform the tower was built on, but couldn't return aimed fire from their position.

One of the guards ran forward, firing on fully automatic, until he could throw himself behind an earth mound shaped like a miniature tank berm.

'We're pinned down!' JT called into his radio.

'On our way boss', said Taff, cutting at the chain-link fence with bolt cutters.

'I'm closer,' said Claudine, as she ran around the outside of the fence trying to gain a firing position. As she did, she took fire from one of the guards who had spotted her. Sparks flew as rounds ricocheted off the fence post.

Claudine rolled on the ground, coming to rest in the prone position, she let off a series of shots to keep the guards honest. She was drawing fire, and exposed as the guard stood up to get a better angle. Paulo had followed his wife and fired three rounds as he moved, the first round hit the guard in the shoulder, knocking him from his feet. Paulo reached his wife and found her bleeding from a wound to her head.

'You're hit!' he said, as he crouched beside her.

'Get down you fool!' said Claudine, dragging her husband down beside her, rounds ripping into the soil beside them.

'Where are you Taff?' asked JT.

'On our way. 10 seconds until we can engage.'

'Get firing!' shouted JT. He heard the team open up from behind the Russians, and a merciful gap in the incoming rounds. Rolling from cover, he took aim at the Russians, shooting one of them twice in the back as they turned to face Taff.

The ground erupted beside him and JT had to roll back into cover. 'Easy, where are they?'

'Two are in the doorway of the main building, one is still in behind the mound of earth, he's keeping his head down, the other two are watching for Taff.'

'Rambo, get up to the tower, take the high ground,' said JT.

Paulo rolled to his right and found a gap between buildings though which he could engage the Russian by the mound. 'I can spook the guy on his own, try to get him to show himself from my position. Tell me when you're ready.'

'Any time you like,' said Rambo, from the tower.

Paulo fired several shots into the earth mound and the Russian tried to jump out of the way, momentarily showing the top of his head above the mound. Rambo dispatched him with a single round, blowing off the rear of the Russian's skull. The man's weapon fired into the air as he fell, bullets arcing harmlessly into the night sky as he died.

'Two left, plus Bergstrom and the woman. Anyone got eyes on them?'

'I'm trying to locate them,' said Easy, sweeping the drone around the facility.

A single shot rang out, everyone recognising the sound of a shotgun. The drone fell from the sky leaving Easy without a camera feed. He reached for another controller, quickly sending a second mini drone into the air.

It took almost three minutes for the drone to reach the facility; three minutes during which the team rearranged their positions, getting ready to tackle the remaining Russians.

Chapter Forty-Five

Laila stood with the pump action shotgun pointing at the main entrance of the building. She had waited in her own accommodation, which was more hut than building, but deliberately away from the Wagner men.

Once the shooting had moved to the far side of the facility, she used the rear entrance to make her way to the door of Bergstroms' locked room. Before entering the building, she had looked up, catching the glint of the accommodation block fire reflected from the drone. Instinctively she'd pulled the combat shotgun to her shoulder, taking down the drone with a single shot.

Inside, she couldn't raise Bergstrom, despite holding her finger on the intercom button. He had told her he would be taking some medication that made him sleep. She already knew he worked, and slept, with noise cancelling headphones. He must surely have heard the explosion she thought, unless he was comatose.

Laila wondered how secure the metal door was, even though she'd felt it heavy and solid earlier. Whoever was attacking this place would surely just blow it open.

Someone was outside the main door, firing sporadically. She counted two shooters. They weren't trying to get inside, so she figured they were Russians.

Grabbing her phone from her pocket she dialled Bergstroms' number, she almost laughed when, after four rings, he answered stifling a yawn. 'Yes, Laila?'

'Open the door, we are under attack, I have to get you out of here now.'

'What do you m-?'

A burst of gunfire cut him off before he finished speaking. He ran to the computer console bringing up the CCTV onto his screens. He could see the burning building and the dead Russians. He saw Major Andreyev, with the weaselly Russian called Povitch, crouched down in the doorway. The camera outside his door showed Laila pointing a shotgun along the corridor, her back against the door. He ran to the door, unlocking it to let her in. She slipped past him to let him close and re-lock the door.

'What about Major Andreyev?' he asked her.

'He is slowing them down, keeping them at bay for now.'

'Who are they?'

'I hoped you might tell me?'

'I don't know.'

'How long before the reinforcements get here?'

'They should be less than 30 minutes away at any time.'

'More Russians?'

'No, they call themselves the 313, Jihadist militia guys. They'll send a small army.'

'They'll need one, whoever is attacking us know what they're doing. We don't know how large a force they are. I suggest we back up your files, and get out of here.'

'What do you mean?' Knut asked, suddenly suspicious.

'You have computers, isn't that what people do, back up files and take them with them?'

'Hmm yes, I suppose they do,' said Knut, removing a hard drive from a computer.

'What about the rest of it?' asked Laila.

'This is the only thing of importance now. I sent the code before I went to sleep, it will already be working its way into their systems, in 48 hours their worst nightmares will come true.'

'Why, what does the code do?'

'It makes me the richest man on the planet.'

'Ok, let's try to get the hell out of here,' said Laila, heading for the door.

'Wait, you're going the wrong way,' said Knut, showing her into his bathroom. He pulled the shower enclosure door back, then undid a catch beside its hinge. Knut put his hand against the tile wall with the shower head, rotating it away from him. It revealed a void with a ladder leading down into a narrow tunnel with electric lighting.

'Where does this lead?' Laila asked him.

'I had a tunnel created that goes outside the fence, past the solar farm. There is a motocross bike waiting in an underground garage.'

'What if the attackers know about this?'

'They won't, the builders thought they were making a cable and pipe duct, for future installation of reverse heat pump technology. I put the bike down there myself.'

Laila hesitated, 'I will need more weapons, give me a moment to get the shotgun.'

'There's no time for that,' said Knut.

'You go ahead, I will catch up, if they are waiting for us at the exit, we will need to shoot our way out. Now go, Mr Bergstrom.' Laila pushed Knut toward the ladder, then turned back out of the bathroom.

Reaching the desk where she had left the shotgun, she extracted a flash drive from her pocket, plugging it into the computer terminal.

The flash drive automatically started downloading computer files, as Laila moved to the steel door and unlocked it. She drew her Beretta Model 71 with its magazine of .22LR rounds. It had been her father's, when he served as a Mossad field agent. He had gifted it to her before he died. Laila had been given her own service weapon from Mossad, but told herself she preferred the lighter weight aluminium alloy frame with it's short barrel for close protection and self-protection work. The truth was, she just enjoyed the idea of her work continuing the legacy of her father.

Moving along the corridor, she called through the main entrance door in Russian, that she was coming out. When she opened the door, she found Major Andreyev and Povitch hunkered down against the concrete walls of the entrance portico.

'Get down you stupid woman. Shut that fucking door,' snarled Andreyev, returning his eyes to the ground in front of him.

'Who are they, that are attacking us?' she asked.

'I don't know, but they have killed all of my men. There must be an army of them out there.'

'Nigerian army or Militia?'

'Which part of I don't know, didn't you understand?' said Andreyev. 'They can't be Nigerian Army, we have people in their ranks who would have warned us.'

'Militia then?'

'No, the local Militia is the 313, they are our allies. They will be here in the next 10 minutes, to wipe out these bastards. Until then we must hold them off. We will need more ammunition, what do you have?'

'I have this,' said Laila, firing her Beretta, shooting Andreyev in the back, before pivoting to Povitch, shooting him in the face as he turned to her.

Laila picked up Povitch's AK-12 assault rifle, she knew it was a marked improvement on the AK-47, but it was no match for the Negev used by the Israeli Defence Forces. She checked the magazine then located a spare in his webbing belt. Tucking the spare mag under her arm she reached for Andreyev who groaned. The tough old bull was still alive. Before she could finish him off, rounds powdered the concrete of the portico wall, forcing her to retreat back inside the building. She locked the steel door behind her, but changed her mind, deciding to leave it unlocked.

Returning to the computer, she saw the flash drive light was now green. She snatched it from the computer, before tucking it inside her sports bra, and heading for the tunnel.

Chapter Forty-Six

'Easy get me a visual on the doorway to that building,' said JT.

A silence from Easy made JT repeat the sentence.

'Yes, sorry I'm just trying to see something. There's maybe six vehicles, coming up the road, fast. I can't make out who or what they are.'

'ETA?'

'I'm not sure, maybe seven or eight minutes, it's not a straight road.'

'Ok, now show me the building entrance,' said JT, his mind racing.

An image appeared on JT's phone screen of a dead Russian with a head wound and a trail of blood leading through the closing door.

'Looks like there is one injured Russian left, plus Bergstrom and the woman. Taff, you and Posty get round the back of the building, let me know when you're ready to breach. We'll hit them from both sides. We need to get the hell out of here. Bob, you, Paulo and Claudine get back to the chopper, be ready for us. If we're not back there in 20 minutes, get going, we'll make our own way back and try to RV with you at the quad bikes.'

'I'm counting six vehicles; they look like pick-up trucks and 4x4s. I'm looking at the map, the road twists and turns so they're at-least five minutes out.'

'Ok, Joe and Cooky get the charges laid, then get up in those towers, ready to give us cover.'

'Roger that,' said Joe, as he and Cooky grabbed the ANFO supplies.

JT and Rambo sprinted to the door then paused until Taff confirmed they were in position. JT just had time to lament they weren't kitted out with flash-bangs but, on the count of three, they threw open the doors, and charged in.

Chapter Forty-Seven

Andreyev had dragged himself through the steel door after struggling to pull it open. The round from Laila's gun had punctured his lung and shattered his rib, but had been slowed down significantly by the extra thick leather strap of his shoulder holster, and the layer of dense muscle in his lats. Regardless, he was fairly certain he would not survive the day, his mind now completely consumed by a burning rage, and desire for revenge.

Pulling himself to his feet, he held his Makarov pistol two handed as he scanned the room. Checking the bathroom, he found the escape tunnel and, grunting at the pain, climbed down the steel ladder. In the distance, up the tunnel, he could see movement as he staggered forward, bent over in the cramped space. What sounded like a motorbike engine was running, masked the sound of his half run, half stagger up the tunnel.

About 40 yards ahead of him was that treacherous bitch Laila. Andreyev knelt down as he took aim. The woman was climbing onto the back of the motorbike as he fired all eight rounds from his Makarov.

He took great pleasure, when Laila fell back from the motorbike. He watched as she rolled bringing up the AK-12 as he inserted his spare magazine into the Makarov.

5.45 mm rounds erupted down the tunnel throwing Andreyev backwards with his legs trapped under him in a grotesque contortion.

Laila clutched at her side. She was bleeding heavily, from a wound that had entered her lower back and exited from her abdomen. The pain was intense as she ripped off her blouse, packing it into either end of the wound. Unclipping the sling from the AK-12 she tied it around her middle to hold the makeshift dressing in place.

'Get on, now!' shouted Knut, as he pulled a lever causing a trap door to fall inwards creating a ramp up out of the concrete vault.

Laila climbed on, placing the AK-12 between their bodies. She gripped her arms around Knut's torso as he revved the engine and the motorbike shot out into the night air.

Chapter Forty-Eight

'A motorbike has just appeared, heading away from the compound, two up,' reported Cooky.

'Which direction?' asked JT.

'Away from the incoming vehicles, it's heading into the bush.'

'Ok, Easy, can you try to track it?'

'Will do, but I only have one more drone, and this one won't last much longer.'

'Do what you can, we're going in, following the trail of blood.'

Rambo tried the steel door, finding it unlocked. With his colleagues stood to the side, he pushed it open, fully expecting a burst of fire from inside. When none came, Taff and Posty rushed the room, panning their weapons left and right.

'Search the place,' said JT, as he looked at the mass of computing equipment. 'Easy, where do I plug this thing in?' he asked.

'I don't think you have time; the vehicles will be here in less than a minute. You'll just have to destroy it.'

'Ok, I'll set the charge.'

'Boss, there's a tunnel over here,' came a shout from the bathroom. 'There's clean air coming in, and by the smell of exhaust, it's where the motorbike left from. There's also a dead Russian in the tunnel, the blood trail led to him, but someone finished the job in there.'

'Ok, get out of here, up the tunnel, I'll be right behind you. Everybody fall back, we're out of here before the cavalry arrive, get going now!'

JT finished setting the charges, rigging up a wire from the steel door so the detonator would be instigated when the door was opened.

He ran crouched, along the tunnel, slowing down to briefly look at Andreyev where he lay, but then racing up the ramp and out into the darkness. He found the team, positioned to give him cover, and they could hear the engines of the approaching vehicles.

JT waved them on, the team running hard into the bush in the direction of where the helicopter waited two miles away.

Running hard for two miles, cross country, while carrying weapons was a tough ask even for SAS trained men, but they kept up the pace, grateful for the comparative cool of the African night.

The sounds of the vehicles faded, overtaken by the tell-tale rattle of AK47s. Confident they were not receiving fire, the team kept running, but stopped briefly when the roar of explosions split the night.

They had failed to get hold of the code, but they had succeeded in their secondary mission of destroying the facility. Now they had to find Knut Bergstrom, and prevent many thousands of deaths by stopping him from unleashing his code.

CHAPTER FORTY-NINE

Back in the Vigilant command and control bunker in the UK, Easy was joined by Hamilton.

'Where can Bergstrom be headed?' Hamilton asked, as he examined the map.

'He's headed West and the nearest town is Kaingiwa, close to the Niger border. There's a couple of little settlements in between, but there won't be much there.'

'How far is that from the helicopter?'

'It's about 70 miles.'

'They won't have enough fuel to re-route there and get back into Benin. We'll need another way for them to intercept Bergstrom and Laila Acker.'

'Bergstrom has slowed down a fair bit, it's rough ground, even though he's sticking to the dirt roads.'

'Then let's hope the team can find a way to reach him, before he disappears into Niger.'

Chapter Fifty

Laila's grip weakened as she continued to lose blood, and with it her strength. The AK-12 slipped from between them, crashing to the ground, as Knut negotiated a badly rutted bend in what could only loosely be termed a road.

'I need you to stop.' Laila grunted.

Knut stopped the motorbike and twisted round to see Laila struggle off the back of the bike. She walk unsteadily in front of the slit headlight. Lifting her blood soaked blouse away, she examined the exit wound in her abdomen.

'I won't make it much further,' said Laila.

'No, it appears not,' said Knut, without emotion.

'Where are we headed anyway, is it far?'

'Oh, another 30 miles or so I should think, but on these roads that will take a couple of hours.'

'Is there somewhere closer, there must be a farm or something out here, I need a first aid kit, then hospital.'

'You've lost the assault rifle, I see,' said Knut, looking back into the darkness.

'It slipped, but I still have this.' She pulled her Beretta from its holster, but it slipped from her blood soaked hand landing at her feet.'

'If you can't hold a weapon, then I'm afraid you are no longer of any use to me,' said Knut, before he opened up the throttle and pushed Laila aside with the bike.

Laila fell to the ground as Knut sped off up the road. She lay back in the sandy soil looking up into the starry sky. She picked out a bright star, that she knew was Saturn. Pressing hard on the saturated blouse, she tried to stem the blood-flow. She doubted she would live too much longer, but wanted to enjoy the stars, for as long as possible.

What she thought at first, was a shooting star caught her eye, but it changed direction, heading back towards her.

Maybe this was an angel coming to find her. She tried to think of the names of the four Archangels of the Talmud. She had never been particularly religious or observant, and she thought now of her father, how he told her he worked to protect their people; it was Yahweh's job to protect their religion.

The angel descended toward her, she heard the flutter of its wings as it came down to her. Then she lost consciousness.

Chapter Fifty-One

Easy took the drone down, to sit on the road next to where Laila lay. The battery was almost done, and it couldn't fly any further from the satellite controller, which was now in the helicopter with the team.

Easy zoomed the camera on Laila's face: she appeared to be smiling. She was still alive, but her breathing was shallow and laboured. He didn't want to watch her die, but felt he couldn't leave her alone. He knew he couldn't be much of a guardian angel from several thousand miles away. He just wished he could say something to comfort her.

'Bergstrom has dumped the woman and ridden off on the motorbike,' he told the team.

'Have you still got eyes on him?' asked JT.

'No, the drone couldn't go any further, sorry.'

'Ok, where is the woman, she might know where he is headed?'

'I can send you the co-ordinates. I've landed the drone beside her, the GPS beacon will help locate her.'

'Ok, how far is she from where we are now?'

'About 10 miles, but you'll have to hurry, she's in a bad way.'

'Ok, Bob can you get me there?'

'No can do I'm afraid, we'll be on vapours as it is by the time we reach the ATVs.'

'Shit, he's going to get away.'

'Wait,' said Hamilton, 'there's a farm two miles south west of your position. Judging by the satellite images, the road to it is well used so they must have a vehicle.'

'Yes. Bob get me there, sharpish please.'

JT slung his carbine across his back, grabbing the winch harness slipping it over his boots and up his legs.

'You lot get back to the ATVs, I'll borrow a vehicle and go check the woman. Get this bird back in the air as soon as you can, then we'll RV somewhere. If I can follow Bergstrom I will, but if not I'll head for the closest border point back into Benin and meet you there.'

'You don't want to go uninvited into Niger, that's bandit country,' said Paulo.

'Don't worry about me, you just get Claudine back to see a doctor.'

'It's just a scratch, I'll stitch it myself,' said an indignant Claudine.

JT put his hand on her shoulder and smiled at her with admiration.

'We're here, I can see a Ute parked up,' said Bob, from the cockpit.

'I'll go down by rope Bob, let's not waste fuel landing,' said JT.

Taff slid open the side door and pulled in the winch hook. He connected the rope to it and to JT's harness, then handed him a spare magazine from his pocket. 'Keep safe down there, Boss, we'll get to you as soon as we can.'

'Ok Taff, just get the team clear, we don't want to be in Nigeria when the shit hits the fan.'

JT shuffled backward, steadying his feet on the lip of the door frame. The turbulence from the rotors buffeted him as he leaned back, then he gave a thumbs up for Taff to start lowering him the 50 feet to the ground.

Stepping out of the harness JT watched as lights started appearing in the farmhouse window. He ran to the door as the farmer appeared looking bewildered.

'I need to borrow your vehicle.' JT shouted

The farmer looked unmoved, just stared until JT swung his carbine round to point at him.

Pushing his hands in the air the farmer shook his head, then turned into the farmhouse followed by JT.

The farmer's wife and children appeared. JT pointed his gun at the floor trying to limit their distress. 'Do you speak English?' he asked the farmer.

'Yes I do,' the farmer replied, in a deep sonorous voice.

'I need to borrow your vehicle; I'm not stealing it, but I need to get to a woman who is injured, she is a few miles from here.'

'Where is she?' asked the farmer's wife.

'On the road to Muchungwe, she doesn't have much time.'

'Give him the keys Chetachi, I will get my things.'

'You cannot go with this man,' said the Farmer.

'The woman is injured. I was a nurse before you brought me to this godforsaken place. Now do as I say, give him the keys!'

The farmer's wife left the room and returned pulling on her coat. She carrying a wooden box that JT knew must be her first aid box.

'Let's go, I will direct you in a short cut, we will save some time.'

CHAPTER FIFTY-TWO

Knut rode the motorbike harder now that he was rid of the excess baggage of Laila. He was concentrating on the road ahead, but trying to figure out what had happened tonight.

Nigeria was always a less than safe place for his operations. The risk of falling out with the Government and Army officials he'd been paying, or blackmailing, was ever present. As was his truce with the 313 militia, he had been paying them well, and knew they were buying weapons for their Jihad activities. Was it them who had attacked tonight?

It didn't make sense. They would know the Wagner Group would hit them back hard in retaliation. There would only be one winner there, in a battle between some religious fanatics and a de facto offshoot of a military super power.

No, something else had happened. It maddened him that he didn't know what, or who, was behind it.

The fact that he had initiated the code the evening before meant the facility was now redundant in his plan, but it had taken him several years, and tens of millions to build it, now it was in flames. The waste of it all bothered him.

Now he was in a race against time. He had to get to the UK, to get Rosa on the plane with him to Cuba, before the code did its job and closed down the skies of Western Europe.

It had taken him several hours the evening before, meant he had to work through his impending migraine, but he had found her. Or at least he found a village in rural England, where she had made a call from a public call box. He'd been unable to get a transcript of the call, but it was to her best friend Maddie in Brighton. It had been followed by a second call, to the trustees of the Orphanages charity two hours later. No-one else would make those two calls one after the other; that meant she was nearby.

He had an existing hack into the mobile phone network, he'd been able to read the text messages from Rosa to Maddie, when they first started dating. It was through them that he'd known what she was thinking, suddenly able to mould himself into the image of a man she would want to marry.

Now, he was quickly able to trace and read a text message from Maddie to another friend called Helen, saying she'd heard from Rosa and that she was ok but keeping her head down.

He had searched for accommodation in the village, finding the old rectory was run as a B and B. That's where she would be. That was where he would be going.

Chapter Fifty-Three

The farmer's wife introduced herself as Adanna. She explained she had trained as a nurse in Lagos, before her father married her off to the farmer.

She directed JT to a ford in the river, that he wouldn't have dared attempt if she hadn't pushed him to keep driving. The water smelled of earth and decaying vegetation, at one point it almost reached the Ute windows.

After sliding a bit trying to gain traction on the far bank, JT found himself on the bumpy, rutted road, having more than halved the distance to travel.

They made good progress and after a few more minutes rounded a corner finding Laila lying in the road.

Adanna jumped out of the vehicle and ran straight to Laila.

JT scanned the bush with his carbine until he was satisfied they were alone.

'She is in a bad way mister,' said Adanna, pressing clean dressings into the wound. 'She has lost a lot of blood. Give me some light, I will give her an IV of saline.'

JT reversed the Ute out of a rut, until the headlights illuminated the two women in the road.

'You come well prepared,' said JT, looking at the drip.

'We are a long way from hospital out here, we need to be able to fix things ourselves,' said Adanna.

'Can you fix her?' asked JT.

'I doubt it, it's a bad wound. She been shot, lost too much blood. But I can try at least to make her comfortable. I have a little morphine for her pain.'

As Adanna inserted the morphine needle into Laila's arm, a bloodied hand reached over to stop her.

'Wait, I must speak,' said Laila, in a croaky voice. 'Give me some water, please.'

JT grabbed a bottle of water from the vehicle. Kneeling beside her he dribbled it gently between Laila's parched lips.

Laila coughed as JT tucked a sack from the vehicle under her head.

'Who are you?' she asked JT.

'My name is JT, I know yours is Laila, you work for Bergstrom.'

'You are English? MI6?' she asked, the surprised look giving way to a pained grimace.

'Yes, I am English. This is Adanna, she is a nurse and will help you.'

'It's too late for that already, but thank you, Adanna.'

'Let me give you some morphine, for the pain,' said Adanna.

'No, I must stay awake while I can. I have something to tell this man. It might be better if you did not hear.'

Adanna looked at JT who nodded and she headed off to sit in the Ute.

'Listen to me very carefully Mr MI6. My name is Laila Acker, I am with Israeli Intelligence.'

'Mossad,' said JT.

'Yes. I was tasked with surveillance on Knut Bergstrom. Through an intermediary, I was placed with him as security. I have been working for him three weeks. We know he has been developing a code, which will allow him to control the computer systems of numerous European Government Agencies,' she paused for a moment, another spasm of pain rolling through her body.

'How do you know about this?'

'We are Mossad, we know everything. My task was to get a copy of the code.'

'Did you?'

'I don't know.' Laila reached her fingers into her sports bra, extracting the flash drive, which she handed to JT. 'This may save lives, or at least prevent chaos. I would love to tell you that my Government were acting in purely good faith, but I have no doubt they would have tried to find an advantage with it. Our country's survival relies on our keeping allies close. You must make sure this gets to the correct hands. You must stop Bergstrom.'

'That's what I'm trying to do. Do you know where he is headed?'

'He said he must be in Cuba within 48 hours. He intends taking his wife with him. If you can find her then you will find him.' Laila arched her back as the pain gripped her.

JT saw the muscles in Laila's jaw tense as she gritted her teeth. He motioned to Adanna, to come forward. 'I think it's time for that morphine now.'

'Can you arrange for my body to return to Israel please Mr MI6. I wish to be buried beside my father and mother, in Haifa, looking down on the sea from Mount Carmel.'

'I'll see that it happens.' JT assured her.

'Promise?' asked Laila gripping his hand.

'I promise.'

Adanna pushed the plunger on the syringe feeding the morphine into Laila's arm.

Laila's eyes rolled back as the drugs took away her pain. Her eyes were almost closed but she could still see the stars in her mind. 'Michael, Gabriel, Uriel and...' her voice trailed as her last breath hissed gently between her lips.

'Raphael child, Raphael,' said Adanna, placing her hand on Laila's face to close her eyes.

'What were those names?' asked JT.

'They were the names of God's four Angels that surround his throne, according to the Tanakh and Talmud. They are the Jewish holy books.'

'How do you know so much about Judaism?'

'There are Jews throughout Africa. Some of them claim to be direct descendants of the tribes of Israel. My mother's people are from Bilad al-Sudan. They were Jews, but were forced to convert to Islam. My family never completely lost their identity.'

'I will need to work out how to get her back to Israel,' said JT.

'We will need to bury her today; it is the Hebrew way. If you cannot fly her body straight to Israel, then I will bury her on my land. Her family can come to collect her, when they are able.'

'You would do that for a stranger?'

'In God's eyes, mister, none of us are strangers.'

Chapter Fifty-Four

Four hours later, JT sat eating a breakfast, of what he learned was unleavened bread, with Adanna and her husband. The man introduced himself as Chetachi Okoro, a hard-working man with hands like shovels. He had the strong back and shoulders of a farmer.

Chetachi had insisted on digging the grave by hand, waving away JT's offers of help.

'This is my land mister; I will be the one who digs and decides who is buried here.' He still viewed JT with suspicion and understandable resentment.

JT could hardly blame him, but won him over a while later, when the chopper returned and JT left behind an almost new ATV quad-bike as an apology.

'Her family are not here to sit Shiva, so I will sit on their behalf.' Adanna informed him.

'I don't know what that means, I'm sorry,' admitted JT.

'It is a Hebrew tradition, when a family stay at home for seven days, to welcome mourners.'

'I don't know that her family will get here within seven days Adanna. I don't even know if she has any family.'

'Then you should return when it is time. You and I will be her family.'

'I'll do that, just as soon as I can, I promise.'

JT hugged Adanna, and felt himself mourning a woman he didn't know, and had met for just a few minutes. He had made a promise to her, a promise he would keep.

Adanna and her family waved as the chopper lifted off. They watched it turn, staying low while heading cross country, toward the border with Benin.

'I will need to keep low to the ground to avoid radar and any Nigerian military aircraft,' said Bob. 'That means travelling a bit slower, but we should be back to the compound in just over two hours. I can pick up the pace, once over the border.'

'Ok, thanks Bob, how is Claudine?'

'She's fine, we'll be picking her up en-route. I'll lay bets she's already stitched up her head.'

'Was it a bad wound?'

'I think a bit of the fence got shot off, the sharp wire hit her rather than a round. She was still bossing Paulo around, so she must be fine. She's a strong woman that one.'

'Yes, I can tell.' JT nodded and thought about the remarkable women he'd met in the last few days. 'Anything from Hamilton on Bergstrom.'

'No updates yet,' said Bob. 'We don't know where he went when the drone lost him.'

JT looked out at the tree tops that felt close enough to touch his feet, 'No, but I think I know where he's going.'

Chapter Fifty-Five

'Easy has uploaded all of the files you sent, but they don't appear to have the code,' said Hamilton.

'Shit, what was on there?'

'A lot of files about the set up in Nigeria, we can see how the code has been transmitted, just not the code itself. It also contained some interesting search history.'

'Such as?'

'Such as, his searching for flight manifests out of Grand Cayman, and his accessing the telephone records of a Maddie Kerson.'

'Who is she?'

'She is the best friend of Rosa, and who she went to stay with, when she left Bergstrom.'

'He's looking to see if she knows where Rosa is.'

'Indeed, and unfortunately, I failed in my duty to persuade Rosa to stay completely off grid whilst she was here.'

'What do you mean?'

'She used the telephone box in the village to call her friend. She tells me she just wanted to let her know she was okay. She hadn't been in touch with her and they usually speak every other day.'

'You think Bergstrom can know it was Rosa calling from a phone box?'

'One call no. Unfortunately, Rosa took the opportunity to make another call later that afternoon.'

'To?'

'To the charity which runs the orphanages on her behalf. She is missing a quarterly meeting, wanted to send her apologies.'

'Bloody hell, you think he'll link them both to Rosa, and to your place?'

'He already has, he searched for accommodation nearby, found my Air BnB place at the old rectory.'

'But Rosa is with you at the church, right?'

'Yes, and I don't particularly want to show her the location of the bunker, so for now she is still here with me.'

'Do we know where Bergstrom is?'

'His jet left Nigeria, enroute to Niamey.'

'Niger?'

'Indeed. He has likely had assistance from Wagner, who are operating in Niger, to get to the airport.'

'Do we know where he's going next?'

'A flight plan has been registered to Dublin.'

'Who else is on board?'

'We don't know, the Niger authorities can be somewhat lax when it comes to details, for a few dollars.'

'Why Dublin?'

'I think possibly because from Dublin it's easy to enter the UK mainland, avoiding checks.'

'I take it you have people in Dublin?'

'I do have some eyes and ears available on the ground yes.'

'So, you'll have him arrested when he lands?'

'As yet, he has committed no arrestable offence in this country, or the Republic of Ireland. We can't arrest him, and we don't yet have the code, so can't just have him shot from the sky.'

'Very funny.'

'I assure you, it has been considered JT. The magnitude of the catastrophe, if his code takes down the systems, is difficult to contemplate. Not only will we have aircraft falling out of the sky when they run out of fuel, the financial impact will completely wreck Western economies. The contagion causing a global meltdown. Millions would starve, the unrest would kill millions more.'

'Wouldn't it be easier to pay the man, then follow the money.'

'He needs to crash the system first. His offer will be to switch it all back on.'

'I still don't understand how he was allowed to get into this position in the first place.'

'He has been playing a very clever and calculated long game. All of this has been years, if not decades in the making. Governments are weak, pushed around by those with their fingers in all of the pies. Greed and stupidity make them easy targets.'

'I thought that was your job, to protect them from themselves.'

'Hmm, that is one interpretation. Suffice to say, I can lead a horse to water...'

'Ok, I hear you. Not trying to lay blame anywhere. What do we do next?'

'I think it's time we got our hands on Knut Bergstrom, and his code, to put an end to this.'

'I take it you have a plan?'

'The beginnings of one yes. There is a German military transport plane leaving Parakou airport, in two hours. I have arranged for them to take you to Militarflugplatz Eggebek in Northern Germany. From there the RAF will take you to Scotland.'

'Scotland?'

'I am sending Rosa to Castle Subhain, with Rory Maxwell. They are booked on a flight to Inverness, leaving shortly. Bergstrom will pick up on the booking name. I've sent a text, on Rosa's behalf to her friend Maddie, saying she's met a charming man, who is a Scottish Laird, and he's taking her to visit his Castle.'

'How did Rory take that news?'

'He is about to spend quality time with a very beautiful woman at his Castle in the Highlands,' Hamilton laughed. 'As you can imagine, he was absolutely furious as he is in the middle of his last case.'

'Can't we just hand all of this over to the regular authorities?'

'Out of the question old chap. If a single detail of this was to reach the public domain, there would be panic. The impact might not be as catastrophic as the code being deployed, but make no mistake, it would be a disaster.'

'So, it's down to us then.'

'Yes, this is a job for Vigilant. It's why we exist after all.'

'Ok where will the RAF flight be landing, there's not an airport close to Castle Subhain.

'You won't be landing.'

'Sorry?'

'To expedite things, you'll be parachuting.'

'That's easier said than done Hamilton, what if the weather is against us? It's bloody Scotland; not exactly known for its calm weather!'

'You'll make it work. Now if you'll excuse me, I have some more logistics to sort out.'

Chapter Fifty-Six

Knut Bergstrom sat in the co-pilot seat of his private jet. He was wearing his noise cancelling headphones and had eschewed his comfortable leather recliner. The less comfortable seat was a price worth paying, to not have to share the cabin with the Wagner Neanderthals.

Their leader was a particularly odious man, who made Knut feel uncomfortable. The feeling was made worse by the burn scars that covered the man's neck and one side of his head. His ear was a shrivelled knot of scar tissue, that made Knut think of the chewing gum he found stuck under his desk in school.

The man's name was Pavlov. When they'd met for the first time, the man had tried to make a joke, saying that he was a dog who salivated only for war.

Under other circumstances, Knut would have asked the Wagner Commanders for someone else, but at such short notice he'd had to take what they could give him. They were desperate to avenge the death of their comrades, in particular Major Andreyev who they seemed to hold in demi-god like esteem.

Knut wondered how he was going to control these men, but while he still didn't know who had attacked his facility, he was taking no chances.

He would have to replace Laila, and made a note to call the broker who had arranged her. She had done her job well, protecting him by taking the bullet from whoever shot at him in the tunnel. He hadn't seen the shooter, as she'd taken him out with some quick shooting of her own. The fact that he'd left her to die on the road didn't register any feeling in him. It was her job to protect him, and she'd done that well. When she was no longer able to do her job, she was no longer of any use to him. It was just a practicality. Still, he thought, he might get the broker to send something to her family, maybe some flowers.

With that thought, Knut pulled on the aviator glasses he'd taken from the co-pilot and closed his eyes. In the dark and near silence, he fell into a restful sleep, dreaming of walking on the beach in Cuba hand in hand, with Rosa.

Chapter Fifty-Seven

Rosa did some shopping at Heathrow Terminal 5, emerging from the changing room of *Armani*, wearing a black parka coat with a fur rimmed hood. She had originally picked up the red coloured version, but Rory told her something more subtle might be better.

'I've no idea what to buy, I've never visited the Highlands,' she told him, as she paid with a credit card she knew Knut could track.

'Warm and dry is all that's important, the Castle is in the middle of nowhere. It's not like there'll be anyone you have to try to impress.'

'Any harm in a girl trying to look her best?'

'Rosa, you know as well as I do, you'd look amazing in a bin bag,' said Rory, then instantly regretting it.

'I'll take that as a sort of compliment,' said Rosa, arching an eyebrow and pouting.

Rory turned, walking to the entrance of the store, he scanned the mass of swarming people moving through the terminal. He registered no threats, but knew, almost hoped, there could be someone watching them. The sunglasses he was wearing felt uncomfortably pretentious, indoors. They hid his eyes, allowing him to look around without it being obvious. They would also make it more difficult for any watchers to identify him. He knew he had no social media presence, and his image wouldn't appear anywhere online linked to the Police. He had almost considered wearing a kilt to go the whole hog, but he'd never been comfortable in a heavy woollen skirt.

Rosa appeared beside him and slipped her arm through his. 'Well your Lordship, what does a girl have to do to get a glass of champagne in this place?'

Rory had a last look around, then got back into character. They were leaving a trail of breadcrumbs for Knut to follow in case he didn't catch the text message sent to Rosa's friend Maddie. The text had told Maddie where they were headed, and how Rosa had been whisked off her feet, by a dashing Scottish Laird. Making a show of gallantly and taking Rosa's bags, Rory smiled, like the very lucky guy everyone who saw them together thought he was.

Rather than use the first class lounge, they took a seat on stools at the Champagne and Seafood bar. The more public space felt safer and the plan was to be seen together. They wanted to make sure Knut had as much chance as possible to spot them, and know where to find them.

Rosa sipped her champagne while Rory had a coffee.

'Darling, you could have just the one glass?' said Rosa, loud enough for everyone at the bar to hear.

'Oh no, it's a drive to Castle Subhain, and it wouldn't do for the locals to see their Laird arrested for drink driving.'

'Tell me again about the estate darling,' said Rosa, placing her hand on his thigh.

Rory felt an uncomfortable but pleasurable rush at her touch, his cheeks reddened a little.

'Well, as you will soon see my dear, the Castle occupies an island within the loch-'

'Oh, say that word again darling, I do love it when you sound all Scottish!' purred Rosa.

Rory laughed, but played along despite thinking Rosa was overdoing it. 'Loch Maree is in the west of the estate. The total land is just over 3000 acres of prime Highland wilderness.'

'Is there a monster in the loch?' Rosa teased, feigning fear at the thought.

'Ocht no, there's only Nessie, she sits happily on the bottom of Loch Ness, waiting to gobble up unsuspecting *Sassenachs*!' Rory made a scary face and lifted his hands towards Rosa, who planted a kiss on his cheek.

'What was that for?' he asked taken aback.

'That my dear Rory, was to say thank you for everything you are doing to help me,' whispered Rosa, as she leaned in to wipe the lipstick from his cheek. 'Hamilton told me you weren't keen on this trip.'

'I just have a lot of work to do,' said Rory.

'Your final case, I know. Hamilton told me that too. I hope this is all concluded very soon, so you can get back to what you're supposed to be doing. Doesn't your wife mind you taking off like this?'

'I'm divorced, and if we don't get this right I'll never be retiring, because all hell will let loose.'

'I'm sorry, about your divorce I mean. I didn't mean to get personal.'

'Occupational hazard, don't worry, it's all in the past now.'

'But soon you'll have a change of occupation.'

'Yes, time for a change.'

'Then perhaps you will remarry?' asked Rosa.

'Who knows, I think I'm maybe a bit past it to be honest. How about you?'

'Am I past it?' Rosa gave him a look of mock offence.

'You know what I meant. You'll have men tripping over themselves to propose.'

'There are men, and then there are *men*, Rory. You never know when you'll meet the right one, but I'll be in no rush.'

'How did you meet Knut Bergstrom?'

'It's a long story, but suffice to say he found me when I was in a low place. I had split up with my ex who, let's just say, didn't treat me very well. Along came Knut and he seemed to just *know* me. He knew just what to say, what to do...it was like he could read my mind.'

'He probably was.'

'What do you mean?'

'Knut has the ability to hack your social media, your telephone messages, and those of your friends. He had the inside track, positioning himself accordingly.'

'That's too horrible to contemplate. You know, I once loved him, and thought he loved me.'

'I think he still does. Let's face it, he's not exactly in your league, so he tried to level up the playing field. I'm sure lots of men would do the same, given the opportunity.'

'Would you?' asked Rosa.

Rory's phone buzzed on the bar top announcing that their flight was boarding.

'Saved by the bell.'

CHAPTER FIFTY-EIGHT

The flight to Germany had been relatively comfortable in the Team Luftwaffe Airbus A400M Atlas transport. The four huge propellers of the Europrop TP400-D6 engines meant it had a cruising speed of 485 mph. Thanks to being almost empty, the pilot was pushing the aircraft over 500 mph, at almost 40,000 feet.

The team had made themselves comfortable, sleeping most of the way, before the very friendly German crew served them a breakfast of coffee and NATO biscuits. On landing at the now disused German air force base, they were met by an RAF C-17 Globemaster. The C-17 with its Pratt and Whitney turbofan engines was a beast, with a top speed of 600mph. It was big enough to accommodate 102 paratroopers, so there was plenty of room for the six man Vigilant team. Inside they were issued flying suits and parachutes, which they all checked over before stowing them safely.

The British Airforce personnel outdid their German counterparts, by providing hot bacon rolls and stainless steel mugs of tea. For JT, this was like the start of so many missions, although he was never a huge fan of jumping out of a perfectly serviceable aircraft. He was looking forward to using the jump skills he'd first mastered, what seemed like a lifetime ago.

The loadmaster told them the flight time would be around two hours, and that the weather report was *reasonable*.

Reasonable wasn't the same as good, and JT started to think they were being too rushed, yet again. He reached up to massage his shoulder, which was still tender from catching Easy back in Grand Cayman, and caught a questioning look from Taff.

He gave him a nod and a thumbs up, then went back to massaging the shoulder.

Once they were allowed to move around the aircraft from their sidewall seats, Taff appeared with some Ibuprofen he'd commandeered from the flight crew. 'Get these down your neck Boss,' he said, pushing the two caplets into JT's hand.

'Thanks Taff.'

'How is it?'

'Still a bit tender. I don't have full range of movement yet but it's on the mend.'

'You best go easy on it when we deploy chutes.'

'Easier said than done,' said JT.

'What's the plan when we're on the ground?'

'Well, if Hamilton's right, then Bergstrom will be coming to the castle to try to get Rosa, to get her to Cuba. Laila Acker said he'd told her he had to be on the way to Cuba within 48 hours, so we'll know soon enough if he's coming.'

'He'll not be coming alone. Not his style,' said Taff.

'No, but we don't know who he has with him. My money is on more of the Wagner guys. That means they'll be well trained and up for the fight.'

'Well, Castles were made for defending against armies, so at least we have that advantage.'

'True, but the armies of 12th century Scotland had swords and axes, maybe arrows. These guys will have automatic weapons, and lord knows what else.'

'Laird,' said Taff.

'Sorry?'

Taff winked, flashing his trademark smile, 'Laird knows what else! Wouldn't want to offend Rory, or our Celtic cousins.'

Chapter Fifty-Nine

Knut and the Wagner troops piled into the Kamov Ka-62 helicopter, waiting for them at Dublin International Airport. The helicopter was courtesy of one of the Russian Oligarchs who called Dublin one of his many homes. He had also greased enough palms to make sure the men avoided Border Control checks.

The weaponry the men had brought with them, was supplemented with two Rocket Propelled Grenades. These however weren't the original Russian RPG-7, rather, these were the American clone, the Precision Shoulder-fired Rocket Launcher better known as the PSRL-1. No self-respecting Russian would ever admit it, but the American version was lighter, at just over six kilograms, and being designed to separate into two pieces, made it much easier to transport.

Knut had received word that Rosa, and an unkown male, had been picked up in a Land Rover registered to the Subhain Castle Estate. That was where she had text her friend Maddie that she was heading with a man called *Ruaridh*.

Knut didn't know who this man *Ruaridh* was, but a search of the land register had confirmed him as the Laird, and owner of the estate and castle.

None of this made much sense, how could Rosa have met this man, then so quickly agreed to run away with him to a Scottish Castle.

He still hadn't worked out who had attacked them in Nigeria. His not knowing was eating at him. It wasn't the authorities or he'd never have been allowed to leave Niger. In fact, his jet would have been grounded in Nigeria. No, something else was going on here It was making him nervous and angry in equal measure.

Knut looked at his watch, the code had been activated more than 16 hours ago. In less than 32 hours, the world would be hit with the biggest shock it had seen since the asteroid caused the Dinosaur extinction event.

Pavlov was passing the iPad pro around his men to show them the aerial photos of the castle. There was a helipad on the little island where the castle stood but that was too risky when they didn't know what lay in store for them.

Instead, they would land in the next valley or *glen,* as the Scots apparently called them, then make their way on foot the mile or so around the hill that formed one bank of the loch. There were fishing boats, tied up to a wooden jetty in the aerial photographs, that they hoped would still be there to transport themselves to the island. If they weren't, then they'd need a new plan. If all else failed, they would just have to use the helicopter and overpower whoever was there.

If there was nothing else Knut could be sure of, it was that these Wagner men were looking for a fight, and pity help whoever got in their way. They were under very strict instructions not to harm Rosa, but everyone else was fair game.

Especially this *Ruaridh* guy. In fact, thought Knut, he might enjoy killing the man himself.

Chapter Sixty

Rory and Rosa approached the Castle, courtesy of a boat rowed by Angus Robertson, the warden of the castle.

Angus was, as ever, clad in green tweed, wearing a plaid shirt with a knitted woollen tie. His *bunnet*, or flat cap, was old with a frayed edge on the peak. The hat also held three beautiful fishing lures known as flies. Each of the flies were colourful representations of gourmet salmon and trout food.

'What are those feathers in your cap?' asked Rosa.

'You'll be meaning the flies,' replied Angus, without turning his head to face her. 'They're hooks for fishing.'

'Do you fish here, in the lake?'

'Not here in the *loch*, no. I fish the river that feeds into the loch.'

'Each one is a designed to look just like a real fly. Angus ties them himself, don't you?' said Rory.

'Aye, gives me something to do in the evenings, there's not so much else to do up here.'

'You have the TV now since we installed the satellite dish.' said Rory.

'That things a carbunkle, no good to man nor beast!' Angus retorted, with some emotion.

'That *carbunkle* means you can always communicate with the outside world.'

'Pah!'

'What if you were to get hurt and need medical attention?' asked Rory.

'There's a public telephone box ten miles down the road. If I can't get to there, then help would be too late getting here anyway.'

'Have it your own way,' said Rory, 'I reckon you probably watch Coronation Street of an evening!'

'They're beautiful, like little works of art.' Rosa said, as she leaned forward examining the flies on Angus's hat, and trying to change the subject.

'Thank you, kind words indeed. As long as the salmon fancy them then they're worth the effort.'

'Are there fish in the lock too?' asked Rosa.

'There's a fair few, the salmon and trout cross the *loch* from the sea, to head up stream for spawning. There's more sport in the river though. I'll be needing to teach you how to pronounce some words properly, if you're to be the Lady of the Castle.' Angus winked at Rory.

Rory rolled his eyes, shaking his head at Angus which earned him a giggle from Rosa.

'Rosa is just visiting Angus, she'll be keen to get back to her jet set lifestyle, just as soon as this is all over.'

'The Castle has a strange power over people, mind Mr Maxwell. Folk fall in love with the place, some even fall in love - in the place!' He tried, but failed, to hide his grin as he enjoyed seeing Rory squirm.

'Oh really, and how is your love life Angus?' asked Rory, attempting to turn the tables.

'Just fine, Mr Maxwell, just fine. You're sharing a boat with the three creatures I love most.' Angus laughed, but anyone who knew Angus would know he was being deadly serious.

Rory had only met Angus once since he assumed ownership of the castle, but already had the utmost respect for the man. He had been recommended by Hamilton, to look after the place, and be on hand to oversee the renovations.

Rosa sat quietly in the bow, flanked by Angus's two Flat Coated Retrievers called *Tor* and *Hamish*. *Skipper* the Jack Russell, sat in her lap, fully alert taking in every sight and sound of the crossing.

'You'll be liking the progress I think, Mr Maxwell.' said Angus, leaning back to pull on the oars.

It was a short journey of 150 metres from the little wooden jetty off the shingle beach, but like many Scottish lochs it ran very deep.

'Please Angus, I've asked you before, Mr Maxwell was my father's name, call me Rory. Is she wind and water tight?'

'I won't be doing that Mr Maxwell. You're Laird here, it wouldn't do for me to be calling you anything but Mr Maxwell. The roof is on and windows replaced, but even with walls nigh on eight foot thick there's no such thing as weatherproof here in a storm. Talking of which, you've timed your arrival well,' he turned his face to the sky and sniffed at the breeze, 'there's rain coming. It feels like a good blaw on its way.'

'What's a good blaw?' asked Rosa.

'It'll be windy,' explained Rory.

'That'll be an understatement I'm thinking, mind you, I'm no Michael Fish!' Angus gave a great guffaw and pulled on the oars, guiding them without looking over his shoulder, to the little bay beneath the Castle wall.

All three dogs suddenly sprung to life, standing rigid with ears pointed, looking eastwards up the loch.

'Here they come,' said Angus, still focused on his rowing.

'Here who come?' asked Rosa.

As if to answer her question, the distant almost indiscernible sound of engines reached them. The noise grew slowly, then all at once was above them as the C-17 flew low over the Castle, before climbing out of the glen and making a turn.

'You've to raise the standard Mr Maxwell,' said Angus. 'She's on the pole waiting for you. Best be quick now; the team will be wanting to see the wind direction.'

The row boat glided with a practiced crunch onto the shingle beach. Rory jumped overboard, knee deep in the cold water of the loch, before running full tilt up the steps of the castle, to reach the big iron studded oak door. The castle had been rebuilt in the 15th century on the site of an earlier iteration. The fact that the door was original, was testament not only to the tough oak and the carpenters who created it, but also to the clever way the castle had been built. The 27 steps from ground level to the doorway into the castle proper, ran in a diagonal up one wall of its square design. The door was set back three feet into the wall, placed in the South East corner of the building. This was the most sheltered position, away from the ravages of prevailing wind and rain when the winter storms lashed in from the sea.

Through the door, Rory had another two flights, of 27 well-worn stairs, to reach the door out of the bulkhead, onto the freshly leaded roof.

He located the flag pole, wrestling momentarily with the ropes before finding the one cord that pulled and released the flag to be raised. He hoisted the flag, tying off the ropes before standing back to look at the flag. Rory hadn't seen it in situ before, and felt a pang of pride at seeing the Maxwell family crest flying over the castle. He knew the Maxwell clan seat was in the Lowlands of the Scottish Borders, but through some bizarre circumstances he was now Laird here in the North West Highlands. The name Maxwell originated from a 11th century Norse chief called Maccus. It made Rory smile to think that almost a millenium after they first tried, a descendant of the Norsemen had conquered Castle Subhain.

The C-17 banked to fly another pass over the castle, the pilot giving a little roll of the wings to indicate he'd seen the flag. The pilot wouldn't be able make out the detail of the crest or clan motto; a stag lying in a holly bush, *Riveresco – I flourish again*.

Rory ran back down stairs, to join Rosa and Angus as they watched the aircraft turn in a slow circle. It reached the desired altitude before six tiny specks appeared from the open cargo bay door, instantly transforming into bobbing canopies, floating toward the earth.

'I'll go fetch them,' said Angus, as he headed back down to the boat. 'Tor and Hamish will look after you until I'm back, but don't let them near the venison on the table,' he called over his shoulder.

Rory and Rosa stood watching the canopies drift across the eastern end of the loch. They dipped behind a thick stand of silver birch trees that grew at the end of the carse, a marshy area where the river entered the loch.

With nothing more to see, they turned and crossed the threshold into the castle.

Chapter Sixty-One

The loadmaster had waved them out of the rear of the aircraft and watched as the canopies opened one after the other. He watched them start their descent as he pressed the close button, lifting the ramp back into place.

Once the ramp was confirmed closed, the pilot lifted the aircraft higher before banking south and west, following the Scottish coastline. Half an hour later the aircraft touched down at RAF Machrihanish, near Campbelltown in the Mull of Kintyre. As they touched down, a helicopter was travelling toward them, over the Irish Sea; heading north to Scotland.

On the ground, the Vigilant team pulled in their canopies, gathering them into a pile which they dragged into the trees before dropping a fallen bough on top of them to keep them in place.

Through the trees they found Angus waiting for them in the Land Rover. 'Welcome back lads,' he said, from the open driver's window.

'Good to see you Angus,' said JT, climbing in to the passenger seat.

Angus noted JT's discomfort as he reached to pull the vehicle door closed.

The rest of the team jumped into the rear, filling the bench seats. From a box beneath their feet, they pulled Heckler and Koch MP7 submachine guns, passing them out.

'I've given them all a wipe down, they're clean and test fired this morning. I have laser sights at the castle if you want them, the other rifles are there too. The sniper rifles are in the box on the roof.'

'How many?' asked JT.

'Two Accuracy International Arctic Warfares. I've swapped out the Zeiss scopes they arrived with, for the original Schmidt and Bender PMII. There's two 10 round box magazines for each of them, with 7.62 NATO rounds.'

'Good work Angus,' called Rambo, from the rear seat.

'There's 40 round mags there too, and spare 20s in the backpacks for the H and Ks.'

'Thanks Angus, when did Rory and Rosa arrive?'

'About half an hour ago, I rowed them over, left the dogs to look after them.'

'Apart from Skipper here?' said JT, stroking the Jack Russell sat in his lap. 'Anything from Hamilton?'

'No, he sent me a message about when to expect you, but nothing since.'

'Well, we know Bergstrom landed at Dublin almost two hours ago, so have to assume he's on his way. Easiest and quickest way to get here is by chopper, where would you land Angus?'

The old soldier had been a paratrooper, and a decorated hero from the Falklands war. He had lived at the castle just a few months, but already knew the place like the back of his hand.

'Assuming they're not daft enough to try the helipad on the island, then they might try to land on the carse, but as you've just found out it's pretty boggy, certainly couldn't safely take a chopper. 'If I were them, I'd land over *Beinn Llath* there,' he pointed out the windscreen at a hulking dark hill, "the glen beyond is dry. There's enough flat ground, obvious from a satellite image or good old Ordnance Survey map.'

'How long would it take on foot, to get to the boats from there?'

'You could yomp it in 40 minutes easy enough going round, or if you're a mountain goat, you could go over the top in 20.'

'Let's assume they don't know this place, what's their plan?' asked JT.

'Depends on who they are,' said Angus, then paused to think. 'If they're expecting you lot to be here, then they'll set up on the shore, so they can get some long weapons on the castle. They'll need to send a team across the loch to storm the castle, or hope they can persuade the occupants to surrender. Then it's down to numbers, and kit I suppose.'

'They can't know we're here, so we have the element of surprise on our side. I reckon our best option is to split their force. We also know they're on the clock, so won't be planning to lay siege for long.'

'If we take the boats over to the island they'll have to swim it, or build a raft,' suggested Angus.

'No, I think we should leave them a boat. If we can split them up, by giving them a chance to reach the island easier, then we can be waiting for them.'

'With rifles on the roof of the castle, and a few of us on the high ground here behind them, we can light work of them I'm sure.' Angus said slowing the vehicle, to avoid a swan standing guard near it's cygnets.

'We need Bergstrom alive; he still has the code, we need him to tell us where it is.'

'You think he'll tell you?'

'I can be very persuasive Angus,' said JT, 'there are thousands, maybe even millions, of lives at risk. We won't be worrying about Geneva Conventions.'

Chapter Sixty-Two

Rory almost bumped into the back of Rosa, when she stopped, frozen at the door of the kitchen. The room was illuminated by lights under the modern kitchen cabinets. They cast their glow across the huge old kitchen table in the middle of the room.

Looking over her shoulder, Rory could see the cause of her discomfort. On the table lay the carcass of a deer. The carcass had obviously been skinned and hung as there was no blood.

'I hope you're not a vegetarian?' Rory asked.

'No, but I could be persuaded,' she replied, still making no effort to move beyond the kitchen door while considering what to do next.

Her mind was made up, thanks to a nudge from Tor and Hamish, as the big black dogs pushed their way in. They took up positions like sentries, sat by the table staring at the overhanging leg of the deer.

Rosa laughed, moving forward to stroke the dogs, rewarded by whooshing tails and happy panting.

'There'll be treats in the cupboard over there,' pointed Rory.

Rosa opened the tall larder cupboard, finding some home baked bone shaped biscuits. She held out both hands, with a biscuit in each. The dogs moved to sit in front of her, simultaneously lifting their front paws off the floor, in a well-rehearsed beg manoeuvre.

Rosa gave each of them their biscuit, surprised by how gently they took them, then watched as they went to lie on a blanket under the table.

'Don't let Angus catch you feeding them too many treats, they're working dogs.'

'Tell me again, how you come to have this place, and Angus?'

'It's in my name, but it's not really mine. It belongs to the whole team.'

'Vigilant?'

'Yes, Vigilant. We took down a gang about three months ago, they had bought this place as a way of laundering their money. Hamilton sorted things so that it was transferred into my name.'

'Who were the gang?'

'They called themselves the Kosanians. They were Albanian people traffickers; you know about the hotel right?'

'The Spa place? Yes, Hamilton has suggested I might want to run the place.'

'That's a great idea. It needs some work after what happened there. Do you know about the women and children?'

'No, not really.'

'Maybe better you don't know.'

'I'm a big girl Rory, I'd rather know.'

'Ok, well the Kosanians had a set the place up, with women and kids being kept for the sex trade. Some had been trafficked in to the country, others were snatched from the streets.

'Oh my god! But you saved them, and arrested these Kosanians?'

'We rescued the women and kids yes, the Kosanians were all killed, along with a paedophile Sheik and his friends.'

'How come I didn't hear anything about this, it must have been on the news?'

'It was written off as a gang war incident. The explosion means there's a team still trying to identify all of the body parts.'

'You seem ok with it, with all of those people dying I mean,' said Rosa, scrutinising his face.

'I've seen a lot of death Rosa, a lot of victims and a lot of human tragedy. These people were sub-human. There's no way a true human being could treat other people the way they did. They are no loss to society.'

Rosa considered this, then asked, 'Did you kill any of them?'

'One, but it was self-defence, she was trying to kill me.'

'She?' asked Rosa horrified.

'She was a Police Officer, or at least she'd joined the Police. Her allegiance was always to the Kosanians, they had planted her in the Met. There was at least one other bent cop involved, he was killed there too, when the Kosanians turned on him. They kidnapped me and were planning to kill me, but I escaped. Thanks to some good fortune and a big help from Easy, I survived.'

'He had a big part in saving me too. Did you know I also had to kill someone?'

'Yes, but in self-defence.'

'Yes, self-defence, but it still makes me sick to think about it.'

'Then try not to think about it, besides we have a long night ahead of us. We'll need clear heads if we're to survive and avert disaster.' Rory took his phone from his pocket checking the signal.

'You can get mobile signal, way out here?'

'Only because of some satellite gizmo Easy set up on the roof.'

'He's quite something that boy isn't he?' said Rosa.

'That he is, but don't let him hear you calling him a boy, he's quite smitten with you, I'm told.'

'I'm old enough to be his mother! He and I are friends, in a very platonic sense.'

'Glad to hear it,' said Rory.

He blushed at the good natured questioning arch of her eyebrow.

'I wouldn't want to see him get hurt is all,' said Rory, turning away to look out of the window. Changing the subject, he continued, 'Let's get this cooking over the fire, there's a clever fan assisted spit roast thing that Angus contrived. It'll be ready in a few hours and the team will want to eat if they get a chance.'

'Where does the electricity come from?' asked Rosa spotting a microwave on the kitchen worktop.

'We put a mini hydro plant on the river. Spent a few weeks building a dam in the summer, getting eaten alive by midges. They seem to like the taste of me!'

'Could you see yourself living here?'

'No, it's a bit remote for me, and it's no fun being midge food from June to August.'

'What about at Palmerston House? Hamilton tells me there's a separate house in the grounds.'

'That's more my thing, easily commutable to London, but rural enough to escape to.'

'That's sounds more my cup of tea too.'

'Talking of tea, can you check that pantry, see if there's any Lapsang Souchong in there? JT is very particular about his tea!'

Chapter Sixty-Three

The pilot spoke to Knut via the radio headset, '45 minutes out sir, where do you want me to put her down?' His soft Russian accent was discernible, but there was something of an Irish lilt in there too. He'd obviously been in Ireland for some time, thought Knut.

'Pavlov reckons the best point is the helipad on the island, but we don't know what sort of welcome party awaits us. What about this other place he suggested, in the valley beyond the hill?'

'That looks viable sir, but I'll only really know when we get a visual of the ground. I can't land if the ground is too soft, this thing might topple, then we'd be in all sorts of trouble.'

'Yes, aircraft crashes are all too common, and about to become more so,' said Knut, almost to himself.

'Sorry?' asked the confused pilot.

'Oh nothing, just put us down safely, as close to the castle as you can, then be ready to take off as soon as we return. We will have an extra passenger, and need to return to Dublin, as soon as humanly possible.'

'I know your jet is fuelled and ready for take-off sir.'

'I will need a helicopter pilot when I move to Cuba. Perhaps you will consider a change of location?'

'Mr Lekyovitch pays me well sir. He looks after my family, back in mother Russia.'

'I understand,' said Knut, knowing exactly the sort of loyalty demanded by the Russian oligarchs, and what happened to the families of those who disobeyed them.

Knut wondered how he'd become so embroiled with these Russians. What had started out as simple security contract, had become messy as their greed, and thirst for power, meant they tried to lean on him. They were about to become even richer, as they positioned themselves shorting the stock markets, especially the airline stocks. They had already made a fortune from the invasion of Ukraine, with the pathetically obvious sanctions imposed by the US and the EU. Knut knew they had front run options on oil and gas sales, knowing the prices would soar. They'd had super yachts and aeroplanes impounded across the world, but those losses were dwarfed by the profits involved.

Russians were obsessed with money, because they thought it would buy them power, but Knut knew that he had the power to *create* money. The sort of money these people could only dream of. He literally had the power to control the future, to control the world. A picture appeared in his mind; of how Rosa would be when her gave her the money, and the power, to transform the lives of the ordinary Cubans. He would become King, and she his beautiful benevolent Queen, in their island paradise.

His thought was rudely interrupted by Pavlov tapping him on the shoulder. The man was mouthing something at him, but Knut couldn't hear him as he was wearing his headset.

Knut looked at the man with his badly scarred face. From this angle, Pavlov's ear resembled the knotted part of a child's balloon. Could he still hear anything on that side, Knut wondered. Pavlov didn't turn his head to the side as Knut would expect someone with only one functioning auditory organ to do. Neither did he appear to have any balance issues. Knut's eyes wandered to Pavlov's good ear. The external ear, which Knut suddenly remembered was called the *Helix*, was scarred in a different way. The soft roll of skin and cartilage, that gave the ear its shell shape, was deformed in the way common among wrestlers, or maybe rugby players. Knut had heard it referred to as a *cauliflower ear,* but it looked nothing like a brassica as far as he was concerned. Instead, it looked the shape of juicy ripe mussel in its shell.

Knut could see Pavlov was getting annoyed and still mouthing away. Without any facial expression, Knut pointed to his headset.

It took Pavlov a second or two to grasp the situation, before he reached up and lifted a spare headset from its hook on the roof.

Pavlov continued to shout, as he had been doing prior to using the headset. Both Knut and the pilot pulled their headphones away from their ears.

Knut gave Pavlov a calm down signal with his hand, and blew out an exasperated sigh. The man was an ignoramus, like so many of the Wagner Group that he'd met. They were, at times, a necessary evil, but the sooner he could rid himself of them the better, he thought.

'My men want to know if we can take what we find at the castle,' he said, eventually.

'What do you expect to find there?' asked Knut, somewhat intrigued.

'I want one of those Braveheart swords, like Mel Gibson, from the movie. Like William Walls!'

'Wallace, his name was William Wallace.'

'I don't give a shit what his name was, I want his fucking sword, ok?'

'Do your job Mr Pavlov, and you can take whatever you like, within reason.'

'What do you mean *reason*? *Reason* is I want it. If I want it, I take it!'

'If it can fit in the helicopter, then help yourself. Just remember, we will have an extra passenger for the return journey back to Dublin.'

'Da, da,' said Pavlov, pulling off his headset.

'Dada indeed, that face looks like Dali had a bad dream,' sighed Knut.

The pilot laughed, and when Knut realised he'd spoken aloud, he looked back to check Pavlov hadn't heard.

'Nekulturny!' laughed the pilot. In response to Knut's blank look he continued, 'He is without culture. He would not know about Dali, or the Dada movement. His type knows only violence.'

'You know about art?' asked Knut, suddenly finding the pilot more interesting.

'Not all Russians are ignorant peasants, Mr Bergstrom.'

'Of course not, forgive my sounding surprised. I have spent too much time with men like Pavlov, of late.'

'No apology is necessary. Men like these have become the international face of Mother Russia. The world sees us as trouble makers and a threat, but the average Russian, he just wants to live in peace. Same as the people of the West. If you give Russian's enough food to feed their family, a house they can call home, and a little Vodka to keep out the cold, then they are happy.'

'What did you say your name was?' asked Knut.

'My name is Timo Yermakov.'

"Yermakov...' repeated Knut, searching his mind to see if the name was familiar.

'I am a descendant of Yermak Timofeyevich. He was a Cossack who conquested Siberia, with Ivan Grozny.'

'Ivan the Terrible.'

'Yes, you know history!' Yermakov said, impressed.

'A little.'

'You know that Grozny does not mean *terrible*, not in the way English speakers think? A better word might be, *formidable*, I think.'

Knut pondered this, wondering how history might name him. His plan was to walk away, without leaving any evidence of his involvement in what the code unleashed. But a King, creating a brand new Kingdom, a great and powerful Kingdom, that would surely be something for history books. Which took him back to the attack in Nigeria. No-one knew of his real plans. Apart that is, from Rosa. Who would she tell? Who would believe her? There was no way any Government could move against him, not as quickly as had just happened in Nigeria. None of it made sense. He needed answers, and there was only one person who could provide them, Rosa.

Chapter Sixty-Four

Angus pulled over at the side of the road, then stood on the footplate to reach the roof box. He handed the rifles down to Rambo and Cooky, who checked them over then put them back in their carry covers, slinging them on their backs.

'Hang on boys,' he said, reaching into the box and pulling out a rucksack. 'There's ponchos and netting in there. The hides on the ridge will give you some cover, but the storm will be here,' he paused, looked down the loch, out toward the sea, 'in about half an hour.'

'I can feel it,' said Rambo. His life in Nepal, and with the Gurkhas before joining the SAS, had been saved a few times by being able to read the weather.

'Thanks for these,' said Cooky, throwing the rucksack over his shoulder, then trotting off behind Rambo.

'They'll be at the hides in 15 minutes. A chopper will be easy enough to see, unless the storm gets too rough up there,' said Angus, climbing back into the driver's seat.

'Are you expecting a big storm?' asked JT.

'Aye, there's going to be a fair dump of rain. As usual up here, it'll be horizontal. It'll be gone by morning, but I'll likely have roads to fix. The culverts will struggle.'

'Will their chopper be able to fly?'

'I wouldn't be happy flying in it, but it's not impossible, if they can get off the ground safely.'

They arrived at the boats tied up at the small wooden jetty.

'Where shall I park the Landy?' asked Angus.

'Leave it where you normally would. We want it to look as if we're not expecting them.'

'I'd usually leave her on the hard standing back there.'

'That's as good a place as any, would you normally leave the keys inside?'

'Aye, sure there's no-one up here to steal it,' said Angus with a grin.

'Do that then, I want them to feel as relaxed as possible when they come over.'

'I'd suggest two trips to get us all over then, leave one of the boats here for them.'

'I agree, they'll be able to come over maximum four at a time.'

'Hit them while they're crossing? They'll be sitting ducks.'

'If we can, we'll let the first group get ashore. They'll either leave three, and have one row back to collect the others, or send both boats back to bring their full force over.'

The team jumped from the Land Rover, everyone climbing into the row boat, leaving just Taff on the shore to park the vehicle, where Angus had suggested. 'Doesn't feel right leaving the keys in the ignition and the doors open,' he said into his radio.

'Nobody steals cars up here. This isn't Swansea!' laughed Posty.

'The old castle was never taken you know,' said Angus as he pulled hard on the oars, 'although a few tried.'

JT looked up toward the imposing stone structure, 'It's not getting taken tonight either.'

Chapter Sixty-Five

A black Jaguar XF Executive, left the Embassy of Ireland at 17 Grosvenor Place, London, driving north past Buckingham Palace Garden toward Piccadilly. In the rear seat sat Padraig O'Mahonney, the recently appointed Irish Ambassador to the UK. O'Mahonney looked a little flustered when he entered the car, immediately pressing the button to lift the privacy screen between himself and the driver.

'I'm in the car Hamilton,' he said, into his phone.

'Excellent, I will meet you at London City Airport in, let's say, one hour.'

'I hope you realise the scrutiny I'll be under, for using the Government jet. There's a perfectly good Aer Lingus service from Heathrow to Dublin.'

'Of course, and I very much appreciate your assistance in this matter.'

'When this is done, we're quits remember, I will no longer be in your debt.'

'Patrick,' said Hamilton, deliberately using the anglicised version of his name, 'you and I go back a long way. Without me, you would not be sitting in that diplomatic vehicle, in fact you'd be lucky to be sitting anywhere at all.'

'That was all a long time ago.'

'Ah yes, indeed it was. Patrick, do you know the Japanese concept of *On*?'

'No, what does that mean?'

'*On*, is a sense of obligation, according to the Japanese. It is a grave matter in their culture, not to fully repay a debt, an obligation that some carry to the grave.'

'You can't keep doing this Hamilton,' said O'Mahonney, 'things are different now!'

Hamilton continued, as if he hadn't heard him, 'Do you know the work of *Yosa Buson*?'

'You know fine well I have no idea what you're talking about. We weren't all educated at Oxbridge you know.'

'Patrick, you have a 1st class Honours degree, from Trinity College Dublin. Political Science, wasn't it? Perhaps, if you had spent some time in the Humanities Department your path may have been more, how can I put it; enlightened?'

'Get on with it! What the hell are you on about Hamilton?'

'*Yosa Buson* was a highly regarded Japanese poet, and painter, of the 18th century *Edo* period. Not as well-known as *Matsuo Basho* or *Kobayashi Issa* perhaps, but some of his *Haiku* are quite wonderful. You do know what-'

'Yes, I've heard of bloody *Haiku*, we Irish are not as backwards as you Brits like to make out.'

'Indeed Patrick, indeed. As I was saying, *Yosa Buson* wrote some excellent *Haiku* but my personal favourite is,' Hamilton spoke in flowing Japanese, '*Fuji hitotsu, Uzumi nokoshite, Wakaba kana.*'

'Okay I submit,' said O'Mahonney, after a pause. 'What does it mean?'

'It translates quite well to English thus; *Only Mount Fuji, is left unburied, by young leaves.*'

Hamilton left a quiet pause for a few seconds, before continuing gravely, 'The lesson I take from it, and I believe you should too, my dear Patrick, is that no matter how hard we try, some things just cannot be buried.'

O'Mahonney let his chin sink to his chest, screwing his eyes shut.

After another pause, Hamilton spoke again, this time sounding friendly and jolly, 'Now Patrick, I intend stopping at Pret a Manger, to pick up a sandwich. Their Reuben on Rye is quite excellent. What can I fetch for you?'

'I'm not hungry,' said a deflated O'Mahonney. Could Hamilton know about Pret a Manger? He couldn't, there was no way, O'Mahonney thought to himself, he'd been too careful.

'Come now Patrick, I hear you're a regular visitor, you enjoy a Chicken and Avocado with Basil sandwich, I believe.'

'How the hell do you know?' hissed O'Mahonney.

'How I know, is not important Patrick. What is important, is that I do know. I also know that Miss Li-Mei, or to use her real name, Miss Caihong, prefers soup.'

O'Mahonney sat in stunned silence.

'Now, when today's little adventure is over Patrick, you and I will sit down to have a proper chat, about your taste for the Oriental. I get the feeling, we may be working together a lot more in future. Now, be a good chap and hurry along to the airport, we have a plane to catch!'

Chapter Sixty-Six

As Timo Yermakov hovered his helicopter above the ground, he scanned for a suitable space on the valley floor to set down his wheels. Gently descending the last 12 feet or so, he felt the buffeting wind stronger than it had been before. It required all of his skill to keep the aircraft level. The landing gear made contact with the earth, the suspension moving in a way that told Yermakov the ground was solid enough, as he eased her down.

The first spots of rain hit the windscreen, as the Wagner men jumped out and spread themselves in a circle. The spinning rotors slowed as the aircraft was shut down, Knut Bergstrom electing to wait until they had come to a complete stop, before removing his head set and climbing out.

Heavy rain drops started hitting the men, blown into their faces by the wind.

'Shit,' said Knut, turning up his collar, 'I'm not dressed for this.'

Yermakov appeared beside him, handing him a padded waterproof jacket, 'Use my jacket, Mr Bergstrom,' he half shouted over the wind.

Knut took the jacket and put in on pulling up the hood. 'Thank you Timo, when we get back, you and I must have a proper conversation about you coming to work for me. I will be paying a lot more than Lekyovitch.'

Yermakov smiled and nodded, then returned to his helicopter.

Pavlov approached Bergstrom, 'I will send two of my men up over the hill. They can report anything they see and provide cover as we make our way around. The road begins down there at the end of the valley. We can be at the Castle in maybe 30 minutes, that is, if you can keep up?' Pavlov grinned, obviously in his element at the thought of some violence and pillaging.

'Don't worry about me Pavlov. Let's go!' said Knut, starting to jog down toward the road.

'Suchev, Drachov, you two get up over the top of this hill. We will meet you on the other side, but until we are in position, you provide cover.'

'Da Ser,' said the small but wiry Suchev, and his taller but equally wiry comrade, Drachov. Both men were ex 7th Guards Mountain Air Assault Division, considered the elite among the Russian Airborne Guards Regiments.

They ran off, following a trail that ascended diagonally up the face of the hill. At just over 2500 feet, *Beinn Llath* was classified as a *Corbett*, one level down from the more famous Scottish mountains over 3000ft; the *Munros*.

As they were running up the hill, the two Russians were completely unaware that they were heading straight for Rambo and Cooky's position.

Rambo and Cooky had already passed confirmation of the helicopter's arrival back to the team at the castle. They had counted 13 out of the helicopter, not including the pilot who had returned to the aircraft. One of the 13 stood out from the rest for two reasons, first - he wasn't carrying an assault rifle, and second – he had a hood pulled up against the rain. That marked him as a civilian among the others who acted like professional soldiers.

From their position in the hide, which was no more than a circle of large stones, set around a natural dip in the brow of the hill, Rambo and Cooky watched the Wagner group men split up. They knew exactly where the two climbers would be heading. The plan they decided was to watch them, then follow the two Russians over the hill. The rain, which by now was getting heavier and reducing visibility to 200 metres, made their job both easier, and more difficult. They would need to stay closer than they'd have liked to keep visuals, but the rain masked any sound they made. It also meant that when they stayed still, they were virtually invisible under their ponchos.

The Russians reached the top of the hill, stopping to catch their breath. They checked out the second hide on the brow of the hill, which was closer to the path they'd used. Rambo and Cooky were less than 60m away in the 2nd hide with weapons trained. It would be an easy shot even in the wind and rain, but for the plan to work they had to let the Russians get off the hill, to join their comrades.

One of the Russians pointed out the second hide through the rain, but didn't make the effort to check it out. Had the roles been reversed, the former SAS men would have cleared the hide, not only to ensure the enemy wasn't using it, but for future use should they need to exfil this way and require a defensive position.

The Russians set off again, heading down the hill using the worn path to zig zag down the steep hillside. That meant they would miss the low hide, sat just 150 metres uphill from the road leading to the jetty. It was from there that Angus would shoot ducks and grouse, as opposed to the two high hides which were for hunting deer.

The low hide was where Rambo and Cooky would head for next. They made their way down the slippery grass and heather clad slope, relishing the cover the weather provided.

As the SAS had taught them, there's no such thing as bad weather; just bad kit.

Chapter Sixty-Seven

JT stood at the head of the stone steps that led out onto the roof of Castle Subhain. The rain was causing a steady stream of water to cascade out of the lead fixture and over the side of the castle wall. As Loch Maree was fresh water, there was no need to conserve abundant rain, but JT found himself thinking it seemed wasteful.

He thought of Adanna and her husband back in Nigeria, trying to farm land with increasingly unreliable rain fall, while here there was too much. It seemed it was the way of the world, but JT knew the disparity between the *haves* and *have nots* was widening ever further.

His thoughts were disturbed by Rory Maxwell approaching up the stairs, handing him a mug of steaming tea. 'Lapsang Souchong, for the Captain of the Castle Guard,' said Rory, with a smile.

'Served by the Laird himself!' said JT, taking the mug.

'You know how it is, one simply can't get the staff nowadays.'

'Bloody Brexit!' they said together, with a laugh.

'How's it looking out there?'

'Visibility isn't great, but I can still see the shore and the boat. Once the daylight goes, we won't see much.'

'Do you think they'll come straight over on the boat?'

'If it were me, I'd set up some firing positions on the shore. Give the guys in the first boatload some cover. If they have decent rifles, then they'll set up slightly higher up the hill, allow them to cover the roof. Then, when the first guys are in position, they can cover the next load.'

'That's when we open up on them?'

'Yes, Angus and Joe will be up here with the rifles. As long as they can see, they can take out the guys in the boat. We need Bergstrom alive, so better if we let him come over, or very close, before we start shooting.'

'What if they have snipers?'

'Rambo and Cooky will either neutralise them, or keep them busy. We'll mop up any that retreat into the water. It's not that far to shore but they'd need to be bloody strong swimmers to do it fully dressed and carrying weapons.'

'I've checked the sight-lines from the windows, the only real blind-spot is if they make it to the castle door.'

'Then we'll leave the door open for them, and deal with them when they come in.'

'Good idea, but I'd rather keep them out if possible.' Rory patted the stone wall, 'this old place has been in the family for thirteen hundred years!' he grinned.

'Thirteen weeks more like!' said JT, laughing along.

'My dear old Great, Great Aunt Morag, a hundred times removed, would turn in her grave listening to you!'

Their laughing had attracted the attention of Rosa, who climbed the stairs to join them.

'I didn't expect to hear laughter, not when those men will be here imminently!' she said.

'You've obviously not met anyone as funny as my friend Rory here then,' said JT, slapping Rory on the shoulder.

'Yes, I'm renowned throughout New Scotland Yard, for my stand-up routine!'

'You certainly are a *stand-up guy*,' offered Rosa, in an attempt to match their mirth. She was anxious, but determined not to show it. At the same time she felt safe with these men, and the castle walls, to protect her from Knut.

A radio message from Rambo interrupted them. 'Two who came over the hill are setting themselves up on the ridge above the road. They'll have eyes on you in a few seconds.'

'Roger that,' said JT. He turned to Rosa, 'Ok Rapunzel, time for you to do your thing. Rory, you know which window will give them the best view.'

'Yes, the master bedroom has the biggest window on that side. Follow me Rosa,' said Rory, squeezing past her on the narrow stairs.

Rosa turned to JT, 'I thought he'd never ask,' she said with a wink.

'Sorry?' asked Rory.

'Oh nothing, my liege!' said Rosa, as she followed him.

Chapter Sixty-Eight

'*Na positzi*,' reported Suchev.

'They are in position,' Pavlov translated for Knut.

'Ask your men to speak in English, I want to be able to understand what is going on.'

'You should learn Russian!' said Pavlov, unamused.

'Thank you for the advice Pavlov, but we are a little short of time for language lessons, so English from now on, please,' said Knut, with an obviously fake smile.

'*Kozyol*,' muttered Pavlov, using a classic Russian insult of calling Knut a *goat*.

'Everyone speaks English from now on!' barked Pavlov. 'We are ten minutes out. Any sign of the woman?'

'Standby...yes, there is a woman with blonde hair, at a window near the top of the castle.'

'That will be Rosa!' Knut said, from beneath his hood.

'Any sign of guards?'

'No sign, there was a man briefly at the same window, beside the woman, but no-one else.'

'A boat?'

'Da, there is a rowing boat tied to a jetty Also there is a vehicle parked nearby.'

'Occupied?'

'No, it does not appear so.'

'That will be the Land Rover that brought them from the airport. There was a driver, so that must mean there are at least three people in the castle,' said Knut.

Pavlov led his group of men around a bend in the road and, for the first time, the castle came into view through the rain. He brought them to a halt, behind the cover of huge boulder.

One of the men ran ahead to check the Land Rover. He tried the door, finding it to be open.

'The vehicle is unlocked, keys in ignition,' he reported.

'Ok, now check the boat,' ordered Pavlov.

A few moments later the man reported again, 'It is a rowing boat, there are oars.'

'How big is this boat?' asked Pavlov.

'It could hold three passengers and one rowing I think, at the most.'

'Ok, wait there, I am sending men forward to join you.'

Pavlov turned, pointed to the three men to his left, then pointed forward with a bladed hand. The three men took off at a sprint, quickly covering the 150 metres and climbing aboard the rowing boat. They set off for the island, completely unaware that they were being watched.

Chapter Sixty-Nine

Angus and Joe knelt along the parapet walk of the crenelated roof. Each wore a poncho against the incessant rain, which also let them blend against the dark wet stone and brooding sky. Their rifles were tracking the approaching row boat making its way slowly, across to the island.

The man rowing, who was obviously inexperienced, was fighting against the wind trying keep the boat on a straight course.

'It'll be bloody Christmas before this lot get here,' said Angus.

'I don't think the Wagner Group has a navy, to be fair to them,' replied Joe, without looking round.

Joe trained his Schmidt and Bender PMII scope on the head of the man rowing. From this distance, he could shoot the man's fingers off the oar and put him out of his misery. Raising the rifle, he adjusted the scope and reacquired the OP, where the two Wagner men were lying, getting drenched by the rain. That won't be any fun he thought to himself. He knew some of the Wagner men were seasoned soldiers, and some were ex Russian Special Forces. He also knew they recruited ex-conscripts, who were just expendable cannon fodder, for a Russian Government who had Wagner fight wars on their behalf.

He thought about the women the Wagner guys had raped and abused in Syria, and the indiscriminate killing they employed wherever they went. He had heard they modelled themselves or at least some of their tactics on Genghis Khan. Khan had used his barbaric slaughter of entire cities as a warning to others. It had worked with countless cities surrendering when he approached rather than fight. The Wagner reputation was not exactly in the league of the brutal Mongol warlords, but they were working on it. Today, thought Joe, it would be time for a little payback.

Two storeys below him, JT was also watching the boat's progress, hidden in the dark window of the dining hall. A further storey down, in the vaulted store room, Taff and Posty waited for the order to engage.

Rory took Rosa from the master bedroom, into a smaller anteroom with just tiny window looking out over the loch. He left her there as he headed downstairs, to take up his position covering the front door.

'The main group are waiting up the road,' reported Cooky. 'Two guys in the OP are still in place below us.'

'Roger that Cooky, the boat is landing now,' said JT. He watched the Russians jump from the boat onto the beach, then a brief silent argument take place, apparently over who was going to row the boat back.

'They're either keen not to row, or keen to get into the castle,' said Angus, from the roof.

'Maybe they think there's treasure in here?' said JT.

'In a way there is,' said Rory, instantly regretting his words as he heard JT snigger.

'First three are taking up positions on the beach, using the other boat for cover.'

'Try not to shoot holes in my boats laddies,' said Angus, 'I'm no' such a great swimmer.'

The team watched the row boat set off heading back to the mainland. This time, the man rowing knew what he was about, he covered the distance in half the time. As he pulled up to the jetty, three more of the Wagner men ran forward, boarding the boat.

'Three more on their way over, last four have left cover, heading for the jetty,' said Cooky.

'Roger that,' replied JT, 'it's almost dark, and they're feeling over confident, just how we want them.'

Chapter Seventy

Three more sets of Russian boots jumped ashore on the island, running forward before pressing themselves against the castle wall.

Two of the men waited tight to the wall, while the other ran out to a position from where he could try to cover the castle door.

'Na posit- sorry, in position sir,' the young Wagner soldier quickly corrected himself, in heavily accented English.

One of the two soldiers sheltering against the wall, spotted the recessed door to the storeroom under the castle. He inched forward and tried to push it open with the barrel of his M4 assault rifle. When it didn't budge, he rotated the old iron ring that operated the latch, hearing a clunk before the door fell open by a few inches. He could smell the musty air from inside, in stark contrast to the clean earthy smell of the rain. Replacing both hands on his M4 he pushed the barrel into the gap, slowly widening the opening while trying to peer into the darkness within.

Behind the door, Taff drew his combat knife, setting his feet on the uneven stone floor. He felt his heart rate increase slightly as he readied himself for the kill. Taking a long silent breath to calm himself he gripped his knife hard. If he could have seen his own face, he'd have seen the faintest glimmer of a smile. He watched as the first couple of inches of the barrel appeared. Even in the low light Taff recognised the sight configuration as that of the Knight's Stoner 1. These American assault rifles were the new weapon earmarked for the Royal Marine Commandos. It was a much better weapon than the SA80, according that is, to his Royal Marine pals. The KS1 came ready to accept a 20 or 30 round STANAG magazine. The magazines were created under Standard Agreement to fit all NATO forces weapons to make them interchangeable. Bloody Gucci kit, Taff thought to himself.

How a Wagner operative came to be in possession of one was a question for another time, but it shouldn't have surprised him really. He knew that arms dealers had no morals when it came to selling their wares. Their only interest was in making profits.

'Hold there until I arrive,' said Pavlov. 'I will enter the Castle first.'

Taff didn't hear the order from Pavlov, but watched the barrel being quickly withdrawn. The heavy old door was left ajar.

The wind was blowing in the opposite direction and the door stayed resolutely in position.

Taff moved position to see through the open door, but as darkness fell, he could only make out the faintest outline of the lone tree that marked the end of the little island.

Chapter Seventy-One

'I will wait here until the castle is secure,' said Knut. 'You can send the boat back for me. If at all possible, keep the man who is with my wife alive. I will deal with him personally.'

Pavlov looked at Knut with a newfound admiration, perhaps this little geek was a man after all. He would enjoy finding out if this man had the steel to take another man's life. Looking at Knut, he doubted it, even if the man had been fucking his wife.

After watching Pavlov and the last three Wagner men row away from the jetty, Knut turned to the Land Rover and jogged over to climb into the passenger seat. The inside of the vehicle felt warm, dry and quiet after being out in the rain. Knut took down his hood and searched the vehicle for something to dry his face. He found a towel and rubbed his face dry. It stank of dog and left hairs attached to the bristles of his chin. Picking the dog hair off, Knut felt the stubble on his face and tried to think of when he last had a shower or shave. He had washed up on the jet before arriving in Dublin, but he knew he must be looking dishevelled. It was not the ideal way to meet Rosa, but then he knew she could hardly be interested in him for his looks.

He thought back to when he had first met her. She had been the most perfect creature he had ever seen. When they were introduced, he could barely make eye contact with her and had stumbled over his words. Rather than laugh at him, she had been kind and touched his arm with her fingertips. He could feel the electricity of it, even now.

Getting access to her social media accounts by tapping her mobile phone had been child's play. It had given him access to her innermost thoughts, and the secrets she shared with her girlfriends.

Rosa's friend Maddie had been a particularly rich resource, she had kept all of the previous two years of messages on her phone. Rosa had changed her phone and number twice in that time. It became clear why, when he read the messages from Rosa about her ex-husband. He had abused and humiliated her, as if she were a mere plaything for him, while he slept with countless other would be WAGs. Terry Waltham was one of those preened and coiffed footballers, that Knut detested. Never without a tan, in designer clothes with Rosa on his arm at glittering events when they were together. The early photographs were of a beaming couple with perfect smiles, and Rosa the picture of health and vibrancy.

Within a year, Rosa had started to look subtly different. No longer was she beaming, but started to look a little demure. Photos of them together showed she stood slightly behind Waltham, rather than at his side.

These were tall-tale signs, but Knut also had the advantage of reading the messages to Maddie, which spoke of how belittled she felt and how Waltham had taken over her life. She was stuck and didn't think she had the strength to leave.

Knut had given her that strength, it was he who engineered for her social media account to be flooded with adverts about Domestic Abuse and how to leave an abusive partner. His master stroke had been obtaining the photos of Waltham with the other girls, especially the younger girl, when he was on international duty with England. The package he sent to The Sun and Daily Mirror newspapers, was enough to end the footballers international career. Knut had been disappointed that Chelsea hadn't seen fit to sack him too.

More importantly it pushed Rosa to leave, and when she did, Knut was waiting. He knew all about her favourite things, from music to perfume, food to charities. He created a version of himself that ticked all of her boxes. His manufactured a version of himself, was good enough that she could even see past his mediocre looks.

Now, here he was trying to get her back. Maybe, he thought, he had built her up to be too strong, and that's why she'd found it so much easier to leave him, than she had Waltham. Knut liked the fact that Rosa had her own mind and opinions, he wanted her to be a wife, not a lap dog. From now on though, he would be more careful. He would make sure that she didn't leave him again, that she *couldn't* leave him again. If that was to be by spoiling her, and giving her the sort of life people could only dream of then all good and well. If that didn't work then he would just have to find other ways to persuade her. She was his wife and would be with him, it was that simple.

The noise of the rain hitting the roof of the Land Rover changed as the rain briefly lost its intensity. Knut wiped away the condensation from the window and looked out toward the island, where he could just make out the intimidating hulk of the castle.

What he'd read about the castle online had said the castle had never been taken by a hostile force. He thought about the ancient invaders, blunting their swords and axes trying to breach the walls to no avail.

Today would be different, Knut Bergstrom was one Viking that they hadn't yet met.

Chapter Seventy-Two

When the rowing boat was half way between the shore and the island, JT gave the order to fire.

From their position, less than 100 metres above the two Russians in their OP, Rambo and Cooky couldn't miss. The sound of their suppressed rifles barely carried on the wind and rain, so the Russians on the island were unaware that their comrades had died, without firing a shot.

Joe's first shot from the roof, hit the man rowing the boat in the centre of his back, shattering his spine, before the round continued its trajectory, ending in the right thigh of one of the two rear passengers.

At the same time, Angus had targeted the man in the bow, and watched his head explode taking him tumbling backwards into the boat. Pavlov was a passenger in the rear of the boat threw himself backwards into the black water. The man with the round in his thigh was madly trying to fashion a tourniquet when Angus dispatched him with another head shot. The lifeless body slumped forward coming to rest in a macabre embrace with the oarsman.

Joe tried to locate the man overboard, but was forced to take cover as the men on the beach opened fire, sending rounds sparking off the stone parapet.

Angus changed position before deftly dispatching the closest of the three men sheltering behind the boat on the beach. He was determined not to damage the boat and waited for another Russian head appear. The remaining Russians made a run for it, sprinting hard across the grass before sliding in a heap against the wall, with Angus's rounds chasing their heels.

The man covering the Castle door had his wits about him, he jumped behind a rock, then laid down cover fire in short three round bursts, trying to keep the snipers on the roof occupied. 'Ataka!' he screamed at his colleagues.

The two Russians who had been waiting at the bottom of the external steps made their way up to the Castle door, followed by one of the men who had escaped from behind the boat on the beach. The biggest of them kicked the door open at the second attempt. The force he'd needed to move the big old oak door caused him to lose balance and he stumbled through the door just as JT opened fire with his MP7. The Russian barrelled into JT's legs knocking him off balance. JT tried to bring the muzzle of his MP7 down to fire but the big Russian sprang up with the agility of a gymnast.

Dropping his own weapon, the Russian grabbed JT's MP7 forcing the muzzle higher and a three round burst arced into the ceiling.

Rory took aim at the Russian but he twisted, turning JT round so that he became a human shield.

JT grunted in pain as his damaged shoulder muscle burned, weakened fibres ripping. The wild eyed Russian grinned when he saw the pain in JT's face. JT tried to headbutt him, but the blow was over extended, barely registering any power. He only succeeded in bursting the lip of the Russian, who spat the blood into JT's face. JT had locked his good arm over the MP7 to keep the Russian from ripping it away, and was trying to line up another headbutt, when movement at the door caught his eye.

'Door!' he screamed at Rory, who was still trying to take aim at the Russian wrestling with JT.

Rory span round, firing at the same time as the new Russian. Rory's rounds went high whistling out into the sky above the Russian's head. Thankfully for Rory, the Russian at the door had been distracted by seeing his comrade wrestling, his bullets shredding the heavy tapestry that covered the wall. Rory threw himself forward, into the alcove of the dining room door, firing blind in the direction of the Russian. He missed again, but succeeded in forcing the Russian to take cover, back outside the door.

Rory frantically looked back to check on JT, just in time to see the big Russian pick him up in a bearhug, driving him through the door into the kitchen.

Rory traded fire with the Russian at the door as they both fired blind, neither daring to break cover.

Knowing that his one good arm would be no match for the big Russian's two, JT thumbed the regulator to fully automatic and pulled the trigger on the MP7 firing the remaining 14 rounds into the woodpile beside the fire. The noise in the stone room was deafening, and for a split second, seemed to disorientate the surprised Russian. JT took the chance to let go of the weapon and aimed a straight fingered strike at the man's throat.

The blow brought tears to the Russian's eyes, but he adjusted his grip to lock up both of JT's arms, squeezing tighter with the bear hug. The air exploded from JT's lungs, as the Russian squeezed up under his ribs against his diaphragm. Very quickly, the world began to shrink, as JT's brain was starved of oxygen, threatening to shut down his consciousness. JT mustered the last of his strength to throw a series of headbutts at the Russian. The first hit the Russian's cheek, causing him to let out an amused tut that told JT he'd connected, but not well enough. He threw another, but this time the Russian was ready, dropping his chin and twisting his face away so that the edges of their foreheads clashed together, the glancing blow saving them both from serious injury.

JT's vision was darkening, but he held back his final headbutt for a fraction of a second, then threw it perfectly to meet the Russians face as he looked back up. This time JT's already bruised forehead connected perfectly with side of the Russian's nose, smashing the bridge and causing an orbital fracture of the left eye socket. There was no more amusement in the Russian's grunt, as he dropped JT and staggered backwards, tripping over an upturned chair.

JT lay on the hard stone floor, willing his lungs out of their spasm and to fill with life saving air. The pain of his shoulder was gone, as his brain focused solely on kickstarting his breathing. The first breath was shallow but the next one was a full painful gasp of air, that shocked JT back into the present. He shook the fuzziness from his head as his eyes regained their focus, just in time to see the Russian getting back to his feet. Blood was running freely from the Russians nose, as he gripped it in his thick fingers to wrench it straight.

JT fumbled for his Glock 19 sidearm but his holster had been twisted around the back of his thigh in the struggle. As he drew it out, a heavy blow from the Russian's boot sent the gun from JT's hand, skittering across the floor.

The Russian pulled a Soviet Army NR40 combat knife from a sheath on his belt. The six inch steel blade caught the light of the fire, glowing gold and red up to the s-shaped guard.

JT pushed with his heels to slide back and away from the Russian, as the big man glowered down at him, coughing out the blood from his mouth. JT reached the wall and as he tried to push himself up into a seated position, his hand touch something on the floor that he gripped.

'This was my Grandfather's knife,' said the Russian admiring the blade. 'He used it to remove the eyes of many Nazis in the Great Patriotic War. The knife was passed to me when he died. In my hand it has removed many more eyes, in Chechnya, Syria and now it will remove your eyes.'

JT looked up at the Russian as he bent forward over him, 'Good story!' he said, as he swung a set of antlers at the Russian. The lethal spikes of bone struck the Russian in the head and face with the top most section breaking off and crashing onto the kitchen table.

The Russian rocked back, standing up straight and pulling the antler free form where its spikes had embedded. As he did a torrent of blood erupted from his neck where a spike had severed his carotid artery. The arterial blood sprayed in time with the beating of the man's heart. He clamped his hand over the wound in a futile attempt to stem the flow of the blood.

JT got unsteadily to his feet, watching the bigger man's confused expression as he realised he was going to die. The Russian's knife slid from his grasp and clanged on the stone floor. JT stopped to pick it up.

'You've dropped something,' he said, as he drove the knife into the Russian's eye, killing him instantly. 'Wouldn't want to ruin your family tradition.'

JT scooped up his Glock and stumbled to the kitchen door. He saw Rory crouched in the dining room doorway, his MP7 now empty. He was about to throw Rory a spare magazine from his pocket, when the Russian entered the castle door, inching forward with his weapon trained on Rory's position.

JT leaned out of the kitchen door and fired several rounds into the chest of the Russian that sent the man staggering backward. A final headshot drove the Russian out the door, and off the edge of the external steps into the darkness.

The Wagner man giving cover fire changed from firing at the roof to shooting at the door, Rory had to crawl forward to push the door back closed. The incoming rounds embedded themselves in the thick oak but had very little impact.

The third man who had come up half way up the stairs retreated, making his way into the recessed storeroom doorway. As he backed up against the door he felt it open slightly and turned to see where the door led. For him the door led to hell, as Taff thrust his combat knife up into the soft flesh under his chin, with such force that his feet were lifted off the ground.

Taff dragged the still writhing body inside, as the man failed to register that he was already dead.

On the shore, Knut was frantically wiping at the window in an attempt to see what was happening on the island. The firing had stopped from the roof, but someone was firing from the ground. It must be the Russians firing, if they'd killed the shooter from the roof then they must be winning, he thought gleefully.

'Get into the Castle!' he shouted into the radio.

'We can't, they have the door covered from the inside,' came the reply from an agitated Russian.

'Then use the RPG for fuck sake, just get into that castle.'

Taff had taken the radio from the dead Russian, he was amazed to hear them speaking English.

'Grigor, do you have the RPG?'

'Yes, I have it, Mikhail. I think we are the only two left'

'Then use the fucking thing, quickly, these fuckers must pay for killing our comrades.'

Grigor picked up the RPG, walking purposefully from his hiding place out onto the grass, to take aim at the castle door. As he lifted the rifle to his shoulder Posty stepped out of the storeroom and shot him with a double tap to the chest. The Russian's finger twitched on the trigger as he fell, the grenade flying high and left hitting the parapet, before exploding by the roof.

'Shit!' shouted JT, running up the two flights of stairs to the roof. He found Angus being tended by Joe.

'He's alright I think, he was hit by the satellite dish when the grenade went off, it probably saved him.'

'Help me get him inside,' said JT.

They picked up the older man, carrying him gently down stairs.

At the bottom of the stairs Rosa was waiting for them. 'Quick bring him in here,' she said, switching on a light in the master bedroom.

As she did, she was briefly visible as Knut looked out from the car.

'What is happening?' he said, into the radio.

'I am the only one left,' said Mikhail. 'Why do the others not come in the boat?'

'Your brothers are all dead,' said Taff in Russian, using the dead Wagner man's radio.

'You will be joining them!' screamed Mikhail, before he ran out of cover shooting at the storeroom door.

Rory stepped out of the castle door and from his high position opened fire on the running Russian. Two rounds caught him in his arm and shoulder. He spun to the ground firing as he fell. After a few seconds, Rory walked down the stone steps where was joined by Taff and Posty. The Russian lay gasping for breath, and speaking in Russian.

'What's he saying?' asked Rory.

'He's praying to his dead mother,' said Taff.

Posty fired a single round into the man's face. 'Well, he can speak to her in person now.'

The three men stood, looking toward the shore, as the Land Rover engine roared to life, the headlights throwing an arc over the water, as it skidded away on the gravel road.

Chapter Seventy-Three

Knut floored the Land Rover sending stone chips and sprays of surface water flying against the underside of the car, out into the air behind him like a comet's tail. The Land Rover's automatic windscreen wipers were on full as they attempted to clear the heavy rain. Knut used the back of his hand to wipe a gap in the condensation on the inside of the windscreen. The car had powerful air conditioning and blower vents to do the job, but Knut had no time to locate and fiddle with the buttons. After fighting the wheel to correct, then recorrect, the steering as he hit ruts in the road, he straightened the vehicle up, pressing hard again on the accelerator. Shocked to see Pavlov emerging from the water ahead of him Knut instinctively slowed as he considered whether to pick the man up or leave him. Pavlov checked left and right then scrambled the few feet up the bank onto the road verge. Somehow he was still holding on to an assault rifle and he held it at high port as he looked into the approaching vehicle. Pavlov ducked his head to protect his eyes from the full beam of the automatic headlights. The headlights gave Knut a perfect view as two shots were fired from the hillside to his left and Pavlov was thrown violently back into the water.

Crouched behind the wheel Knut threw the vehicle around the bend, clipping a boulder on the way past. No bullets had hit the car but he expected one any second. Undeterred he kept his foot to the floor, shouting into the radio, 'Timo get the engines started I'm on my way back, be ready to take off right away.'

'Yes Mr Bergstrom,' came the reply, the whine of the engines starting was audible through the radio.

'Do you have your wife?' asked Timo as he reached for the rotor switches.

'No, not this time, I'll have to return for her.'

'Ok, sorry to hear that sir,' said the implacable pilot.

Three minutes later, Timo saw the Land Rover appear as Knut took it off road and it bucked down toward the helicopter.

Knut jumped from the driver's seat, running in a crouched position to the cockpit door.

'Get us out of here Timo!' he shouted, as he pulled himself into the co-pilot seat.

'What about the Wagner men?'

'They're all dead. So will we be if you don't get us out of here.'

Timo pulled back on the collective as he used the throttle to push the rotors to achieve lift off. Once in the air, he took her up to 150 metres before dipping the nose with the cyclic, to head west and out to sea, safely away from the hills.

Knut noticed the position lights were blinking, creating a halo effect in the rain. 'You need to kill the lights,' he told Timo.

'You think they'll try to shoot us down?'

'Maybe, and I'm not keen on making it easy for them.'

A few miles south, Knut's phone pinged as it picked up a signal. He skimmed the messages, then sent one to his pilot back in Dublin. After five minutes without a reply, he tried calling his pilot's mobile number. The phone rang out, and with it so did Knut's patience.

'Timo, I take it you can fly fixed wings too?'

'Yes of course, I also pilot Mr Lekyovitch's jet.'

'How much does Lekyovitch pay you?'

'He pays me well.'

'How much, Timo?'

'150,000 US.'

'Ok, well now you work for me. Your salary just doubled, You're coming with me to Cuba.'

'Seriously?'

'Yes Timo, seriously.'

'But my family, they are in St Petersburg-' began Timo.

'We can bring them over, once it's safe to fly again,' said Knut.

'What do you mean, "once it's safe to fly again"?'

'In approximately,' Knut looked at his watch, '10 hours, the entire Western European Air Traffic Control System will fail. You and I will be well on our way to Cuba so will miss the excitement.'

'But that would be catastrophic!' Timo gasped.

'Yes, it's meant to be, but from that catastrophe, great things will come.'

'Such as?'

'Such as you having enough money to move your whole family to Cuba. Such as not having to answer to anymore Bratva Oligarchs. There's an outside chance that Russia might end up at war with the West, and you don't want your family anywhere near St Petersburg when the Americans have itchy fingers.'

Timo fell silent, concentrating on flying while Knut went back to his phone.

***

From the top of the hill, the rain meant it was impossible to see the floor of the valley. Rambo had thrown himself down the scree slope, jumping in bunny hops whenever the scree slowed down. Through the rain he could make out the ethereal glow of the car headlights and a few seconds later the position lights of the helicopter had blinked into view before disappearing as they were apparently switched off.

Rambo walked down the rest of the way off the hill and took up a position where he could observe the Land Rover which sat with the driver door wide open and the engine still running. After a minute he moved around the rear of the vehicle and approached the open door. Clearing the vehicle, he checked for booby traps, then climbed in.

'Sorry Boss, I missed them. The chopper was in the air when I got off the hill.'

'Roger that, we did what we could. Get back here and we'll regroup.'

Travelling slowly and with the hazard lights flashing, he drove the road to the castle to pick up Cooky who had jogged around the hill via the road.

The two men returned to the jetty, then climbed the hill to drag down the bodies of the two dead Russian snipers.

'What's the plan for the Wagner bodies, boss?' asked Cooky, when he'd dragged Pavlov's body from the water's edge.

'Good question, let's pile them up for now. We can sort it later,' replied JT.

'I'll go row over for the lads,' said Taff. 'We'll pick up the other boat too.'

Rory walked into the room, 'Best give the boat a good scrub, or Angus won't be happy when he wakes up.'

'How is he?' asked JT.

'Rosa is playing nurse. He's only just conscious, but he's breathing fine, the old buggers got the heart of a stag. He'll have a sore head for a bit, but looks like the satellite dish came off second best. Talking of which, any joy getting hold of Hamilton or Easy?' asked Rory.

'Nothing, we're hoping the weather will clear enough that we can get some sort of signal.'

'I saw the satellite dish, it was wrecked,' said Rory

'Yeah, Posty has rigged something up, but the signal isn't strong enough, maybe because of atmospherics.'

'And if it doesn't work?'

'Then we're screwed. If Bergstrom gets that code into those systems we might as well stay here, at least we're not under a flight path.'

'Do you think he'd really let planes fall out of the sky?' asked Rory.

'I don't know, but Hamilton was taking it very seriously. If he doesn't know what's real and what's not, then what hope do we have?'

'So now we just have to wait, see what happens?'

JT rubbed at his shoulder and stared into the fire. 'We've no contact with the outside world, it may already be happening.'

Chapter Seventy-Four

The Vigilant team sat around the solid wooden kitchen table, in a gloomy silence. It was just two hours since the battle with the Wagner men had begun. They had survived, and defeated their enemy, but the mood was one of failure. The room smelled of a mix of bleach mingled with roast venison, as Rory had mopped and scrubbed the blood from the kitchen floor.

They had managed to gather the bodies of all the Wagner men into a pile on the beach. They were a real mix in appearance, from tall blonde haired men to smaller, eastern featured guys. They had two things in common; first, they had all been dangerous killers, and second, their killing days were now over.

The Wagner weapons had been stockpiled and the team discovered that the Russians had failed to use a second RPG, which if deployed effectively, might have seen things end very differently.

Other than Angus, the only injuries the team had suffered was that Joe had been hit by a chip of rock in the shin, which now sported a bandage, carefully applied by Rosa. JT's face was already bruised with a decent swelling that was threatening to force his eye closed. He held a bag of ice against his forehead with another strapped to his shoulder.

Angus was now awake, and sat up in bed with Rosa holding an ice pack to his head, the news of which had brought a little temporary cheer. He had also told them where he kept his personal supply of whisky. The bottles were all sealed but unlabelled, and came with a double warning from Angus; don't waste a drop and never try to drink cask strength whisky neat.

JT served up plates of roasted venison with mash and Angus's home made Buckthorn jelly. There was a tradition of JT cooking for his men, but tonight it was more function than pleasure.

Taff looked around the table then stood to say his traditional Grace, but then changed his mind. 'Right guys, we're all feeling it, but we did our level best tonight. We succeeded in keeping that lovely lady upstairs safe. You all know I'm not a religious man, but I reckon that if I'm wrong and there is a God up there, then Bergstrom won't be allowed to succeed. So now Gentlemen, charge your glasses to drink a toast with me. To Laird Rory, our gracious host, to Rosa, our lovely nurse, to Angus for this meat and for sharing his whisky. We don't know what tomorrow holds, so be happy we've survived today. To Her Majesty the Queen!' Taff raised his glass, then swallowed the contents, the others did the same.

A second bottle of whisky sat in the middle of the table. The men all picked at their food, despite it being delicious, sipping the golden spirit from their mugs.

'It sounds like the wind is calming down,' said Posty. 'I'll nip back up and have a fiddle with the array. You never know we might pick something up.'

'Thanks Posty, go for it,' said JT.

At that moment, they all felt as if they were the survivors in some dystopian disaster movie. The future seemed as bleak as it had ever done.

Chapter Seventy-Five

Knut Bergstrom removed his headset before climbing out of the helicopter after waiting for the rotors to come to a complete stop.

The rain that had lashed Scotland hadn't reached this far south, but there was a bit of breeze in the night air. He was exhausted after the tension of the last few hours, and heartbroken that he hadn't managed to reach Rosa and bring her home.

He'd spent the journey back from Scotland contemplating a future without Rosa, and knew that he just couldn't let that happen. He would return for her, he would bring a better army than these Wagner imbeciles, who had let him down so badly. How could they have failed so badly, he wondered. 12 men with modern weapons, should have been more than enough to take the castle. The weather hadn't helped, but even so...his thoughts were interrupted by a vehicle approaching.

The airport had sent a car, to drive him from the helipad to his jet, but he wanted to walk and set off across the General Aviation apron, followed by the airport vehicle with its flashing yellow lights. The airport staff had tried to tell him it was forbidden to walk there, but he ignored them, setting off regardless.

Timo had climbed into the vehicle without completing his post landing checks, or securing the helicopter. He knew his boss, Mr

Lekyovitch, was waiting for them aboard Bergstrom's private jet, and he wanted to be there if the two men were going to negotiate over his services. It was important that Lekyovitch didn't think Timo had betrayed him by leaving without his permission, his family would suffer the consequences.

Timo thought about what Bergstrom had said earlier, about it not being safe to fly, and puzzled over what it might mean. He was used to dealing with men with huge egos and a god complex. All too often, they thought the lives of others were without value, they could order a death, as easily as they could order a cocktail.

Knut stopped momentarily looking at a dark grey jet parked adjacent to his own. He could see from the markings that it belonged to the Government of the Republic of Ireland. The steps of both aircraft were down but unlike the Government jet his own was in darkness.

He'd had enough of incompetence for today, and determined that he would buy Timo from Lekyovitch to replace his own pilot, no matter the price. He was going to Cuba. He would watch the world fall apart from somewhere warm and comfortable, far away from these islands, with their depressingly damp weather. Stopping at the bottom of the steps he understood why the British had set off to conquer the world. Their achievements, considering Great Britain was such a tiny island on the global scale, were truly amazing. Knut thought to himself that had he been stuck in this miserable place, he too would have boarded a ship and headed for India or the New World.

With that thought, he was chuckling to himself as he boarded his plane.

Chapter Seventy-Six

The automatic lights came on as Knut stepped aboard, and he turned left to look into the cockpit, checking for the pilot. The cockpit was empty, so Knut poured himself a large drink from his personal collection in the galley, before stepping through the curtain into the cabin.

His glass almost slipped from his grasp, but he caught the heavy crystal tumbler before it fell, then licked the rum from his hand where it had sloshed over the rim.

'Welcome aboard, Mr Bergstrom,' said a distinguished looking man in a suit and tie, who was also pointing a silenced pistol in his direction.

Knut looked around, and saw his pilot was bound and gagged, in a seat at the rear of the cabin. He could see Viktor Lekyovitch was sat in a seat, facing the man holding the gun. Another pair of feet lay across the floor beside the pilot, which Knut guessed belonged to Lekyovitch's body guard.

'Who are you?' asked Bergstrom.

'We'll get to that, but in the meantime, take a seat here, beside our mutual friend, Mr Lekovitch.'

'It's Lek-yo-vitch!' growled the older Russian.

'Of course it is Viktor,' said the man, without taking his eyes off Knut. 'Now, please sit, Mr Bergstrom, or may I call you Knut?'

'If you tell me your name, then you can call me whatever you like.'

'Excellent, Knut it is then. You may call me Hamilton.'

Knut took the empty seat beside Lekyovitch.

'Be a good chap, and fasten your seatbelt please Knut, aeroplanes can be dangerous places. I'd much rather you didn't get hurt; un-necessarily.'

Knut did as he was told, fastening his seatbelt after placing his glass on the little side table by the window. 'Ok, now are you going to tell me what you want?' asked Knut.

'I want an explanation Knut,' said Hamilton.

'Explanation of what exactly?'

'Come now, let's not play games Knut. I am interested in your plan involving this.' From the seat beside him Hamilton lifted the hard drive that Knut had carried back from Nigeria.

'I don't think you would understand,' said Knut.

'You shouldn't underestimate me Knut, our friend here Mr Lek-yo-vitch,' said Hamilton, parroting the Russian's pronunciation, 'made that mistake earlier, and now his life is in my hands.'

'What do you know?' asked Knut.

'I know that you fled Nigeria, bringing this hard drive with you. I also know that you have gained access, through *StromSec,* to a lot of rather essential IT systems.'

Knut laughed, 'You won't be able to stop it. You're too late. I am the only one who can remove the virus. You'd never break the encryption on that hard drive in time.'

'Ah, well in that case you have nothing to lose by telling me the whole story. From the beginning, if you please.'

Knut looked up the ceiling of the cabin then reached forward and downed the rest of his rum.

'Black Tot, Master Blender's Reserve rum?' asked Hamilton.

Knut was surprised, 'Yes, it's my favourite rum, but how did you know?'

'A good guess. I'm more of a whisky man myself. My preference is for a 21 year old Macallan.'

'It's good, but you should try one of these,' said Knut, weighing the glass in his hand, considering if he could throw it at Hamilton.

'On this occasion, I'll leave that one to you.'

'Suit yourself.'

'Now, you were about to tell me your story,' said Hamilton, gently waving the silenced Browning in his direction.

'It's not much of a story really. As *StromSec*, I won the contracts for lots of Government Cyber Security. Their systems have suffered from years, if not decades, of under investment as each Government can only think in terms of electoral cycles. The idiots make no real planning strategies for longer than four, or at the most five years. This means their security is always playing catch up, never ahead of the game. I was surprised at just how easy it was, to hack my way in, free to wander through their files and systems. Which Government Department is it you work for, Hamilton? British Secret Service?'

'Oh, that's a difficult one to answer. Let's just say I work with some that you'd have heard of, but others that you won't.'

'I doubt it, I have been through the Home Office, Foreign Office and Justice Ministry systems numerous times. They are like Swiss cheese, and what's even better is, that those idiot Civil Servants gave me the keys.'

'How did you persuade them to give so many contracts to *StromSec*?'

'It was easy really. My Russian associates, like Viktor here, have people in virtually every Government department, in every Western European country,' Knut paused as something occurred to him, 'with the possible exception of Lichtenstein, but then no-one cares about Lichtenstein, do they?'

'You bribed your way in then?'

'Bribed, coerced or just asked nicely, these people despise the Governments and Countries they work for, most were happy to do my bidding.'

'How did that work on a practical level?' Hamilton asked, his face showing no emotion.

'It's very simple. Each of them was sent a series of emails over a few months. Embedded in each email was a fragment of code. No one fragment was enough to trigger firewalls or virus protection but when the last fragment was opened it activated all of the others and *hey presto*; the code was inside their system.'

'Very clever, very clever indeed.'

'Thank you, but I prefer the term, *genius*,' said Knut, without a hint of humour. He was getting warmed up now, and ready to reveal to Hamilton just how smart his plan was. 'The code ran in two parts; one was sacrificial and allowed the other to do its work.'

'Sacrificial?' asked Hamilton.

'Yes it did some minor damage within the system, but was deliberately clunky enough to be detected, once it had done its job. At the same time, *StromSec* released details of the same code, saying we had identified it as hackers attempted to use it on one of our existing clients. After that, the phone didn't stop ringing. Everyone wanted to sign us up, begging for my protection. Meanwhile, the true code was lying dormant, awaiting my signal.'

'What does that code do, when it is activated?'

'It shuts the whole lot down,' said Knut, looking quite pleased with himself.

'I see, and what pray tell, do you envisage will be the impact?'

'Chaos, pure and simple chaos.'

'The world is already in a constant state of chaos, mostly just beneath the surface.'

'When the Air Traffic Control systems shut down,' Knut was enjoying himself as he looked at his watch, 'in just a few hours, none of the aircraft will be able to land. Here at Dublin, there are over 300 flights land per day. Of those, some 15% are transatlantic, and those huge jet liners have less than an hour of fuel left, by the time they reach Ireland. Now, let's say five of those forty-five transatlantic flights have flown too far across the Atlantic, making it impossible to return to the US or Canada. When when they can't land, they will be forced, eventually, to ditch into the sea. Each of those aircraft carry approximately 500 passengers. That's 2,500 fatalities from Dublin alone. Add in the Aer Lingus European flights, and I imagine 10,000 fatalities is a very conservative estimate. Now think of a bigger airport, like Heathrow, Schiphol or Charles de Gaulle, and you begin to see much bigger numbers. I'm thinking maybe half a million? That of course doesn't include casualties on the ground.'

'Why would you want to kill all of those people?' asked Hamilton, still a picture of calm and showing no emotion.

'I'm not interested in those people, although there are far too many humans on the planet to be sustainable. No, I am interested in the chaos it will cause.'

'Why?'

'Why? Isn't it obvious? I will hold the key to switch the systems back on. I will be able to name my price.'

'So, it's all about money?'

'Everything is about money; because money is power. When the world has paid my demands, then I will be King.'

'The financial markets would go into free fall, and the world economy plummet. Anarchy, riots, wars, banks forced to close; money won't be much good to you then.'

'That's where you're wrong. Viktor here, and a select group of his fellow Oligarchs, have been positioning themselves for the inevitable market crash. They have enough futures contracts and shorts that will see the balance of power forever shift to the East. The corrupt West, and especially the United States, has had a hegemony for too long.'

As Knut finished speaking he winced, a sudden sharp pain causing him to shift in his seat.

'Ah, there's a political ideology at play then?' asked Hamilton, apparently oblivious to Knut's pained expression.

'No,' Knut replied, a little frustrated, 'I don't care about mere politics.'

'Then how does this benefit you?'

'I will be in Cuba. With the USA and her allies fatally wounded, they won't have the strength to attack Cuba, or to interfere with my future.'

'And Rosamunde?'

'Rosa is my wife, and I'll have her brought to me, just as soon as I have things set up in Cuba.'

Knut clutched at his stomach and had to fight the urge to vomit.

'Are you ok old chap?' asked Hamilton.

'I'll be fine.' Knut wiped his mouth with the back of his hand. He looked at the gun in Hamilton's hand, 'you won't be needing that, will you Hamilton?'

'Really? Why not?'

'Because you need me alive. I am the only one who can get past the encryption in that hard drive. I alone can turn the systems back on. As I said, I will be King.'

Hamilton considered the man who would be King. 'Perhaps it is something to do with your name? Did you know that King Knut, which was more often spelled C-A-N-U-T-E, was the King of England, before becoming King of Denmark, and later Norway? He even had some influence here in Dublin, through his alliance with good old Sigtrygg Silkbeard. Like you, he took an army to Scotland expecting an easy victory, but the Scots are a canny lot. They let him leave thinking he'd lost the battle, but won the war. In reality of course, they simply carried on, as if he'd never been.'

Knut wretched, his eyes screwed shut as waves of painful nausea enveloped him.

'Now,' continued Hamilton, 'the most recognisable tale, of that more famous Knut, is that he tried, but failed, to halt the waves. Now it seems, it is your turn.'

'You've...you've poisoned me?' moaned Knut, as the sweat dripped down his face, another agonising wave of pain bending him double.

'The Strychnine like mix, strictly speaking, is a bio-toxin. It is virtually undetectable when mixed with a strongly flavoured drink, like rum for example. Your body is under attack, being *hacked* as it were. You are losing control of your bodily functions as the intruder interrupts messages from your brain. Your little plan, as you described it earlier, makes a fitting analogy for what is happening inside your system. You are being shut down, and it will be fatal.'

'But you need me, for the encryption!' Knut grunted, the pain making him jump in his seat.

'No, actually I don't. You see, my dear Knut, you are not the only genius working in the cyber world. I have an incredible young man in my team, who has defeated your encryption. He is clearing your code from the many systems, as we speak.'

'I don't believe you. No-one is that good, or that quick.' Knut's voice was barely audible as he struggled for breath.

'He had a bit of a head start, did our Ezekiel. You see, a certain Mossad operative, by the name of Laila Acker, who I believe you knew and left to die in the Nigerian dust, supplied us with a thumb drive. She had downloaded all of your files, with the exception of the aforementioned hard drive.'

'If you have the drive here...then your genius can't have accessed it...' Knut was panting, his shirt soaked in sweat. His arms twitched violently as he lost control of his nerve impulses, his back arching. Grinding his teeth as he tried to speak, his face contorted in pain. The sour smell of urine announced his bladder vacating.

'Au contraire, he finished with it half an hour or so before you arrived.' For the first time a little smile played across Hamilton's lips as he spoke. 'The Irish Government were kind enough to let us work in their aeroplane, parked next door.' Hamilton gestured with his gun hand to the window, through which the Irish jet was visible.

Lekyovitch took his chance, having unclipped his seat belt he threw himself at Hamilton, knocking the pistol from his hand. The former SVR man remembered his training and still regularly worked out with his bodyguards. He was able to pin Hamilton to the seat, with a forearm across his throat, while he wrenched at the gun. Hamilton grunted in pain as his grip gave way, losing the gun to the bigger, stronger man.

Lekyovitch stood up from his seat, pointing the gun at Hamilton. He watched dispassionately as Hamilton carefully manipulated his dislocated finger back into place. Both men looked at Knut who was frothing at the mouth, drooling down his chin. His tongue was bleeding where he had involuntarily bitten through it. They watched on, as spasms continued to wrack Knut with agonising jolts, but as he was struggling to breathe he barely moaned. His arms and legs were now rigid, his previously intelligent eyes showing nothing but confusion and desperation.

Knut found himself thinking about the young Nigerian man who was crucified outside the squat. He tried to look down at his own stomach, where his tortured brain was imagining his own intestines spilling out into his lap. Another spasm made his back arch and his head snap back so violently, there was an audible crack. He battled the pain in an attempt to think clearly, trying desperately to picture Rosa on their wedding day. Instead the last image he saw in his minds eye, before the darkness finally took him, was of Rosa slamming the door when she left.

'Well now Mr Hamilton, it seems our positions are reversed,' said Lekyovitch, turning his attention back.

'Yes indeed Viktor. I should have remembered that you are ex Sluzhba Vneshney Razvedki.'

'You know what they say, once SVR always SVR.'

'Yes, I should imagine they do.'

'How did you know he would pour himself a drink?'

'As you well know, a player should never reveal his cards.' said Hamilton, a picture of calm.

'You were bluffing about cracking his encryption yes?'

'Oh, I never bluff Viktor,' said Hamilton, looking past him. 'You might wish to look behind you.'

'Do not insult me Hamilton, I am not about to fall for something so childish,' said Lekyovitch, with a sneer.

'Suit yourself.' said Hamilton, as Timo Yermakov crashed a vodka bottle into the head of his boss, knocking him unconscious.

Lekyovitch fell across his seat, landing face first into the pool of drool, blood and urine in Knut's lap.

Hamilton raised an eyebrow and permitted himself a chuckle when he looked at Lekyovitch's position, 'Oligarch to piss poor, oh how the mighty have fallen!' He turned to Timo who stood, still holding the bottle, staring at Lekyovitch, 'Thank you. We have yet to be introduced, but I assume you are Lekyovitch's pilot?'

'Yes, or I was. My name is Timo Yermakov.'

'Thank you once again, Timo Yermakov.'

'It's ok, I was listening to what these men were saying, they are monsters.'

'Yes, I think that's a fair description. Now, perhaps you would be so kind, as to check if they have any decent whisky back there; in a sealed bottle. I think we deserve a drink, while we figure out what to do with these chaps.'

Chapter Seventy-Seven

Timo brought the helicopter down gently onto the helipad that formed the middle section of the island. The rain had cleared and the sun was threatening the horizon making the low clouds glow rose gold on top of the eastern mountains.

The rotors came to a stop before the door opened, and outstepped a man wearing an overcoat with the collar turned up. Bent forward, the man's face was hidden from the watching eyes behind the trained weapons, pointed at him from the roof of the castle.

The pilot walked round the nose of the aircraft, opening the rear door then helping drag someone with their hands tied behind their back and a black hood over their head.

After cutting a zip tie from the ankles of the hooded man they marched him toward the castle.

The trained weapons were lowered when the man in the overcoat lifted his head and waved, 'Good morning Gentlemen, be with you in a jiffy,' called a smiling Hamilton

JT stood with Rory at the top of the castle steps, watching as the men made their way directly to a rusty old door in the base of the castle wall.

The door squealed and screeched as it was opened and the hooded man was pushed inside.

Inside the room, Timo was gestured to leave before the hood was removed.

Viktor Lekyovitch blinked rapidly, trying to take in his surroundings. 'Where is this place?' he asked, his voice betraying just a hint of panic.

'For the foreseeable, you may consider this place *home*, Viktor,' said Hamilton.

'You know you are a dead man, Hamilton, my Bratva brothers will hunt you down and kill you. They will let you live, just long enough to watch your family, and everyone you care about, die.'

'Oh Viktor, enough of the theatrics,' laughed Hamilton. 'No-one is going to die, although it is possible, that before long, you might wish to.'

'Untie my fucking hands and I will kill you myself!' growled Lekyovitch.

'I will arrange to have some breakfast brought down to you,' said Hamilton, ignoring Lekyovitch's threat. 'Be a good chap, and make yourself comfortable on the... hmmm, there doesn't seem to be any furniture in here, does there? Make yourself comfortable, on the cold stone floor. I'm sure your SVR training will have prepared you to cope with such deprivations.'

Hamilton stepped backwards out of the door, before pushing it closed and working the big rusty bolt into place.

Lekyovitch let out an animalistic roar in the darkness of his cell, which made Hamilton smile, as he walked around the corner to the castle steps.

'Good morning, Hamilton,' said JT, as Hamilton was climbing the stairs.

'Good morning, Gentlemen, good morning!' said a smiling Hamilton, taking in JT's arm in a sling. 'Any possibility of some coffee, for my new friend and I?'

'Are you going to introduce your friend?' asked JT.

'Of course,' said Hamilton, suddenly realising Timo had waited at the bottom of the stairs. 'Come on up Timo, they won't bite, I promise!' he said, as the two Flat Coated Retrievers bounded down the stairs wagging their tails. 'Where is the Jack Russell?' he asked Rory.

'Upstairs keeping an eye on Angus, he was knocked unconscious last night. Skipper hasn't left his side.'

'As it should be,' said Hamilton. 'Aren't you going to invite me in?'

'You hardly need an invitation!' laughed Rory.

'Oh, but I do, you are after all the Laird, and this is *your* castle, sire,' said Hamilton, with a cheeky bow.

'Bugger off and get in man,' said Rory, smiling while rolling his eyes. 'Tor, Hamish, heel!' he called to the dogs, who stopped circling Timo and, still wagging their tails, bounded up the stairs into the castle. 'Come on Timo, the kettle is on.'

Timo was shown into the kitchen where the team had assembled and were sitting around the kitchen table.

'Lads, this is Timo, Timo this is the lads,' said JT.

'Hello,' replied Timo, as his eyes scanned the weapons on the table.

'Tea or coffee Timo?' asked Posty, from the end of the table.

'Coffee please, if I may?' Timo replied.

'Grab a pew,' said Joe as he shuffled up the bench.

Hamilton returned from briefly checking on Angus. 'Angus appears to be in good hands, he also appears to be enjoying being tended to, by his very beautiful nurse!'

'Hamilton, we've been off line for a few hours, but from your cheery disposition, I'm assuming you managed to thwart Bergstrom's plan?' asked JT.

'Yes, thankfully we did.'

'Is that him down in the dungeon?'

'No, no, Bergstrom is dead,' said Hamilton, without emotion.

'So, who is in the dungeon?'

'Thank you Taff,' said Hamilton, as his coffee was passed up the table, 'it's been a long night.'

'The dungeon?' pressed JT.

'Ah yes,' said Hamilton, sipping his coffee, 'Viktor Lekyovitch.'

'Who is Viktor Lekyovitch, when he's at home?' asked Rory.

Hamilton smiled at Rory's accidental joke, 'Lekyovitch is a Russian Oligarch who, until a few hours ago, was Russia's man in Dublin.'

'He's not anymore then?' asked Rory.

'No, although they may not realise it, just yet.'

'Are you going to explain what happened?'

'Yes of course, but you first, tell me about last night, while I drink my coffee.'

'There's not too much to tell really. They came with a force of 12 men, not sure who they were but they were Russians, so we assume they were Wagner Group.'

'Yes, they were,' said Timo, 'I flew them here.'

'I take it you flew the one who escaped back out, we figured it must have been Bergstrom?'

'Yes, he came to collect his wife. He thought you might shoot at the helicopter, so we left in a hurry.'

'We wanted him alive,' said JT.

Timo nodded.

'The 12 men attacked the castle, but either they didn't know we were here, or they were poorly trained. We dealt with them, without too much difficulty.'

Hamilton looked at JT's sling and raised an eyebrow.

'I had a bit of a wrestle, with a Russian bear...'

'So, you wrestled *Mishka* and live to tell the tale!' said Hamilton.

'Let's just say it was an eye for an eye.'

'The bear didn't stand a chance against *The Monarch of the Glen*!' said Rory, finishing his sentence for him, with a nod to the antlers on the floor.

'Sir Edward Landseer,' said Hamilton, picking up the reference.

'I believe *you* are the Laird, not me,' said a confused JT.

'I'll explain later!' said Rory with a wink.

'It hangs in the National Gallery in Edinburgh, well worth a visit, it's rather impressive.' said Hamilton.

JT was too tired, and in too much pain, to care what they were talking about. 'Other than my shoulder, Joe's shin and Angus falling foul of a stray RPG, we did our thing without casualties. We've recovered the 12 Russian bodies, we'll need to dispose of them.'

'I can help, with the helicopter?' offered Timo.

'That'd be good, thanks,' said JT, as he puzzled over what Hamilton might have planned for the pilot. 'We've also secured some decent weapons. These Wagner guys had the new KS1s, that the Royal Marines are waiting on to replace their old SA80s. They're good kit and in short supply, so Christ knows where they got them from.'

'That is one of many questions Mr Lekyovitch may be able to help us with,' said Hamilton, placing his mug down on the table.

'Mr Lekyovitch is not the sort of man to voluntarily answer questions. He is a very rich and powerful, a personal friend of the people running the Kremlin, including the President,' offered Timo.

'Yes, Mr Lekyovitch does have friends in high places, but both he and lots of his cabal, are about to lose their shirts, or Dachas if you will.'

'I don't understand,' said Timo.

'They have all placed what are essentially very large bets on the collapse of world markets. The collapse was to be a knock on effect and consequence of Bergstrom's plan. That plan will no longer become reality. As such the bets will lose, and the huge amounts of capital backing them will be lost. These people were so convinced that their bets were a sure thing, they've over committed themselves, they will lose everything.'

'That will cause ructions in the Kremlin,' said Rory.

'Indeed, it may create a power vacuum that will allow Mr Putin to strengthen his grip even further on the country. Who knows, he may even use some of the billions, earmarked for lining the Oligarchs pockets each year, to lift some of his people out of poverty?' said Hamilton.

'That's not how it works in Mother Russia,' said Timo. 'They will find a way to rebuild the Oligarchs, those who have been faithful to the President. Or they will replace them, with more loyal allies.'

'Sadly, I think you are entirely correct. Such machinations always present opportunities. Who knows, we may find someone with more agreeable sympathies to ourselves, being pushed into a position of power.'

'A spy?' asked Rory.

'An ally is often as good as a spy,' said Hamilton.

'How did you get Bergstrom?' asked JT, itching to be able to understand the missing pieces.

'That was of course a team effort and involved all of the Vigilant Team. Easy was able to crack the encryption of Bergstrom's hard drive.

The encryption, that Bergstrom thought was impregnable, turned out not to be so. Thanks, in very large part, to Laila Acker and the thumb drive she passed to you.'

'I still don't understand Mossad's involvement,' said Rory.

'They were on to Bergstrom, but didn't fully understand his plans. They have assets in Russia, who were picking up on background information through the Oligarch circles. It seems they have at least one of them working for Israeli intelligence, either through choice or coercion. When Bergstrom was in the market for a new personal security person, to replace the man he sent to bring Rosamunde back to him, the Israelis used a broker to suggest Laila to him. She was feeding back information, but when we raided the University in Nigeria, she took what she thought was a download of the code.'

'But it wasn't the code,' said JT, thinking of the dying woman who's hand he had held.

'No, not the code, but it contained details of how the code was delivered. Easy managed to reverse engineer it, and in doing so could read the encryption keys backwards - or something like that. I confess I glazed over slightly when he explained it all!'

'So, she didn't die in vain then?' said JT.

'Most certainly not, it's no exaggeration to say her actions saved the world.'

'She's buried in Nigeria, I promised I would take her home to Israel.'

'I know, and that's already in hand JT. I have arranged with an old Israeli friend of mine to facilitate this. Timo here will fly down, in the helicopter outside, to Nigeria, to collect Laila's body. Then he will fly her home to Israel, where she will receive the highest honours of her Government, and a hero's funeral.'

'I want to be there too,' said JT, 'I made a promise.'

'Indeed, and I anticipated you wanting to do so. You will accompany Timo on the journey.'

'What happens afterwards?' asked JT.

'Afterwards, I would suggest that you get that shoulder looked at, and if necessary, you have surgery to repair it.'

'I meant for Timo. There will be questions asked in time about Lekyovitch, they'll expect Timo here to answer them.'

'Timo's family are shortly leaving St Petersburg and flying to Tel Aviv. A new life awaits them in Israel, they will keep them safe until the Russians lose interest.'

'My family and I are not Jews, but we will have a good life in Israel, thanks to Mr Hamilton,' said Timo.

'You saved my life Timo, it's the least I can do.'

JT gave Hamilton a taste of his own medicine with a raised eyebrow.

'It's a long story, for another time,' said Hamilton.

'What about Bergstrom?' asked Rory.

'Bergstrom is currently flying to Cuba aboard his jet.'

'I thought you said he was dead?' said JT.

'He is very dead. His pilot has been instructed to fly to Cuba, as the filed flight-plan said they would. When he lands in Cuba, he will tell the authorities that he found Bergstrom dead in his seat. It will take a few days for a post-mortem to determine the cause of death. I have someone ready to tell the world it was an accidental overdose.'

'Won't the pilot tell them what really happened?'

'No, he thinks he would be implicated in the murder. He has the perfect incentive to keep quiet.'

'What happens to *StromSec*?' asked Rory.

'Well, that will depend. In due course, Rosamunde will inherit the company, she is after all still officially, Mrs Bergstrom. The company itself was very profitable outside of his nefarious plans, but without

Bergstrom himself, it will require a revamp. It will be up to her what she does with it, but I hope she will employ others to keep the company running. We can put its reach and contracts to good use.'

'To spy on our Government Departments?'

'Not our own Government Departments, but you never know when a little leverage might be useful, when dealing with Foreign Governments. That reminds me, we need to have a chat about a little Sino-Irish espionage issue, that I'd like us to have a look at.'

'Chinese?' asked Rory.

'Yes, the details are a little sketchy at the moment, but they were running an Irish asset in London. I now have that asset on a string, and intend to root out the Chinese operations in the UK. That is something else Mr Lekyovitch will be given the opportunity to assist with.'

'Always the spy huh Hamilton?' said Rory.

'Always the pragmatist my dear Rory. You of all people, have an inkling of how these things work.'

'Yes, I do, but I don't have to love it.'

'We cannot love, what we do not understand,' said Hamilton, sagely.

'Did I hear my name being mentioned?' asked Rosa, as she walked in carrying a tray.

'Yes, and I'm afraid I have some bad news for you,' said Rory, standing up.

'Knut is dead, isn't he?' said Rosa, laying the tray down by the sink.

'Yes,' he said, unsure of how to comfort her, or if she even needed comforting.

'That's not bad news. From what you guys have told me, he was a monster. A would be murderer of thousands of people. He's not the man I thought I knew. It was all a lie. I know that he'd have left me to be killed by those men in Grand Cayman too, so no, that's not bad news at all.' A tear ran down her cheek as emotions boiled to the surface.

Rory stepped forward and offered her a handkerchief. Rosa took it, then buried her face into his shoulder, weeping.

Chapter Seventy-Eight

JT stood at the side of the grave in *Hof Hacarmel* cemetery, on the outskirts of Haifa in Israel. The sun was shining, reflected from the white marble gravestones. Laid out in neat rows, the resting place of Haifa's residents since 1937 was beautifully kept.

Arriving early, JT had walked around the *Bereaved Parents* plot, adjacent to the Military section, where fallen Israeli Defence Force soldiers were buried. The idea that parents would want to be buried next to their children, made perfect sense to him, in the same way as Laila's wish had been to be buried next to her parents.

He had been given a yarmulke to cover his head and a prayer shawl to wear, but out of deference he stood slightly apart from the other mourners.

The eulogy had been in Hebrew, but Laila's younger brother Seif had approached afterwards, thanking him in American accented English.

JT felt himself becoming emotional when the mourners sang the Kaddish at the graveside, and although invited, decided not to follow them as they retired to the Acker family home. Despite never being religious himself, he found he often enjoyed the communing of people at such events, whether they were sad or happier times. There was something about belonging, about being part of something bigger than yourself, that appealed to him. Maybe that's why he'd joined the Army, and why he still felt the loss of leaving the Regiment.

From inside his sling, he withdrew the stone that Adanna had given him back in Nigeria, to be placed on Laila's grave. Bending down, he placed the stone carefully, offering the little blessing that Adanna had taught him.

He thought about the next step for him. He would be heading to Bordeaux, to spend some time with Esmé as they tried to rekindle their marriage.

The rest of Vigilant would take a well earned rest, before gearing up for their next mission. JT knew Hamilton was busy planning it now, so it wouldn't be long before they were all back in action.

Rosa was staying on with Angus at the Castle, and would remain there until the furore over Knut Bergstrom's death had subsided. She had already decided that she wanted to turn *StromSec* into a not-for-profit, and that they would develop a team dedicated to tackling fraudsters and scammers online.

Rory was returning to New Scotland Yard, to finally finish his last case before he retired. His retirement plan was to oversee the redevelopment of the hotel at Palmerston House on behalf of Vigilant. It was to be made into a retreat for Police Officers and Military Personnel suffering from PTSD.

As JT stood up, he could see the sea below him and knew that this was exactly where Laila had wanted to be buried.

Through the *Soldier's Gate*, he saw a group of men patiently waiting for him. They were his team. They were *Vigilant*.

The End

Also By

HACKED is the second book in the SAS: *VIGILANT* series.
The first book of the series **RETRIBUTION** is also available (use the link below).
The third book in the series is in development, be sure to subscribe for details on the release date at simondaleybooks.com
Subscribers will receive a free short story featuring a character from **HACKED** as a thank you for joining
Team Vigilant.
I hope you enjoyed reading **HACKED** as much as I enjoyed writing this, my second novel. The Vigilant characters are now a very real part of our family!
I would be extremely grateful if you could leave a brief review of **HACKED**. Reviews will help other readers find my books, but, from a purely personal point of view, I am really keen to know if you enjoyed what I've written.
Writing a book is a labour of love and all consuming. I am proud of the work I have produced and always happy to discuss the characters and plot. There are links to my social media platforms at simondaleybooks.com and I'd love it if you want get in touch!
Thanks again for reading and for your support, Simon.

Acknowledgements

Writing can be a reclusive and individual pursuit. The space, freedom and push for me to get words out of my imagination and onto a page only come with the support of my amazing family.

To Caroline, Erin, Bobby and Frank, my eternal thanks for putting up with me when I've been completely self absorbed.

Caroline deserves another special thanks for her excellent cover design.

About the Author

Simon Daley lives and writes between Scotland and the US. He worked in law enforcement for over 30 years. His experience in Counter Terrorism and working with numerous agencies has given him an insight that he uses in his writing.

His favourite hobbies, away from reading and writing, are his dog Frank, tennis and soon to be marathon training.

Printed in Great Britain
by Amazon